STRONGWOOD

OTHER BOOKS BY LARRY MILLETT
PUBLISHED BY THE UNIVERSITY OF MINNESOTA PRESS

———————

Sherlock Holmes and the Red Demon

Sherlock Holmes and the Ice Palace Murders

Sherlock Holmes and the Rune Stone Mystery

Sherlock Holmes and the Secret Alliance

The Disappearance of Sherlock Holmes

The Magic Bullet

STRONGWOOD

A Crime Dossier

LARRY MILLETT

A MINNESOTA MYSTERY
WITH SPECIAL APPEARANCES BY SHADWELL RAFFERTY
AND SHERLOCK HOLMES

UNIVERSITY OF MINNESOTA PRESS
MINNEAPOLIS · LONDON

Published by the University of Minnesota Press
111 Third Avenue South, Suite 290
Minneapolis, MN 55401-2520
http://www.upress.umn.edu

Library of Congress Cataloging-in-Publication Data
Millett, Larry, 1947–
Strongwood : a crime dossier / Larry Millett.
"A Minnesota Mystery with Special Appearances by Shadwell Rafferty and Sherlock Holmes"
Includes bibliographical references.
ISBN 978-0-8166-9093-0 (hc)
1. Minneapolis (Minn.)—Fiction. 2. Mystery fiction. 3. Legal stories. I. Title.
PS3563.I42193S77 2014
813'.54—dc23

                                    2014001724

Printed in the United States of America on acid-free paper

The University of Minnesota is an equal-opportunity educator and employer.

21 20 19 18 17 16 15 14   10 9 8 7 6 5 4 3 2 1

To Lexy, a wonderful daughter and a great reader

AUTHOR'S INTRODUCTION

ON THE DAMP, GLOOMY EVENING OF NOVEMBER 9, 1903, A YOUNG MAN AND A young woman met in an office building in downtown Minneapolis for what turned out to be a lethal encounter. The woman was Adelaide Strongwood, age twenty-one, and when she left the building the man she had met there, twenty-six-year-old Michael Masterson, lay dead on the floor, blood pouring from a bullet wound to his chest. Strongwood was arrested and later indicted by a grand jury on a charge of first-degree murder, all the while proclaiming that she had acted in self-defense.

Her case became a sensation, especially because she was both very beautiful and exceptionally well spoken. The *Minneapolis Tribune*, then the city's largest morning newspaper, immediately took to Strongwood's defense. In December, a few weeks before she went on trial, the newspaper published a series of seven articles by Strongwood in which she described her background, her relationship with Masterson, and the events that ultimately led to his death at her hands. It is hard to imagine any newspaper today offering a criminal defendant such an opportunity for self-justification, but the *Tribune* went even further by contributing five hundred dollars to the cost of her defense.

Rival dailies, such as the *Minneapolis Journal*, depicted Strongwood in a far less flattering light. Her widely disparate treatment in the press reflected the degree to which her case divided the city along class lines. Strongwood came from a working-class background while Masterson hailed from a wealthy and influential family of industrialists. The fact that much of Strongwood's legal defense hinged on painting the worst possible portrait of Masterson as a cruel and dissolute playboy only served to exacerbate those sharp divisions.

By the time Strongwood's trial began in Hennepin County District Court on January 11, 1904, all of Minneapolis–St. Paul and much of the nation seemed to be following the case. The stakes could not have been higher for Strongwood, since capital punishment was still a possibility (it would not be outlawed in Minnesota until 1911). Her trial, which lasted just over three weeks, drew tremendous publicity, and not only in the Twin Cities. Newspapers from as far away as New York City, Chicago, and Denver had correspondents on the scene, as did several national magazines. Yet the case, like so many others that once blazed across the front pages of newspapers, is now all but forgotten.

I first stumbled across the case while researching one of my historic mysteries featuring Sherlock Holmes and Shadwell Rafferty. To my surprise, I discovered that Rafferty, and to a lesser extent Holmes, had become entangled in the Strongwood affair, which was—and still is, to my way of thinking—a fascinating story. I began gathering information about the case and was able over a period of several years to amass a rich collection of documents, including books, newspaper and magazine articles, letters, and even copies of private journals, all preserved by various historical societies.

The case, I soon came to realize, was populated by a large and formidable cast of characters, beginning with Strongwood and including a rich mix of people from both the high and low ends of Minneapolis society at the dawn of the twentieth century. Many were described in considerable detail and pictured (in the form of engraved drawings) in a now hard-to-find book titled *The Trial of Adelaide Strongwood, Including an Introduction to the Case, a Description of the Principals, and Select Testimony*. Published in 1904 by the *Tribune* as a sort of instant potboiler, the book features lengthy excerpts of trial testimony obtained directly from a stenographer hired by the newspaper, and it remains the single most important source of information about the case.

My first thought was to write a fictionalized account of the Strongwood affair, but I found the historic record so compelling that I decided instead to let the documents, including the trial testimony, speak for themselves. I have pieced them together, much like a collage, in a way that I hope will convey a sense of the enduring mystery at the heart of the case.

Readers should be aware that I have been very selective in editing the trial testimony, eliminating some witnesses entirely and abridging the testimony of others in order to move the story along. Addie Strongwood was the chief witness at the trial, but I found it necessary to substantially edit even her testimony in order to focus on key moments in both her direct and cross-examinations. In addition, I deleted the attorneys' opening statements, which were not especially enlightening, and substantially abridged their closing arguments. I also skipped over many of the objections and legal arguments made during the trial. The presiding judge's rulings and statements from the bench were edited as well. My goal was to create a sleek, compelling version of what was, in actuality, a long trial with a good deal of repetitive testimony and highly technical legal maneuvering.

All the documents and excerpts from trial testimony in my account are identified in short headings preceding them. I also inserted explanatory footnotes when appropriate to help readers better understand references in the documents to now-obscure people, places, or events. A line in the section break indicates where I edited documents.

The jury's verdict, rendered on February 5, 1904, came as a surprise to many. I invite you now to read on and see whether it will be a surprise to you as well.

Larry Millett
St. Paul, 2014

ONE

Few criminal trials in recent memory have produced as great a sensation in the Northwest as that of Adelaide Strongwood, who stood accused of murdering Michael Masterson, scion of one of the wealthiest manufacturers in Minneapolis. Miss Strongwood's trial, held before Judge Charles Elliott in the Hennepin County District Court in January and February 1904, became a spectacle avidly followed by almost every resident of the city. The many shocking details that emerged during the three-week-long trial, culminating in the dramatic testimony of Miss Strongwood herself, are still the source of discussion, as is the verdict ultimately rendered by the jury of twelve men good and true. It is the belief of the publishers of this book that the question of whether justice was indeed done in this case is best left to the reader, who will now have before him all of the relevant information needed to reach a well-considered judgment.

Miss Adelaide, or as she preferred to be called, "Addie," Strongwood, aged twenty-two at the time of her trial, is a character who needs little introduction. Remarkably well spoken, calm of manner, and possessing startling physical beauty, she was at all times the center of attention in Judge Elliott's courtroom. Usually dressed in a fall suit consisting of an A-line skirt and tailored jacket over a high-neck blouse with a silk jabot, she never failed to present a fashionable yet dignified appearance. Her piercing blue eyes, which suggested great presence of mind, drew much comment from courtroom observers, as did her luxuriant black hair, which was invariably pinned up in back so that only a few loose tendrils curled at her finely formed face. Despite her humble beginnings, she carried herself at all times with a regal air, and not even the faintest shadow of doubt ever seemed to trouble her visage. Only once during her hours on the witness stand did she succumb to the tears that come so easily to many members of her sex.

From the very beginning, Miss Strongwood proclaimed her innocence by reason of self-defense, and even penned her own account of the events leading up to Mr. Masterson's death. This document, handwritten by Miss Strongwood during her confinement in the Hennepin County jail, appeared in the *Tribune* in seven parts, beginning on December 14, 1903. It is a measure of Miss Strongwood's certainty of mind, perhaps the sovereign feature of her character, that her attorney advised against such an account on the grounds that her words could become impeachable at trial. Her response to this concern, as later reported in the *Tribune*, was characteristically direct: "You cannot," she said, "impeach the truth."

———————

Both of the lawyers in the case—Mr. Frederick H. Boardman for the prosecution and Mr. J. Winston Phelps for the defense—are well known to the citizens of Minneapolis. A Canadian by birth, Mr. Boardman settled in Minneapolis in 1878 and quickly earned a sterling reputation as a practitioner of the law. He was elected to the position of Hennepin County attorney in 1900, and in that capacity he became a champion of the people when he successfully prosecuted the gang of thieves and charlatans led by Dr. Ames.[1] A compact, elegant man with sharp gray eyes and a fine brushy mustache, Mr. Boardman is known for his courtly manners, probing intellect, and subtle sense of humor. Unfailingly courteous, even toward the most hostile of witnesses, he is nonetheless a tenacious advocate in the courtroom who has sent many a miscreant to prison.

Mr. Phelps is equally renowned for his efforts at the bar. Tall and gaunt, like a figure from one of El Greco's paintings, he is fond of flamboyant attire and is considered one of the great "talkers" of the city. He is no popinjay, however, for

———————

1. Minneapolis Mayor Albert A. ("Doc") Ames headed a notoriously corrupt administration before being forced to resign in July 1902. His activities received national attention six months later when *McClure's Magazine* published a now-famous article by muckraker Lincoln Steffens titled "The Shame of Minneapolis: The Ruin and Redemption of a City That Was Sold Out." Much of the corruption involved the city's police department under the leadership of Fred Ames, the mayor's brother. Fred Ames was ultimately sentenced to six years in prison for his crimes.

beneath his colorful plumage lurks a fierce bird of prey. Witnesses have been known to tremble before the force of his cross-examinations, and his skills in this regard were amply displayed during Miss Strongwood's long trial.[2] The presiding judge, the Honorable Charles B. Elliott, was appointed to the municipal court bench in Minneapolis in 1890 at the tender age of twenty-nine. He was elevated to the district court only four years later, and despite his youth he is now regarded as one of the "wise old men" of the bench by virtue of his profound knowledge of the law and his calm but firm judicial demeanor.[3]

The trial was held in the stately courtroom on the third floor of the new Municipal Building.[4] With its beamed ceiling, arched windows, and frescoed arabesques, this noble room provided a dignified setting for what proved to be a dramatic and fiercely contested trial.

———

The twelve men "good and true" who served as jurors in the case were as follows: Samuel Ahern, janitorial supervisor, Richfield Township; C. M. Calvin, architectural draftsman, Minneapolis; Col. J. R. Camp, U.S. Army, retired, and now a well-known writer of boys' stories, Edina Village; Marion Carroll, government worker, Minneapolis; Alexander Deane, university professor, Minneapolis; K. R. Greshwalk, thespian, Richfield Township; Corey James, skate-shop proprietor, Minneapolis; J. M. Lucey, illustrator, Minneapolis; Henry Mallander, lens grinder, Robbinsdale; David Persons, jobber, St. Louis Park; Matthew Edwards, mapmaker, St. Anthony Village; S. M. Singham, merchant, Minneapolis; and Andrew Vogel, advertising salesman, Minneapolis. Col. Camp was the jury's foreman.

———

2. Phelps was unquestionably the most successful, and controversial, defense attorney of his day in Minneapolis, and was especially notorious for his support of radical causes. He was first introduced to readers in *Sherlock Holmes and the Secret Alliance*, which concerns a murder case in Minneapolis in 1899.

3. Elliott was appointed to the Minnesota Supreme Court in 1905 and went on to a long career that included a stint as an associate justice of the Supreme Court of the Philippine Islands. He also authored several law books. He died in 1935.

4. Now known as Minneapolis City Hall, this massive building—a notable example of the so-called Richardsonian Romanesque style—opened in 1895, although portions weren't completed until 1906.

List of Major Exhibits

Prosecution

1. .41-caliber Remington Model 95 double derringer

2. Coroner's report and findings re the autopsy of Mr. Michael P. Masterson, November 12, 1903

3. Partial photograph of a woman, found in Mr. Michael Masterson's left hand, November 9, 1903

4. Affidavit of Miss Lorna Smithers, office manager at Masterson, DeLaittre and Sons, Minneapolis, November 23, 1903

5. Letter from Mr. Michael Masterson to Mr. Philip Masterson, September 18, 1903

6. Letter from defendant to Mr. and Mrs. Philip Masterson, September 15, 1903

7. Seven articles written by the defendant for the *Minneapolis Tribune*, December 14–20, 1903

8. Help-wanted advertisements in the *Chicago Tribune*, May 3, 1903

9. Job application form filled out by the defendant at Masterson, DeLaittre and Sons, Minneapolis, July 15, 1903

10. Note handed by the defendant to Mrs. Philip Masterson, October 24, 1903

11. Report by Inspector Donald Gordon, Minneapolis Police Department, re a search of Mr. Michael Masterson's apartment, November 11, 1903

12. Letter from the defendant to Mr. and Mrs. Philip Masterson, November 2, 1903

13. Affidavit of Miss Ellen Morse, friend of Mr. Michael Masterson, December 16, 1903

14. Merchandise delivery receipt from John S. Bradstreet and Company, Minneapolis, September 8, 1903

15. Report on examination of bullets found at scene of Mr. Michael Masterson's death, by Mr. J. W. Smithington, ballistics expert, November 25, 1903

16. Sheet of paper with words "I, Adelaide Strongwood" and a Waterman Ideal fountain pen, both found by police in room 413 of the Windom Block, November 9, 1903

17. List of items found in Mr. Michael Masterson's pockets, as prepared by Inspector Robert McCall of the Minneapolis Police Department, November 9, 1903

18. Affidavit of Miss Emily Litton, clerk at the Robertson Secretarial Agency, January 28, 1904

Defense

1. Letter from Mr. Michael Masterson to Mr. Theodore Masterson, August 14, 1903
2. Report by Inspector Donald Gordon, Minneapolis Police Department, re an interview with Herbert Speed, pawnshop owner, November 14, 1903
3. Time card of Miss Greta Hauser, office worker at Masterson, DeLaittre and Sons, Minneapolis, August 10, 1903
4. Affidavit of Mrs. Jackie Lee, brothel owner, Minneapolis, December 8, 1903
5. Article in the *Minneapolis Journal* re a cotillion at the George Partridge residence, April 12, 1903
6. Affidavit of Dr. Richard Forsyth, veterinarian who treated Mr. Michael Masterson's cat, January 5, 1904
7. Article in the *Minneapolis Times* re Mrs. Violet Cutter, midwife, November 27, 1901
8. St. Paul Police Department records re Mr. Frank Kendall, 1898–1903
9. St. Paul Police Department records re Mr. Joseph Mugliano, 1896–1903
10. Note re "Muggy" found by police in Mr. Michael Masterson's coat pocket, November 9, 1903
11. Ledger sheet from records of Minneapolis Police Chief Frederick Ames, July 16, 1902

List of Witnesses in Order of Testimony

Prosecution

* Mr. Olaf Wangstad, elevator repairman[5]
  Patrolman Michael Sweeney, Minneapolis Police Department
* Inspector Robert McCall, Minneapolis Police Department
  Dr. Randolph Porter, Hennepin County coroner
* Miss Marie Dornquist, housemaid for Mr. and Mrs. George Van Dusen
* Miss Lorna Smithers, office supervisor, Masterson, DeLaittre and Sons
* Miss Greta Hauser, office worker, Masterson, DeLaittre and Sons
* Miss Emma Crosby, friend of Michael Masterson
* Mr. Herbert Speed, pawnshop proprietor
* Mr. Earl Duggers, Pinkerton detective
* Mrs. Philip (Bernice) Masterson, mother of Michael Masterson

---

5. An asterisk indicates a witness whose testimony is included in this account of the case.

Mr. Ernest Coxhead, chauffeur for Mr. and Mrs. Philip Masterson
* Miss Constance McBride, housemaid for Mr. and Mrs. Philip Masterson
Mrs. Hilda Jacobson, rooming house proprietor
* Mr. Daniel Wellington, clerk, John S. Bradstreet and Company
* Mrs. Violet Cutter, midwife
* Mr. Jonathan Jakes, friend of Michael Masterson
* Mr. Frank Kendall, billiard hall proprietor
* Mr. Joseph Mugliano, barber

Defense
* Inspector Donald Gordon, Minneapolis Police Department
* Mr. Samuel Marks, cigar shop proprietor
* Miss Adelaide Strongwood, defendant

PART ONE OF "AN ACCOUNT OF MY LIFE AND THE INCIDENT FOR WHICH I HAVE Been Unjustly Accused of Murder," by Addie Strongwood, *Minneapolis Tribune*, December 14, 1903

I will begin by stating that I did not murder Michael Masterson in cold blood, as the calumnies of the press would have it, and that I am in every way a woman wronged. If there does indeed abide in this world some measure of justice—a dubious proposition, I am beginning to believe—then it is not I who should be standing trial before the people of Hennepin County but those who in their low viciousness and cruel cunning abetted in the crimes against me. I feel upon me the heavy weight of falsehood, as did the prophet Isaiah: "None calleth for justice, nor any pleadeth for truth: they trust in vanity, and speak lies; they conceive mischief, and bring forth iniquity."

The truth is that I loved Michael, more than the world will ever know. I gave him my heart, which is the greatest thing a woman has to give, and I gave it to him so completely that I will never be able to give it in that way again. Yet instead of love from Michael I was met only with treachery on that fateful day in room 413 of the Windom Block.[6]

---

6. Located at Washington and Second Avenues South in downtown Minneapolis, the Windom Block was a four-story office building constructed in 1882. Once home to the offices of the Pillsbury Company, famed flour millers, the building by 1903 was already in decline, its tenants including a saloon and a barber college. The building was razed in about 1910 to make way for a federal building that still occupies the site.

My trial is now but a few weeks away, and while I am hopeful that the truth in all of its mighty splendor will emerge from the proceedings to come, I have decided to take advantage of the offer made to me by Mr. William J. Murphy[7] of the *Minneapolis Tribune* to write my own account of the events that led to Michael Masterson's death. My attorney, Mr. J. Winston Phelps, who is well known in this city as a champion of justice, has advised me to remain silent until my day in court arrives, but as I am the only person in a position to tell the truth without prejudice or distortion, I believe that I must go ahead and make my case to the public. Untruths have already been piled upon my good name like dirt slung into a freshly dug grave; I do not propose to let men with shovels bury me in their lies.

Of all the falsehoods that have circulated since that day which changed my life forever, none is more loathsome than the claim that I planned Michael's killing like some patient spider weaving its web. While it is true that I armed myself before going to the Windom Block, I did so only for the purpose of defending myself should the need arise. My intent was only to convince Michael to do the right and honorable thing. His response to my heartfelt plea was sudden and brutal, and it was in that moment life or death for me. I chose to defend my life, as any man or woman would in such dire circumstances, and had I failed to act I have no doubt that I would today be among the unremembered dead in the potter's field at Lakewood or some other lonely burial ground.[8]

It has been reported by the press since my arrest that I was raised as a "street waif" and was known, in the words of one especially malicious article in the *Journal*, to be a "wild and unruly" girl destined from an early age to a life of immorality and crime. Nothing could be further from the truth. To set the record straight, I will now describe the early years of my life, which were indeed difficult but hardly as impoverished and unhappy as certain sensation-minded writers have made them out to be.

I was born in the Third Ward[9] of the city of Minneapolis, on the 20th day of December in the year of Our Lord, 1881. I was named Adelaide, after my

---

7. William J. Murphy was publisher of the *Tribune* from 1891 until his death in 1918. Murphy Hall, home to the University of Minnesota's journalism program, bears his name.
8. Lakewood Cemetery, in the lake district of south Minneapolis, was founded in 1871. Many of the city's most famous business, civic, and political leaders are buried at Lakewood, which is the city's largest cemetery.
9. The Third Ward was located on the North Side of Minneapolis in what was then, and now, largely a working-class neighborhood.

grandmother, long dead, but I was from the very beginning called Addie. It was remarked later by my mother that having been born so close to the shortest, darkest day of the year, my purpose must be to bring some measure of light to the world. How forlorn that hope seems now as I write these words in the dreary confines of the Hennepin County jail, untouched by the golden warmth of the sun! I am only happy that my mother has not lived to see me in such circumstances or to know the terrible agonies I have endured.

My father, John Strongwood, was a hand at Mr. Curtis Pettit's flour mill[10] near Portland Avenue by the Falls of St. Anthony, and insofar as I know he was a man well regarded by one and all. Father hailed from good Puritan stock in New Hampshire, and I do not doubt that my life would have been much different had he survived to see me born and to protect me from the perils of the world. Instead, he died at the age of thirty-two, one month before my birth, when the main shaft of the Pettit Mill, above the wheel pit where he was making repairs, suddenly broke loose and came crashing down upon him like the very thunder of the heavens. He lay trapped, I have been told, for six hours, in agony all the while, until death—that blessed relief of the tortured and oppressed!— finally claimed him. May he forever rest in the peace of God's bosom.

Mr. Pettit paid my mother $100 for the trouble of losing her husband. I suppose that is what a life was worth in those days in the great city of Minneapolis; I doubt the value has risen much since then. My mother, Martha Strongwood, née Dougherty, was then left to raise me, supporting herself as a laundrywoman and operating a respectable boardinghouse on Sixth Street North, near the Church of St. Joseph, where I was baptized on a bitterly cold January day.[11] She loved me, I know now, more than she could ever say or than I could ever hope to understand.

I spoke my first words at a very tender age and once I began talking, according to my mother, I never stopped. She thought me a brilliant child—as all mothers must think their children to be—and told me once that I had been born to startle the stars. Perhaps I have done so now, although I am inclined

---

10. The Pettit Mill, built in 1878 after the original mill was destroyed by an explosion, operated until 1891, when it was converted into a grain elevator. The building was torn down in 1931, its foundations now forming part of Mill Ruins Park along the downtown Minneapolis riverfront.

11. St. Joseph's Catholic Church, built in 1889 at Fourth Street and Twelfth Avenue North, was for many years a prominent monument on Minneapolis's North Side. The twin-towered church was razed in the 1970s to make way for a new interstate highway.

to think that the stars, hurtling across the dark vault of the heavens, have no need to concern themselves with my petty affairs. By the time I was a mere eight years of age, I had already begun to write stories and poems, as I had an unusual facility with language, and I also became a voracious reader, eager to understand the world. I also enjoyed playacting, and had my circumstances been more favorable, I might have attempted a career on the stage.

Mother died in 1890. I remember seeing her in her coffin, in the front parlor, a rosary wrapped around her gray, still hands. I do not think I cried, for I had learned even at a tender age to steel myself against life's misfortunes and calamities. As I had no relatives in the city, nor anyone else to support me, I was sent to the Catholic Orphanage for Girls, where I was instructed to walk meekly before God and to obey others. I will admit I found such lessons hard to accept and that I chafed under the order imposed by the stern Sisters of Notre Dame.

Even as a young girl, I was not afraid to stand up for myself, and the nuns were no doubt pleased to be rid of me when, at age sixteen, I was sent out into the world to work as a maid. My second place of employment in this capacity was in the mansion of the Van Dusen family.[12] It was in that great house, a fairy-tale castle of round towers and swooping roofs, that I grew to womanhood, faithful in my duties but also anticipating the time when I would be able to find some better opportunity. It is now well known, thanks to the newspapers, that I was dismissed by Mrs. Van Dusen in April of this year for supposedly stealing two silver spoons. What has not been reported is that the real culprit was in fact another maid employed in the household who had long resented me. As for subsequent events at the Van Dusen mansion, I can only state that once I left that vast house under a false cloud of suspicion, I never returned and so know nothing of any criminal acts allegedly committed there.

My unjust dismissal from the Van Dusen household caused me much anguish, as might be imagined, but I did not dwell upon it. Instead, I resolved to find some new place where I could make a better life. By this time, working in domestic service had become extremely tiresome to me, and as I had reached the age of majority, I determined to seek some other line of endeavor. Mr. Van Dusen, who was of a kindly disposition and always treated me well, had spoken often of his fondness for Chicago and of the opportunities that city

---

12. The Van Dusen Mansion, built in 1893 for George and Nancy Van Dusen, still stands at 1900 LaSalle Avenue in Minneapolis and is listed on the National Register of Historic Places. It is now used as an events center.

offered to anyone eager for work. I therefore decided that Chicago would be my new home. I arrived there on a rainy morning in late April and immediately began making the rounds of employment agencies. Alas, I found the great city by the lake, with its overwhelming bustle and thick forest of buildings, to be an unwelcoming place, and despite the most vigorous effort on my part I was unable to secure a permanent position as a secretary or clerk.

So it was this past summer that I returned to Minneapolis and soon, to my happy surprise, obtained employment with the well-known manufacturing firm of Masterson, DeLaittre & Sons.[13] It was in that company's offices, on Nicollet Island just above the Falls of St. Anthony, that I first met Michael Masterson, under circumstances that I will relate shortly. Oh, how I wish now that the Mighty Hand which moves us through this troubled world had never seen fit for such a meeting to occur! But our route is not ours to choose, for as the Bible tells us, "Lest thou should ponder the path of life, her ways are moveable, and thou canst not know them."

EXCERPTS FROM THE DIRECT TESTIMONY OF OLAF WANGSTAD, ELEVATOR repairman, Mr. Boardman for the prosecution, January 11, 1904

Q: Now, Mr. Wangstad, on the night of last November ninth you were called to the Windom Block here in downtown Minneapolis to repair the building's elevator. Is that correct?

A: Yes, sir, I was. The car, it wasn't leveling up right, so I had to go to the penthouse to make some adjustments.

Q: Tell us what occurred as you were on your way to the penthouse.

A: Well, sir, I was on the fourth floor, where the stairway to the penthouse is, when I heard boom, boom, two gunshots, very loud.

Q: What time was this?

A: I would say it was quarter past nine or thereabouts.

Q: You were certain you had heard gunshots?

A: Oh yes. I hunt when I can, so I know very well what a gun sounds like.

---

13. Masterson, Delaittre and Sons was among several manufacturing firms that once occupied the southern end of Nicollet Island. All of these companies are long gone, and most of the old industrial district is now a park. Several remnants of the island's industrial past remain, however, including the Island Sash and Door Works, built in 1893 and now the Nicollet Island Inn.

Q: Could you tell where the shots had come from?

A: Sure, they came from down at the end of the hall. I saw a light on in one of the offices there.

Q: Now, after the gunshots, did you hear anything else?

A: Not that I remember.

Q: You didn't, for example, hear any loud sobbing or crying?

A: No, nothing like that.

Q: All right. What did you do next?

A: I started down the hall to see what the trouble was, but then I saw the door open—

Q: You mean the door to the office where the lights were on?

A: That's right.

Q: Did you see someone at the door?

A: No, not that I could tell. The door opened a little ways and then it closed again.

Q: As if someone was peeking out the door?

A: Could be.

Q: What did you do next, Mr. Wangstad?

A: Well, now I'm thinking I'd best be careful if there's somebody with a gun behind that door. I didn't want trouble, if you know what I mean, so I said to myself, Olaf, you should go look for a copper.

Q: And did you do so?

A: Yes, sir. I went back downstairs and I was lucky because there was a copper right out there on Washington Avenue.

Q: Was this police officer later identified to you as Michael Sweeney?

A: Yes, sir, that is who it was.

———

Q: Now, when you and Officer Sweeney reached the fourth floor of the Windom Block, what happened?

A: Well, the copper, that is, Sweeney, he starts calling out, "Police, police, what is going on?" Pretty soon, a young lady, she comes out the door and walks right toward us.

Q: Was that young woman Miss Adelaide Strongwood, the defendant in this case?

A: Yes, sir, it was her all right.

Q: How did she appear? Was she crying or upset?

A: No, she didn't seem that way at all.

Q: What happened next?

A: Well, Sweeney, he asked her if there had been some trouble and she just looked right at him calm as she could be and said, "Yes, I have just shot a man and I believe he is dead."

————————

FROM THE JOURNAL OF J. WINSTON PHELPS, NOVEMBER 14, 1903[14]

930 pm—cold rain & snow—met Miss Strongwood or Addie as she prefers to be called for first time at jail this afternoon—taller than I thought & much prettier—riveting blue eyes like jets of gas—could burn a hole right through you—no tears or outbursts of sentiment—very businesslike & organized—laid out whole tale as well as any lawyer could—was defending her honor, etc & no choice but to shoot Masterson—strange aspects to her story, tho—asked about plea to manslaughter—she wouldnt hear of it.

————————

Asked how much her defense would cost—told her not to worry as I delighted in sheer pleasure of chewing upon such a fine & well-publicized bone of contention & in any event Tribune has put in $500 for cause of justice—1st Amend a beautiful thing when theres money behind it!

————————

14. Phelps maintained a journal from 1889, when he tried one of his first high-profile cases, that of two brothers accused of rioting during a streetcar workers' strike, until 1913, when he for some reason decided to stop recording his daily thoughts and activities. The four volumes of the journal that remain at the Hennepin History Museum in Minneapolis are marked by numerous missing pages. It is not known why these pages were removed or who did so. It's possible that Phelps himself tore out the pages sometime before his death in 1921 in order to delete references to his sexual activity. Phelps was in all likelihood a gay man, and while it would have been unheard of at the time for him to "come out," his sexual orientation seems to have been widely known, judging by various comments made during the Strongwood trial. Fortunately, only a few journal pages are missing from the period of the Strongwood case. The numerous entries that remain, written in Phelps's eccentrically punctuated style, offer many insights into his trial strategy and how he obtained and assembled evidence.

EXCERPTS FROM THE DIRECT TESTIMONY OF INSPECTOR ROBERT McCALL, Minneapolis Police Department, Mr. Boardman for the prosecution, January 11, 1904

––––––––

Q: Now, Inspector McCall, you were called to the Windom Block, which is an office building here in Minneapolis, on the night of November ninth of last year. Is that correct?

A: Yes, sir.

Q: What was the nature of the call?

A: I was informed that a man had been shot and was believed to be dead.

Q: Where did the call come from?

A: From headquarters. I was told that a patrolman had found the body and that I was to take charge of the investigation.

Q: What time did you arrive at the Windom Block?

A: It was half past ten by my watch.

Q: In the evening?

A: Yes, sir.

Q: Describe the situation you encountered.

A: Well, sir, there were a number of people milling about the place and several police patrolmen standing guard outside. I was informed that the body was in room four thirteen, on the fourth floor, so that is where I went.

Q: All right. Tell us in your own words, Inspector, what you found in room four thirteen.

A: I found the body of a young man, lying on the floor. He appeared to be deceased.

Q: Was there a pool of blood beside his body?

A: Yes, sir, there was great deal of blood.

Q: Now, was the man on the floor later determined to be Michael Masterson, based on identification he carried?

A: Yes, sir.

Q: What did you do next?

A: I immediately examined Mr. Masterson for any signs of life. I found none. He was not breathing and had no pulse. I also noted that his eyes were fixed and dilated.

Q: In point of fact, when Dr. Randolph Porter, the county coroner, arrived about fifteen minutes later, he pronounced Mr. Masterson dead.[15] Isn't that correct?

A: It is, sir.

Q: Very well. Now, describe to the jury, if you would, the position and appearance of Mr. Masterson's body, based upon the notes you made at the scene.

A: Certainly. Mr. Masterson was lying on the hardwood floor of the office between a rolltop desk and an overturned chair. He was wearing a blue serge suit, a white shirt, and black oxfords. His body was in the prone position, that is to say, facedown on his stomach. His right arm was thrust outward. His left arm was tucked under his body. His legs extended in typical fashion from the torso.

Q: I see. Now, at some point you turned over Mr. Masterson's body, did you not?

A: Yes, after Dr. Porter arrived and said we could do so. Another detective, Inspector Gordon, helped me turn the body over. When this was done, I saw a large bloodstain in Mr. Masterson's shirt, near the center of his chest. Dr. Porter said I should go ahead and unbutton the shirt.

Q: What did you find when you opened up Mr. Masterson's shirt?

A: There was wound near the center of the chest.

Q: What sort of a wound did this appear to be?

A: I have seen many such wounds in my time, sir. It clearly had come from a projectile entering the body.

Q: You mean a bullet?

A: Yes, sir. It looked as though it had penetrated the heart.

Q: Dr. Porter's autopsy report, which has been admitted into evidence here as Prosecution Exhibit Two, later confirmed that Mr. Masterson died of a bullet that went through his heart and lodged in his back. Isn't that right?

A: Yes, sir, it is. Death would have been all but instantaneous.

Q: Now, Inspector, did you find anything else when you turned over Mr. Masterson's body?

A: We did, sir. Mr. Masterson had a torn photograph in his left hand. It was clenched between his thumb and forefinger.

Q: Very well, let me show you Prosecution Exhibit Three. It is a photograph, about four by four inches in size, with beveled corners. The upper left

---

15. In his testimony, Dr. Porter stated that he pronounced Michael Masterson dead at 10:36 p.m. The coroner also testified that the body displayed no signs of rigor mortis or lividity, indicating that death had occurred within the past two hours.

corner of the photograph, perhaps a square inch or more, has been ripped away. Is this the photograph you found in Mr. Masterson's hand?

A: It is, sir.

Q: Describe the photograph to the jury, if you would.

A. Well, it shows a young woman's torso from the front. The woman is naked. As you said, sir, one corner of the photograph, where the woman's face would have been, is gone.

Q: I see. I assume you searched the scene for the missing portion of the photograph?

A: Yes, sir, we searched very thoroughly, but we were unable to find it. It must have been discarded somehow before we arrived.

[Objection, Mr. Phelps. Speculation. Sustained.]

Q: Even though the face of the woman in the photograph cannot be seen, do you know her identity?

A: Yes, sir. It is the defendant, Miss Strongwood.

Q: And how do you know this, Inspector?

A: Well, sir, because she told us so.

———

Q: In addition to the photograph, what else did you find upon Mr. Masterson's person?

A: We found quite a few items in his pants and coat pockets. I made a list of them.

Q: Let me show you Prosecution Exhibit Seventeen. Is this the list you prepared?

A: It is.

Q: Please read it to the jury.

A: Of course. Let me just put my reading glasses on. All right, here is what I wrote down: "Baume pocket watch with chain. Two five-dollar gold pieces. Leather wallet containing twenty-two dollars in currency, an identification card with Mr. Masterson's name and address, and a blank check from Mr. Masterson's account at the First National Bank of Minneapolis. Handkerchief embroidered with the letters MPM. Door key, probably to Mr. Masterson's residence. Slip of plain white paper with the words 'Muggy, Thomas Western, 1 a.m. Tuesday, red barrel,' handwritten in pencil. Business card for 'Best Billiard Hall, 450 Wabasha St., St. Paul, F. Kendall, proprietor.' Small ivory-handled pocket knife." That covers it.

Q: Thank you. We will explore the significance of some of these items a bit later. In the meantime, please describe for us in more detail the office in which Mr. Masterson's body was found.

A: I will be happy to do so, sir. The office was approximately twelve-by-sixteen feet in size, with two windows facing to the southeast. Both windows were shuttered. An overhead electric fixture provided the only light. We were later told by the building owner that the office had been vacant for some time. As far as furniture goes, there was a rolltop desk along the wall between the windows, a high stool of the kind used by clerks, and an office chair. The chair had been tipped on its side and was near the center of the office.

Q: Did you notice anything else?

A: Yes, sir, I did. There was a hole in the plaster wall a foot or so above the desk.

Q: A bullet hole?

[Objection, Mr. Phelps. Leading the witness. Sustained.]

Q: Let me rephrase the question. What sort of hole did you find in the wall?

A: We examined it and saw that it had been made by a bullet, which was lodged there.

Q: Now, let me show you Prosecution Exhibit Fifteen, which is a report submitted by Mr. J. W. Smithington of Chicago, who is a well-known ballistics expert. His report, which the defense does not contest, states that the bullet found in Mr. Masterson's body and the bullet lodged in the wall were both fired from Miss Strongwood's derringer. Is that correct?[16]

A: Yes, sir. Mr. Smithington had no doubts in that regard.

––––––––

Q: Let us continue with our look at the scene of Mr. Masterson's death. You stated that there was a rolltop desk in the room. Was anything on this desk?

A: Yes, sir, there was a black Waterman Ideal fountain pen[17] and a sheet of paper.

Q: Let me show you Prosecution Exhibit Sixteen. Is this the piece of paper you found on the desk?

––––––––

16. Ballistics evidence was ruled admissible in Minnesota courts as early as 1879. However, it wasn't until the 1920s that forensic ballistics came into widespread use in criminal prosecutions.

17. The Waterman Pen Company was founded in New York in 1884 by Lewis Waterman, who patented a system whereby air pressure controlled the flow of ink from the reservoir. The Waterman Ideal, made of hard rubber and featuring a gold nib, was the most popular American fountain pen of the early 1900s.

A: It is, sir.

Q: What if anything is written on it?

A: There are three handwritten words. The first word is "I," followed by a comma, and then the words "Adelaide Strongwood."

Q: Just those three words and nothing else?

A: Yes, sir, that is all it says.

———

Q: Now, Inspector McCall, after leaving the office where Michael Masterson lay dead, you went into an adjoining room to speak to Miss Strongwood. Is that correct?

A: Yes, sir.

Q: And in that room did you find a forty-one-caliber Remington double der-ringer[18] Miss Strongwood had surrendered to Patrolman Michael Sweeney?

A: Yes, the gun was there.

Q: Did you examine the weapon?

A: I did. There were spent rounds in both barrels.

Q: What happened next?

A: I asked Miss Strongwood if the weapon belonged to her and she said it did. I then asked whether she had used the weapon to shoot Mr. Masterson and she answered "yes."

Q: Did she appear nervous or upset to you?

A: Not that I could tell.

Q: What about her physical appearance? Were there any signs that she had been involved in a struggle?

A: No, nothing like that. She was wearing a black wool jacket and a gray skirt and her entire appearance was very neat. Nothing looked out of the ordi-nary. As I said, she was very composed.

Q: You found her behavior to be unusual, I take it?

A: Very unusual. Women, as we all know, are fragile creatures and become emotionally distraught all too easily. Given what had just happened, I should have thought she would be making quite a scene.

[Objection, Mr. Phelps. Irrelevant, speculation, etc. Overruled.]

———

18. The Remington Model 95 double derringer featured superimposed barrels and was a very popular weapon for many years. It was introduced in the 1860s and remained in production until 1935.

Q: Tell the jury what occurred next.

A: I informed her that Mr. Masterson had been declared dead and asked if she had anything to say about it. She looked me straight in the eye and replied, "It had to be, as Michael was untrue to me in every way that a man can be, and now he has paid the price for his crimes." At least, those were her words as I recall them.

Q: What else did she tell you?

A: She stated that she had been lured to the scene and that Mr. Masterson had tried to kill her with the help of a hired assassin. When I asked her who this supposed assassin was, she claimed not to know his name. I said I found her story hard to believe.

Q: How did she respond?

A: She said that what the police thought did not matter to her because she knew in her own heart the truth of what had happened. I then told her that it was the truth we wished to hear and that she could unburden herself by confessing to Mr. Masterson's murder.

Q: What did she say to that?

A: She just shook her head and said, "It was not murder. It was simply what needed to be done." I must tell you, it sent a chill down my spine, the way she said that. It was very cold.

[Objection, Mr. Phelps. Opinion, irrelevant, etc. Overruled.]

Q: At this point did she show any regret about what had happened?

A: There was nothing like that. I do not think she shed a single tear.

————

Excerpts from the direct testimony of Miss Adelaide Strongwood, defendant, Mr. Phelps for the defense, January 27, 1904

————

Q: Now, Addie, you heard earlier in this trial the testimony of Inspector Robert McCall regarding your behavior when he interviewed you shortly after Mr. Masterson's death. You appeared very calm to him. Were you in fact without emotions or deep feeling at that moment?

A: Oh no, my heart was pierced with anguish, even though I knew I had acted in self-defense. A life was gone, the life of a man I thought I once had loved. How could any woman not feel the deepest sorrow at such a time? It was all I could do not to break out in tears. But I knew I could not let myself go, not with the police accusing me of murder and demanding that I confess to the crime. I had to keep my mind clear, despite the grief and horror I felt.

Q: And when you were taken to jail that evening, how did you react?

A: All the emotions that I done my best to keep in check burst out like the waters of a mighty torrent. I think I cried the whole night long.

————

EXCERPTS FROM THE CROSS-EXAMINATION OF INSPECTOR ROBERT McCALL, Mr. Phelps for the defense, January 12, 1904

————

Q: Inspector, you have stated that you and your men searched for the missing part of the photograph in Mr. Masterson's hand but could not find it. You made a minute search of the office, I suppose.

A: Yes, sir, every inch of it, to no avail.

Q: Could the missing piece have been tossed out one of the windows?

A: No, sir, the windows were all bolted shut.

Q: And you searched the hallway outside the office as well?

A: We searched everywhere.

Q: Was Miss Strongwood's person also searched?

A: Yes, sir. One of the matrons at the jail made a very thorough examination.

Q: I see. Well, then, could she have swallowed the evidence, as it were?

A: We investigated that possibility, sir.

Q: I imagine you did. We need not go into the specifics of how this was accomplished, but am I safe in assuming you found nothing to suggest that she had ingested the missing portion of the picture?

A: That is correct, sir. It would have turned up in the normal manner had she done so.

Q: So, in fact, you have no idea where the missing portion of the photograph might be. Isn't that right?

A: Yes, sir, we have yet to locate it, assuming it still exists.

Q: Isn't it entirely possible that Mr. Masterson himself tore Addie's face from the photograph in a moment of rage before bringing it to Windom Block that night?

[Objection, Mr. Boardman. Calls for speculation. Sustained.]

———————

EXCERPTS FROM THE DIRECT TESTIMONY OF MISS MARIE DORNQUIST, VAN Dusen family maid, Mr. Boardman for the prosecution, January 13, 1904[19]

Q: Now, Miss Dornquist, tell us if you would about a conversation you had with the defendant in the early months of last year, not long before she left the employ of the Van Dusens. I am referring specifically to a conversation regarding Miss Strongwood's desire to become a wealthy woman.

A: Well, she talked about that all the time, if you want to know, but I remember this one time when she just went on and on about it, saying as how she would be richer than Mrs. Van Dusen one day and have the finest mansion in Minneapolis.

Q: Did the defendant say how she intended to achieve such wealth?

A: Oh, she talked about that all the time, too. She said she would find a rich man and wrap him around her finger. She said men were all fools and could be played easy as could be if a person knew how.

Q: What do you suppose she meant by "playing" a man? Seducing him, perhaps?

[Objection, Mr. Phelps. Speculation, leading the witness, etc. Sustained.]

Q: All right, let us move on and explore the matter of the defendant's departure from the Van Dusen household, which I am informed took place in April of last year. Is that correct?

A: I believe so.

Q: Why did she leave?

A: It was on account of the stolen spoons.

———————

19. *The Trial of Adelaide Strongwood* offered this description of Dornquist: "The next to testify was the maid, Marie Dornquist, a very petite young woman, nineteen years of age, with sharp pointed features and coal black hair tied up in a bun. She wore a white blouse and navy blue skirt, spoke in a quiet voice, and appeared rather nervous on the stand, especially during Mr. Phelps's probing cross-examination."

Q: I see. Now, as I understand it, you were with Mrs. Van Dusen when she found two silver spoons from her best service in the bottom of a drawer in the defendant's room in the attic of the mansion. Is that correct?

A: Yes. Mrs. Van Dusen told me to come along with her as she had reason to believe Addie was a thief. I was right there when Mrs. Van Dusen opened the drawer and found the spoons.

Q: Then what happened?

A: Oh, I remember that very well, sir. Mrs. Van Dusen said, "I knew it! I knew that girl could not be trusted."

Q: And Miss Strongwood was terminated that very day. Isn't that right?

A: Yes, sir. Mrs. Van Dusen is not the sort of woman who would tolerate a thief in her household.

———

Q: Did you have occasion to speak with the defendant after she was let go by Mrs. Van Dusen?

A: Yes.

Q: When and where did this conversation occur?

A: Well, sir, she was cleaning out her room that very day and as I was passing in the hallways she called me in.

Q: I see. What did she say to you?

A: I will never forget it, sir. She looked at me with those terrible eyes of hers and said, "Mrs. Van Dusen will pay. Mark my words, she will pay dearly for what she has done to me."

Q: So Miss Strongwood was very angry, I take it.

A: Oh yes, sir, angry as a nest of hornets.

Q: Did she say anything else to you, such as how Mrs. Van Dusen might be made to pay?

A: No, not exactly.

Q: All right, what else did Miss Strongwood say to you during the conversation in her room?

A: Well, she called Mrs. Van Dusen a bad name, if you want to know the truth.

Q: And what was this name?

[Objection, Mr. Phelps. Irrelevant. Overruled.]

A: Oh, I would rather not say, sir.

COURT: The witness is instructed to answer the question.

A: She called her a bitch, sir.

Q: Thank you, Miss Dornquist. No further questions.

Excerpts from an article in the MINNEAPOLIS JOURNAL, January 2, 1904[20]

The social set in Minneapolis has begun decamping to warmer climes. Among those already on their way are Mr. and Mrs. George Van Dusen, who left yesterday for their winter residence in Pasadena, California.

The couple's departure comes only a week or so before the trial of their former maid, Addie Strongwood, is to begin in Hennepin County District Court on charges that she murdered her lover, Michael Masterson. It had been thought that Mrs. Van Dusen might be called upon to testify at the trial, but that clearly will not be the case now that she and her husband are bound for California.

———

FROM THE JOURNAL OF J. WINSTON PHELPS, JANUARY 13, 1904

830 pm—long day in court & much arguing—Judge Elliott an ass but no surprise there—will have at little Miss Dornquist tomorrow—dont think she did much damage on direct—even so will have to explain what Addie meant by making Mrs. Van Dusen "pay."

Boardman trying to sneak in the "fire" angle any way he can—Addie of course denies it all—matters not as Boardman is without proof.

———

EXCERPTS FROM THE CROSS-EXAMINATION OF MISS MARIE DORNQUIST, MR. Phelps for the defense, January 14, 1904

———

20. The *Journal* was Minneapolis's leading afternoon newspaper in the early 1900s. Regarded as the newspaper of the city's upper classes, it was generally far more critical of Addie Strongwood than its morning rival, the *Tribune*.

———

Q: I would be curious to know, Miss Dornquist, if you considered Addie to be a friend during the time the two of you worked for the Van Dusens?

A: I guess so.

Q: That does not sound like a ringing endorsement of your affection for her. The truth of the matter, Miss Dornquist, is that you didn't like Addie one bit, did you?

A: I should not say that.

Q: Really? Come now, let us be honest. Isn't it a fact you resented her beauty and intelligence? Isn't it a fact that you were jealous that so many handsome young men courted her, while you were not so fortunate in that regard?

A: No, that's not true.

Q: I see. Perhaps I am mistaken then. Would I also be mistaken in noting that, according to the police department of this city, a complaint was lodged against one Marie Dornquist on February 2, 1902, alleging that the said Miss Dornquist attempted to steal silver earrings valued at ten dollars from Grand Jewelers at 408 Hennepin Avenue? Am I mistaken as well that the report states you were caught red-handed leaving the store with the earrings hidden in your purse? I am anxious to hear your response, Miss Dornquist.

A: That is a lie. I did not steal those earrings.

Q: I see. The earrings, I take it then, must somehow have fallen, unbeknownst to you, into your purse, which then latched itself tight, no doubt much to your chagrin. Is that your story?

A: No. It was a misunderstanding. I never intended to steal anything.

Q: Well, I am happy to hear that. Still, the police report suggests that you are a young woman who likes the gleam and shimmer of silvery things. Perhaps those pretty spoons caught your eye as well. Perhaps you even stole them and put that in Addie's room to get her fired because you hated her so. Isn't that what actually happened, Miss Dornquist?

A: No, no. That is not true. I am not a thief.

Q: How reassuring. Now, let us turn to another portion of your direct testimony that requires more than passing scrutiny. You stated that after Addie was let go, you and she had a talk during which she vowed that Mrs. Van Dusen would be made to "pay" for her actions. Correct?

A: Yes, sir.

Q: But Addie didn't say specifically how she intended to make Mrs. Van Dusen pay, did she?

A: No, she didn't go on about it, at least as I remember.

Q: Isn't it entirely possible, Miss Dornquist, that Addie meant her words in a very literal way? To wit, that she expected to receive her full week of wages from Mrs. Van Dusen for services rendered, even if she had been let go?

A: I don't know, sir.

Q: But it makes sense, does it not, that Addie simply wanted the money owed her. Wouldn't you agree?

[Objection, Mr. Boardman. Leading question. Sustained.]

Q: Well, let me ask you this: did Addie at any point during your conversation say that she intended to cause physical harm to Mrs. Van Dusen or anyone else in the Van Dusen household?

A: No, she did not say that.

Q: She didn't say she was going to lie in wait and attack Mrs. Van Dusen?

A: No, sir.

Q: She didn't say she was going to steal something from her?

A: No, sir.

Q: She didn't say she was going to set the house on fire?

A: No, sir.

Q: In fact, there really was nothing threatening about her words, was there?

[Objection, Mr. Boardman. Leading question. Sustained.]

———

Q. All right, let's talk about Addie's alleged name-calling. Is Mrs. Van Dusen an easy woman to work for?

A: I have had no trouble, sir.

Q: That is not what I asked. How long have you worked at the Van Dusen home?

A: It will be three years in March.

Q: And during that time, how many maids or other staff members have been let go by Mrs. Van Dusen on one pretext or another?

A: Oh, I really don't know, sir. There have been some, I'm sure.

Q: "Some" is a vague term, Miss Dornquist. Let us get down to the specifics. Would you say the number exceeds five?

A: I would think so, yes.

Q: Ten?

A: It could be that many, yes.

Q: Fifteen?

A: Ten would probably be about right, sir.

Q: Well, then, let us split the difference and say that perhaps a dozen maids and other servants have been let go during your three years at the Van Dusen mansion. That's an average of four or so a year. Quite a bit of turnover, wouldn't you say?

[Objection, Mr. Boardman. Calls for opinion. Sustained.]

Q: Very well, let me rephrase the question. Isn't Mrs. Van Dusen in fact a notoriously difficult and demanding woman who thinks nothing of firing employees on the merest whim? And doesn't that make her—I hate to say it, but I must—exactly what Addie and no doubt other servants have called her?

[Objection, Mr. Boardman. Calls for speculation. Sustained.]

Q: I withdraw the question, Your Honor. I have nothing further of this witness.

EXCERPTS FROM THE DIRECT TESTIMONY OF MISS LORNA SMITHERS,[21] OFFICE supervisor, Masterson, DeLaittre and Sons, Mr. Boardman for the prosecution, January 14, 1904

———

Q: Miss Smithers, in your capacity as a supervisor at Masterson, DeLaittre and Sons, is one of your duties the hiring of new office girls as needed?

A: Yes.

Q: And how do you go about selecting a new employee, such as Miss Strongwood was last year?

A: I look for young women of high moral character who can be relied upon to be thorough, honest, and industrious at all times. I will not stand for lazy or foolish girls.

Q: Do you also look for girls who may have some previous experience in secretarial or clerking work?

A: Of course. It is always best to hire an experienced girl if that is possible.

———

21. A *Minneapolis Journal* reporter described Smithers as "a small but energetic woman, in her middle years, with an oval face, a prominent pointed nose and gold, wire-rimmed glasses. She speaks quickly and precisely and appears to know her business very thoroughly."

Q: Very well. Now, I call your attention to Prosecution Exhibit Nine, which is an application form for work at your company. Do you recognize it as such?

A: I do.

Q: And could you tell us who submitted this application, dated July 15 of last year?

A: Yes, it was Adelaide Strongwood. Her signature is right there at the bottom.

Q: I see. Now, on the fourth line of the application there is request for information regarding previous employment. Is that correct?

A: Yes.

Q: Please read to the court what is written on that line of Miss Strongwood's application?

A: Of course. It says, "Employed as secretary for Stillwell Industries, Chicago, Illinois, April 1903 to July 1903."

Q: Thank you. Now, to your knowledge, is that a true statement, Miss Smithers?

[Objection, Mr. Phelps. Calls for conclusion, assumes facts not in evidence, etc. Overruled.]

A: It is not a true statement.

Q: How do you know that?

A: For the simple reason that I have had occasion to check the reference. There is in fact no firm named Stillwell Industries in Chicago.

Q: Very well. And in fact, you have submitted an affidavit, which is Prosecution Exhibit Four, have you not, describing in considerable detail how you were able to ascertain that there is indeed no firm by the name of Stillwell Industries in Chicago or anywhere else in Illinois?

A: Yes.

MR. PHELPS: Your Honor, in order to save us all from further tedious inquiries, the defense will stipulate as to the nonexistence of Stillwell Industries.

COURT: Then let it be so stipulated on the record. Do you have additional questions for this witness, Mr. Boardman?

Q: I do, if it may please the court. Now, Miss Smithers, in going over Miss Strongwood's application to work at Masterson, DeLaittre and Sons, was it your considered judgment that she was the best candidate for the position that was available?

A: No, there were at least two other girls who looked more qualified and able than she was.

Q: How interesting. Why, then, did you hire Miss Strongwood?

A: Because I was told to.

Q: By whom?

A: Why, by Mr. Masterson himself.

Q: You mean, Michael Masterson?

A: No, I mean Philip Masterson.

Q: Michael's father, the owner of the company?

A: Yes.

Q: How did this come about?

A: How was I told to hire Miss Strongwood? Is that what you are asking?

Q: Yes.

A: Well, I received a note from Mr. Masterson.

Q: I see. What did this note say?

A: As I remember, it said that Mr. Masterson was aware of a certain Miss Strongwood who had applied for work and that I was to hire her at once.

Q: Did the note say anything else?

A: Yes. It said she was to start at twelve dollars a week.

Q: Twelve dollars a week? That is quite a lot for a new clerk, is it not?

A: I should say so. Most of the girls begin at eight.

Q: Did Mr. Masterson indicate why he wished Miss Strongwood to receive such high wages?

A: No.

Q: Tell me this, Miss Smithers: Did Mr. Philip Masterson, as owner of the company, often send notes to you directing you to hire a particular person?

A: Absolutely not. Such a thing had never happened before in my experience.

Q: So you found it unusual?

A: Very unusual.

Q: And Mr. Masterson, I believe you said, offered no explanation for his intervention on behalf of Miss Strongwood?

A: None whatever.

Q: Let us return now to the matter of how Miss Strongwood came to leave the firm. Did she leave of her own accord or was she let go?

A: She was let go for cause.

Q: When was this?

A: September eighteenth of last year.

Q: Less than two months before Michael Masterson was killed, is that correct?

A: Correct.

Q: Now, you indicated earlier in your testimony that you learned Miss Strongwood had entered false information on her application. Is that why she was terminated?

A: That was the stated reason, yes.

Q: How did you learn of this false information?

A: I am afraid I cannot recall exactly. I believe it might have been mentioned to me by one of the other office girls who knew Miss Strongwood. There were irregularities, or so I was informed, regarding the company in Chicago she said she had worked for.

Q: You mean Stillwell Industries?

A: Yes.

Q: As you've told us, you were quickly able to determine that there was no firm by that name in Chicago. What did you do next?

A: I went to Miss Strongwood and asked for an explanation.

Q: And what did she say?

A: She offered no explanation. She just shrugged and said that she supposed she would be let go now. I said I certainly could not have a dishonest employee and then she laughed. I'll never forget that. She laughed and said I did not know half the story, or something like that.

Q: Were you surprised by her rather nonchalant response to the news that she would be let go?

A: Yes, I had never seen a girl act like that before.

Q: Then what happened?

A: Well, normally I would have let her go at once, but I thought it best to check first with Mr. Masterson, as he seemed to have a special interest in her.

Q: That would be Philip Masterson?

A: Yes.

Q: And when you reported the situation to Mr. Masterson, what was his response?

A: He agreed that Miss Strongwood should be terminated at once.

Q: He had no doubts in this regard?

A: None that I was made aware of.

———

EXCERPTS FROM THE CROSS-EXAMINATION OF MISS LORNA SMITHERS, MR. Phelps for the defense, January 14, 1904

Q: When was my client hired by your firm, Miss Smithers?

A: I believe she began work on July twentieth of last year.

Q: And was her work satisfactory?

A: For the most part, yes.

Q: Well, what part wasn't satisfactory?

A: I am not sure I can give you any specifics in that regard.

Q: Why is that?

A: Well, I would have to look at my records to see.

Q: And that, no doubt, would be a laborious process. So you are in essence telling us that her work was satisfactory except when it wasn't, even though you can't tell us why it may have been unsatisfactory. Does that about sum it up?

A: I am not sure I would put it that way.

Q: Then how would you put it?

A: I would simply say that her work generally was satisfactory.

Q: All right, I can see that we are waltzing merrily around this particular question with no end to the dance in sight, so let us move on. You stated that Miss Strongwood was hired upon the direct order of Mr. Philip Masterson. Is that correct?

A: Yes.

Q: You also stated, did you not, that Mr. Masterson gave no reason as to why he wished you to hire Miss Strongwood?

A: That is correct.

Q: Nor was a reason given as to why she was to be paid twelve dollars a week, was it?

A: Correct.

Q: So, it would be fair to say, would it not, that you have no knowledge as to why this apparent favoritism was shown to Miss Strongwood?

A: Yes.

Q: And would it also be fair to say that you have no reason to believe that Miss Strongwood herself requested or expected such favoritism?

A: I have no knowledge of what she may have done to gain such favor, if that is what you are asking.

Q: In fact, to your knowledge, she may have done nothing whatsoever to cultivate favor. Isn't that right?

A: I suppose so, but it is peculiar nonetheless.

Q: I agree, Miss Smithers. Isn't it possible that the person who wanted to see Miss Strongwood hired was in truth Michael Masterson, and not his father? [Objection, Mr. Boardman. Speculation. Overruled.]

A: I wouldn't know.

Q: Well, isn't it a fact that Michael had quite an eye for the young ladies and would often come through the office to talk with your girls?

A: He would come to the office sometimes, yes.

Q: And flirt with the girls?

A: I really could not say.

Q: And isn't it possible that he could have spotted Miss Strongwood among the girls applying for jobs and decided that she was a girl he would very much like to pursue and so told his father that she should be hired on some pretext or other?

A: I have no knowledge of that.

———

Q: You stated that my client was hired in July and was terminated some two months later, this past September, after you discovered a discrepancy on her employment application. Tell us again, if you would, how you made this belated discovery.

A: As I told Mr. Boardman, I am not positive as to how I learned of the discrepancy, as you call it. But I think it may have come from one of the office girls.

Q: Any girl in particular?

A: Not that I can recall.

Q: So perhaps you learned of the discrepancy is some other way?

A: Perhaps.

Q: My dear Miss Smithers, you have suddenly become a sworn enemy of anything that smacks of specificity. You say the discrepancy came to your attention, but you really can't say how. Did a bright blue bird fly in through your window with a little note attached to its beak saying, "Check Miss Strongwood's employment application"?

A: You are being ridiculous, Mr. Phelps.

Q: Perhaps, but you are being evasive. Now, I must ask you again: exactly how did the alleged discrepancy come to your attention?

A: I told you. I can't recall.

Q: Ah, so it might have been that bird after all.

[Objection, Mr. Boardman. Mocking witness. Sustained.]

Q: Let me submit to you, Miss Smithers, that you do in fact know who ordered you to take another look at my client's application. It was Philip Masterson himself, was it not?

A: I do not recall anything like that.

Q: Don't recall or won't recall?

[Objection, Mr. Boardman. Badgering the witness. Overruled.]

A: As I have said before, I do not recall.

Q: How peculiar, given the razor-sharp memory you displayed on direct examination. Well then, let us test your apparently failing memory on another point. Regarding the application from my client Mr. Boardman showed you a little while ago, do you remember anything unusual about it? Anything at all that might cause you to take note?

A: No, it was our standard application for employment.

Q: Filled out in the standard way?

A: I think so.

Q: Let me show you the application again, which is Prosecution Exhibit Nine. Now, what do you notice about the much disputed line regarding my client's previous employment in Chicago with what we now know to be the nonexistent Stillwell Industries?

A: I'm not sure what you mean.

Q: Oh, come, Miss Smithers, do I have to draw you a diagram? The line is printed in all capital letters, is it not?

A: Yes.

Q: And what about the rest of the application?

A: The rest is handwritten.

Q: In cursive?

A: Yes.

Q: Does that strike you as odd?

[Objection, Mr. Boardman. Calls for conclusion. Overruled.]

A: I really couldn't say.

Q: So if I told you that next week, on account of my birthday, there will officially be eight days instead of the usual seven, you would see nothing peculiar about that, I presume.

[Objection, Mr. Boardman. Badgering the witness. Sustained.]

Q: Then let us get to the nub of this supposed falsehood. Isn't it a fact that Miss Strongwood made no mention of previous employment on her original application and that the printed reference to Stillwell Industries was added later upon the direct orders of Philip Masterson himself, who wanted a pretext to get rid of her because of her involvement with his son? It was printed because forging Miss Strongwood's handwriting would have been too difficult and might have raised suspicions. Isn't that what actually happened, Miss Smithers?

A: It did not, sir, and that is an outrageous claim.

Q: No, what is outrageous is that my client was the victim of such a bold and malicious fraud.

[Objection, Mr. Boardman. Defense counsel is testifying. Sustained.]

Q: No further questions, Your Honor.

PROSECUTION EXHIBIT NUMBER FIVE, LETTER FROM MICHAEL MASTERSON TO Philip Masterson, his father, dated September 18, 1903

Dearest Father:

Greetings from the Palmer House![22] I'm sure you won't be surprised to hear that Jake[23] and I are having a swell time in Chicago. We have already been to the art museum, which is as fine as you said it would be. We saw Uncle Peter and stayed at his "little" place on the North Shore[24] last night. He is doing just fine and says business has never been better. Didn't see Cousin Theo, who was

---

22. The Palmer House, one of Chicago's most opulent hotels, was built in 1875 by businessman Potter Palmer. A new hotel of the same name was built on the site in 1920s and remains a Chicago landmark.

23. "Jake" is a reference to Jonathan Jakes, a close friend of Michael Masterson, who later gave crucial testimony at the trial. Peter Masterson was a wealthy Chicago merchant, whose son, Theodore, had apparently been quite close at one time to his cousin, Michael. It is unknown why the cousins had a "falling out," but the ill will between them was to have consequences in the Strongwood case because of several key pieces of evidence Theodore Masterson very probably leaked to the defense.

24. The North Shore is an area along Lake Michigan where many of Chicago's wealthiest families built mansions.

off on one of his gallivants but I guess he'll be coming up to Mpls. soon. Don't know if I'll see him, tho, or even want to, as you are all too aware of our falling out. I have tried not to think of the business with Miss Strongwood while we're here, but it is still preying on my mind. I am well aware of how upsetting it has been to you and Mother, but I must assure you again that I never made any promises to her as she claims. Father, did you let her go today as you said you would? It was certainly the right thing to do.

I hardly need add that she is a schemer of the lowest sort, and I rue the day I met her. You warned me long ago that there would be a certain class of women interested only in my money and my name who would use all of their female wiles to entrap me. How right you were, Father, and how ignorant I was to ever doubt your wise counsel! I hope you can forgive me, as I do not wish to see our family's good name sullied in any way.

We'll come back Tues. or Wed. on the noon Burlington but first we're going to the McVickers tonight to see Weber and Fields, who always put on a funny show.[25]

Your obedient and loving son,
Mikey

FROM THE JOURNAL OF J. WINSTON PHELPS, NOVEMBER 16, 1903

930 pm—call from Shad[26] this evening & had long talk—said hed heard Addie was my client & found her case most interesting, especially as it was a

---

25. "Burlington" refers to the Burlington & Quincy Railroad, which provided regular passenger service between Chicago and the Twin Cities. The McVickers Theater, on Madison Street in Chicago, was designed by the famed architects Louis Sullivan and Dankmar Adler. It was demolished in 1922. Comedians Joe Weber and Lew Fields formed a popular vaudeville act in the early 1900s.

26. "Shad" refers to Shadwell Rafferty, a St. Paul saloonkeeper and part-time detective who was well known in the Twin Cities at the time, especially for his connections to Sherlock Holmes. Rafferty first met Holmes and Dr. John Watson in St. Paul in 1896 during the case later recounted in *Sherlock Holmes and the Ice Palace Murders*. The trio also became involved in *Sherlock Holmes and the Rune Stone Mystery*, concerning murderous events in western Minnesota in 1899. Later that year, they met again in Minneapolis to investigate the case that became the subject of *Sherlock Holmes and the Secret Alliance*. It was while looking into the doings of the Alliance that Rafferty first met Phelps, and the two men became friends thereafter.

rich man she killed—offered to be of help—accepted at once as it never hurts
to have a bulldog in your corner.

———

Asked about note found in Mastersons pocket re Muggys Thomas Western—a
St. Paul street address perhaps?—Shad said it was & that he knows all about
Muggy!—seems my ship has come in & theres a fat Irishman at the tiller.

EXCERPT FROM THE *TRIAL OF ADELAIDE STRONGWOOD*

———

It should hardly come as a surprise that no witness in the case spent more time
on the stand, or underwent a more rigorous examination, than Miss Strongwood herself. Her direct testimony commenced on January 27 and concluded
the following morning. Mr. Boardman's cross-examination consumed an even
longer number of hours, and it wasn't until five o'clock on the evening of January 29 that Miss Strongwood finally stepped down.

———

EXCERPTS FROM THE DIRECT TESTIMONY OF MISS ADELAIDE STRONGWOOD,
Mr. Phelps for the defense, January 27, 1904

Q: Good morning, Miss Strongwood.
A: Good morning to you, sir.
Q: May I call you Addie?
A: Of course. Everyone does.
Q: Addie, I am going to begin with the question which, as you and everyone
   else in this courtroom knows, is at the heart of this matter: Did you, on
   November 9, 1903, go to office number four thirteen of the Windom Block
   here in the city of Minneapolis and shoot down Michael Masterson in cold
   blood, having premeditated his murder because he refused to pay you ten
   thousand dollars?
A: No, I did not.

Q: Did you in fact shoot and kill Michael Masterson?

A: I did.

Q: Why did you do so?

A: To protect my own life, Mr. Phelps. I had no choice, yet I will regret to my dying day that I was forced to do what I did. Michael had once been a friend to me, or so I thought.

Q: But in that room at the Windom, he was not your friend, was he?

A: No, he was as a wild beast, lusting for blood.

Q: Addie, there has been much testimony at this trial concerning the alleged theft of two silver spoons at the Van Dusen home in Minneapolis while you were employed there as a maid. Did you purloin those spoons and put them in a drawer in your room?

A: I did not. I was not raised by my dear mother to be a thief. I have never stolen anything in my life.

Q: Yet those spoons were found in your drawer. How do you suppose they got there?

[Objection, Mr. Boardman. Calls for speculation. Sustained.]

Q: All right, let me ask you this: Did you keep your room in the Van Dusen mansion locked while you went about your duties during the day?

A: No, I saw no need. I had nothing of great value in the room and no reason to believe anyone in the household would wish to steal from me.

Q: So if, say, a maid or anyone else in the household wished to enter your room while you were gone, I suppose there would be nothing to stop them.

A: That is correct.

Q: One of your fellow maids at the Van Dusen mansion was a girl named Marie Dornquist. Is that right?

A: Yes.

Q: Were the two of you friends?

A: We certainly knew each other, but I would not say we were friends.

Q: You did not like her for some reason?

A: I would say it was more a matter that I did not trust her.

Q: Why?

A: She was very fond of gossip and was always saying malicious things behind people's backs. My mother once told me that gossips were the scourge of the world, and I believe so to this day.

Q: Did she gossip about you in a malicious way?

A: I was informed so, yes.

Q: In fact, didn't she regularly attribute to you statements which in fact you had never made, just to embarrass and belittle you?

[Objection, Mr. Boardman. Hearsay. Sustained.]

Q: Did you ever tell Miss Dornquist that you hoped to find a rich man and, I quote, "wrap him around your finger"?

A: No, I never said such a thing.

Q: And did you ever state to her that all men were fools who could be played?

A: No, that is entirely ridiculous.

Q: Did you ever state that you intended to become richer than your employer, Mrs. Van Dusen?

A: I remember saying to Marie that I dreamed of being wealthy one day and having a fine house and a handsome husband and a beautiful family. I will readily admit that I dreamed of such a life. What poor girl does not?

Q: Indeed, Addie. I do not think we can fairly criticize you for that.

———

Q: Now, Addie, I wish to turn to the matter of your initial employment at Masterson, DeLaittre and Sons. As you are aware, there has been testimony to the effect that you entered false information on your employment application. Is that true?

A: It is not.

Q: So when asked about previous employment in Chicago, you did not write in the name of Stillwell Industries as a company for which you had worked?

A: I most certainly did not. I have no idea how that information appeared on the application form. I can only surmise that someone put it there later in an attempt to discredit me.

Q: In fact, you entered nothing in the section of the form asking for previous employment. Is that correct?

A: That is correct.

———

Q: Addie, questions have also been raised about your wages at the Masterson firm. You were hired, as I understand it, at a wage of twelve dollars per week.

A: Yes.

Q: Was that, to your knowledge, higher than the typical beginning wages for a clerk?

A: I did not know it at the time, if that is your question, but I have since learned that it was indeed a high wage.

Q: Do you know why you received a higher-than-average wage?

A: I do not.

Q: So you were not aware that anyone in the company, Philip Masterson, say, or even Michael, had intervened on your behalf to specify the wages you were to receive?

A: I had no knowledge of any such thing, nor any reason to suspect that it might be so.

———

Q: During the time you and Michael were together, did he ever state that he had intervened with his father to hire you?

A: No. I do not recall that we ever discussed the circumstances of my employment.

Q: To sum up, as far as you knew, you were hired in the normal way and paid the normal wages for the position you held. Would that be an accurate statement?

A: Yes, it would. I requested no favors and was not aware that any had been granted to me.

———

EXCERPTS FROM THE CROSS-EXAMINATION OF MISS ADELAIDE STRONGWOOD, Mr. Boardman for the prosecution, January 28, 1904

Q: Good afternoon, Miss Strongwood.

A: Good afternoon, Mr. Boardman. I trust this day finds you well.

Q: I believe it will be a very fine day, especially now that I have the opportunity at last to ask you a few questions. Let us begin with this: Have you ever noticed, miss, that you have in recent years been surrounded by a great deal of trouble?

A: I believe all of us encounter our share of troubles in this world, Mr. Boardman.

Q: But in your case, trouble seems to follow you wherever you go, does it not? There is, of course, Mr. Masterson's death. Before that, there was the business of the falsified employment application, and before that the missing spoons at the Van Dusen mansion, and before that—well, you get the picture, don't you?

A: I am sure I do not, Mr. Boardman, but I am hopeful you will eventually explain yourself.

Q: It will be my pleasure to do so, Miss Strongwood, when the time comes. But first, let me ask you this: Do you suppose it's just bad luck that you've had so many difficulties of late, what with allegations of theft, forgery, and now murder lodged against you?

A: I do not believe in luck, Mr. Boardman, but I do believe that my life and yours and all the other lives on this earth move according to a plan that none of us can see or comprehend.

Q: You believe in the Almighty, then.

A: Of course.

Q: God is watching over you and guiding the path of your life?

A: I believe God watches over all of us, as we are His creation.

Q: Therefore, there can be no accidents, can there? Mr. Masterson's death, from a bullet fired from a gun in your hand, was no accident, was it?

A: As I have never denied pulling the trigger, then I could hardly claim it to have been an accident. But I will state once again that I never intended to kill him. I wished only to stop him from taking my own life.

Q: We shall see what the evidence has to say about that.

———

Q: Now, Miss Strongwood, you testified, did you not, that you believed you were hired in the normal way to work at Masterson, DeLaittre and Sons and that you were unaware that your starting wages were much higher than those of other girls working there?

A: Yes, that is what I believed.

Q: Did you ever have cause to wonder upon your good fortune in this regard?

A: I am not the sort of person to wonder upon things, as it is of little use.

Q: I see. So you are telling us that even though you had no previous experience as a clerk and listed none on your employment application, and even though you were hired at the munificent sum of twelve dollars per week, you had not the faintest idea that you were receiving special treatment. Is that your story?

A: It is not a story, Mr. Boardman. It is the truth as I know it.

Q: Ah yes, the truth. You speak often of the truth, don't you, Miss Strongwood?

A: I believe in the truth, as we all must.

Q: So you have never told a lie, I take it?

A: I have always endeavored to be truthful, but I am no more a perfect specimen of humanity than I would imagine you are, Mr. Boardman.

Q: I suspect, Miss Strongwood, that you may be considerably less perfect than most, but as Mr. Phelps is sure to object to this observation, I withdraw the remark. Now, in your devotion to truth telling, Miss Strongwood, why did you not mention, on the Masterson company's employment form, your work as a maid at the Van Dusen household?

A: I did not think it relevant. I did not see that working as a maid would have prepared me in any way for the tasks of a clerk.

Q: Yet your work as maid, if satisfactory, would have resulted in a favorable letter of reference from your employer, would it not? Do you suppose Mrs. Van Dusen would have written such a letter on your behalf?

A: I think both you and I would be surprised if she had done so.

Q: In fact, you didn't mention anything about working at the Van Dusen household on your employment application, did you? You lied, in other words.

A: No, I did not lie. I simply chose to omit my experiences there, knowing that the false allegations made by Mrs. Van Dusen might harm my chances to secure new employment. I believe any girl in my situation, which was quite desperate, would have done the same. I very much needed a job, as there was no one else who could support me.

———

Q: I am still curious, Miss Strongwood, about how you came to be hired. Despite your lack of experience or obvious qualifications, Mr. Philip Masterson insisted that you be brought on as a clerk, and at an unusually high rate of pay. Why do you suppose he did that?

A: I have stated before that I have no idea.

Q: A mystery, in other words.

A: I suppose you could say that.

Q: But it isn't really a mystery, is it, Miss Strongwood? It was Michael Masterson who arranged to have you hired, was it not?

A: If he did so, it was without my knowledge, and for reasons which I cannot fathom.

Q: Really? Isn't it true that you knew Michael Masterson well before your supposed first meeting with him in the company offices?

[Objection, Mr. Phelps. Speculation. Overruled.]

A: That is not true.

Q: So you are telling the jury that there is no possibility you could have known Michael Masterson before you went to work for his father's company. Is that correct?

A: I will simply say that I have no recollection of ever meeting him before that time.

Q: Ah, so now you are stating that, well, perhaps I could have met him but I just don't remember. Is that it?

A: No, I am stating that I have no memory of ever meeting him, and since I do not have such a memory, it is very unlikely that I ever did meet him. Will that satisfy you, Mr. Boardman?

COURT: Miss Strongwood, it is the prosecutor who asks the questions, and not the other way around. Do not engage him in any debates. Simply answer his questions to the best of your ability. Is that clear?

A: Yes, Your Honor.

Q: Very well then, Miss Strongwood, let us test your memory. After you were let go by Mrs. Van Dusen, you decided to seek your fortune in Chicago. Is that correct?

A: Yes.

Q: And when did you arrive in Chicago?

A: It was the last week in April, I believe.

Q: April of 1903?

A: Yes.

Q: And when you got to Chicago, you have stated in an article you wrote for the *Minneapolis Tribune* that you were unable to find employment as a clerk or secretary. Is that correct?

A: Yes.

Q: Very well, let me show you Prosecution Exhibit Eight. Please tell the jury what it is.

A: It appears to be a page from the classified section of the *Chicago Tribune*.

Q: And what date appears on the page?

A: It looks to be May third, 1903.

Q: Were you in Chicago at that time?

A: Yes.

Q: Searching for a job?

A: Yes.

Q: Now, turning your attention back to Exhibit Eight, what does this page from the *Chicago Tribune* consist of?

A: Advertisements for jobs.

Q: Jobs employers are seeking to fill?

A: Yes.

Q: What sorts of jobs?

A: It says here clerks, secretaries, and bookkeepers, or so it would appear.

Q: And how many openings are there for, say, clerks and secretaries?

A: Do you want me to try to count them?

Q: That will not be necessary. By my count, there are one hundred and thirty-six such positions being offered. Does that seem about right?

A: I will take your word for it, Mr. Boardman.

Q: And yet, for some reason, even with all of these positions available, you were unable to find a job in Chicago, or so you have stated. Is that right?

A: Yes.

Q: At how many establishments did you apply for employment?

A: A great many. I do not know the exact number.

Q: And they all turned you down, correct?

A: Yes.

Q: Your lack of experience perhaps worked against you?

A: I could not say.

Q: Well, what did the employers you applied at tell you?

A: Often, they simply said they were not hiring or the job I was seeking had already been filled.

Q: Did they ever mention to you what your pay might be? I wager it was not twelve dollars per week.

[Objection, Mr. Phelps. Calls for speculation. Sustained.]

Q: Let me rephrase the question. Did you apply for positions offering a specified wage?

A: I may have. You must understand that I was going from one company to another all day long, and it is hard to recall the specifics of each one.

Q: Well, do you recall anyone offering a clerk or secretary job at twelve dollars a week?

A: No, I do not.

Q: And yet you return to Minneapolis after failing utterly to find a position in Chicago, and, presto, you are hired at once for a job paying this most generous sum. You must have counted your blessings.

A: I felt very fortunate, yes.

Q: Ah, so fortune smiled upon you, like bright rays of sunshine, and Mr. Masterson had nothing to do with it. Do you really expect us to believe that?

———

EXCERPT FROM AN ARTICLE IN THE *ST. PAUL PIONEER PRESS*, JANUARY 8, 1904

———

It has been reliably reported that two famous visitors from England, Sherlock Holmes and Dr. John Watson, passed through St. Paul last night on their way to Rochester to consult with Dr. Will Mayo, the famed surgeon.[27] There is speculation that one of the duo is quite ill and will require Dr. Mayo's services at St. Mary's Hospital.

———

27. Dr. William J. Mayo was the oldest son of Dr. William Worrall Mayo, an English-born physician who established a medical practice in Rochester in the 1860s. By 1904 William J. Mayo and his brother, Charles, had already become renowned surgeons, attracting patients from as far away as Europe. In 1921 the brothers were among seven founders of what is now known as the Mayo Clinic.

TWO

I began work at the firm of Masterson, DeLaittre & Sons on July 20 of 1903, in the company's offices adjacent to their factory, where equipment is made for the flour mills of Minneapolis and other cities. More than once, as I sat at my high desk, I wondered whether the shaft that long ago broke in Mr. Pettit's Mill and killed my poor father had come from my employer's plant, and if so, whether some imperfection in its manufacture had caused Papa's sad end. It was a useless thing to think of, of course, as the past is a knot which cannot be untied, never more so than when we are the ones who find ourselves bound up in it.

There were, I suppose, a dozen or so girls who worked in the offices, at a row of desks along windows that faced out toward St. Anthony Falls and its mighty row of mills.[1] When the windows were open and the wind swept in from the south, I could hear the roar of the falls, once so wild and picturesque but now harnessed to the dreary, unceasing work of industry. Still, I thought the falling water a beautiful sound, carrying with it my own cargo of dreams, and sometimes I imagined myself floating down the mighty river all the way to New Orleans, where magnolias bloom and Creole belles dance in the tropical moonlight. But dreams avail for naught unless they can be made real, and in hope of doing just so I applied myself with the utmost diligence to my work, which consisted of preparing and sending out bills to the far-flung customers of Masterson & DeLaittre.

---

1. St. Anthony Falls is the only major waterfall on the Mississippi River and by 1903 powered more than twenty flour mills, including two of the largest in the world, the Washburn A and the Pillsbury A. Minneapolis continued to produce more flour than any other American city until the 1930s.

It was exactly three weeks after I started my employment at the firm that I first met Michael Masterson. The scene remains vivid in my mind, etched there by the indelible stylus of fate. I was at my desk, reviewing a bill going out to Mr. Lawrence at the Wabasha Roller Mill Co.,[2] when I looked up and saw Michael standing at the doorway to our office. No, that is not quite right. He was leaning, his left shoulder against the door frame, his head slightly tilted, his fine dark eyes roaming the room, like some young sultan surveying his domain. I thought him the most perfectly stunning man I had ever seen. In an instant, his eyes caught mine. I looked away, feeling that it would be impolite to meet his gaze, as I was certain by his manner and his attire, which consisted of a handsome white linen suit of the latest cut, that he must be a young man of some means, though I did not know then that he was the son of one of the firm's founders.

I will confess that I watched out of the corner of one eye as he stepped into the room, spoke briefly to Miss Smithers, the office manager, and then left as quickly as he had appeared. I noticed, too, that before he vanished through the doorway he glanced in my direction. It was the sort of glance that all women instinctively know, and so I was not surprised when, the very next day, he again paid a visit to our office and made a point of stopping at my desk.

"You must be new," he said in a blithe manner, as if the topic was of little concern to him. "I saw you here yesterday. I am Michael Masterson. My father owns the place. Fancy that. And you would be?"

Although I was unaccustomed to such directness, I found Michael's attitude to be refreshing. Hedgers and hawers and circlers have never appealed to me. "I am Addie Strongwood," I told him, looking steadily into his eyes for the first time. "You are right, sir, I am new here. It is less than a month since I started."

"And how do you like it so far?"

"I have nothing to complain of," said I, "though as I'm sure you are aware, the work is of a rather routine nature."

Michael nodded and said, very gaily, "Now, isn't that the trouble with work in general? No excitement. There are remedies for tedium, however, especially for a pretty young girl such as yourself."

"And what might those be?" I asked.

---

2. The Wabasha Roller Mill Company, in Wabasha, Minnesota, was founded in 1882 and produced flour under the trade name "Big Jo." James G. Lawrence was the company's president for many years. The company was later acquired by International Multifoods, Inc.

He smiled, in a dazzling way, as if he had saved up all the radiance of his being for me. He said, "I do not suppose you have ever heard of Mr. Carlton's fancy club down on Washington Avenue? It is a charming place, with a fine little band. I would be happy to take you there one evening."

In fact, I had heard of the club and knew it to be a thoroughly disreputable establishment. "It is not a place for a proper woman," I told him straight out, "and it is disturbing to me that you would think I would ever go there, with you or anyone else."

My words stung, as I had intended them to, and Michael seemed at once angry and abashed. I do not think he was accustomed to a woman, especially a poor working girl, talking to him in so forthright a way.

"Well," said he, "I certainly would not want to offend your royal highness. Pardon me for thinking you a mere common woman." With that remark, he spun around on his heels and marched away.

"Now you've done it," said Greta Hauser, the girl who worked next to me. "You'll never see him again, I wager."

Oh, how I wish now that dear Greta's words had proved true! Yet do not the Proverbs tell us, "Lest thou should ponder the path of life, her ways are moveable, thou canst not know them"? So it was that only a few days later, as I left the office, I found Michael waiting for me outside the main doors on Merriam Street.[3]

"I thought I might catch you," he said, grasping my wrist in a way I found unpleasant. "I wish to apologize for what I said the other day. It was not right, I am sure."

I pulled my wrist away and said, "Perhaps you confuse me with one of the young women of the type I suspect you are accustomed to 'seeing,' if that is the right word. You must know that simply because I am of a poor family does not mean I am without the virtue which all good women guard as their most sacred possession."

"Of course not," he said. "And I will admit that you are right in thinking that I have perhaps fallen into some bad habits. I wish to make amends, if that is still possible. I think you are a splendid young woman and I should like to get to know you, if you will allow that, but only in an entirely proper manner."

---

3. Merriam Street still exists at the southern tip of Nicollet Island. It is named after St. Paul entrepreneur John Merriam, who along with William Eastman, once owned the entire island.

He seemed perfectly sincere, and there was in his eyes a look of genuine regard that I found appealing.

"And just how to you proposed to make amends?" I asked.

"There is a picnic Sunday at Minnehaha Park for the Young Men's Commerce Club, to which I belong. It is fine group, and a number of the unmarried gentlemen will be bringing along lady friends, all women of the best sort. I would be privileged if you would agree to join me."

"I rather doubt I would fit in among such elite company," I said. "I am not a fancy woman."

"Oh, you will fit in perfectly," Michael said with a wide smile. "Why, you will dazzle them, I'm sure. Come now, what do you say? I know we would have a grand time."

"I will think about it," I said, but as I am sure you who are reading these words will understand, I knew I could not say no, for does not every normal girl dream of a summer afternoon in the park with a handsome young man?

As it turned out, it was indeed an afternoon to remember. Michael met me outside the old mansion on Portland Avenue where I had a small room, and we took the streetcar down to the park. The day was glorious—if only August were the only month on the calendar!—and the park presented the gayest possible scene, with crowds of well-dressed men and women strolling along the walkways or sprawled out on blankets with their picnic baskets. There were children everywhere, too, and as I watched them clamber about I remembered how as a little girl I had come to the park with my dear mother, always eager to race down to the bottom of the cool, shady glen and let the spray of the falls wash like holy water across my face.

We went at once to look at the falls. There had been heavy rains through all of the summer, and the falls, which sometimes grows quiet as autumn approaches, was thundering down into its misty chasm. The rush of the water thrilled me—it seemed like the force of life itself hurtling to some grand and mysterious conclusion—and Michael took my hand as we stood at the edge of the precipice.

"You must be careful here," he warned. "I am sure people have fallen in and been carried away."

"I doubt that will happen to me," I said. "But if it did, would you jump in after me?"

He laughed and said, "Why, I'd make a perfect swan dive and rescue you. I would be your knight in shining armor, Addie."

It was my turn to laugh. "It is hard to swim in armor, Michael. I imagine you would sink like a stone."

We continued to joke in this manner for some time, even as Michael tightened his grip on my hand. Then he asked, "What would you think if I kissed you?"

"I would think you to be a very forward young man," I replied, slipping from his grasp. "Come along now. I would like to meet your friends."

The club to which Michael belonged had put up a large tent in a grassy spot not far back from the glen, and I felt a nervous twinge as we entered, for I knew nothing of his friends other than that they all were all of a far loftier social class than my own. Michael, however, assured me that I would be perfectly welcome, telling me none of his friends were "high hats" or "snobs."

As soon as we entered, a hubbub enveloped the tent, where cold cuts, bread, salads, and fruit were arrayed on two tables, along with punch, iced tea, and lemonade. There were cries of "Mikey Boy" all around and several young men rushed up to greet him. So, too, did two young women. They were smiling, but I saw no warmth in their eyes as they inspected me as if looking for signs of some dread disease.

"Well now, who is this bauble on your arm?" one of them, whose name I later learned was Emma, asked Michael, all the while staring past me as though I were as invisible as the very air.

Michael, who appeared on most familiar terms with Emma, made a slight bow in my direction and said, "Why, this is Miss Adelaide Strongwood, whom I had the good fortune of meeting not long ago at my father's offices. She is a sweet girl, and very talented."

"I am sure she is," Emma replied, continuing to ignore me. "I am sure she will have a good time with you. Most ladies do."

A gangly, red-haired young man who looked as though he might have been assembled by a plumber's apprentice now entered the tent and rushed up to Michael.

"Saw you coming in, Mikey Boy," he said without preamble before turning his watery gray eyes in my direction. "And you must be Addie. I have heard about you. I think Mikey is in love and I can see why."

Feigning embarrassment, Michael said, "Do not mind this insensitive cur,

Addie. He is my oldest chum, Johnny Jakes. He is harmless, or so the ladies tell me."

The two of them went on joshing for several minutes, and for reasons which I could not readily identify I took an immediate dislike to Mr. Jakes. My perceptions in this regard were to prove well founded, and as I look back on what happened between Michael and me I am struck by remorse, for I should have followed my head rather than my heart. But a woman's heart is the engine of her being, and its mighty turnings can easily overwhelm all sensible doubts. So it was with Michael. I was aware that he and perhaps his friends might well pose some great danger to me, yet my heart would not listen to such objections, and so I ventured into the darkness in the eternal hope of finding love.

EXCERPTS FROM THE DIRECT TESTIMONY OF MISS GRETA HAUSER, CLERK AT Masterson, DeLaittre and Sons, Mr. Boardman for the prosecution, January 15, 1904[4]

———

Q: Now, Miss Hauser, I turn your attention to July twenty-seventh of last year. I believe it is a day you remember better than most because it is your birthday, if I am not mistaken.

A: Yes, sir, that is right. My twenty-third birthday.

Q: Now, can you tell us about a conversation you had that day, during your lunch hour, with the defendant?

A: Yes, sir. As you said, since it was my birthday I remember that Addie and me were talking in the lunchroom. She'd only been in the office for a week or so, I think, but we were already on friendly terms because our desks were next to each other. We were talking about this and that, as girls will do, and then she asked, kind of all of a sudden, who is that young man I saw this morning in the counting room. She described him and said he was very handsome and I knew it must be Mikey.

Q: One moment, Miss Hauser. By "Mikey," whom do you mean?

———

4. According to *The Trial of Adelaide Strongwood*, Hauser was "a heavy, dark-haired girl, rather homely in appearance, who seemed eager to answer all of the questions put to her."

A: Oh, I'm sorry, sir. That would be young Mr. Masterson. Everybody called him Mikey.

Q: I see. Now, what else did the defendant say to you about this young man?

A: Well, she said she thought he must be very rich, being the son of the company owner and all.

Q: Did she also say she would like to meet him?

A: She sure did, but mostly I remember her talking about how handsome he was.

———

Q: Let me turn your attention to Prosecution Exhibit Seven, which consists of a series of articles written by the defendant and published last December by the *Minneapolis Tribune*. Now, I call your attention to the article that appeared on December fifteenth. Have you read it?

A: Yes, sir, I have.

Q: Very good. In this article, the defendant gives an account of what she describes as her first encounter with Michael Masterson, which would have occurred on or about August tenth of last year, in the offices where both of you worked. She suggests this was the first time she had ever seen Mr. Masterson. To your knowledge, is that an accurate statement?

A: No, sir, because as I just said she told me on my birthday in July that she'd seen him in the counting room.

Q: So she did. Now, in the same article the defendant claims that after rebuffing an advance by Mr. Masterson, you told her that she would never see him again. Do you recall this conversation?

A: No, sir. I don't think I ever saw her with Mr. Masterson in the office.

Q: Not even once?

A: No, sir, not even once.

———

From the Journal of J. Winston Phelps, January 6, 1904

1130 pm—wearying day—spent 3 hours with Addie this pm at jail, reviewing trial evidence, etc—still cant get a real handle on her—beginning to think shes playing poker with everybody, myself included—been reading about Parker girl[5] & wondering if Addie cut from same cloth—hope not.

———

Still dont know why Masterson DeLaittre hired her in first place & at such high wages—she claims to have no idea but something smells of dead fish—did young Masterson bring her up from Chicago & give her a job just to have her?—not sure—dont think Boardman knows either but could be wrong—I fear more surprises await.

———

EXCERPTS FROM THE CROSS-EXAMINATION OF MISS GRETA HAUSER, MR. Phelps for the defense, January 15, 1904

———

Q: I note, Miss Hauser, that in your direct testimony you referred to Mr. Masterson as "Mikey." Is that right?

A: Yes, sir.

Q: Am I to take it, therefore, that you knew him quite well?

A: Well, sir, I know him. I mean, I knew him. All the girls in the office did.

Q: Did you know him well enough to be on very close terms?

A: We were most certainly not on close terms, sir. He was just someone who was familiar to us because he liked to stop in at the office.

Q: I see. Now then, I have but a few other small matters to ask you about. You testified, did you not, that you have read the article Miss Strongwood wrote for the *Minneapolis Tribune* on December fifteenth of last year?

A: Yes, sir.

Q: I have here the article, which has already been introduced by the prosecution. I would like you to read aloud, for the court, the first sentence in the article's third paragraph. Can you do that?

A: Yes, sir. It reads, "It was exactly three weeks after I started my employment at the firm that I first met Michael Masterson."

———

5. This is very probably a reference to Mabel Parker, a beautiful and clever young woman who was accused in 1903 of running a check forgery scheme in New York City. Her case was widely followed in Twin Cities newspapers, in part because she was said to have been raised in Minneapolis. Her first trial ended in a hung jury, but she was later tried again and convicted.

Q: Thank you. You would agree, I presume, that Addie does not state that she first "saw" Mr. Masterson on the day in question, but only that she first "met" him?

A: Yes, sir, that is what it says.

Q: So she was being truthful in this regard, wouldn't you say?

[Objection, Mr. Boardman. Calls for conclusion. Sustained.]

———

Q: Very well, let us move on to one final matter. Does the firm of Masterson, DeLaittre and Sons require of employees such as yourself the use of a time clock to record hours of work on any given day?

A: Yes, sir.

Q: Let me show you Defense Exhibit Three. Look at it, please, and tell me what it is.

A: Well, it looks like my time card.

Q: Your name is written on it. Is that correct?

A: Yes, sir.

Q: And does the signature appear to be yours?

A: Yes, sir.

Q: And what is the week and year indicated atop the card?

A: Let me see. It says the week of August tenth, 1903.

Q: Now, for Monday, August tenth, 1903, and for Tuesday, August eleventh, what does the card show?

A: It is blank for both days, sir.

Q: What does that mean, Miss Hauser?

A: I guess I wasn't at work. I was sick last summer, so I missed some days.

Q: In fact, you missed the very days when Miss Strongwood said she first met with Michael Masterson and talked with him. Isn't that right?

A: Well, I don't know. It is all mixed up, if you ask me. I mean, Addie said I made some remark to her after Michael left, so if I wasn't there, I don't see how that could have happened, either.

Q: Since you seem a bit confused in your testimony, Miss Hauser, allow me to suggest that you never saw Miss Strongwood and Mr. Masterson together in the office because you weren't there the day they met, and that as for the remark attributed to you by my client, that was merely a small mistake of memory on her part in that the remark was probably made by another girl in the office. Isn't that an entirely reasonable explanation for what happened? [Objection, Mr. Boardman. Calls for a conclusion. Sustained.]

Q: I have no further questions, Your Honor.

EXCERPTS FROM THE DIRECT TESTIMONY OF MISS EMMA CROSBY, FRIEND OF Michael Masterson, Mr. Boardman for the prosecution, January 15, 1904[6]

———

Q: Miss Crosby, you have testified that you were among a party of people who attended a picnic at Minnehaha Park on August sixteenth of last year. While at the picnic, did you have occasion to observe the behavior of the defendant in this case, especially as it related to Michael Masterson?

A: I certainly did. It was quite scandalous, if you ask me.

[Objection, Mr. Phelps. Opinion on part of witness. Sustained.]

COURT: Simply tell the jury what you observed, Miss Crosby, not what you thought. Will you do that?

A: All right. Well, the first thing I noticed was she was fawning all over him, touching him all the time in a very suggestive manner, blowing him little kisses, that kind of thing. They acted like lovers.

Q: So it would be fair to say, would it not, that from what you saw they were a close couple?

A: Oh yes, very close. Regular lovebirds.

[Objection, Mr. Phelps. Opinion on part of witness. Overruled.]

Q: Did you see other specific forms of behavior on the defendant's part during the picnic which led you to believe she had a very close relationship with Mr. Masterson?

A: Well, they shared a big bowl of ice cream at one of the picnic tables and I saw her feeding him spoonfuls and talking to him like he was a little baby. She was sweet on him, all right, sweet as could be.

———

6. Crosby was described in *The Trial of Adelaide Strongwood* as "a pert and attractive young woman, with delicate features, straw-colored hair, and exceptionally large green eyes. She wore a finely tailored dress and matching jacket, but her manner was perhaps less refined than her appearance, for she displayed a voluble temperament and often seemed impatient with the questions asked of her, especially by Mr. Phelps."

Q: I see. Now, did you at any point during the picnic have occasion to talk to the defendant?

A: Michael introduced her when they came into the tent, but that was about all there was. I don't think she wanted to talk to any of us ladies. She wanted Michael all to herself. At least, that's what it looked like to me.

————

Excerpts from the cross-examination of Miss Emma Crosby, Mr. Phelps for the defense, January 15, 1904

————

Q: Miss Crosby, am I correct in stating that your father is Walter Crosby, a well-known mill owner in this city?[7]

A: Yes.

Q: So it would be fair to say, would it not, that you are a member of a wealthy, socially prominent family here in Minneapolis?

A: I suppose so, but I don't see how that matters.

Q: No, I imagine you don't. In any case, let us return to the picnic at Minnehaha Park last August. You were there in the tent, you said, when Mr. Masterson and Addie arrived. Did her appearance with Mr. Masterson come as a surprise to you?

A: I don't know what you mean.

Q: Really? I thought my question was very clear, but apparently not. Let me try again. Did you know, before the picnic, that Mr. Masterson was going to bring Addie to the event?

A: I can't say that I recall one way or the other.

Q: My, my, my, how fleeting are the memories of youth. So you can recall all manner of things about the picnic, including Addie's supposedly outlandish behavior, but you can't remember the salient fact that you knew she was coming with Mr. Masterson and that you were in consequence very angry because you yourself had designs on him.

————

7. Walter Crosby was connected to the Washburn–Crosby Company, forerunner of General Mills, Inc., which is still based in Minneapolis.

[Objection, Mr. Boardman. Badgering the witness. Overruled.]

A: That is not true.

Q: So you had no interest whatsoever in Mr. Masterson. Is that what you are saying?

A: I am just saying that I was not angry the way you have said I was.

Q: Not even the least bit upset?

A: No.

Q: Not even the tiniest twinge of jealousy?

A: No.

Q: Well then, it would appear you are a most sensible young woman when it comes to matters of the heart. I assume, therefore, that you had no strong feelings about Addie either. Is that right?

A: Yes.

Q: In other words, you didn't dislike her simply because she showed up with Mr. Masterson, correct?

A: I had no reason to dislike her. I hardly knew her.

Q: How commendably opened-minded you are, Miss Crosby. So you formed no opinion about Addie, experienced no jealously or anger, even though she was seeing a young man with whom you yourself were on friendly terms. Am I right in saying that is your testimony?

A: Michael and I were merely acquaintances. I resent the implication that we were anything more.

Q: Perish the thought, miss. Yet during your own testimony not half an hour ago in this courtroom, you went on at some length about how Addie and Mr. Masterson appeared to be enjoying each other's company at the picnic. Indeed, it seems you were watching the two of them quite intently. Why did you do so, if, as you tell us now, you really didn't have much interest in Mr. Masterson?

A: It was just something I happened to notice, that is all.

Q: I see. Speaking of noticing things, do you read the *Minneapolis Journal*?

[Objection, Mr. Boardman. Irrelevant. Upon promise that relevancy to be shown, objection overruled.]

Q: I call your attention to Defense Exhibit Five, which is an article that appeared in the *Journal* on April twelfth of last year. It is an account of a cotillion at the

Lowry Hill home of Mr. George Partridge[8] of this city. The article includes a list of those who attended the affair, which by the sound of it must have been exceedingly grand. Now, if you would, please read to the court and the jury the portion of the article that I've underlined.

A: "Mr. Michael Masterson, son of Mr. and Mrs. Philip Masterson, was accompanied by Miss Emma Crosby, daughter of Mr. and Mrs. Walter Crosby."

Q: Do you always go to dances, Miss Crosby, with young men with whom you are the merest of acquaintances?

A: I go to many dances with different young men.

Q: Ah, so you are in great demand. Would it surprise you to learn, however, that according to the society pages of the *Journal,* you went to no fewer than four prominent social events with Mr. Masterson last year?

[Objection, Mr. Boardman. Assumes facts not in evidence. Sustained.]

Q: So you are prepared to maintain, I take it, that no matter what the newspapers say, you and Mr. Masterson were no more than acquaintances and, as a result, you would have no reason to be jealous of my client. Is that correct?

A: Yes.

Q: By the way, how many other male acquaintances took you to four events last year?

A: I don't recall.

Q: Of course you don't. All right, let's talk a bit about Mr. Masterson, your frequent escort. How did he treat you?

A: I'm not sure what you mean.

Q: Well, was he always a perfect gentleman?

A: Michael was never unkind to me, if that's what you're asking.

Q: No, that wasn't my question. Let me put it bluntly. Did Mr. Masterson ever make advances to you that you found it necessary to resist?

[Objection, Mr. Boardman. Irrelevant. Overruled.]

A: I do not see how that should be of any concern to you.

COURT: It is not your duty, Miss Crosby, to decide whether a question is appropriate. That is the job of this court. Therefore, I instruct you to answer the question.

A: Michael could be a bit forward at times.

---

8. George Partridge's mansion, built in 1897 and demolished in 1954, contained one of the largest private ballrooms in Minneapolis and was the scene of many glittering social events. The mansion was located at 1 Groveland Terrace, overlooking Hennepin Avenue.

Q: Isn't it a fact that he tried on more than one occasion to take liberties with you, Miss Crosby?

A: I don't know what you mean by that.

Q: Well, unless I am mistaken, I am speaking English, not Hindi. Are you saying you do not know what is meant by a man trying to take liberties with a woman? If so, my dear Miss Crosby, I fear for your well-being.

[Objection, Mr. Boardman. Argumentative, badgering the witness. Sustained.]

COURT: I must remind you again, Mr. Phelps, to watch yourself.

Q: My apologies, Your Honor, though I am merely trying to get the truth from a witness who seems reluctant to answer my questions. Now, Miss Crosby, we can agree, can we not, that Mr. Masterson was a man who could be a bit pushy and aggressive around women?

A: Sometimes he was that way, yes.

Q: In fact, didn't he on several occasions attempt to touch you in a way that you found highly offensive?

A: As I said, he could be a little forward at times.

Q: In fact, didn't you literally have to fend him off more than once because he was, as you put it, so "forward"?

A: I would not go that far.

Q: Your circumspection is admirable, Miss Crosby. In fact, didn't Mr. Masterson even go so far as to brag about some of his conquests and suggest that you should join his "harem," as he called it?

[Objection, Mr. Boardman. Question "goes beyond the bounds of decency." Sustained.]

Q: That will be all of this witness, Your Honor.

REPORT FROM SHADWELL RAFFERTY TO J. WINSTON PHELPS, DECEMBER 4, 1903

Win:

Wash[9] typed up these notes, which should give you plenty of ammo in your battle on the Strongwood girl's behalf. Keep them private if you can. I'll testify to what we found out if I have to but would rather not as you must understand. Who knows better than you, Win, that lawyers are the very demon spawn espe-

---

9. "Wash" refers to George Washington Thomas, Rafferty's longtime friend and business partner.

cially when they can get a poor Irishman up on the stand and beat him like an old carpet?

Wash and I spent two days this week canvassing the brothels along 1st and over on 11th.[10] It's just as you suspected. Masterson and Jakes were regulars. The two of them liked to visit with the ladies together and sometimes the lads would entertain a half dozen of the choicer doves at once. Not the sort of sporting life a poor man could afford. Here's something else to pique your lawyerly interest: the two lads had a nickname in the trade. Ladies called them "cruel boys" because they liked to inflict pain with their pleasure.

They beat up one of the girls at Ida Dorsey's with a belt last fall and Ida who as you know is not a person to be on the wrong side of told them in no uncertain terms never to come back or there would be hell to pay.[11] Ida would make quite a witness if you could figure out a way to get her on the stand and not blow up on you but would not advise it. Jurors in your fair city don't much like either Negroes or madams, so that's two strikes against Ida right away. Suppose you could try to get an affidavit from her but wouldn't hold out much hope. She is not the cooperative sort when it comes to lawyers.

One other thing Ida said is that after she tossed out Masterson and Jakes they threatened to have the coppers close her place down and run her out of town on a rail and that a "nigger" had no business in Mpls. anyway. That's when Ida said she got out her Winchester riot gun and told the lads they were welcome to have a go at her. Would like to have seen that!

Wash and I found three other places on 1st where the lads were also steady customers. Jackie Lee who owns one of the houses there will give an affidavit if you wish but won't testify. Said lads could be "a bit rough" with her girls. No reports of trouble in any of the other places but the madams may have been covering up. A customer with plenty of cash in his pocket can get away with most anything short of murder or mayhem in a whorehouse so long as he keeps on coming back.

Have to tell you one other thing and this you definitely don't want to circulate. Wash happened to talk to a girl at Jackie Lee's and she swore up and down

---

10. Like most American cities, Minneapolis once had a substantial brothel district, even though prostitution was supposedly illegal. Many of the brothels in Minneapolis were along the riverfront on First Street. A few were also located on Eleventh Avenue South near the river.

11. Ida Dorsey was a prominent Minneapolis madam whose former brothel, now apartments, still stands at 212 Eleventh Avenue South in downtown Minneapolis.

she'd seen your client in Chicago last year in one of the Levee dance halls (she couldn't remember which joint but thought it had the word pink in it).[12] As you know reputable women are as rare there as rain in the Sahara. The girl said she saw your Addie with a man and remembers her because she was wearing a fancy dress that made her stand out. Don't know what to make of this but as Wash is going to Chicago soon he can have a look. Now this girl could be wrong but if she's right you better talk to your client pronto. Could be she's not what she appears to be.

Will go up to Fargo in a few days to look into that case you heard about. Hope I can get the young lady to talk but you never know.

Best,
Shad

ARTICLE IN THE MINNEAPOLIS JOURNAL, APRIL 13, 1903

What could have been a terrible tragedy was narrowly averted early this morning at the home of Mr. George Van Dusen, the well-known grain merchant whose mansion on LaSalle Avenue has long been one of the ornaments of the city.

A fire of incendiary origin erupted at two o'clock, when the entire household was asleep, and had not an alert servant sounded the alarm, lives might easily have been lost. There can be no doubt that the fire was set, for a note was found in the main hallway of the mansion stating, "This is just the beginning. Watch yourselves."

The fire was discovered by Mr. Van Dusen's chauffeur, Thomas Rawlings, who was awakened by what he described as a sudden flash of light outside the window of his apartment in the home's carriage house.

Mr. Rawlings arose to investigate and was startled to see flames of considerable height in the basement of the mansion. The loyal servant, still in bedclothes, ran across a small courtyard to the mansion's rear door. Gaining entry with his key, he raced up the stairs to alert members of the family as well as other servants sleeping in the attic. Mr. and Mrs. Van Dusen, their children, and

---

12. The Levee, located just south of the Loop, was Chicago's most notorious red-light district.

three servants were able to escape the mansion before flames could spread to the upper floors.

The fire department was summoned, and two companies reached the mansion within a matter of minutes. The fire, which had all but consumed a large pile of firewood stored in the basement, was quickly extinguished with only minor damage to the rest of the home.

Chief Daly of the fire department told a *Journal* reporter that the blaze was "most definitely the work of a malicious human hand." The chief said the remains of two broken kerosene lamps were found in the basement, where a window was also broken. "It appears the arsonist smashed the window and then threw the lamps down onto the woodpile," the chief said. "Given enough time, there is no doubt the fire would have gone up through the walls and into the rest of the house."

The chief said the note left in the hallway, presumably by the incendiary, was "a very strange thing" and that he had never encountered its like before.

Mr. Van Dusen declined to speak with the *Journal* but Chief Daly said he has been told there is a "prime suspect" in the arson. "There was a servant dismissed just last week for theft, and the police will soon be talking with her, if they are not already. I should not be surprised if she is charged by the end of the day."

The *Journal* has learned exclusively that the servant in question is a girl named Adelaide Strongwood, who lost her job as a maid for the Van Dusens last Thursday upon allegations that she had been stealing from the household.

A *Journal* reporter was able to locate Miss Strongwood, who is now living not far from the Van Dusen home. She vigorously denied any agency in the arson and stated that "a campaign of vilification" has been mounted against her by someone in the Van Dusen household. She added, "I have done nothing wrong, and there is not one shred of evidence against me. It is all lies and innuendo."

EXCERPTS FROM A SUMMARY REPORT BY INSPECTOR ROBERT McCALL, Minneapolis Police Department, April 15, 1903

Re: Adelaide Strongwood and fire of incendiary origins at the Van Dusen mansion

At the request of Chief of Police Lindstrom, I have prepared, with the assistance of Insp. Donald Gordon, this summary report relating to the incendiary fire at the Van Dusen mansion, 1900 LaSalle Ave., on April 13.

Mr. and Mrs. George Van Dusen were interviewed by Insp. Gordon on the morning following the fire. The Van Dusens were accompanied by their attorney, Mr. Peter Marrinan. Mrs. Van Dusen stated she was sure the fire was the work of a former housemaid named Addy [sic] Strongwood, who was terminated on April 9 for theft. She further stated that Miss Strongwood was "capable of anything" and had a violent, quarrelsome temper. Mrs. Van Dusen went on to say that Miss Strongwood had made statements suggesting she would seek revenge against the family for what she believed was her unjust dismissal. Mrs. Van Dusen also said the note left behind at the house threatening further reprisals was "just like her (Miss Strongwood), as she was always an insolent girl."

Upon further questioning, Mrs. Van Dusen revealed that a key to the rear door of the mansion had gone missing after Miss Strongwood's departure and had not as yet been found. It was her opinion that Miss Strongwood had taken the key and used it to gain entry to the mansion. Mrs. Van Dusen demanded that we arrest the Strongwood girl at once. Insp. Gordon said we would certainly question the girl but of course would need evidence to press charges. Mr. Marrinan then asked whether it might be possible to trace the writing on the note to Miss Strongwood, but we informed him this would be very difficult to do as the note was printed in pencil in block letters of the simplest sort on what looked to be very ordinary paper.

———

Miss Strongwood came to police headquarters voluntarily on the afternoon of April 14 for initial questioning. She stated at once that she had "nothing to do" with the fire at the Van Dusen mansion and therefore did not know who the incendiary was. Miss Strongwood did not deny that she was angry over her dismissal but stated that this was "hardly cause to set a house on fire."

Insp. Gordon then came in and inquired as to Miss Strongwood's whereabouts on the night of the fire. Unlike most subjects in such circumstances, Miss Strongwood made no effort to proffer an alibi, stating only that she had been in her quarters in Mrs. Ruud's rooming house on Portland Ave. from eight o'clock that evening and had not left for any reason until seven the next morning. She said that to her knowledge no one else had seen her during those eleven hours, but that she rarely went out at night, preferring to spend her time alone in her room. She further stated that she had just moved into Mrs. Ruud's after being let go by the Van Dusens and had as yet made few acquaintances at this new place of residence.

Insp. Gordon then began pressing her very hard and suggested that someone had seen her in the vicinity of the Van Dusen house at or about the time the fire was set. (In fact, this was not true). Miss Strongwood did not flinch and stated very firmly that she would like to confront the supposed witness and expose him for the liar that he was. She further stated that she would not put it past the police to "invent" evidence against her and that she would not stand for it.

I then asked her about the key missing from the Van Dusen home and she stated she had not taken it and knew nothing of it. She said we were welcome to search her room at Mrs. Ruud's, and later that day Insp. Gordon and I did so. We found no key or any other evidence, such as paper similar to that used to write the threatening note, that might suggest Miss Strongwood was the incendiary. We did discover that her quarters, on the third floor of the Ruud house, are within twenty feet of a rear fire escape, and that she might easily have left the house and returned to it sight unseen during the darkness of night. Upon interviewing other occupants of the house, however, we were unable to locate anyone who saw her come or go during the night hours, nor have we found anyone who saw her at or near the Van Dusen mansion at the approximate time the fire was set.

Insp. Gordon tried "sweating" Miss Strongwood for two hours but did not get anywhere, as she gave as good as she got. She is very strong-willed and intelligent, far different from the usual girls of her class, and I doubt she can be broken. Unless a witness can be located who puts her at the scene of the fire, I do not see at this point how she can be charged with the crime, but that is of course a matter for Mr. Boardman to decide.

EXCERPTS FROM A PRETRIAL HEARING BEFORE JUDGE CHARLES ELLIOTT regarding the admissibility of testimony pertaining to the fire at the Van Dusen mansion, January 7, 1904

MR. BOARDMAN: Your Honor, it is our contention that it is necessary to make the jury aware of the act of incendiarism at the Van Dusen mansion, since there is strong circumstantial evidence to suggest that it was linked to Miss Strongwood's dismissal as a maid there for theft of household property. As you know, the matter of the theft of the silver spoons is one the state believes goes to the character of the defendant and is therefore an important part of our case. The state is of the view that this is a very simple request and one that is entirely appropriate under the circumstances.

———

COURT: Mr. Boardman, just how would you make the jury aware, as you put it?

MR. BOARDMAN: It would be a simple matter, Your Honor. The state proposes to call Inspector McCall of the Minneapolis police as a witness. He would be asked to narrate the circumstances of the fire and the questions raised thereby. Naturally, he would do so in a very professional and straightforward manner.

COURT: Mr. Phelps, you appear on the verge of apoplexy. I take it you oppose this motion.

MR. PHELPS: Emphatically, Your Honor. It is not only prejudicial in a blatant way but it is also patently ridiculous, since I would happily wager a thousand dollars that not a single juror we select will be unaware of the supposed connection between my client and the fire. The newspapers of this city have speculated about it for days on end, despite an utter lack of proof that my client had anything to do with it. Mr. Boardman wishes to introduce this matter into the trial for the sole purpose of trying to further prejudice the jury against my client. It is such a transparent ploy, Your Honor, that I am surprised a lawyer of Mr. Boardman's experience and judgment would think for even a moment that he could get away with it.

———

MR. BOARDMAN: My learned colleague, I believe, protests too much, though I do appreciate his kind words as to my sagacity. The fact of the matter is that

Miss Strongwood did indeed come under suspicion and with good cause. I hardly need remind Your Honor of the house key stolen at the time Miss Strongwood left the Van Dusen house or of the incriminating statements attributed to her, some published in the newspapers of which Mr. Phelps speaks so poorly, regarding her desire to gain revenge against Mrs. Van Dusen. The jury in this case, it seems to the state, has a right to know just what kind of woman the defendant is.

MR. PHELPS: This is simply outrageous and I will not stand for it. My client was never charged in the fire and, as I have repeatedly stated, there is not one scintilla of evidence connecting her to it. Nor are the statements regarding Mrs. Van Dusen attributed to my client true, and I note that "attributed" is Mr. Boardman's own word, not mine. Your Honor, if Mr. Boardman wishes to accuse my client of attempting to burn down the Van Dusen mansion, then I suggest he file charges and bring her to trial for that offense. But he most certainly cannot be allowed to try her here for a crime with which she has not been charged. To even raise the issue would be cause for an immediate mistrial as far as I am concerned.

COURT: All right, Mr. Phelps, hold your horses. You have made your point. The court agrees that, at this point, there is no valid legal reason for bringing the fire at the Van Dusen mansion into this case. Mr. Boardman, your motion is denied, but without prejudice. Should some new evidence appear, the court would be willing to reconsider its ruling. That will be all, gentlemen.

FROM THE JOURNAL OF J. WINSTON PHELPS, DECEMBER 8, 1903

8 pm—fine day thanks to some manna from heaven—anonymous letter arrived this afternoon from Chicago—appears to be copy of one sent by young Masterson to cousin named Theo—can only guess Theo sent it to me for reasons unknown—letter leaves no doubt "Mikey the Masher" liked bawdy houses in Chicago, New Orleans, & elsewhere—one problem, tho, & it could mean big trouble—letter suggests Masterson knew Addie in Chicago & then got her job in Mpls—Addie denies it up & down but who knows?—hope to god Boardman doesnt have goods to impeach her—if so, we could be left swinging in the wind.

———

Still convinced best strategy is to put Masterson on trial & show jury he was a rotter & cad, etc—Addie will give a good account of herself—trouble is, jurors like a weepy woman & she is not that—wish she were—but it wont matter if they see Masterson for what he really was.

EXCERPTS FROM THE DIRECT TESTIMONY OF MISS ADELAIDE STRONGWOOD, Mr. Phelps for the defense, January 27, 1904

———

Q: We have been discussing your experiences in Chicago, Addie, followed by your return to Minneapolis last year. You have stated that as far as you know, you obtained your position at Masterson, DeLaittre and Sons without the help of anyone in the Masterson family, is that correct?

A: Yes.

Q: Now, I wish to call your attention to Defense Exhibit One, which is a copy of a letter sent by Michael Masterson to his cousin Theodore Masterson in Chicago on August 14 of last year. Would you please read this letter to the jury.

A: Of course. "Teddy boy, how are you, you salty dog? I hear via the grapevine you were down in New Orleans last week visiting friends. Did you make it to the Arlington?[13] The circus there has some of the wildest animals you'll ever see, tho the Levee can hold its own in that regard. Jake and I will go down to New Orleans in the winter if we can. Speaking of the fair sex, Teddy boy, I have to tell you what I have set myself up with at the office. Can't go into the details here (I'll tell you my little secret next time we meet) but suffice to say it started in Chicago and I now have a new girl to work on. My oh my what a fine wench she is. Naturally she claims to be a respectable woman. All the girls do. Don't you hate that? I want unrespectable woman, and the more the merrier. When I get a good picture of her on the sly, I'll send you a copy. You'll be jealous, old sport, I guarantee it. I'm playing her right now and in any case

———

13. The Arlington was an opulent New Orleans brothel operated by a madam named Josie Arlington.

she owes me. She won't be easy but the ace of spades[14] will be mine sooner or later. Mikey the Masher. P.S. Don't forget to tell me all about New Orleans."

Q: Thank you. Do you know what the word "Arlington" in the letter might refer to?

A: No.

Q: Would it surprise you to learn that the Arlington is a well-known brothel in New Orleans?

[Objection, Mr. Boardman. Assumes facts not in evidence. Sustained.]

Q: I withdraw the question, Your Honor. What about the term "ace of spades"? Have you ever heard that it means something other than the card of that name?

A: No, I cannot say I know the term.

Q: Do you believe, Addie, that you are the girl referred to in this letter?

A: It certainly sounds that way.

Q: The references to you are not very flattering, are they?

A: No. It is apparent that Michael simply thought of me as another of his possible conquests. It is very sad to think that he saw me in such a crude light.

Q: Now, the letter also suggests that Michael somehow set you up with your job and that he may even have met you in Chicago. Is that in fact true?

A: As I have testified, I know of no such thing. I suppose it is possible Michael saw me in Chicago and perhaps became infatuated for some reason, but whatever he may have done he did on his own. I knew nothing of it.

———

Q: I want to ask you, Addie, about the picnic you attended with Michael Masterson in August of last year at Minnehaha Park.

A: Very well.

Q: Was it a pleasant event?

A: For the most part, yes.

Q: But not entirely, I take it.

A: There was an uncomfortable incident.

Q: Did this incident involve Miss Emma Crosby?

[Objection, Mr. Boardman. Leading the witness. Sustained.]

———

14. A Victorian-era slang term for sexual intercourse.

Q: Very well, we will do this the hard way. You mentioned an incident, Addie. What sort of incident was this?

A: There were some harsh words directed toward me by one of the other girls at the picnic.

Q: And who was the girl who spoke these harsh words?

A: Emma Crosby.

Q: The same Emma Crosby who testified here earlier?

A: Yes.

Q: How did it come to happen that she spoke to you in a cross manner?

A: It was very peculiar. Michael and I were walking back from the falls to the picnic tent when she came up and began to berate me in a very offensive tone of voice.

Q: What specifically did she say?

A: She said I was nothing but a little tramp and that I had no business being with Michael, as she was his girl. She even used a word I was very shocked to hear, especially from someone of her class.

Q: What was this word?

A: I could not repeat it, Mr. Phelps, most certainly not with so many ladies present here.

Q: Was it a four-letter word that begins with the letter "f"?

A: Yes.

[Courtroom disruption. Brief recess.][15]

Q: Thank you, Your Honor. Now, Addie, let us return to your encounter with Miss Crosby. How did Michael react to her verbal assault?

A: He seemed mortified that she had done such a thing and spoke to her very sharply.

Q: What did he say to her?

A: He told her that she was not his girl and that she was "acting like a lunatic." I remember those were his exact words. He said she should leave at once and that he never wished to see her again.

Q: And how did Miss Crosby react to this?

---

15. According to the *Minneapolis Tribune*, the "disruption" occurred when Emma Crosby, who was seated in the rear of the courtroom, stood up and shouted at Addie Strongwood, "Liar. You are nothing but a dirty little liar." The *Tribune* went on to report that Crosby, "who appeared to be convulsed with anger, then shouted, 'How can you let her say such awful things?' At this point, Judge Charles Elliott ordered that Miss Crosby be removed from the courtroom and instructed jurors to disregard her remarks."

A: She tried to slap Michael but he grabbed her wrist and twisted it a little until she gave out a cry of pain. Then he said, "Now get out of here and leave us alone or I will make trouble for you."

Q: And did she leave?

A: Yes.

Q: Did she say anything as she left?

A: Yes. She told me I "deserved" Michael—that was her word—and that she would get back at me one day.

Q: What else, if anything, did she say?

A: She said I would learn soon enough what a liar and cheat Michael was. I wish now that I had taken to heart what she said.

Q: So you don't hate Miss Crosby, do you?

A: No, of course not. I believe that despite her anger she was trying to warn me about Michael.

———

Q: There is one other point I wish to raise regarding Miss Crosby's earlier testimony. She stated that she saw you and Michael together in the picnic tent at Minnehaha Park and that you were acting in a scandalous way. Specifically, she said you were touching him in a lewd manner, blowing him little kisses, and generally acting like the two of you were lovebirds. Is that true?

A: Absolutely not. I never did any of those things and if you were to ask anyone else who was at the picnic whether they saw what Miss Crosby claims, they would agree with me.

[Objection, Mr. Boardman. Speculation on part of witness. Sustained.]

COURT: Miss Strongwood, I must caution you not to speculate on what others might have thought or seen.

A: Of course, Your Honor.

Q: In any case, Addie, your behavior at the park that day was entirely ladylike and appropriate. Am I correct?

A: Yes. I have never behaved in any other way.

———

EXCERPTS FROM THE CROSS-EXAMINATION OF MISS ADELAIDE STRONGWOOD,
Mr. Boardman for the prosecution, January 28, 1904

————

Q: Let's take a closer look at the letter from Mr. Masterson to his cousin, Theo. It is the sort of joshing letter that contains some perhaps rather crude innuendos, which a young man might write. Yet it also contains some very interesting information, does it not, about how the two of you met?

A: I do not see it that way.

Q: Ah, so you continue to insist that you did not meet in him Chicago?

A: Yes I do, because it is not true.

Q: But does he not say in his letter that "it started in Chicago," to use his own words, and that he set you up with a job in the office?

A: I do not believe that is precisely what the letter says. In any event, all I can say is that if he saw me in Chicago or if he did any favors for me, I was not aware of it. I do not think I can be any clearer than that.

Q: So Michael was lying?

A: I do not know.

Q: And, of course, there could be no possibility, could there, that you are lying to cover your tracks?

A: No. I speak the truth.

Q: So you say, Miss Strongwood, so you say.

————

Q: You have given us a rather dramatic account of your encounter at Minnehaha Park with Miss Emma Crosby. Bitter words exchanged. An obscenity uttered. A twisted wrist. Vows of revenge. It is quite a story. And yet I note that none of this was mentioned in the account of the picnic you provided in the *Minneapolis Tribune* last month. Why is that?

A: I did not think it germane at that time.

Q: Not germane? How very strange. The real reason you included nothing about your supposedly harsh encounter with Miss Crosby in the *Tribune* article is that you hadn't gotten around yet to making up the whole thing. Isn't that right?

A: I do not make things up, Mr. Boardman.

Q: But Miss Crosby, on the other hand, why, she is the greatest fabulist since Aesop. Is that what you would have us believe?

A: I cannot speak for Miss Crosby. I can only speak to what I heard and saw.

Q: Let us return to the picnic. You have testified that you never acted in a forward or suggestive manner toward Mr. Masterson. Isn't that right?

A: Yes.

Q: And you also stated, did you not, that others who were at the picnic would confirm your stellar conduct, correct?

A: Yes.

Q: Do you recall the testimony of Mr. Jonathan Jakes?

EXCERPTS FROM THE DIRECT TESTIMONY OF MR. JONATHAN JAKES, MR. BOARD-man for the prosecution, January 25, 1904

Q: You attended a picnic at Minnehaha Park in August of last year at which Miss Strongwood and Michael Masterson were present, did you not?

A: Yes, I was there.

Q: Did you have occasion to observe how Miss Strongwood was acting toward Mr. Masterson?

A: Oh yes. She was on very warm terms with him that whole afternoon.

Q: How so?

A: Well, you know, she was rubbing her hands through his hair, kissing him, sort of draping herself all over him, if you know what I mean.

Q: Were you accustomed to seeing behavior like this from a young woman?

A: No, not at all.

Q: What about Mr. Masterson? How was he responding to all of this attention, if that is the right word, from Miss Strongwood?

A: He seemed a bit embarrassed. I even saw him push her hand away once.

Q: And did her conduct cause something of a stir among the other guests?

A: Oh yes, everybody was talking about it.

[Objection, Mr. Phelps. Hearsay. Sustained.]

STRONGWOOD

Excerpts from the cross-examination of Miss Adelaide Strongwood, Mr. Boardman for the prosecution, January 28, 1904

Q: Mr. Jakes's account of your behavior at the picnic would seem to confirm Miss Crosby's, would it not?

A: Mr. Jakes is a well-known liar.

Q: Really? Well known by whom? By you, Miss Strongwood?

A: I doubt I am the only one who knows him to be a prevaricator of the rankest kind.

Q: I must say I am beginning to see a pattern here, Miss Strongwood. You seem to be surrounded by liars. Michael Masterson, of course. Mr. Jakes. Miss Crosby. Miss Hauser, your coworker. Miss Dornquist, the maid who was supposedly your friend. Mrs. Van Dusen. Why, it is a veritable devil's cauldron of deceit in which you have been immersed.

[Objection, Mr. Phelps. Prosecutor is testifying.]

COURT: I suggest, Mr. Boardman, that you get to the point.

Q: Of course, Your Honor. Miss Strongwood, you were in fact behaving in a very suggestive way toward Mr. Masterson at the picnic. Isn't that true?

A: No.

Q: You were luring him into a trap with your feminine wiles, so that you could one day get him to marry you and then get your hands on his fortune. You were toying with him. Isn't that correct?

A: No, it is not. I would characterize your statement as ridiculous.

Q: Ridiculous? Really? So you never wished to marry Michael. Is that what you are telling us now?

A: No, I did not say that. There was a time when I thought that I might marry Michael, but it was not to be.

Q: Because he saw through your tricks, didn't he? Saw that you were, just as his parents had feared, a fortune hunter. You never cared for him at all, did you?

A: That is a lie. I loved Michael with all my heart and then he betrayed me.

Q: Ah, so I am a liar now as well. I have been added to your great list of prevaricators, as you call them. Everyone in the world, it seems, is a liar, except for you. Is that what you're saying, Miss Strongwood?

[Objection, Mr. Phelps. Argumentative. Overruled.]

A: It will be up to the jury to decide who is telling the truth and who is not, Mr. Boardman.

Q: Indeed it will, Miss Strongwood. Indeed it will.

———

ARTICLE IN THE *ROCHESTER DAILY BULLETIN*, JANUARY 10, 1904

All of Rochester is abuzz today with the news that the world's most famous detective, Sherlock Holmes, and his longtime companion and amanuensis, Dr. John Watson, are in town. The two Englishmen, traveling under pseudonyms in the vain hope of keeping their presence a secret, arrived last night by train from St. Paul and went immediately to the Cook House.[16] Neither man has spoken to the press, but Mr. Holmes was seen walking down First St. in the wee hours of the morning, smoking his familiar briar pipe and looking, according to one witness, "as though he were deep in thought."

No purpose for their visit has been announced, but it did not require any great feat of detection on the part of the *Bulletin* to deduce that Dr. Watson is to be a patient at St. Mary's. The good doctor, whose thrilling accounts of Holmes's adventures have made him every bit as well known as the great detective, is said by a trustworthy source to have been ill for some months now. He is to consult today with Dr. Will Mayo, whose reputation as a surgeon is such that he is now known and admired throughout the world.

It is to be fervently hoped that whatever condition is afflicting Dr. Watson will be quickly attended to and that the patient will enjoy a rapid recovery.

———

16. The Cook House, long gone, was a prominent Rochester hotel of the day.

THREE

Part Three of "An Account of My Life and the Incident for Which I Have Been Unjustly Accused of Murder," by Addie Strongwood, *Minneapolis Tribune*, December 16, 1903

The afternoon Michael and I spent at Minnehaha Park was for the most part quite pleasing, and when he took me home early in the evening he said he would like to see me again and that we might have a "future together," as he put it. Naturally, I was thrilled to think that a young man of his lofty situation would take an interest in me, but at the time I could not help but feel dark clouds of doubt gathering at the back of my mind, for I was acutely aware, after meeting Michael's friends at the park, that they viewed me as a low sort of interloper. To their way of thinking, I am sure, I was someone from a place so far across the tracks, as is commonly said, that no bridge of sufficient length could ever be built which would deliver me into their circle as an equal. Michael, of course, did not understand this, or at least he professed not to, even as I warned him of the chasm, as wide in its way as the great canyon of the Colorado, that separated our circumstances.

And yet I was in love, or so I thought, for Michael was handsome and charming and gay, and I saw him often that August. We went to band concerts at Lake Harriet, strolled along the river gorge, and enjoyed an ice cream social at the home of one of his friends on Park Avenue amid surroundings far more lavish than any I had ever known.[1] I particularly remember one warm Saturday night when Michael took me to Mr. Gibbs's famous restaurant atop

---

1. Park Avenue just south of downtown Minneapolis was once home to the city's most impressive array of mansions. Most of the big houses that still remain have been converted to institutional or business use.

the Metropolitan Building.[2] We enjoyed an elegant dinner served on Haviland china,[3] and I was, if not in heaven, very near to it. Afterward, we went to the roof garden, where a band played, and we danced to Strauss's grand waltzes. I was enchanted, as any girl would be, to be dancing beneath the stars on a soft summer night, and for the first time I let Michael kiss me. I am sure there are those who will think it improper for me to have done so, but I do not care for such opinions. If a young woman in love cannot kiss her lover, then what is the point of being in love?

Later, we walked up the spiral stairs to the observation tower and stood at the iron railing to look out across the city and its sparkling tapestry of lights. I had never seen such a view before, and I felt as though I had for a moment become as free and airy as an angel, removed from all the heavy burdens of the terrestrial world. We had been taking in the view for some time when Michael suddenly touched my shoulder and said, "Have you ever thought of getting married, Addie?"

I was surprised to hear Michael utter these words, but I noted that he was speaking in general terms, and so replied in kind. "Every young woman thinks of marrying."

"I suppose so, but of course it has to be the right man," he said, sounding unusually solemn.

"Of course," said I.

"Well, you should know that it is no different for a young man such as myself," Michael continued. "I know there will be a time when I will have to settle down. In fact, Mother and Father would be very happy if I would do so, the sooner the better."

"I see. Do you have a young woman in mind with whom you wish to 'settle down,' as you say?" It was, I readily admit, an audacious question, but I have never found much value in the usual sort of womanly coyness, and I sensed that Michael had something he wished to tell me.

"I have been thinking about you, Addie."

---

2. The twelve-story Metropolitan Building, built in 1890 and demolished in 1962, was Minneapolis's tallest office building in the early 1900s. The building was especially notable for its iron and glass light court, which was among the grandest spaces of its kind in the nation. Jasper Gibbs was an African American entrepreneur whose restaurant was considered one of the city's best.

3. Haviland china is a type of porcelain made in Limoges, France.

My heart skipped a beat, but I maintained my composure. "And have these thoughts led to a conclusion?"

Michael turned to me and grasped my hand. My heart was racing now, spurred by a potent mixture of hope and doubt. Michael said, "I wish I could tell you that I have reached a conclusion, but I cannot. There are issues that must be dealt with, and I am not sure how to proceed."

"What sort of issues?" I asked, though I feared I knew the answer.

"It is my parents," he said. "I think you can understand what I mean."

I understood only too well. "It is what I have been telling you all along, Michael, is it not? We are from distant places, even though we grew up in the same city. Your parents, I assume, would not want you marrying a common girl such as myself."

"They have never said so," Michael replied.

"Perhaps not, but surely you must have cause to believe that they would never approve of such a match."

Michael said, "Well, I think if they met you, they might feel differently."

"Then perhaps you should introduce me to them," I said.

We had by this time been "seeing" each other for at least a month, yet Michael had never mentioned, up to this moment, his parents, nor had he given any indication that I would be welcome in their home, which was said to be one of the most splendid mansions on Lowry Hill.[4]

Michael said, "Yes, I guess that would be the thing to do. But just give me a little more time, Addie. Everything has to be done just right. Maybe in a week or two I will take you to the house and introduce you."

"Are you sure you really wish to do that?" I asked, then said, "I have been thinking, Michael, and I am not sure I see the 'future together' you talked about not long after we first met. Perhaps it would be best if we parted ways. I assure you that I will always think highly of you and consider you a friend."

Michael grew very agitated as I spoke these words. Finally, he burst out: "No, no! I refuse to let you go like that. Just give me time. If my parents cannot accept you, then so be it. All that matters is what we want for ourselves. Promise me, Addie, that you will give me a chance to work this out."

---

4. Lowry Hill is a steep glacial ridge at the southwest edge of downtown Minneapolis. Thomas Lowry, after whom the hill is named, built the first mansion there in 1874, on what is now the site of the Walker Art Center. The Masterson family's mansion, built in 1893, was located on Groveland Terrace just south of the present-day Walker. The mansion was torn down in 1933.

What could I say? I kissed Michael softly on the cheek and said, "I promise. But you must be true to your word. You cannot let others, not even your parents, whom I am sure you love dearly, decide what is right for you."

I can see now how foolish I was at that moment, allowing the dictates of my own heart to overwhelm my better judgment. But the truth was, I still believed in Michael and still thought that he believed in me as well. As August turned to September, Michael remained affectionate and kindly, or so it seemed, yet he still made no effort to acquaint me with his parents, despite my repeated requests that he do so. I began to think that he was simply frightened that his parents would reject me, and therefore did not wish to risk an introduction.

So it was that I finally decided to make my own introduction, as it were, by writing a letter to his parents in which I stated my love for Michael and frankly mentioned the possibility of marriage. Much has been made of this letter in the press, including allegations that I was merely trying to "blackmail" his parents. How far from the truth are such invidious claims! My letter was a heartfelt plea for understanding, but it was also a test of sorts, and when I received no response I came to realize that Michael and I could never have a life together.

Michael, I know now, never intended to introduce me to his parents or to take my hand in marriage, as he intimated that night on the rooftop of the Metropolitan Building. Indeed, it was only under the most unpleasant of circumstances that I ever encountered his mother, to deliver to her a brief note concerning the child—Michael's child—that I carried in my womb. This note, too, has been fodder for the bullies of the press, when in fact it was a genuine cry for help at a desperate moment in my life.

After I wrote to Michael's parents, his behavior toward me changed and as a result, my ardor began to cool. He no longer invited me to social occasions with his friends, suggesting instead that we spend our evenings at dance halls and other low establishments, which I steadfastly refused to do. Michael's personal behavior also became increasingly aggressive and even threatening at times. Although we had kissed more than once, Michael seemed to believe that he was entitled to "a little more affection," as he put it, but I made it clear to him that I was not that sort of girl.

It saddens me now to think of all that happened between Michael and me. Yet the unfortunate truth is that Michael's real motives, which he hid behind his charming facade, were always of the basest sort. Even now I shudder to contemplate his perfidy and the utter blackness of his heart. As the Bible tells us, "They that plow iniquity, and sow wickedness, reap the same." So it was with Michael.

Before I close this chapter of my story, I must first rebut one of the more egregious lies that has been told in the effort to make me out as a cold-blooded murderer. I am referring to the story that appeared yesterday morning in the *Minneapolis Journal,* a newspaper which, unlike the *Tribune,* makes no pretense of fairness, or honesty. The story made certain ridiculous claims regarding my purchase of a derringer at Mr. Speed's pawnshop a few weeks before Michael's death.

The real story, which the *Journal* could not be bothered to tell, is that I bought the derringer out of a very sensible fear for my own safety stemming from the widely publicized depredations of the man known as the "Park Avenue Prowler."[5] Indeed, it was the *Journal* itself that first reported upon his series of attacks, in which one young servant girl was horribly violated and another nearly so. As is well known, these attacks occurred in an alley near 26th and Park. At that time, I lived but a few blocks away on Chicago Ave., and like other women in the neighborhood I was terrified by the news that such a vicious criminal was on the loose.

I make no apologies for the fact that as news of these assaults spread, and as it became all too evident that the police of Minneapolis were incapable of preventing further outrages, I determined that I must find a way to defend myself against a possible attack. A woman cannot hope to match a man's physical strength, but as Annie Oakley so magnificently demonstrated during a sharpshooting exhibition at one of Mr. Cody's Wild West shows I once saw in Minneapolis, she is every bit as able as the male of the species to use a gun to good effect.[6]

Of course, I could never hope to emulate Miss Oakley's skills, but I thought that if the prowler should attempt to harm me, I would at the least be able to frighten him away by displaying a gun. Indeed, until the prowler was finally caught, I slept with the weapon—a derringer with two barrels—under my pillow.

The derringer, it now seems, is the great piece of evidence against me, and Mr. Boardman has in the pages of the *Journal* suggested that I brought the

5. No references to the "Park Avenue Prowler" have been found in Minneapolis newspapers from 1903, suggesting that the case was not quite as "widely publicized" as Addie Strongwood made it out to be.
6. William F. ("Buffalo Bill") Cody and his touring Wild West Show performed in Minneapolis in 1896, 1898, and 1900, all years during which Annie Oakley was part of the troupe. The best guess is that Addie Strongwood saw the performance on August 13, 1900, since she would have been eighteen years old by that time. The show also made a stop in Minneapolis in 1902, but Annie Oakley had left by then.

weapon with me to the Windom Block expressively for the purpose of ending Michael's life. Indeed, I recall Mr. Boardman stating that "the mere fact" I had the gun in my possession was sufficient to demonstrate my "intent to commit a murderous act." By this distorted logic, then it must be assumed that every policeman in Minneapolis who carries a revolver at his side does so with the aim of shooting someone before the day is done.

I have said from the very beginning of my ordeal before the law that I took the derringer to the Windom Block out of fear that Michael might attempt to harm or even kill me. Given what had happened only a few weeks earlier (a terrible episode that I will soon share with the *Tribune*'s readers), it should hardly come as a surprise that I felt the need to carry some means of protection with me when I went to see Michael and to ask him, for once in his life, to do the decent and honorable thing.

My intentions that awful night were to obtain justice, not to exact revenge. I hoped that Michael, despite all the evil he had done to me, might finally agree to settle accounts, as it were, so that I could go forward with my life. I wish now, as I have a thousand times since then, that our last encounter might have ended in understanding instead of blood. But I had no possibility of surviving his ungovernable fury unless I chose to act to save the one thing that I will never be willing to give up without a fight, and that is my life. Dear readers, in such a circumstance as I faced that night in the Windom, I believe any one of you would have done the same.

EXCERPTS FROM THE DIRECT TESTIMONY OF MR. HERBERT SPEED, OWNER OF the North Star Pawnshop and Emporium, Mr. Boardman for the prosecution, January 18, 1904[7]

———

Q: Tell me, Mr. Speed, do you sell guns in your shop?

A: We sell just about every kind of firearm there is. Rifles, shotguns, pistols, derringers. We have it all. We are the largest and best-stocked shop of its kind in the Northwest, if I may say so.

———

7. The *Minneapolis Journal* described Speed as "a tall, thin man, somewhat stooped over, about fifty years of age, with a rather choleric manner. His brown eyes are very quick and alert, perhaps reflecting his years in a line of work that requires great canniness as well as the ability to quickly appraise his fellow man as a condition of success."

Q: And so you have. Now, on or about October thirty-first of last year, did the defendant in this case come into your store and inquire about purchasing a gun?

A: She did.

Q: And you have no doubt, I take it, that the defendant you see here in court today is the same woman who was in your shop?

A: No doubt at all. It was Miss Strongwood for sure.

Q: You must have many customers in your shop every day, Mr. Speed, and yet you seem to remember the defendant quite well. Why is that?

A: Well, it is unusual to have a woman come in looking to buy a gun, so she stood out from the crowd, if you get my drift.

Q: Of course. Now, Mr. Speed, tell us in your own words what happened after Miss Strongwood came into your shop.

A: Well, I will say that she seemed to know exactly what she wanted. She marched right up to the front counter and said, "I wish to buy a small gun, one that can be easily handled. What can you show me?" So I said that we had quite a few and was there a particular type she was looking for, and she said, and I will never forget this, that she didn't want some "lady's toy," as she called it, but the real thing. Something that meant business. All right, I said, but can I ask what you intend to use the gun for? That's when I got quite a surprise, because she looked me right square in the eye and said, "I intend to get rid of a varmint." Well—

Q: Hold on for a moment, Mr. Speed. I want to be very clear about what you just said. You testified that Miss Strongwood said she wished to "get rid of a varmint." Not a group of varmints but a single varmint. Is that correct?

A: Yes, sir, that's what she said.

Q: All right. Please continue.

A: I thought it a funny thing for her to say, so I kind of joked and said, "It must be a pretty big varmint you intend to shoot." But she didn't seem to think that was very amusing and made it clear she didn't have any time to waste and would I show her some guns.

Q: And did you do so?

A: Sure. I'm in business to sell things and if the lady don't want to make small talk, so be it. But she sure did seem in a hurry, like she couldn't wait to get her hands on a gun.

[Objection, Mr. Phelps. Speculation on part of witness. Sustained.]

Q: Just tell us if you would, Mr. Speed, what happened next.

A: Well, I showed her some real nice Colt revolvers I had on hand, but she said they were too big, so I said maybe she would prefer a derringer. I had a nice Remington double in stock and she picked it out right away.

Q: By "Remington double," do you mean a two-shot, double-barreled derringer made by the Remington Arms Company?

A: Yes. It is a nice little gun. Very reliable.

Q: Let me show you Prosecution Exhibit One, which is a forty-one-caliber Remington Model Ninety-Five double derringer. Is this the gun Miss Strongwood picked out?

A: Sure looks like it.

Q: Now, when you sold the gun to Miss Strongwood, did you issue a sales receipt to her?

MR. PHELPS: In order to save us all time, Your Honor, the defense is prepared to stipulate that the gun Mr. Boardman just showed the witness is in fact the same one my client bought at the pawnshop.

COURT: Is that stipulation agreeable to you, Mr. Boardman?

MR. BOARDMAN: It is, Your Honor.

COURT: Then you may proceed.

Q: I have only one more question for you, Mr. Speed. How much did Miss Strongwood pay for the gun?

A: Well, I told her it was worth at least twenty dollars but she wouldn't hear of it. No, sir, she wanted to bargain for it. I guess she had done some looking around, so we went back and forth as to the price. She was a tough one, I'll tell you that. I finally sold it to her for ten dollars, with a box of ammunition thrown in. She insisted on that.

Q: And how did she pay for her purchase?

A: Cash on the barrelhead. It's the only way I do business.

Q: Thank you. Your witness, Mr. Phelps.

EXCERPTS FROM THE CROSS-EXAMINATION OF MR. HERBERT SPEED, MR. PHELPS for the defense, January 19, 1904

Q: Good morning, Mr. Speed. I have only a few trifling questions, which I am sure you will have no great difficulty in answering. Let me begin by asking whether it is true that after the unfortunate death of Mr. Masterson, you contacted the police to inform them that you had sold a derringer to my client sometime before?

A: Yes, I did. I felt it was my duty to let the police know of this fact.

Q: Commendable of you, Mr. Speed, very commendable. You are a friend of the police, I take it?

A: Well, I don't know. I was just trying to be a good citizen, that's all.

Q: I see. Have you always been a good citizen, Mr. Speed?

A: I have done my best.

Q: What more could we ask of you, sir? By the way, does your definition of good citizenship include the act of receiving stolen property, an offense which the police have accused you of on more than one occasion, have they not?

A: Why, that is a rank falsehood and I resent it. I have never been convicted of any crime.

Q: So those police reports to which I have referred are merely scurrilous lies. Is that your position?

[Objection, Mr. Boardman. Argumentative, assumes facts not in evidence, etc. Sustained.]

Q: I withdraw the question, Your Honor. Now, Mr. Speed, when you did your civic duty and summoned the police to inform them of my client's purchase of a gun, what exactly did you tell them?

A: Well, I just told them what you said, that I'd sold her the gun. I showed them the receipt and that was about all there was to it, I guess.

Q: A brief interview indeed. Just to make sure I understand you correctly, you simply said to the police that she'd bought the gun—an entirely legal purchase, I might add—and the police then went on their way. Is that how you remember it?

A: Yes, I'd say so.

Q: So you didn't mention to the police my client's supposed comment that she wished to "get rid of a varmint," did you?

A: I'm not sure. I might have.

Q: Really. Well, let me show you Defense Exhibit Two, which is a report filed by Inspector Donald Gordon of the Minneapolis Police Department, following his interview with you at your pawnshop on November thirteenth of last year. Go ahead now, sir, and read it. Take your time. No rush, no rush at all…Finished?

A: Yes.

Q: Good. Did you find any mention in Inspector Gordon's report of the now infamous "varmint" remark which you have attributed to my client?

A: No, I didn't see it there.

Q: No, you didn't, because Inspector Gordon in fact says not one word in his report about any incriminating statements that my client supposedly uttered to you while buying the gun. Isn't that correct?

A: Well, I still think I mentioned it to him.

Q: Do you now? That is most interesting. I fear we can only conclude that Inspector Gordon, a decorated veteran with nearly twenty years of service on the force, must be the biggest dunderhead since Humpty Dumpty. How else, sir, to explain his astonishing oversight?

[Objection, Mr. Boardman. Calls for speculation. Overruled.]

A: I cannot say. I guess you will have to ask him.

Q: You may be assured, Mr. Speed, that I shall, and I do not think you will like his answer. Let us not thrust and parry any longer, sir. Isn't the plain truth of the matter that you never mentioned my client's alleged statement about killing a varmint until you gave a long interview to a reporter for the *Minneapolis Journal* on November seventeenth?

A: That is not how I recall it.

Q: Oh, come now, why keep up the pretense? You made up the "varmint" remark out of whole cloth, did you not, just so that you would get front-page play in the newspaper? I wager it made you feel like a real big wig, an important man.

A: That's not true. I would not tell a lie like that.

Q: How reassuring. You are a regular George Washington, and I can entrust you with my cherry tree any day. Is that what you are claiming?

[Objection, Mr. Boardman. Mocking the witness. Sustained.]

Q: My apologies, Mr. Speed, if I have offended you. Still, when it comes to the matter of truth telling, I am curious about something you said earlier. Did you not testify that you told my client, as she was preparing to buy the gun, that it was worth "at least twenty dollars"?

A: I guess I did.

Q: Well, sir, was it?

A: Was what?

Q: Good Lord, man, you know what I mean. Was the Remington derringer worth twenty dollars?

A: It could have been.

Q: I am surprised to hear you say so, Mr. Speed, since I have always assumed that it is the business of a man in your line of work to know the value of everything you buy and sell. Isn't it a fact that the derringer in question can be purchased new for nineteen dollars and seventy-five cents direct from the Remington factory in Massachusetts, and that used models can be found for as little as five dollars right here in Minneapolis? And isn't it also a fact, sir, that you lied to my client about the value of the weapon, hoping you could sell it to her for far more than it was worth? Lying is what you do every day, isn't it, Mr. Speed?

A: I do not have to listen to such talk from a dirty queer. I—

COURT: Mr. Speed, you will watch your language or be found in contempt. You are here to answer defense counsel's questions, whether you like them or not. Is that clear?

A: Yes, sir.

COURT: Now then, Mr. Speed, answer the question.

A: Well, all I can say is that like anybody else I try to get the highest price I can for what I sell. That is all I was doing. I do not see that I did anything wrong. It's just business.

Q: And if you have to lie in order to get a good price, or make a name for yourself in the newspaper, then I suppose that is just business, too. Is that how you look at it, Mr. Speed?

A: I did not lie to the newspaper. What I said in that article was all true.

Q: As true, no doubt, as that twenty-dollar price you quoted for a derringer worth less than half that amount. I have no further questions of this witness, Your Honor.

EXCERPTS FROM THE DIRECT TESTIMONY OF INSPECTOR DONALD GORDON, Minneapolis Police Department, Mr. Phelps for the defense, January 26, 1904

————

Q: Inspector Gordon, when you interviewed Mr. Herbert Speed at his pawnshop on November thirteenth of last year, did he at any point during your interview mention anything whatsoever about Miss Strongwood stating that she wished to purchase a gun in order to "kill a varmint"?

A: No sir, he did not.

Q: Did you in fact ask him about any conversation he may have had with Miss Strongwood?

A: Yes.

Q: And what did Mr. Speed say?

A: As I recall, he said she was all business and didn't make much small talk.

Q: You are certain of this?

A: I am.

Q: Let me ask you this: Had Mr. Speed attributed the "varmint" remark to my client, would you have put that information in your report?

A: Of course. It would be considered an incriminating statement. I would not be much of a detective if I left a thing like that out.

Q: Thank you, Inspector. I have nothing further.

LETTER FROM SHADWELL RAFFERTY TO J. WINSTON PHELPS, DECEMBER 7, 1903

Waldorf Hotel[8]

Fargo

Dec. 7

Win:

Ever been to Fargo? Flattest damn place in the world. Coldest too or so I'm beginning to think. -10 when I got here and still heading down. Wash says I should be well protected from the cold because I'm "nice and fat." Imagine that! Fortunately the Waldorf has a well-stocked bar frequented by drummers who enjoy buying a drink or two for a jolly old Irishman like myself so I am not suffering. Now as to the business at hand there is good news as I have found the girl we heard about from your informant.[9]

---

8. The Waldorf, with 160 rooms, was Fargo, North Dakota's largest and most luxurious hotel in 1903. It remained in business under various names until 1951, when a fire destroyed the building.

9. The "informant" Rafferty refers to was in all likelihood Theodore Masterson, who seems to have provided Phelps with a good deal of incriminating information about Michael Masterson and his parents.

Name is Mary McDonald. She's at the Crittenden Home[10] up here and in a family way. Child due pretty soon by looks of it. Ladies who run the home didn't want a thing to do with me but as you know I can be a persuasive fellow and managed to see the girl. Of course she didn't want to talk about what happened—who can blame the poor thing?—but I kept at her and got the story more or less.

Facts are these: Young Masterson and his bosom buddy Jakes had their way with the girl last April down in Chicago where she was working as a clerk at the Palmer House. The lads were staying there on one of their whoring expeditions and spotted her of an evening as she was leaving. No time here to give you all the foul details but the gist of it is that they talked her into dinner at a fancy restaurant and plied her with plenty of gin. May even have administered something from Mr. Finn's pharmacy.[11] Next thing she knows they are all in a cheap hotel room on South Wabash a few blocks from the Palmer House and she is doing things she never would have done if she were sober. She said the lads were both charming at first and told her how beautiful she was etc. but then they became very insistent and so got what they wanted. Not a pretty story but an old one in this world of ours.

Just to be sure I showed her the pix of Masterson and Jakes you gave me and she left no doubt they were the ones. Could hardly get her to stop crying after that. Pitiful case all the way around. She was too ashamed to go to the coppers not that they'd have cared anyways. Found out later she was with child and once it became obvious, she went back home to Fargo. Now here's what's really interesting: even tho the lads lied to her about their names she figured out who young Michael was by checking the registry at the Palmer House. So she wrote to his parents explaining her situation and begging for money to support the child. All she got back was a letter from some fancy pants lawyer saying he'd destroy her if she ever tried to blackmail the family again. Oh they're sweethearts that Masterson clan.

So now poor Mary is in the care of devout church ladies along with all the other fallen girls of Fargo. Pity how things are done isn't it? The girl feels

---

10. Rafferty made a spelling mistake here. The Florence Crittenton (not "Crittenden") Home was established in Fargo in 1893. It was one of many homes for unwed mothers founded with the help of New York businessman Charles Crittenton, who took on a life of good works after his daughter, Florence, died at age four.

11. "Mr. Finn's pharmacy" refers to a Mickey Finn, a kind of knockout drug named after a Chicago bartender who supposedly pioneered its use.

everything is her fault and her life is ruined. Of course it could be worse for if the damn Papists got their hands on her why you can bet the good sisters in black would be pleased to remind her every day just what an awful miserable sinner she is.

Rub is she won't testify under any circumstances as she told me more than once. Won't sign an affidavit either. Guess that lawyer put the fear of God in her. Suppose you could try a subpoena but what good would it do? She can't travel as she is and likely will be too late by the time she can even if you persuade her to testify.

I will tell you this, Win, when you get that weasel Jakes on the stand and I know you will, I want you to hurt him and hurt him hard in the way only you can. He is moneyed trash of the worst kind. I would greatly enjoy meeting him in a dark alley and having an old-time Irish conversation with him if you know what I mean but I can't as it would harm your case and probably get me sued. Not for the first time I might add.

I'll give you more particulars—times, places, etc.—when I get back next week.

Shad

FROM THE JOURNAL OF J. WINSTON PHELPS, DECEMBER 9, 1903

———

4pm—letter from Shad—he found woman weve been looking for in Fargo—name is Mary McDonald—what a witness she would be!—would blow Boardman & his case right out of the water—looks hopeless, tho, as Shad says she wont testify—rotten luck all around.

———

EXCERPTS FROM THE DIRECT TESTIMONY OF MRS. PHILIP (BERNICE) MASTERSON, mother of Michael Masterson, Mr. Boardman for the prosecution, January 20, 1904[12]

———

Q: Mrs. Masterson, I know this will be difficult for you, but I must ask some questions about your late son, Michael.

A: He was the jewel of my life, Mr. Boardman. My one and only son. I cannot tell you how much I miss him.

Q: My deepest condolences, Mrs. Masterson. I hesitate to bring up yet another painful matter, but your husband also died last year, did he not?

A: Yes, on December twenty-first.

Q: And what was the cause of death?

A: The doctors said apoplexy, but I have no doubt that it was Michael's murder that killed him, too. That little hussy murdered both my husband and my son.

COURT: Mrs. Masterson, stop. I must warn you that you are not here to deliver opinions about the defendant or anyone else. The court understands that you have strong feelings in this matter, but that does not give you license to go beyond what the law allows. Do you understand?

A: Yes, Your Honor. I am sorry.

COURT: Very well. All right, Mr. Boardman, go on.

Q: Thank you, Your Honor. Now, please tell us a little about Michael. How would you describe him to this court?

A: Oh, I hardly know where to begin. He was lively, warm-spirited, energetic. The life of every party. Very bright. Very loving. Just a wonderful young man.

———

———

12. *The Trial of Adelaide Strongwood* offered this description of Mrs. Masterson: "Wearing a subdued black dress as befitting her state of mourning for both her only son and her beloved husband of many years, she presented a most striking appearance as she took her seat in the witness chair. Tall and stately of manner, with strong, sharp features and reddish-gray hair held neatly in a bun, she seemed to command the entire courtroom. She answered questions put to her in a steady voice, but she also displayed instances of fiery emotion, especially during the combative cross-examination of defense counsel Phelps."

Q: Mrs. Masterson, when did you first become aware that your son was seeing the defendant in this case, Miss Adelaide Strongwood?

A: I cannot tell you the exact date, but it was sometime last August.

Q: How were you made aware of Michael's relationship with the defendant? Did he himself tell you?

A: No. You know how young men are. They do not always discuss with their mothers the things that they should. I found out when I went down to the office one afternoon to see Philip about some small matter and ran into Miss Smithers.

Q: The office manager?

A: Yes, I know her quite well. We were talking and I rather casually asked her if she had hired any new girls of late and she mentioned Miss Strongwood. She then went on to tell me that Michael appeared to be interested in the girl and had even taken her out to a picnic at Minnehaha Park, I believe.

Q: Now, before we go any further, Mrs. Masterson, I must ask you this: Did Miss Smithers make you aware of any special circumstances regarding the hiring of Miss Strongwood?

A: No, not that I recall.

Q: So she did not, for instance, mention that Miss Strongwood had been hired at an unusually high beginning wage?

A: No, nothing like that.

Q: However, did you subsequently learn anything from either your husband or son regarding the terms of Miss Strongwood's engagement with the firm?

[Objection, Mr. Phelps. Leading the witness. Overruled.]

A: Yes. Philip told me sometime later that Michael had asked that she be hired. Philip said he should never have done it but that Michael had been very insistent.

Q: Did Philip tell you why Michael wanted Miss Strongwood to be hired?

A: Yes. He explained that Michael had told him he'd met the girl quite by accident during a business trip to Chicago and had been tremendously impressed by her intelligence and how hard she worked. Michael believed she would be an excellent clerk and would quickly earn her keep at our firm.

Q: And was it Michael who insisted on paying her twelve dollars a week?

A: I cannot be sure. I only learned later how much she was being paid.

Q: Very well. Let us now go back to your talk with Miss Smithers. You mentioned that she told you Michael had began seeing Miss Strongwood. Were you surprised by this news?

A: I would say "disappointed" would be a better word.

Q: Why so?

A: I had always stressed to Michael that a young man in his position would be the target of a certain kind of girl who would be interested in his money above all else and that he should therefore be wary of becoming entangled with anyone who was not of his social class.

Q: You were, to put it bluntly, afraid that she might get her claws into Michael. Is that correct?

A: Yes. It has happened all too many times with young men like Michael. He was sometimes innocent in the ways of the world, and I did not wish to see him get hurt. A mother must always protect her son if she can.

Q: Of course. Did you later talk to Michael about his relationship with the defendant?

A: Yes. It was just a few days later, I think. He was going out for the evening and I asked him if he would be seeing Miss Strongwood.

Q: How did he react?

A: He was surprised that I knew of the relationship but did not deny it.

Q: What happened next?

A: I told him that I wished he had informed me that he was seeing one of the office girls and that I thought it to be a bad idea.

Q: What did he say in response?

A: He said the girl—that would be Miss Strongwood—was just someone he had befriended and that he had no real feelings toward her.

Q: Did he mention at this time that he had helped secure a job for Miss Strongwood?

A: No. I imagine he was too embarrassed to talk about it.

[Objection, Mr. Phelps. Speculation. Sustained.]

COURT: Mrs. Masterson, remember to tell the jury only what you know, not what you believe.

A: Certainly, I will try to do so.

Q: So, in any event, it would be fair to say, would it not, that Michael didn't indicate that he was in love with Miss Strongwood?

A: That is correct.

Q: From his point of view, in other words, the defendant was merely an acquaintance. Is that right?

A: That is what Michael told me.

Q: And I presume he never stated to you that he hoped to marry Miss Strongwood, did he?

A: Of course not. The very idea of such a thing would be ridiculous.

———

Q: I would now turn your attention to Prosecution Exhibit Six. Would you look at this document, Mrs. Masterson, and tell us whether it is in fact a letter you received from Miss Strongwood dated September fifteenth of last year?

A: Yes, it is. I remember it only too well.

Q: I would like you to read the letter out loud to the jury, if you would.

A: Very well. "Dear Mr. and Mrs. Strongwood. It is with a heavy heart that I feel compelled to write to you about my relationship with your dear son, Michael. I do not know how well aware you are of our situation, but for some time now Michael and I have been seeing each other regularly, under the most proper of circumstances of course, and during that time we have fallen in love. Michael has on more than one occasion stated his desire that we become man and wife, but owing to the differences of class that separate us, I have been reluctant to accede to his wishes that we wed. Yet as you must surely realize there is no gulf between a man and a woman so wide that it cannot be bridged by love, and so I now must ask you to accept the fact of our love and that Michael I wish to spend our lives together. I know Michael has been reluctant to speak to you about our relationship, fearing that you will not approve of it, and I pray you do not think me impertinent for writing to you in this way. My only aim is to assure you that I will be a good wife to Michael and that all I desire of him is the love in his heart. His fortune, which I will readily admit is many times larger than my own, means nothing to me. Michael, I must tell you, does not know that I have written this letter. He will of course learn of it from you, and once he does it is my fervent hope that we will all be able to meet one day and that you will then learn firsthand of my sincerity as well as my abiding love for your son. Cordially, Adelaide Strongwood."

Q: How did you react to this letter, Mrs. Masterson?

A: I thought it perfectly outrageous and appalling. Michael had never said he was in love with her and yet here she was, claiming he wanted to marry her.

Q: May I assume that your late husband, Mr. Philip Masterson, also read the letter?

A: Of course. He was as appalled as I was. It was then that he told me about how Miss Strongwood had come to be hired and how he wished he had not listened to Michael.

Q: Did he say anything else?

A: Yes, he said he thought the letter was a naked ploy and nothing more and that he would take a good hard look to see how she had come to be hired in the first place. He told me, "The girl wants money, just you wait and see, and that is all there is to it. But she will not get it, not now or ever." Poor Philip was very upset.

Q: And did your husband in fact take "a good hard look" at the circumstances under which Miss Strongwood had come to be employed by his company?

A: Yes, and it didn't take him long to learn that she had lied on her employment application regarding her past work in Chicago.

Q: What did your husband do upon making this discovery?

A: He made sure that she was let go at once.

Q: You mean, I take it, that she was terminated as an employee of Masterson, DeLaittre and Sons?

A: Yes. She was told to leave immediately and also to stay away from Michael.

———

Q: Let me ask you, Mrs. Masterson, if you talked to Michael after receiving the letter from Miss Strongwood?

A: Yes, Philip and I showed him the letter that very evening.

Q: And what did Michael say?

A: He professed utter shock. He said he had gone out with her a few times and liked her well enough but had never so much as breathed a word of marriage to her.

Q: And did he also acknowledge that he had helped her to get a job at your husband's company?

A: Yes, but he said he did so only because he thought she was deserving of a chance.

Q: What else did Michael say?

A: As I recall, he said, "I do not know what this girl is up to, but I assure you I shall never see her again."

Q: Was anything else said during your meeting with Michael?

A: Yes. Philip said, in the strongest terms, that if the girl tried to blackmail us, he would see her thrown in jail. He also made it very clear to Michael that he must live up to his word and never see her again under any circumstances.

Q: And did Michael so promise?

A: He did.

Q: So at that point, you and your husband thought the matter was done with. Is that correct?

A: Yes. How wrong we were.

———————

Q: Mrs. Masterson, I call your attention to the afternoon of Saturday, October twenty-fourth of last year. Were you at that time shopping in Mr. Dayton's establishment here in Minneapolis?[13]

A: I was.

Q: Can you tell us what happened as you were leaving the store?

A: Yes. I had just stepped out onto Nicollet to meet my chauffeur when she approached me.

Q: By "she" do you mean the defendant?

A: Yes, Miss Strongwood.

Q: You recognized her at once, I take it.

A: To be honest, no. I had seen her only once before, at the factory. It took me a moment to realize who she was.

Q: Did her sudden appearance seem to you to be an accidental encounter of the sort that might occur when two people run into each other on a busy street?

[Objection, Mr. Phelps. Speculation. Overruled.]

Q: You may answer the question, Mrs. Masterson.

A: No, it hardly seemed an accident at all. She was waiting for me, by my automobile, as Mr. Coxhead I'm sure will testify to.

[Objection, Mr. Phelps. Assumes facts not in evidence. Sustained.]

———————

13. This is a reference to Dayton's Department Store, which had just opened in 1902 in a new building at Seventh Street and Nicollet Avenue. The building, expanded several times, is now occupied by Macy's and remains the city's largest department store.

COURT: Mrs. Masterson, we will let your chauffeur speak for himself at the appropriate time.[14] Simply tell us what you saw, if you would.

A: Of course. As I said, she was standing there and as soon as she saw me, she came right up, bold as could be.

Q: All right, what happened next? Did she speak to you?

A: No, that is the strange thing. She said absolutely nothing. She just came up to me, grabbed my arm, and pressed a folded piece of paper into my hand. Then she rushed off. It all happened very quickly.

Q: How did you react to this peculiar encounter?

A: I must say I was frightened. I thought for a moment she intended to harm me. [Objection, Mr. Phelps. Speculation on part of witness. Overruled.]

Q: What did you do next?

A: Mr. Coxhead asked if I was all right and I said I was. He helped me into the backseat of the automobile and I told him to take me home.

Q: Now, while you were on your way back to your home, did you look at the piece of paper which the defendant gave you?

A: Yes. Naturally, I was curious.

Q: Let me show you Prosecution Exhibit Ten. Is this the note you received from the defendant in front of the Dayton's store?

A: Yes. I could hardly forget it.

Q: Please read its contents to the jury.

A: "I fear I am carrying Michael's child. We must talk at once or I cannot be responsible for the consequences. Addie Strongwood."

———

Q: Mrs. Masterson, did you or your husband ever meet face-to-face with Miss Strongwood as a result of her letter or the note she passed to you?

A: No.

Q: Why not?

A: I should think it would be obvious. She was trying to blackmail us. What purpose could be served by meeting with such a conniving creature? Besides, neither of us believed for one moment that Michael would have consorted with a girl of her kind.

14. Ernest Coxhead's brief testimony followed Mrs. Masterson's, and he corroborated her version of the encounter with Addie Strongwood.

Q: Did you show Michael the note?

A: Of course.

Q: What was his reaction?

A: He said it was the most perfectly ridiculous thing he had ever heard. He even joked, as I recall, that the girl must be smoking opium if she believed he had ever been intimate with her.

Q: But Michael didn't view the whole situation as a joke, did he?

A: Oh goodness, no. He understood that he—indeed, that our entire family— was under attack by this girl. He agreed that we would have to do something to stop her and silence her wild allegations.

Q: And did you in fact decide to take action?

A: Yes. Philip decided right then and there that we must take the matter up with our attorney, Mr. Moody, to see what could be done about Miss Strongwood. We met with him the very next morning.

Q: For the record, your meeting was with Mr. Darwin Moody, an attorney here in Minneapolis, is that correct?

A: Yes.

Q: I take it that you showed Mr. Moody the letter from Miss Strongwood regarding her supposed love for Michael as well as her note claiming to be carrying his child?

A: We did.

Q: And what did he advise you to do?

A: He suggested that we hire a private detective to look into Miss Strongwood's background, to see what kind of girl she really was.

Q: And did you in fact hire a detective?

A: Yes.

Q: And the man you hired was Mr. Earl Duggers of the Pinkerton Agency. Is that correct?

A: Yes.

Q: I will not ask you what Mr. Duggers discovered, since he has already testified to that.[15] But would it be fair to say that his findings were deeply disturbing to you and your husband?

[Objection, Mr. Phelps. Vague, calls for opinion, etc. Conference before the bench. Sustained.]

---

15. Mr. Duggers's testimony can be found in chapter 5.

Q: Now, getting back to the subject of your various communications with Miss Strongwood, you and your late husband received at least one other missive from her, only a week or so later and not long before Michael's death, isn't that right?

A: Yes, it was the blackmail letter we had feared all along.

FROM THE JOURNAL OF J. WINSTON PHELPS, JANUARY 20, 1904

1030 pm—cold & getting colder & damn furnace doing little good—ought to have left this dump[16] years ago but too much trouble now—maybe will warm up tomorrow when I get great battleax, Mrs Masterson, on the stand—would like to make her squirm as she is a true bitch—have to be cautious, tho—don't want to sound like Im berating mother of poor dead Michael—god but I hate rich people & all they do—of course who am I to complain, what with a big silver spoon lodged firmly in my mouth.[17]

EXCERPTS FROM THE CROSS-EXAMINATION OF MRS. PHILIP MASTERSON, MR. Phelps for the defense, January 21, 1904

Q: I promise I shall not detain your for too long, Mrs. Masterson. I know you have spent several hours testifying as to matters that must still be very painful to you. Still, there are a few items I should like to clarify. Now, let me begin by asking you a very simple question, if you do not mind. Were your parents wealthy?

---

16. Phelps lived in La Veta Terrace, an ornate Victorian row house at Seventeenth Street and Nicollet Avenue in Minneapolis. His apartment there is described in *Sherlock Holmes and the Secret Alliance*. Built in 1887, La Veta Terrace was demolished in 1932.

17. Phelps came from a wealthy family and enjoyed a substantial income beyond what he earned from his legal practice.

[Objection, Mr. Boardman. Conference before the bench. Objection overruled
but Mr. Phelps cautioned not to "stray too far."]

A: No, my parents were not wealthy.

Q: Your father, in fact, was a millwright, was he not, and later a machinist at Mr.
Pray's factory here in this city?[18]

A: Yes.

Q: A working man, in other words.

A: Yes. He worked very hard and always tried to better himself.

Q: I am sure that is the case and that he was a very fine man indeed. But he was
not, as you have said, a wealthy man who came from a wealthy family, and yet
here you are, his daughter, who married at age twenty-one, did you not, one
of the wealthiest young industrialists of Minneapolis, Mr. Philip Masterson?

A: Philip was still making his way in the world when we were married, Mr.
Phelps. I would hardly have called him wealthy.

Q: Ah, but was not his father a member of the well-known Masterson family
of industrialists and financiers with interests in Boston, New York, Chicago,
and other cities as well as Minneapolis?

A: I do not see the point of this inquiry, Mr. Phelps.

Q: Then I will state it quite baldly. You were a young woman of twenty-one,
from a poor family, who married a young man from a very wealthy family.
And yet when your own son proposed to a girl from circumstances much
like your own, you reacted, as you have told us, with a sense of outrage, if
not downright horror. I am merely trying to discover why that was so. Perhaps you can enlighten us?

A: In the first place, I do not believe that Michael ever proposed to her, as you
claim. Nor do I believe her intentions were ever to achieve a state of marriage. She was trying to get money out of us. That was all there was to it.

Q: I see. So it would be fair to say that from the very start, even though you
never spoke one word to my client or made any effort to meet her and
see what kind of person she might be, you assumed she was a tramp and
certainly not worthy of your son. And you made this assumption solely
because she, like you, came from poor circumstances. Is that your testimony, Mrs. Masterson?

18. Pray Manufacturing, founded by Otis A. Pray in 1878, made milling equipment at a large factory com-
plex near St. Anthony Falls. The company went bankrupt in 1886 and the factory is long gone.

A: You are twisting my words. I have nothing against the working people. I simply thought Michael would do best by marrying into his own class. It is a well-known fact young men of his kind are at risk from women who are interested only in their money.

Q: Ah, I see. And is there no room in this hard equation for love? Or is it your contention that the only true love is the love of the dollar?

[Objection, Mr. Boardman. Argumentative. Sustained.]

Q: Let us move on. You also testified on direct examination that you feared for your son because he was something of an "innocent"—I believe that is the word you used—in the ways of the world. Is that correct?

A: Yes.

Q: Mrs. Masterson, I have no desire to embarrass you, but you are aware, are you not, of the affidavit that has been submitted as Defense Exhibit Four regarding your son's activities at a certain notorious brothel in this city?

[Objection, Mr. Boardman. Irrelevant. Overruled.]

A: I do not know of such things.

Q: Yet if, in fact, your son was visiting our local sporting houses on a regular basis, he can hardly be called an "innocent," can he?

A: I will let you be the judge of that.

Q: Very well, let me be more blunt. Mrs. Masterson, do you have any reason to believe your son was a virgin before he met my client?

[Objection, Mr. Boardman. Conference before the bench.]

Q: I withdraw the question, your honor.

———

Q: Now then, Mrs. Masterson, let me clarify something you testified to earlier. You stated, I believe, that Michael told you and your husband that he had met Miss Strongwood in Chicago and out of admiration for her character had put in a good word for her so that she would be hired at Masterson and DeLaittre. Is that that correct?

A: Yes, that is what he told us.

Q: Here is my question: Do you have direct knowledge of this supposed meeting in Chicago?

A: I am not sure what you mean.

Q: Well, did you personally witness the meeting?

A: No.

Q: Did you see pictures of the two of them meeting?

A: No.

Q: Did anyone else who was at this meeting confirm to you that it had in fact taken place as Michael described it?

A: No, but I see no reason why Michael would have lied about it.

Q: We shall see about that, Mrs. Masterson. In the meantime, however, I wish to learn more about your reaction to the note from Addie informing you that she might be carrying Michael's child. You have testified that you and your husband showed the note to Michael and that he denied any possibility of paternity. Is that correct?

A: Yes. He completely rejected Miss Strongwood's claim. He said it was well known that she was a girl with the loosest sort of morals. Any one of a number of men, he believed, could have been the father, if she was indeed with child.

Q: She must be a tramp, in other words, inviting many men into her bed? Is that what Michael told you?

A: Words to that effect, yes.

Q: And you believed him?

A: Of course.

Q: He was, I take it, in your eyes a young man who was always honest and upright?

A: Yes.

Q: He would never tell a lie?

A: No, I always had complete trust in Michael.

Q: A fine moral character?

A: Yes.

Q: A good boy, in other words?

A: Yes, a very good boy.

Q: Not the sort of boy who would frequent bawdy houses or hold orgies at his apartment or hide such unsavory activities from his beloved mother. Is that what you are saying, Mrs. Masterson?

[Objection, Mr. Boardman. Argumentative. Sustained.]

Q: I withdraw the question, Your Honor.

———

Excerpts from the direct testimony of Miss Adelaide Strongwood, Mr. Phelps for the defense, January 27, 1904

―――――

Q: Addie, tell the court why you wrote the letter to Mr. and Mrs. Masterson speaking of your love for Michael and his desire to marry you. You weren't trying to blackmail them in any way, were you?

A: No, and it never occurred to me that my letter could be interpreted in such a sinister light. My only aim was to inform Michael's parents of the depth of our relations, since I feared Michael himself was reluctant to do so. I certainly meant no harm or for my letter to be regarded in any way as a threat.

Q: Your intentions were on the up-and-up, in other words?

A: Yes.

Q: In fact, you hoped that as a result of your letter, you might one day be able to meet Mr. and Mrs. Masterson. Is that correct?

A: Very much so. Michael, for whatever reason, was reluctant to introduce me to them, so I decided to take matters into my own hands.

Q: And what sort of response did you hope to receive from your letter?

A: I hoped that Mr. and Mrs. Masterson would write back to me and tell me how they felt about my connection to Michael. To be honest, I feared that they would not approve, but I thought it important to know one way or the other. Otherwise, I was not sure my relations with Michael could move forward.

Q: I see. And did the Mastersons ever reply to your letter?

A: No, I did not hear a word, but as I am not ignorant in such matters, I could only assume that their silence meant that they would never welcome me into their family.

Q: And it was at this point, I take it, that you began to think about ending your relationship with Michael?

A: Yes, I saw no other choice.

Q: Now, you must pardon me for asking this, Addie, but I cannot avoid the question: Had you and Michael ever been intimate at the time you wrote the letter?

A: Absolutely not.

Q: Had Michael ever attempted to achieve that goal?

A: Michael certainly tried, but I indicated to him in no uncertain terms that I would not do so. I must say that as his intentions in this regard became ever more obvious, I in turn became cooler toward him. It was just one more reason why I began to suspect we could not go on together.

———

Q: Addie, we will discuss in due time the painful and violent circumstances under which you came to be with child, but before we do so, tell the jury why you delivered the note to Mrs. Masterson regarding your fear that you might be in such a condition.

A: I was desperate. There is no other word for it. I could not be absolutely certain that I was carrying a child, but I thought it all too likely given what had just happened to me. I hoped that Michael's parents would understand my dire circumstances and be of some assistance.

Q: And why did you put the note in Mrs. Masterson's hand rather than, say, sending a letter through the mail?

A: I had tried sending a letter before and received no response. I believed a note, put directly into Mrs. Masterson's hand, would convey the urgency of the situation.

Q: Were you attempting to blackmail the Mastersons?

A: No, not at all. That was the farthest thing from my mind. I was simply seeking help from the grandparents of my child.

———

EXCERPTS FROM THE CROSS-EXAMINATION OF MISS ADELAIDE STRONGWOOD, Mr. Boardman for the prosecution, January 28, 1904

———

Q: Let me ask you about the letter you wrote to Mr. and Mr. Masterson in which you, stated, among other things, that Michael had proposed marriage to you. Who else was aware of this supposed proposal?

A: I do not believe, Mr. Boardman, that I ever said Michael had proposed to me. I only said that he had expressed a desire to wed one day.

Q: Well, however you wish to term it, this alleged interest in marriage on Michael's part was known to no one other than the two of you before you wrote the letter. Is that correct?

A: I believe so.

Q: And yet Michael told his parents there was in fact no such interest on his part. Isn't that right?

A: That is what Mrs. Masterson testified to. I know only what Michael told me.

Q: Exactly. Conveniently enough, you were the only person in possession of such knowledge, or so you tell us. So you could have made it all up, couldn't you?

A: I did not make it up.

Q: So you say. Now, here is the problem I am having, Miss Strongwood. On one hand, you have stated in several different forums, including your wondrous tales in the *Tribune*, that you believe Michael never wanted to marry you, never intended to marry you, and lied about pretty near everything. So why, then, would Michael ever have bothered to tell you in the first place that he wanted to marry? What exactly would he gain from this lie?

A: I do not know. I can only speculate that he perhaps thought that by professing his love for me and his desire to wed he might gain the favors he was so clearly after.

Q: String you along, in other words. Yet you've said you made it very clear to Michael from the start that you were not the type of girl to surrender your virtue outside the bonds of marriage. So, we get back to my question: What did Michael hope to gain by his lie?

A: And I have answered your question, Mr. Boardman, to the best of my ability.

Q: Oh, I doubt that. The truth is that Michael never suggested marriage. The truth is that it was you who were stringing him along, hoping to entrap him in your snare. The truth is that you planned to seduce him in order to have a child and thereby force him to marry you so that you could get your hands on his fortune. The truth—

[Objection, Mr. Phelps. Prosecutor is testifying, assuming facts not in evidence, failing to ask a proper question, etc.]

COURT: Mr. Boardman, let us hear a question from you, if you have one. Otherwise, I suggest you move on to a new field of inquiry.

Q: I will do so, Your Honor. We have heard a good deal of testimony about the note you handed to Mrs. Masterson outside the Dayton's store. You stated in the note that you feared you might be carrying Michael's child. But you didn't know, when you wrote that note, that you were in fact in that condition, did you?

A: No, I was not certain, but there had been one prominent physical indication that I was indeed with child.

Q: But you didn't know for sure, and yet you went to all the trouble of delivering a note to Mrs. Masterson that, well, maybe, just maybe, you might be impregnated with her son's child. Why would you do such a thing unless your goal was to strike fear of scandal into Mrs. Masterson's heart and perhaps extract a nice chunk of money from her and her husband? That was your real goal, wasn't it?

A: No, it was not. I simply wanted to alert Mr. and Mrs. Masterson to the strong possibility that Michael's cruel assault had left me with child.

Q: We will talk more in due time about Michael's supposed assault, an attack that Mr. Jakes stoutly denies and that Michael, of course, cannot deny, since he is, conveniently enough for your purposes, dead.

A: If you are suggesting that there was no assault, Mr. Boardman, then you are sorely mistaken. I would never lie about such a thing, not when that which I value above all else was taken from me.

———

Q: By the way, how is that you happened to find Mrs. Masterson in front of Dayton's so that you could deliver the note to her?

A: Well, I had heard that she frequently shopped there, and I thought it might be a place where I could give her the note.

Q: I see. Who was your source of information regarding Mrs. Masterson's shopping habits?

A: I do not recall.

Q: Is that so? And yet your memory is normally all but photographic, is it not, judging by the articles you've written for the *Tribune*? Entire conversations reproduced word for word. Quite amazing. Yet you cannot remember who passed on such an important piece of information regarding Mrs. Masterson?

A: That is what I have said.

Q: Yes, it is, but I wonder. Isn't it a fact that you called the Masterson residence on October twenty-first of last year and, by means of a ruse, learned when Mrs. Masterson was likely to be at the store?

A: I did no such thing.

Q: And isn't it also true that you staked out the store for hours, watching and waiting so that you could pounce on Mrs. Masterson when she came out the door?

A: I had to wait for a time, yes, but I did not "pounce" on her as you have said. I merely handed her the note and left. My intentions, as I have said repeatedly, were entirely honorable.

Q: Just as they were honorable, no doubt, when you sent a blackmail letter to the Mastersons demanding ten thousand dollars for the baby you were supposedly carrying. Is that what you would have us believe?

[Objection, Mr. Phelps. Misstatement of facts, etc.]

Q: I withdraw the question, Your Honor.

———

EXCERPTS FROM THE DIRECT TESTIMONY OF MISS CONSTANCE MCBRIDE, downstairs maid at the Philip Masterson home, Mr. Boardman for the prosecution, January 22, 1904

Q: Miss McBride, did you answer a telephone call at the Masterson home last October twenty-first regarding a matter at the Dayton's store here in Minneapolis?

A: Yes, it was a clerk from Dayton's who said there was a concern with something Mrs. Masterson had bought and she asked when she would be in the store again so they could fix the matter.

Q: Was this clerk, I assume, a woman?

A: Yes, it was a woman's voice.

Q: What did you tell her?

A: Well, I said Mrs. Masterson was almost always at the store on Saturday afternoons and she could talk to her then.

Q: What happened next?

A: Why, nothing happened. The girl just said "thank you" and hung up.

———

CROSS-EXAMINATION OF MISS CONSTANCE MCBRIDE, MR. PHELPS FOR THE defense, January 22, 1904

Q: Just one question, Miss McBride. Could you identify the voice of the clerk who called you from Dayton's if you heard it again?

A: Oh, I don't think so, sir. It was a poor connection.

Q: Miss Strongwood, with the court's permission, would you stand up and speak a few words to Miss McBride.

DEFENDANT: Good afternoon, Miss McBride. It is a lovely day and I hope you are doing well.

Q: That should be sufficient, Addie. You may sit down. Now, Miss McBride, is that the voice you heard over the telephone?

A: It could be or it could not is all I can say. I don't know. Like I said, it was a bad connection.

Q: No further questions, Your Honor.

LETTER FROM SHERLOCK HOLMES TO SHADWELL RAFFERTY, JANUARY 17, 1904[19]

Cook House
Rochester, Minnesota
17 January
My Dear Rafferty:

It was of course most kind of you and Mr. Thomas to come down for a visit on Saturday and see the patient, who I am confident now will make a full recovery. I have been informed by no less an authority than Dr. Will—by the way, how informal you Americans are!—that my long-suffering companion is a cured man and that the surgery presented no complications. You will be astonished to learn that no fewer than 200 stones were found in his gall bladder,

---

19. This letter was found among Rafferty's papers, left behind after his death in 1928. It is known that Holmes and Rafferty kept up a steady correspondence during their long friendship, but only two letters from Holmes that relate to the Strongwood case have been found.

and while this may indeed seem an extraordinary number, Dr. Will assures me that it is far from the record in this regard, which stands at over 3,000![20]

Dr. Watson, as you might imagine, has been a most difficult patient, as he does not relish being on the other end of the stethoscope, as it were, but he is nonetheless most pleased to be rid of the attacks that had become so excruciating to him in recent months. Did I mention during your visit that the poor doctor had suffered an especially ferocious attack just days after the successful conclusion of the curious affair involving Professor Presbury?[21]

Speaking of "affairs," I have found the matter of the Strongwood girl in Minneapolis to be of more than passing interest, particularly after learning of your involvement with it. Have been following it in the newspapers here. What a remarkable young woman your Miss Strongwood appears to be, and you were quite right in noting her resemblance to Mrs. Cubitt.[22] Ah, how thrilling and full of danger at every turn was our long chase in that affair! Young Miss Strongwood's case, however, presents an entirely different challenge. I am thinking now that I will come up to Minneapolis one day next week to observe the trial as there is nothing like seeing the dramatis personae in person. My regards as always to Mr. Thomas.

Your Friend,
Sherlock Holmes

---

20. Drs. William J. and Charles Mayo pioneered new approaches to gall bladder surgery in the 1890s. By 1904, when Dr. Watson arrived in Rochester, more than 300 gall bladder surgeries a year were being performed by the Mayos and doctors associated with them. The patient with 3,000 gallstones was a woman, who apparently made a full recovery.

21. The Presbury "affair" of which Holmes writes occurred in September 1903 and later became the subject of Dr. Watson's story "The Adventure of the Creeping Man," first published in 1923.

22. Holmes is referring here to Elsie Cubitt, whom he first met in 1898 during an investigation that served as the basis of Dr. Watson's exciting tale "The Adventure of the Dancing Men." Two years later, when Cubitt was abducted, Holmes and Dr. Watson set off on a mission to rescue her. Rafferty later joined the team, as recounted in *The Disappearance of Sherlock Holmes*.

FOUR

Part Four of "An Account of My Life and the Incident for Which I Have Been Unjustly Accused of Murder," by Addie Strongwood, *Minneapolis Tribune*, December 17, 1903

So many falsehoods have been circulated regarding my relationship with Michael Masterson that it could well be the labor of a lifetime to refute them all. The most scurrilous attacks have come in the pages of the *Journal*, where I have been treated as little more than a clay target in a shooting gallery. Firing off lies like scattershot, so that they might try to wound me no matter how wild their aim, my enemies have been cruel and unrelenting. Yet is not the truth the mightiest of armor? I believe it to be so, and I wear it proudly.

Among the most hurtful of the lies promulgated against me is that I set out to entrap Michael, even going so far as to falsely claim that I was carrying his child. The truth is that I was indeed with child, albeit only briefly, and that Michael was the father. The further truth, which even now I can hardly bear to think of without the utmost feelings of horror and revulsion, is that I was violated by Michael in a manner so brutal and degrading that it can scarcely be accounted for except as the Devil's very own work. I see now that, when it came to Michael and his ways, I would have been well advised to heed the words of the Bible: "Be sober, be vigilant; because your adversary the devil, as a roaring lion, walketh about, seeking whom he may devour." Michael tried to devour me, and it is only by the grace of God that I survived his depredations.

Most of the other prevarications that have been spread like ordure across the pages of the *Journal* in recent weeks hardly require a response from me. I am confident that when my day in court arrives, and my accusers are finally forced to speak their specious words in public, the world will finally see where the truth, in all of its sacred beauty, actually lies. Yet I cannot let one claim, made only days ago by Mr. Jonathan Jakes, pass without comment. I am sure, dear readers, that you know the nature of this claim and how deeply poisonous it is. The fact of the matter is that none of the events so graphically described by Mr. Jakes occurred. I can only surmise that he concocted his absurd story in a pathetic attempt to heap shame upon me in the eyes of the public. He will not, however, succeed in this meretricious endeavor, and his Great Lie will be fully exposed at the appropriate time. Like Michael, Mr. Jakes is a prince of deception who is sure to spend eternity in a very hot place.

It is now my painful duty to describe the terrible events of September 26, 1903, a day that will forever lodge in my memory, as though carved into my very bones. I fell victim to Michael's brutal violation at a time when I considered my concourse with him to be all but over, for the reasons which I have enumerated previously in these pages. There was, I finally came to realize, but one thing Michael really wanted of me, and I was not prepared to give it. When I was let go from my position at Masterson, DeLaittre & Sons, upon the flimsy basis of evidence that had obviously been forged, I believed that I had been officially dismissed, as it were, from the Masterson family. The very day that I was told never to return to the company, Michael called me from Chicago and expressed great surprise that I had lost my job, claiming my termination was the handiwork of his parents and not his own.

"I do not think that it matters," I told him. "If your family does not want me, and if you value your family, which I believe you do, then I see no avenue by which we can continue our relationship."

"Why, Addie, it is not a dead-end street yet between us," he said. "Just give me another chance. I will be back next week and we can talk then. You must know that I really do love you."

So spoke the champion of deceit, although at that time I was not sure what to think. I still wished to believe in Michael and so I clutched at hope as a drowning man might grasp at a frail piece of driftwood. Yet I also knew, or most certainly should have known by then, that Michael's words and deeds were rarely one and the same.

I did not hear from Michael until the next Friday, when he called once again. He sounded earnest and apologetic. "Addie, you must meet me tomorrow night in Loring Park.[1] I have something to show you that I believe will change your mind about me."

Although I was reluctant to do so, I agreed to meet him, if only to tell him that I had meant what I said on the telephone and that I believed our days together were indeed finished. Oh, what a foolish, foolish girl I was in agreeing to see him one last time! Regret, I know, is a cold meal little worth the trouble of dining on, and yet hardly a day goes by when I do not think of what I should have done at that moment, as opposed to the course of action I so unwisely followed.

So it was that late on the afternoon of September 26, I took the Chicago Ave. streetcar downtown and then walked to Loring Park. The evening was cool but pleasant, the smell of burning wood lingering in the air. A few ducks glided across the park's pretty little pond, but in a few short weeks they would be flying south to escape the icy grip of winter. I felt that my emancipation was also near, for once free of Michael and his demanding ways I intended to find a job, perhaps in some other city, and begin my life anew. How I wish now that the guiding hand of providence had taken me in that direction!

It was dusk when I reached the park, and I followed one of the footpaths to the little bridge that crosses the channel connecting the two portions of the pond. There I found Michael, dressed in a gray trench coat and black fedora and smoking a small cigar. As always, he looked handsome and dashing, and he greeted me with a broad smile.

"Dearest Addie, how wonderful to see you!" he said, and attempted to kiss me on the cheek.

I rebuffed him, however, for I did not wish to incite any false expectations. "Good evening, Michael," I said. "I hope you are enjoying this fine weather."

"I didn't come to talk about the weather, as you surely know," he replied in a rather stern voice. "The subject must be you and me and nothing else."

I saw no point in denying him his wish. "Very well, Michael, then I will tell you what I came here to say. I know you wish to change my mind, but I cannot see how such a thing could happen. We must say good-bye to each other."

Michael usually maintained an air of debonair disregard for matters of the heart, yet I expected that he would react to my announcement with at least some display of emotion.

---

1. Loring Park, established in 1883, remains the largest green space in Minneapolis's downtown area. It was initially known as Central Park, but the name was changed in 1890 to honor Charles Loring, first president of the Minneapolis Park Board.

Instead, he merely grinned at me and said, "So, I am to be tossed out with the refuse of the day, is that it? I am surprised, Addie. Did you not tell me many times how much you loved me? I am wondering what happened to that love of yours."

"I did love you," I said, "but I do not think you ever really loved me. I fear it is not love which moves you, Michael, but only base desire."

"That is not true!" he protested. "I have always had the warmest feelings toward you."

Said I: "If that is so, then why have you never introduced me to your parents? Why do you hide me from your friends? Why do you treat me as I fear you might treat a common woman of the streets? I am not sure, Michael, that you are an honorable man, and I cannot abide that!"

These were harsh words, I know, but I believe that the truth of the heart should never be compromised by false speech. Michael's immediate response was to stare at me for several moments, with eyes that were hard and cold. But to my surprise, he soon seemed to brighten again.

He said, "You have got me wrong, Addie, and I can prove it to you." He then stated that if I would accompany him to his apartment, which was nearby, he would show me something that "absolutely proved" his devotion to me and his desire to be joined in marriage.

Once again, I acted the fool. I should have pressed him to explain what this supposed "proof" was. Better yet, I should have walked away from Michael then and there. And yet I did not. The only explanation I can offer for my heedless behavior is that somewhere in the deepest chambers of my heart I still wished that Michael and I could be together. The Proverbs tell us, "Whoso rewardeth evil for good, evil shall not depart from his house," but the evil that awaited me at Michael's apartment was beyond anything I could ever have imagined.

Michael's place of residence was in the Virginia Flats,[2] and it was a matter of only a few minutes to walk there. Naturally, I felt uncomfortable entering his apartment, as it was not something that as a respectable woman I would normally do, but I still held out some tiny grain of hope that I had been wrong about Michael and that he would in some way prove his fealty to me.

What actually happened inside that apartment was the greatest horror any woman can experience. I should have known that something was amiss the

---

2. The Virginia Flats, a four-story brick apartment building, was located between Hennepin and Lyndale Avenues just south of Loring Park. The building was demolished in the 1960s to make way for Interstate 94.

moment we arrived at the door to the apartment, which was on the third floor. Instead of using his key to enter, Michael knocked on the door and shouted, "Are you there, Jake?"

"Whom are you talking to?" I asked.

"Why, Addie, it is just my friend, Mr. Jakes, who is staying with me for a few days. Don't worry, he won't bother us. Beside, we'll just be a minute." He then said, "Jake, Miss Strongwood is with me. I just want to show her something. You'll have everything ready, won't you?"

From the other side of the door came words from Mr. Jakes that will haunt me to the end of my days. "Oh yes, I'll be ready for her."

Oh, that I had never entered that apartment! How different my life would be and how different Michael's as well. There would have been no confrontation in the Windom Block, nor would I now be locked behind cold iron bars awaiting an unknown fate. But of course, out of foolishness and hope, I did go inside with Michael, and so my nightmare began.

I had hardly stepped inside when I saw Mr. Jakes, lounging on a blood-red divan and wearing a sweater of similar hue, so that he seemed almost a devil come up from some burning netherworld. He was smoking from a hookah placed on a low table and stared insolently at me without uttering a word. Although smoke hung heavily in the air, I caught the scent of something else. It was a sweet yet sickly aroma, and it brought back a sudden rush of memory to my early childhood and a day when I had visited my dying mother at the city hospital.

My attention, however, was soon turned to other matters. "Don't mind Jake," Michael said. "He's just being his usual idle self. If you'll just come over here to the window, Addie, I will show you what you came to see."

The window was at the far end of the room, well past the divan where Mr. Jakes, a smirk on his unpleasant face, sat smoking. I followed Michael past Mr. Jakes, who continued to stare at me in a most discomfiting way. There was a low table in front of the window, and atop it sat a leather-covered scrapbook.

"Ah, here it is," Michael said, sounding as though he had made a great discovery. "If you'll just look right here, you'll see what I wanted to show you."

I bent over to look at what appeared to be a newspaper clipping, and as I did so I suddenly felt a powerful arm around my throat and a rough cloth being pushed over my face. The cloth had the same sweet, deathly odor I had smelled as I entered the room, and my senses were so quickly overwhelmed that I lost all ability to resist my attacker. I remember, before losing all consciousness, seeing Michael's face. He was looking at me with such burning malevolence that I believed, before I passed into darkness, that I was about to die.

ARTICLE IN THE *MINNEAPOLIS TRIBUNE*, DECEMBER 18, 1903

Mr. William J. Murphy, publisher of the *Tribune,* stated today that he will "fight tooth and nail" any effort by Hennepin County Attorney Frederick Boardman to suppress the writings of Miss Adelaide Strongwood, who is accused of murdering Mr. Michael Masterson and who will soon go to trial in the case in Hennepin County District Court.

For the past four days, the *Tribune* has featured articles written by Miss Strongwood in which she describes the circumstances of the case from her point of view and professes her innocence on the grounds of self-defense. The *Tribune* has made these articles available to readers as a public service, and has offered to make a similar amount of space available in it pages to the family or friends of Mr. Masterson to present his side of the story. Thus far, no one has accepted that offer.

Yesterday afternoon, Mr. Boardman took to the pages of the *Journal* to criticize Miss Strongwood's articles as "prejudicial to a fair trial" and to condemn the *Tribune* for what he called "an unprecedented instance of interference by the press in a murder case." Significantly, however, Mr. Boardman has yet to file any legal motions in regard to the matter, and it is fair to say that his failure speaks volumes.

"The First Amendment to the Constitution of the United States enshrines our most sacred right, which is to speak freely, in the press or anywhere else, without fear of government sanction," Mr. Murphy said. "Miss Strongwood is simply exercising this right, and Mr. Boardman's ill-timed criticism is without foundation."

Mr. Murphy went on to say that he is confident that a jury will "come to the correct conclusion" when it hears all the evidence in the case and that nothing that has appeared in Miss Strongwood's articles will "prevent the jury from doing its duty as it sees fit."

"The *Journal,*" he added, "is merely engaging in sour grapes by publicizing Mr. Boardman's complaints. The *Journal* has been scooped, and it knows it, on this story, and it has nothing to do now except make whatever small noise it can in hopes of distracting attention from Miss Strongwood's articles in the *Tribune.*"

Excerpts from the direct testimony of Mr. Daniel Wellington,[3] clerk at John S. Bradstreet and Company,[4] Mr. Boardman for the prosecution, January 22, 1904

Q: Mr. Wellington, you are a clerk in the furniture division of Mr. Bradstreet's firm on Nicollet Avenue here in Minneapolis. Is that correct?

A: Yes.

Q: And how long have you been so employed?

A: For a little more than five years.

Q: Let me call your attention to Saturday, September fifth of last year. Were you at work on that day?

A: I was.

Q: Now, did you have a customer who was familiar to you that morning?

A: Yes, Michael Masterson stopped by to look at some new furniture.

Q: And how do you happen to remember the date of his visit to the store?

A: Well, it is on the sales receipt of the furniture he bought.

Q: Very well. Mr. Masterson had been a customer before, I take it?

A: Oh yes, he had purchased quite a few items from us about a year before when he moved into a new apartment.

Q: Would that be his apartment in the Virginia Flats?

A: Yes.

Q: Now, what was Mr. Masterson looking for on September fifth?

A: He said he wished to buy a new divan for his apartment.

Q: Did this request come as a surprise to you?

[Objection, Mr. Phelps. Leading the witness. Overruled.]

A: To some degree, yes. I recalled that he had bought a divan from us when he was furnishing his apartment and so I naturally asked him if it had proved unsatisfactory in any way.

Q: How did he respond?

---

3. "A handsome young man, he made an interesting impression as a witness," the *Minneapolis Times* said of Wellington. "He was the picture of sartorial splendor in a midnight blue pin-stripe suit cut in the latest fashion, and his words were always perfectly modulated, yet at times he sounded rather too much like an overly obsequious salesman."

4. John Bradstreet was Minneapolis's most prominent interior decorator of the time and provided furnishings for many of the city's leading families.

A: He said the divan was perfectly all right but that it had become badly stained and he therefore wished to replace it.

Q: I see. What color was this divan that had become stained, do you recall?

A: I looked up the sales record in our files. It was dark red shade known as Cabernet, after the wine of that name. A very lovely color, if I may say so.

Q: That is most enlightening, Mr. Wellington. Now, sir, did you in fact sell Mr. Masterson a new divan to replace the red one?

A: Yes. A very nice tufted divan, imported from France. One of our very best items of furniture.

Q: And what color was this new divan?

A: Light brown, with slight overtones of yellow. An extremely nice piece.

Q: Was this light-brown divan duly delivered to Mr. Masterson's apartment in the Virginia Flats?

A: It was.

Q: And when was it delivered?

A: Our records indicate Mr. Masterson received the divan on September eighth.

Q: And do your records also show that he signed a receipt stating that he had in fact taken delivery of the divan?

A: Yes.

Q: I will show you now Prosecution Exhibit Fourteen. Is this the receipt of delivery for the divan signed by Mr. Masterson?

A: It appears to be, yes.

Q: Now, Mr. Wellington, do your records also indicate what happened to the old divan—the red one?

A: Yes, it was taken away.

Q: And how do you known this for certain?

A: It is indicated right here on the receipt. The deliverymen made a note of it.

Q: Thank you, Mr. Wellington. I have no further questions.

FROM THE JOURNAL OF J. WINSTON PHELPS, DECEMBER 19, 1903

9 pm—pretty snow tonight but bitter cold will no doubt follow—early Xmas present arrived in mail today—another missive from anonymous angel in Chicago—quite the thunderbolt from on high & couldnt be more timely— my seraphim says clerk Wellington who has been quoted in Journal & is sure

to testify about the damned red divan was a friend of young Masterson & even attended parties at his place—further seems these parties were regular orgies with whores aplenty on hand for all the lads.

———

Still, divan is a big problem & Boardman will do his all to exploit it—Addie says it was just a slip of memory but dont see how as she probably remembers first time she suckled at her mamas tit—trouble is, if she owns up to being in Mastersons apartment before Sept 26th, Boardman will have plenty of fun & turn her into a wanton woman & Jezebel, etc—will try to gloss it all over with usual smoke & mirrors but dont know what jury will think.

EXCERPTS FROM THE CROSS-EXAMINATION OF MR. DANIEL WELLINGTON, MR. Phelps for the defense, January 22, 1904

Q: Mr. Wellington, how did the prosecution come to know about Mr. Masterson's purchase of a new divan on September fifth of last year?

A: I told Mr. Boardman about it.

Q: I see. What led you to get in touch with the esteemed prosecutor?

A: Well, I read the defendant's account in the newspaper and I noticed that she had mentioned the red divan and I thought it was odd, being that I knew we had sold Michael, I mean, Mr. Masterson, one of a different color only a few weeks before.

Q: Just doing your civic duty, were you?

A: Yes, you could say so.

Q: Do you suppose you might have had some other motivation beyond civic duty?

A: I don't know what you mean.

Q: Let me spell it out then. You were actually a friend of Mr. Masterson. Isn't that right?

A: I knew him, yes.

Q: Well enough to attend parties at his apartment?

A: Yes, I was there a few times.

Q: They were pretty lively parties, were they not?

[Objection, Mr. Boardman. Vague and irrelevant. Conference before the bench.]

COURT: The objection is overruled. You may proceed, Mr. Phelps, but do not wander from the issue we discussed.

Q: I understand, Your Honor. Now, Mr. Wellington, at these aforementioned parties, were there often young women in attendance?

A: There were some, yes.

Q: Were these the kind of women who could be called respectable?

A: I am not sure what you mean.

Q: Oh please, spare us the sanctimonious nonsense, Mr. Wellington. There were hired women, were there not, prostitutes, who were brought to these parties to provide favors for the men?

A: I couldn't say. There were many people at the parties. I didn't know most of them.

Q: So if you saw young women at these parties who were dressed in provocative attire and drinking and smoking with the men, you just assumed they were friends of the family, or schoolmarms on vacation, is that it?

[Objection, Mr. Boardman. Calls for conclusion on part of witness. Sustained.]

Q: In fact, these parties were orgies, were they not?

[Objection, Mr. Boardman. Irrelevant and beyond the scope of the direct examination. Sustained.]

Q: I withdraw the question. Let us be more specific then. Would it be fair to say that at these parties there were frequently, shall we say, amatory activities on Mr. Masterson's red divan?

A: I really couldn't say.

Q: Is that so? Did you close your poor innocent eyes lest they might be offended?

[Objection, Mr. Boardman. Badgering the witness. Sustained. Mr. Phelps cautioned.]

Q: My apologies, Your Honor. Isn't it a fact, Mr. Wellington, that when Mr. Masterson bought the new divan, he joked to you about how the red one had become so badly stained?

A: I don't recall him saying anything like that.

Q: I see, yet another unfortunate memory lapse. I am finished with this witness, Your Honor.

STRONGWOOD

Jonathan Jakes of this city, who is sure to provide most interesting testimony at the upcoming trial of Michael Masterson's accused killer, Miss Addie Strongwood, spoke at some length to a *Journal* reporter yesterday and made a number of shocking allegations. Mr. Jakes was a lifelong friend of Mr. Masterson and so possesses an unusual degree of knowledge regarding all the circumstances of the case.

It was Mr. Jakes himself, son of the well-known industrialist T. B. Jakes,[5] who asked for the interview in order to refute what he called "entirely false" claims by Miss Strongwood in a series of articles she has written for the *Tribune*. He said it seemed "extremely odd" to him that the *Tribune*, a newspaper that purports to offer its readers the truth, would allow "such shameful lies to be circulated about Mr. Masterson by the very person who cruelly took his life."

Mr. Jakes stated that virtually all of what Miss Strongwood has written in the *Tribune* is a "made-up story" and that he will prove it to be so when he is called upon to testify at her trial. Contrary to Miss Strongwood's assertions, Mr. Jakes said that it was she, not Mr. Masterson, who sought to prolong their relationship and that she was "desperate to find a rich man to marry."

"She is a very dangerous woman," Mr. Jakes stated, "and no man would ever be advised to turn his back on her. That is what Michael did, and we all know what happened to him."

Mr. Jakes also made the shocking allegation that Miss Strongwood, who has vigorously defended her virtue in the pages of the *Tribune*, seduced him one evening when Mr. Masterson was out of town.

"I was stunned," Mr. Jakes said, "at how brazenly she approached me, even though she knew I was Michael's closest friend. She is the most flirtatious and forward woman I have ever met, and nothing like the girl she pictures herself to be in the *Tribune*."

———

5. Thomas B. Jakes owned a company in Minneapolis that manufactured water pumps and similar products. It appears from various court documents that the company went bankrupt in 1918 and was later dissolved.

EXCERPTS FROM THE DIRECT TESTIMONY OF MR. JONATHAN JAKES,[6] FRIEND OF
Michael Masterson, Mr. Boardman for the prosecution, January 25, 1904

Q: I wish to turn now to certain events that occurred on the evening of Saturday, September twenty-sixth, 1903. Tell us, if you would, Mr. Jakes, where you were that evening.

A: I was staying at Michael's place.

Q: At the Virginia Flats on Hennepin Avenue?

A: Yes.

Q: Why were you staying at his apartment? You have a place of your own, do you not?

A: Yes, but Michael was seeing some friends out of town overnight and he wanted me to take care of his cat. So I told him I would stay over.

Q: Where did Michael say he was going?

A: He has friends in Duluth. That's where he said he would be.

Q: And what time did he leave?

A: I'm not really sure. It might have been around noon. I think that's when he said he was going to catch a train up to Duluth.

Q: Very well. Now, what time did you arrive at his apartment?

A: It was about five as I recall.

Q: And Michael was gone when you arrived?

A: Yes.

Q: To your knowledge, could Michael have met with Miss Strongwood that evening in Loring Park, as she has claimed in one of her articles written for the *Tribune*?

A: I don't see how, since he was out of town.

––––––––

Q: Now, did anything out of the ordinary happen that evening when you were staying in Michael's apartment?

––––––––

6. In *The Trial of Adelaide Strongwood,* Jakes was depicted as follows: "He is a gangly young man of twenty-five or so, well over six feet, with a freckled face, a prominent nose, thin red hair combed to the back, and pale blue eyes. His voice is high and rapid, his manner quick and alert. On the witness stand he often seemed ill at ease, frequently shifting in his chair or daubing sweat from his forehead with a handkerchief. Under the probing cross-examination of Mr. Phelps, he became particularly voluble and made several outbursts that drew the ire of Judge Elliott."

A: I should say so. It was about seven o'clock, I think, and there was a knock on the door. I went to answer it. It was Miss Strongwood.

Q: What did she want?

A: She asked for Michael, but I told her that he was out of town and wouldn't be back until the next day.

Q: I see. How did she react?

A: She did not seem surprised, if that's what you mean. I had the feeling she knew Michael was gone.

[Objection, Mr. Phelps. Speculation on the part of the witness. Sustained.]

Q: Did you notice anything else about Miss Strongwood's demeanor?

A: Well, I could tell she had been drinking quite a lot.

Q: How could you tell this?

A: Well, she smelled of gin and she seemed wobbly on her feet.

Q: Had you ever seen her in such a state before?

A: No, but Michael told me once, he said, "That girl likes her gin."

[Objection, Mr. Phelps. Hearsay. Overruled.]

Q: By "that girl," you mean the defendant?

A: Yes.

Q: All right, what happened next? Did you invite her in?

A: No, she sort of invited herself in.

Q: By the way, how was Miss Strongwood dressed?

A: I guess it wasn't what you would expect. She had on a red dress that was, well, kind of low in the front, like she was on her way to a fancy ball.

Q: Did she in fact say she was going to some formal event later?

A: No.

Q: All right. Now, when Miss Strongwood came into the apartment, what happened next?

A: Well, she waltzed right over to the divan and sat down and said I should sit down beside her, as she had something she wished to tell me.

Q: Before we go further along these lines, let me ask you, Mr. Jakes, what color was the divan that Miss Strongwood sat down on?

A: Kind of a light brown, or maybe tan, I guess you could say.

Q: But not blood red or anything close to that color?

A: No.

Q: Had there once been a red divan in the apartment?

A: Yes, but Michael had gotten rid of it a few weeks before, as I remember. He didn't like the color for some reason.

Q: Or perhaps it was badly stained?

A: Not that I ever noticed.

Q: All right, let us return to Miss Strongwood's visit. Smelling of gin, she has, according to your testimony, invited herself into the apartment. She has taken a seat on the light-brown divan. She has invited you to sit down beside her. How would you describe her tone of voice?

A: She was very insistent, I guess that is the best way I could put it.

Q: What did you do next?

A: I sat down on the divan.

Q: Then what happened?

A: Well, she told me to sit closer. Said I should not be a stranger to her, or something like that.

Q: Did you move closer?

A: No, I wasn't feeling real comfortable about the whole thing, if you want to know the truth, but it didn't matter because she moved over right next to me and put an arm around my shoulder.

Q: How did you react?

A: I wasn't sure what to do. I'd never seen a proper girl act like that before.

Q: Very well. What happened next?

A: She kissed me on the cheek.

Q: I see. How would you describe this kiss?

A: What do you mean?

Q: Well, was it the sort of simple, affectionate kiss a mother might give to her child or was it something more passionate than that?

A: Oh, it was warm all right. The way she was acting I thought she wanted to, well, you know, be intimate with me.

[Objection, Mr. Phelps. Speculation on part of witness. Sustained.]

Q: Very well, let me put the question to you this way: Were you in fact intimate with Miss Strongwood later that evening?

A: I regret to say that I was.

DEFENDANT: "You lie, Jakes. You are nothing but a liar and God will judge you for it."[7]

COURT: Miss Strongwood, you will sit down and you will be silent. If there is another outburst you will be found in contempt and removed from this courtroom. Do you understand?

DEFENDANT: Yes, Your Honor. I am very sorry, but—

COURT: You will say no more, Miss Strongwood, not one more word. Mr. Boardman, please resume.

Q: Thank you. Now, Mr. Jakes, let us go back a bit to when you and the defendant were on the couch in Mr. Masterson's apartment. Did she tell you anything about Mr. Masterson while you were sitting there?

A: She did. She said Mikey—that is, Mr. Masterson—wanted to stop seeing her because he didn't feel she was good enough for him, but that she wasn't going to let him get away with it on account of the fact that she had something over him.

Q: Did she explain what she meant by having "something over him"?

A: No.

Q: Do you have any idea as to what she might have meant?

[Objection, Mr. Phelps. Calls for speculation. Conference before the bench. Sustained.]

———

Q: Did Miss Strongwood tell you that night that she was carrying Michael's child?

A: No.

Q: Did she tell you she had been intimate with Michael?

A: No.

Q: Did Michael ever state to you that he had been intimate with her?

A: Yes.

Q: Under what circumstances?

———

7. The *Minneapolis Tribune* reported that "Miss Strongwood, trembling with anger, rose from her chair, shook her fist at Mr. Jakes, and called him a liar who would have to answer to God for his prevarications." The *Minneapolis Journal* offered a far less sympathetic account, writing that "the defendant, perhaps hoping to convince the jury of her virtuousness, made quite a scene by shouting out that Mr. Jakes was a liar."

A: He told me they'd gone out one evening in late August to a club and, you know, had some drinks, and that she came back with him to the apartment later. He said he'd had too much to drink and the next thing he knew she was next to him and then it happened.

Q: They were intimate?

A: Yes.

Q: How did Michael feel about what had happened?

A: He was very worried.

Q: Why?

A: He thought that she had gotten her hooks into him right from the start in Chicago and that now she wanted blood.

Q: What did he mean by that?

[Objection, Mr. Phelps. Speculation. Sustained.]

Q: Did Michael tell you what he meant when he said Miss Strongwood "wanted blood"?

A: Yes. He said he thought she was after his money and had been all along and that she would try to say she was, you know, in a family way, because of what they had done, even though he thought she had been with other men.

Q: Now, you testified that Michael told you Miss Strongwood had "gotten her hooks into him" in Chicago. Did he ever say how that had happened?

A: Not in any detail. He just said he'd met her there at a dance hall and they'd talked and then he'd gotten a job for her here.

Q: At Masterson, DeLaittre and Sons?

A: Yes.

Q: Did he say why he'd arranged to have her hired?

A: He just said she was pretty and he liked her and she really needed a job.

———

Q: Now, returning to the night of September twenty-sixth, about what time did Miss Strongwood leave the apartment?

A: I think it was a little after midnight.

Q: Did the two of you have a conversation before she left?

A: Yes.

Q: What did you talk about?

A: Well, she said I would be well advised not to tell Michael what had happened between us, as it would do her no good, and that maybe she would see me again sometime if I was nice to her. It was hard to understand everything she said because she was still, well, you, know, under the influence.

Q: Of alcohol?

A: Yes.

Q: Did she say anything else?

A: Yes, and it was a funny thing to say. She said she'd heard my father was even richer than Michael's and that no matter what happened, somebody was going to have to pay.

Q: How did you react to this statement?

A: I wasn't sure what to make of it, but I said I was beginning to think she was playing me for a fool and that I regretted what we had done.

Q: What was her response?

A: She just laughed and said, "Oh, don't be an even bigger idiot than Michael." I'll never forget that.

Q: And then she left?

A: Yes.

Q: At about midnight?

A: I think so.

Q: Did you spend the rest of the night at the apartment?

A: Yes, I stayed until the next morning.

Q: What time did you leave?

A: About eight.

Q: Did you lock the door when you left?

A: No, I couldn't find the key.

Q: You didn't remember where you had left it, was that it?

A: No, I knew exactly where I had left it, on the table by the door.

Q: And it wasn't there?

A: No.

Q: Did you look for it?

A: Everywhere I could think of, but I couldn't find it.

Q: What did you think happened to it?

[Objection, Mr. Phelps. Calls for speculation. Sustained.]

Q: Did you leave the door open when you left?

A: No, I stopped by the caretaker's office on my way out and explained the situation. She said she would go up and lock the door.

Q: And did she do so?

A: As far as I know, yes.

Q: Let me turn your attention now to Sunday, September twenty-seventh. Did Michael return to his apartment that afternoon?

A: Yes. He called me at about one o'clock and said he was back, so I went over to see him.

Q: In his apartment?

A: Yes.

Q: Did you talk with him about Miss Strongwood's visit the night before?

A: Yes.

Q: Did you tell him everything that happened, including that you and Miss Strongwood had been intimate?

A: Yes, I felt terrible about it and told Michael how sorry I was.

Q: What did he say?

A: I thought he would be very angry but he wasn't. He said she was really nothing more than, well, I don't want to use the word, but you know what I mean.

Q: I must ask you to use the word, Mr. Jakes. I am sure the jury will recognize the necessity of stating the full truth in this matter.

A: Well, he said he thought she was a whore, and that she had just proved it.

Q: What else did he say?

A: He said he would never see her again, under any circumstances.

Q: And did he, to your knowledge, live up to his word?

A: Yes. I don't think he ever went out with her again until she killed him.

Q: You miss Michael, don't you?

A: Very much.

Q: He was a good friend?

A: He was the best friend a man could have.

———

Q: Mr. Jakes, did you tell Michael about the missing key to his apartment?

A: Yes.

Q: How did he react to this news?

A: He was very upset.

Q: Why?

A: He told me he believed Miss Strongwood had taken it and that she might sneak in and try to murder him.

[Objection, Mr. Phelps. Hearsay, speculation, etc. Conference before the bench.
Overruled.]

Q: Did he say why he felt that way?

A: He just said she was a scary woman and that he wouldn't put anything past
her.

Q: Did he say anything else?

A: Yes, he said he would have the locks changed right away.

———————

LETTER FROM SHADWELL RAFFERTY TO J. WINSTON PHELPS, DECEMBER 11, 1903

Win:

Salutations from Osakis.[8] Know you are not of the piscatorial persuasion
but you should see the beauty I pulled thru the ice yesterday. 25 lbs. easy. A
pike for the ages. Will have it mounted on the back wall for the good drinking
men of St. Paul to admire.

Writing to tell you just got telegram from Wash who as you know is down
in Chicago. Did his usual fine job of digging around in the muck and mire and
guess what—you were right! Young Masterson was whoring at Everleighs[9]
pretty much every month. Wash talked to Ada herself. Lad was well known
to the place as was his pal Jakes. Of course you will never get anyone to testify.
The sisters have the best damn shysters there are—no offense to your noble
profession, Win—and all the girls will dummy up anyway.

Now here is some info re the thing you were worried about and it is not
good news I'm afraid. As you will no doubt be hiding this letter somewhere it
can't be found I will just say that Wash dug up some disturbing news re your client when she was living in Chicago. He will send info to you direct. Don't know
the details and don't care to in case I must testify before this business is done.

Did you see *Pioneer Press* story regarding yours truly? Can't imagine how that
fellow found out I've been working for you but that is what those newshounds

———————

8. Osakis is a community located on Lake Osakis in west-central Minnesota. It appears that Rafferty, an
avid fisherman, stopped at Osakis for a few days after his trip to Fargo to interview Mary McDonald.

9. Everleigh's was the most sumptuous and expensive brothel in Chicago's Levee District. It was operated by sisters Ada and Minna Everleigh from 1900 to 1911.

are paid to do. Back in St. Paul Sunday if you want to call. Been thinking about Miss Strongwood and her story and you must tread carefully, Win, as I think there are secrets all around and maybe neither of us knows the half of them.

All the best,
Shad

ARTICLE IN THE *ST. PAUL PIONEER PRESS*, DECEMBER 10, 1903

An interesting piece of intelligence has emerged regarding Shadwell Rafferty, who is among this city's most prominent citizens and certainly its most renowned saloonkeeper. It has been learned that Rafferty, who has also made quite a name for himself as a detective and whose adventures with a certain Sherlock Holmes of London hardly need recounting here, is now looking into the case of Adelaide Strongwood, the Minneapolis girl accused of murdering her lover. A reliable source has informed the *Pioneer Press* that Rafferty is working with Miss Strongwood's attorney, J. Winston Phelps, in an effort to establish her innocence.

To which we can only say: the prosecution has been duly warned! Rafferty has solved many a mystery in his day and there's no better man to have in one's corner in a fight. Can we assume, with Rafferty on the case, that Sherlock Holmes and Dr. John Watson will soon join him?

EXCERPTS FROM THE CROSS-EXAMINATION OF MR. JONATHAN JAKES, MR. Phelps for the defense, January 26, 1904

Q: Well, Mr. Jakes, it is quite a tale you've told, quite a tale. Let us see, however, how it bears up under close scrutiny. Now, going back to that fateful Saturday, you testified that Mr. Masterson left town to visit some friends and that you were asked to take charge of his apartment and his cat during his absence. Is that correct?

A: Yes.

Q: Tell me about this cat, if you would. It's a tomcat, is it not?

A: I guess so.

Q: And what is this tomcat's name?

[Objection, Mr. Boardman. Irrelevant. Conference before the bench. Overruled.]

Q: I ask you again, Mr. Jakes. What was the cat's name?

A: I really can't recall. It was some silly name or other.

Q: Oh, come now, Mr. Jakes, don't be shy. You know full well the cat's name. It was called Balling? It is spelled b-a-l-l-i-n-g. Isn't that correct?

A: If you say so.

Q: Do you deny that was the cat's name, because if you do, I would be happy to produce an affidavit from the veterinarian, Dr. Forsyth, who treated the cat for a broken leg last year and whose records show that its name was indeed Balling?

A: I don't really care about the cat's name.

Q: Ah, you are not a lover of the feline species. Is that it? But don't you agree, Mr. Jakes, that Balling is a rather odd name for a cat? Did Michael ever say why he chose such a queer name?

A: I imagine you would know more about queer things than I would.

COURT: Mr. Jakes, confine yourself to answering the question put before you. Your commentary is neither desired nor welcomed.

A: Like I said, it was just some silly name Michael came up with.

Q: Might it have been in fact a reference to your and Michael's favorite activity in the apartment vis-à-vis young ladies?

[Objection, Mr. Boardman. Calls for speculation. Sustained.]

Q: I withdraw the question, Your Honor. Let us explore the topic of Mr. Masterson's overnight visit, shall we, sir? You said he went to Duluth. Is that correct?

A: Yes.

Q: Who was he seeing there?

A: I wouldn't know.

Q: Well, can you tell us the names of any of his friends in Duluth?

A: Like I said, I wouldn't know.

Q: How convenient. There's no way to check your story, is there, since even though Michael was supposedly your bosom buddy you don't seem to know a single one of his friends in Duluth?

A: I don't know all of his friends. Why should I? You're being ridiculous.

COURT: Mr. Jakes, I must caution you. Simply answer defense counsel's questions without engaging in any commentary. Do you understand?

A: Sure, I understand.

Q: At the risk of being accused of ridiculousness, Mr. Jakes, let me ask a few more questions about Mr. Masterson's visit to Duluth. You said he left about noon, is that right?

A: Yes.

Q: Did you see him off at the depot?

A: No.

Q: Did you in fact see him at all that day?

A: No.

Q: So all you know is that he told you over the telephone that he would be leaving for Duluth around noon. Is that your testimony?

A: Yes.

Q: And he would have had no reason to lie about the trip, would he?

A: Not that I know of.

Q: Michael was always honest with you?

A: Yes.

Q: Not the sort of man who would tell lies?

A: No.

Q: Now, as I remember, you stated in your direct testimony that you arrived to take charge of Mr. Masterson's apartment at about five o'clock. Is that right?

A: Yes.

Q: And at that time, presumably, Mr. Masterson would already have been in Duluth, correct?

A: I assume so.

Q: I see. Well, sir, would it surprise you to learn that your friend, Mr. Masterson, was seen just a few blocks away from his apartment at six o'clock that very night, even though he supposedly told you he was in Duluth?

A: I wouldn't know anything about that.

———

FROM THE JOURNAL OF J. WINSTON PHELPS, JANUARY 25, 1904

7 pm—wonder of wonders!—call late this afternoon from man named Marks—owns cigar shop at Franklin & Lyndale not far from Virginia Flats—read

Tribune re that liar Jakes & said Masterson cant have been in Duluth on Sept 26 as Jakes testified—knows that because Masterson was in his cigar shop just before 6 pm—Marks willing to swear to it!—will impeach that little prick Jakes now.

———

EXCERPTS FROM THE DIRECT TESTIMONY OF MR. SAMUEL MARKS, CIGAR SHOP owner, Mr. Phelps for the defense, January 26, 1904

Q: Where is your cigar shop located, Mr. Marks?

A: At Franklin and Lyndale.

Q: How far is that from the apartment building known as Virginia Flats?

A: Oh, it would be two or three blocks, no more.

Q: A short distance, in other words.

A: Yes.

Q: Did you know Mr. Michael Masterson?

A: Yes. He would stop in the shop pretty much every week.

Q: And you knew him by name. Is that correct?

A: Yes, he had a standing order for Juan Lopez coronas, one of the nicest Cuban cigars I sell. I would call him when a shipment came in and he would stop by to pick them up.

Q: I call your attention to Saturday, September twenty-sixth, of last year. Did Mr. Masterson stop by your shop that evening?

A: Yes. He came not too long before closing.

Q: What time do you close on Saturdays?

A: Six o'clock.

Q: Now, you will pardon me for asking, Mr. Marks, but how is that you remember Mr. Masterson coming into your shop on that particular evening, among so many others?

A: It was the fire right across the street. Mr. Berman's tailor shop. Nearly burned down the whole building.

Q: The fire department was there?

A: Yes.

Q: Quite a spectacle, I'm sure.

A: Oh yes, more excitement than I'd seen in a long time.

Q: And it was during all of this excitement that Mr. Masterson came into your shop?

A: Yes, that's why I remember seeing him that night.

Q: Did you talk with him?

A: Sure. He said he was glad it wasn't his place that was burning down. I remember that.

Q: How long was Mr. Masterson in your shop?

A: Not long. He bought his cigars and left.

Q: And this was right before six o'clock at night?

A: Yes. He was my last customer of the day.

Q: Did you see him at all after he left?

A: He walked across the street to look at the fire. I saw him standing there with the rest of the crowd.

Q: Did he seem to be in any kind of hurry?

A: No.

Q: Then what happened?

A: Well, I closed up shop, and I went over to look at the fire myself.

Q: Did you see Mr. Masterson in the crowd?

A: No, but I saw him walking away down Lyndale.

Q: Which direction was he heading?

A: North.

Q: Toward Loring Park?

A: Yes, he was going in that direction.

———

EXCERPTS FROM THE CROSS-EXAMINATION OF MR. JONATHAN JAKES, MR. Phelps for the defense, January 26, 1904

———

Q: So your story, Mr. Jakes, is that Michael Masterson went to Duluth at noon and did not return until the next day. Is that correct?

A: Yes.

Q: Even though he was seen at six o'clock that night in a cigar shop just a few blocks from the apartment?

[Objection, Mr. Boardman. Assumes facts not in evidence. Sustained.][10]

Q: All right, we will establish Mr. Masterson's whereabouts on the night in question later. In the meantime, let us not fiddle around any further, Mr. Jakes. The truth is that Michael Masterson didn't go anywhere. The truth is that you and Mr. Masterson were together in that apartment all night. The truth is that you lured Addie there. The truth is that you drugged and viciously assaulted her. Isn't that right?

A: No, nothing like that happened.

Q: Ah yes, that's right. It was instead, you've told us, the night of your great conquest. Seized by a sudden onset of lust, the great seductress Addie Strongwood, reeking of alcohol, practically drags you kicking and screaming into the boudoir. What do you suppose came over her? Was it your irresistible good looks and scintillating personality that did the trick?

[Objection, Mr. Boardman. Mocking the witness. Sustained.]

Q: All right, let's talk about your amorous exploits, Mr. Jakes. Your testimony thus far leaves the impression that you and Mr. Masterson are wholesome young lads, and that the two of you, like lambs being led to the slaughter, were both seduced by the evil wiles of my client. Are you in fact a wholesome lad, Mr. Jakes?

[Objection, Mr. Boardman. Irrelevant, badgering witness. Sustained.]

Q: Let us try another tack, Mr. Jakes. You testified earlier that you and Mr. Masterson were the best of friends. Isn't that correct?

A: Yes.

Q: In fact, you attended school with him at Andover Academy in New Hampshire, did you not?

A: Yes.

Q: The two of you spent a good deal of time together. Isn't that right?

A: I suppose so.

Q: What did you do to amuse yourselves?

A: Just the usual sorts of things.

Q: I see. Going to shows?

A: Yes.

Q: Visiting with friends?

---

10. At the time Judge Elliott made his ruling, Samuel Marks had not yet testified. His testimony came later, when the defense presented its case.

A: Yes.

Q: Riding around in Michael's new motorcar?

A: Sometimes.

Q: All perfectly normal activities for young men about town. Am I right?

A: Yes.

Q: Now then, Mr. Jakes, you were also a frequent visitor at Mr. Masterson's apartment. Isn't that correct?

A: I was there quite often, yes.

Q: Did you attend parties there?

A: Yes.

Q: In fact, it would be fair to say, would it not, that Mr. Masterson had numerous parties at his apartment?

A: I don't know if "numerous" is the word I would use.

Q: Pray tell us, sir, what would be a better word?

A: He had parties once in a while. That is how I would put it.

Q: These were, I assume, polite gatherings at which everyone drank root beer, nibbled on cake, and discussed the latest trends in social thought. Is that the kind of party you're talking about?

[Objection, Mr. Boardman. Irrelevant. Conference before the bench. Overruled.]

Q: Isn't it a fact, Mr. Jakes, that these parties of which you speak were, to put it bluntly, sex parties in which you and other young bloods spent the night with whores?

[Objection, Mr. Boardman. Irrelevant, beyond the scope of direct examination. Conference before the bench.]

COURT: Objection overruled. Mr. Phelps, I am going to allow you some leeway as to your inquiries into the character of this witness, but you must not go beyond the bounds of decency.

Q: Thank you, Your Honor. You may answer my question, Mr. Jakes.

A: They were just parties, that's all I can say.

Q: No, I believe you are required to say more than that, sir. Let me ask you again: Were there prostitutes at these parties?

A: There may have been.

Q: Don't you know whether there were prostitutes in attendance, Mr. Jakes? After all, why hire prostitutes to entertain you and your friends of an evening if you don't know they're there? Wouldn't make much sense, would it?

A: I'm not sure I understand the question.

Q: Really? I believe my friend Dr. Will Johnston over on Robert Street in St. Paul would have an easier time removing one of your molars with a tweezers than I am having in getting you to answer a simple question. Now sir, yes or no, were there prostitutes at parties you attended in Michael's apartment?

A: I don't really recall.

Q: My oh my, how fickle is the memory of youth. Come now, have you ever consorted with prostitutes, Mr. Jakes?

A: I don't see why that matters.

COURT: Mr. Jakes, the court determines the relevancy of questions in this matter, not you. You are instructed to answer the question.

A: I have on occasion.

Q: You are whispering, Mr. Jakes. Speak up. You have "on occasion" visited with prostitutes. Did Michael Masterson sometimes join you on these forays?

A: Sometimes.

Q: Let us attempt to enter the dangerous realm of specificity, Mr. Jakes. Just how many times did the two of you visit one of this city's palaces of carnal recreation, say in the year before Mr. Masterson's death? Once a month? Twice a month? Dozens of times?

A: I don't really recall.

Q: Very well, Mr. Jakes, let me put it to you this way: If I were to ask Miss Ida Dorsey, who runs a notorious house of ill repute on Eleventh Avenue South not five blocks from here, if she ever saw you and Mr. Masterson at her establishment, her response would presumably be that the two of you are as unfamiliar to her as the Baby Jesus, is that what you are saying?

[Objection, Mr. Boardman. Assumes facts not in evidence. Sustained.]

Q: Do you deny that you and Mr. Masterson were customers at the brothels of this city?

A: I don't deny it, but there are lots of young fellows who do what we did.

Q: And even more, I venture, who do not. Be that as it may, isn't it a fact, Mr. Jakes, that you and Mr. Masterson were well known to virtually every madam of this city as frequent and well-paying customers and that you were also known for your rather peculiar tastes?

[Objection, Mr. Boardman. Beyond the scope of direct examination.]

Q: I withdraw the question, Your Honor. So, let us be clear about this. You and Michael Masterson were frequent visitors at our local whorehouses. Veritable regulars, is that correct?

A: As I said, we visited such places once in a while, like most young fellows do, but I would not use the word "frequent."

Q: I see. Let me show you Defense Exhibit Four, which is an affidavit prepared and duly signed by Mrs. Jackie Lee, who operates a brothel on First Street South not six blocks from here.[11] Seems you were at her place, what, a dozen times this year alone?

A: I do not recall the number of times.

Q: Too busy having fun, I suppose, beating up on the girls. Is that it?

[Objection, Mr. Phelps. Assumes facts not in evidence. Sustained.]

Q: So, your story is that you and Mr. Masterson were just sowing your wild oats now and then. Is that right?

A: Yes.

Q: In fact, didn't the two of you plant a mighty field of oats in the whorehouses of Minneapolis, Chicago, New Orleans, and God knows where else? Indeed, you were even frequent visitors to the Everleigh sisters' famed establishment in Chicago, were you not?

A: I wouldn't necessarily say so.

Q: Is that a fact? And I suppose you will deny as well that you and Michael enjoyed punching the girls around just for the fun of it? The truth is, the two of you were holy terrors, were you not? Come, sir, speak up and tell us about the wonderful things you and Michael did while sowing your wild oats.

[Objection, Mr. Boardman. Assumes facts not in evidence, badgering the witness, etc. Sustained.]

COURT: I think you have made your point, Mr. Phelps. It is time to move on.

Q: You've stated here that Michael Masterson told you he was seduced by my client. Is that correct, Mr. Jakes?

A: Yes.

Q: Is this the same Michael Masterson who went with you to whorehouses from here to New Orleans and many points in between and bragged of his many sexual conquests?

A: Those are your words, not mine.

---

11. Mrs. Lee stated in her affidavit that Michael Masterson and Jonathan Jakes were "regular customers" at her establishment but were sometimes "rough on the girls," though she offered no specific details regarding their behavior.

Q: No, sir, they are facts. How in God's name do you expect us to believe that "Mikey the Masher," the great seducer, was somehow seduced against his will by my client? It is arrant nonsense and you know it, don't you, Mr. Jakes?

[Objection, Mr. Boardman. Argumentative. Sustained.]

Q: It was you and Michael who did the seducing, wasn't it? It was the two of you who took what you wanted and took it by force. Isn't that what really happened, Mr. Jakes?

A: No, I deny that.

———

Q: Now, before we move on to some other matters, Mr. Jakes, tell me this, if you would: Do you own a camera?

A: Yes.

Q: What sort of camera?

A: A pocket Kodak.[12]

Q: What about Mr. Masterson? Did he also own a camera?

A: Yes. He had the same one as mine.

Q: What sort of pictures did the two of you take?

A: I don't know, just the usual things.

Q: Family, friends, vacation outings?

A: That's right.

Q: And maybe the occasional drugged and defenseless naked woman?

[Objection, Mr. Boardman. Irrelevant and immaterial, etc. Conference before the bench. Overruled.]

COURT: You may answer the question, Mr. Jakes.

A: No, that is nonsense.

Q: We shall see about that. By the way, did Mr. Masterson have a darkroom in his apartment?

A: No, not that I ever saw.

Q: How about you, Mr. Jakes? Do you have a darkroom at your place of residence?

A: Yes, a small one.

———

12. Kodak introduced its first folding pocket camera in 1897. An improved version, the No. 1 Folding Pocket Kodak, appeared in 1899 and is probably the camera Jakes owned. The camera used roll film that produced a 2¼- by 3¼-inch negative.

Q: Well now, that's curious. You've just testified that your camera is one of the Kodak pocket models, which if I am not mistaken, uses roll film. Am I right?

A: Yes.

Q: And that film is developed by Kodak, is it not? You simply mail the roll to them and they send back the developed pictures.

A: That's right.

Q: Of what avail, then, is your darkroom, Mr. Jakes? Could it be that you use it to develop pictures of naked woman you've taken on the sly?

A: That is not true.

Q: Well then, do you own other cameras that require you to develop the film yourself?

A: I used to, but I don't anymore.

———

Q: Now, you have testified that Michael Masterson told you he'd met Addie in a dance hall in Chicago. Is that right?

A: Yes.

Q: Did he say when this supposed meeting was?

A: No.

Q: Did he provide any additional details at all?

A: Not really.

Q: You weren't at this alleged meeting, were you?

A: No.

Q: Didn't see it with your own eyes?

A: No.

Q: So all we have is your word that Michael told you about this meeting?

A: I suppose so.

Q: And you're an honest, upright fellow who, when he's not busy whoring and drinking and carousing, always tell the truth. Is that what you wish us to believe?

[Objection, Mr. Boardman. Argumentative, etc. Sustained.]

Q: I withdraw the question, Your Honor.

———

Q: Let us turn, Mr. Jakes, to the curious matter of the missing apartment key. You say you left it on a table and then, voilà, it was gone. Is that correct?

A: Yes.

Q: Isn't it entirely possible you simply misplaced it?

A: I doubt it.

Q: Well, you were busy that night, were you not?

A: I don't know what you mean.

Q: Of course you do. You were helping your friend, Mr. Masterson, as he went about ravishing Addie. Isn't that right?

A: No one ravished her.

Q: Well, whatever you were doing, you weren't wearing any clothes, were you, so the key might easily have slipped out of your pocket. Isn't that right?

A: I remember putting it on the table, as I said.

Q: It is amazing, Mr. Jakes, how selective your memory is. Some matters you seem to remember with pinpoint precision, yet in others your memory seems beset by persistent fog. It could lead a person to believe you are not being truthful, couldn't it?

[Objection, Mr. Boardman. Argumentative. Sustained.]

Q: I withdraw the question. Now, sir, you have also testified that Michael Masterson was supposedly afraid of Addie?

A: Yes.

Q: Curious, isn't it? A strapping lad like Michael afraid of a young woman who probably weighs little more than a hundred pounds. Isn't the real truth the other way around? Wasn't Addie deathly afraid of Michael and his vicious temper?

A: No, that is not true.

Q: Isn't it? So you would have us believe Michael was trembling with fear, poor fellow. Well, come to think of it, perhaps he was. But what he really feared was that his brutal assault on Addie might come back to haunt him. He was afraid she might in some very public way seek justice for what he had done to her and so expose his utter villainy. Isn't that what he really told you that Sunday afternoon in his apartment?

A: No. He never said any such thing.

———

STRONGWOOD

FROM THE JOURNAL OF J. WINSTON PHELPS, JANUARY 26, 1904

8 pm—remarkable day!—hardly know where to begin—when trial opened this am saw Shad sitting in back row trying to look inconspicuous—hard to do in his case—we talked during recess—Shad said he just wanted to see things for himself, etc, so I went about my business with Jakes—think I nailed the little bastard & jury will hate him—thats what I want—if jurors hate Jakes theyll hate Masterson too & Addie will prevail.

———

After adjournment Shad came up & introduced me to friend of his—tall bearded fellow dressed in bohemian fashion wearing floppy hat—reminded me of art professor Id known, in every sense of the word, at Harvard—three of us chatting away when Shad says, "Im guessing you dont recognize my friend"—"no, I dont," says I—then the "professor" speaks up in a different voice & says, "It is a pleasure to meet you once again, Mr. Phelps. You perhaps remember me from the affair of the Secret Alliance"—damn but I nearly soiled my pants—Sherlock Holmes!

After reminiscing about Alliance & Mary McGinty & late Wm McKinley[13] Holmes asked to see the photo of Addie—assured me his interest not prurient (as tho I would care!)—once I brought the picture he took out a small ruler & measured it very carefully—after a long pause he says, very mysteriously, "I doubt this is a Kodak"—asked what he meant but he would say no more.

———

Holmes said hed be back in the morning to hear Addies testimony—told him shes one of most extraordinary people Ive ever met—"I have no doubt she is extraordinary," he says, smiling like the proverbial Cheshire cat, "but what I do not know, Mr. Phelps, is whether she is extraordinary in a good or a bad way"—cant say I disagree.

———

13. Mary McGinty was a labor radical who played a key role in *Sherlock Holmes and the Secret Alliance*, a case that brought Holmes and Dr. Watson to Minneapolis in October 1899, at the same time that President William McKinley was visiting the city. McKinley was assassinated two years later in Buffalo, New York.

Excerpts from the direct testimony of Miss Adelaide Strongwood, Mr. Phelps for the defense, January 27, 1904

———

Q: Now, Addie, I wish to go over some of the details of what happened on the night of September twenty-sixth in the apartment of Michael Masterson. I know how difficult and painful this must be for you, but it is important that the whole truth come out.

A: I understand.

Q: You stated in the article you wrote for the *Tribune* last month that when you met Michael that evening in Loring Park, it was your intention to end your relations with him once and for all. Is that correct?

A: Yes. I knew we could not go on.

Q: Even so, you agreed to go back with him to his apartment. Tell us again why you did so.

A: I cannot explain it except to say that my heart was riven. On one hand, I was all but sure that Michael did not love me, and yet despite all that had happened between us, I held out the merest thread of hope that somehow I might be wrong and that Michael was the kind and loving man I had once thought him to be. When he promised to show me something that would prove his love, I could not help myself. My heart pulled me like a team of horses to that apartment. Of course, I should not have gone. I know that all too well now.

———

Q: Addie, you have heard the testimony earlier of Mr. Jonathan Jakes, testimony in which he claimed that you were drunk or nearly so and seduced him when you came to Michael's apartment. Were you in fact drunk that night?

A: How could I be? I have never had a drop of alcohol in my life and never intend to. A woman who consumes liquor, especially in the presence of men, can only put herself in jeopardy.

Q: How true that is. What about Mr. Jakes's claim that you seduced him? Were you in fact intimate with Mr. Jakes that evening?

A: I will simply say this, Mr. Phelps: I would just as soon douse myself in kerosene and set myself on fire from head to toe as touch that loathsome man. He is a liar through and through.

Q: And you have already stated here, have you not, that you were never intimate of your own free will with Michael Masterson. Isn't that right?

A: Yes.

Q: Now, getting back to Mr. Jakes, would it be fair to say that you frequently had to rebuff his advances, even when he knew you were seeing his supposed best friend?

A: Yes, all the time. He even told me once that he and Michael were "used to sharing things"—those were his exact words—and that they could share me as well. I found his remarks so revolting that I complained to Michael.

Q: How did Michael react?

A: He acted as though he was very angry and said he would tell Mr. Jakes to stop bothering me.

Q: And did Mr. Jakes stop bothering you thereafter?

A: No. If anything, his behavior grew worse. It was just one more reason why I began to doubt Michael's true feelings toward me.

———

Q: Before September twenty-sixth of last year, had you ever been to Michael's apartment?

A: Never.

Q: You are certain?

A: Absolutely. A young woman who values her reputation does not visit a gentleman's apartment unless it is a social event at which others are present. As I have stated, Michael did not make a habit of inviting me to parties with his friends after the picnic at Minnehaha Park, and so I had no occasion to see his apartment. Even so, I did know a little bit about it.

Q: I see. I see. Most interesting. Well then, tell me how you came upon this knowledge.

A: It was through a conversation I overheard at the office one day.

Q: When you were working at Masterson, DeLaittre and Sons?

A: Yes. The girls there talked all the time about what they were doing after work, who they would be going out with, that sort of thing. One afternoon

I overheard one of the girls say something about being invited to a party at Mikey's apartment.

Q: You mean, the apartment of Michael Masterson?

A: Yes, that is what I believe she meant, since everybody called him Mikey.

Q: Go on.

A: As I said, one of the girls mentioned she was going to a party there and then another girl spoke up and said, "Just don't let him get you on his famous red couch." I thought it an odd thing to say and didn't really understand at the time what it meant.

Q: When did you overhear this conversation?

A: I cannot be sure, but it was not long after I began working at Masterson and DeLaittre last summer. I think it was before I had even met Michael.

Q: Do you remember the name of the girl who made the statement about the couch?

A: No, and the fact of the matter is that I could not. You see, Mr. Phelps, I never actually saw her. I was eating my lunch in the cafeteria and it was just something I heard being talked about behind me. I paid no great attention to it at the time, but for some reason her remark stuck in my mind. It is strange how the memory works sometimes.

Q: Indeed it is. So you believe, I take it, that your erroneous memory of a red divan in Michael's apartment on the night you were assaulted may stem from that overheard conversation?

A: I would not presume to say so, but I think it possible.

Q: And you readily admit, do you not, that your memory of the divan being red, as you stated in your article in the *Tribune,* was incorrect?

A: Yes. I am not afraid to say that I was wrong. I wish my memory were perfect in every detail, but it is not.

Q: Of course, the situation you found yourself in that night may also have affected your memory. Isn't that so?

A: Yes. I remember much of what happened, but some of the smaller details are unclear to me. I can only assume that the substance used to render me unconscious may have caused some loss of memory.

———

Q: In regards to your memory of that evening, do you recall your picture being taken at any time?

A: No.

Q: Now, Addie, as difficult as this is, I must ask you to look at Prosecution Exhibit Three, which shows the torso of a woman. It is the very same torn photograph that was found in Michael Masterson's hand on the night of his death. Are you the woman in this photograph?

A: Yes, I am afraid so.

Q: Do you know when and where this photograph was taken?

A: I believe it was taken that night in Michael's apartment when I was drugged and then ravished.

[Objection, Mr. Boardman. Speculation. Sustained.]

Q: Addie, did you willingly or knowingly pose for this photograph?

A: Absolutely not. It is repugnant to me in every way that such a photograph was ever taken. I cannot tell you how shocked I was when Michael tried to use it to blackmail me.

———

FROM THE JOURNAL OF J. WINSTON PHELPS, JANUARY 27, 1904

10 pm—still beastly cold—makes me wonder why I stay in this godforsaken place—must get to Ocean Springs[14] once this damned trial is over or I will turn into an iceman.

Have always said a good lawyer should fear his client above all other people & so it was today with Addie—quite a little bombshell she dropped this morning re how she suddenly remembered hearing about red couch in Mastersons apartment—had no idea she would change her story—fear Im the poor horse in this affair & shes riding me to who knows where—curious to see what Boardman will make of it on cross-exam tomorrow—could get nasty.

———

14. The resort community of Ocean Springs, Mississippi, became a popular destination for Midwesterners in the early 1900s in part because it was easily reached by rail from Chicago.

Holmes & Shad at trial again today watching Addie on stand—had lunch at the Dutch Room[15] & much good conversation—among other things Holmes said torn photo of Addie "most remarkable feature" of case & one that most puzzled him—he then posed three "crucial" questions to chew on with our beef sandwiches.

First question: how long after shooting of Masterson did police arrive at office?—told him as far as I knew first copper on scene arrived with Wangstad the elevator man within 5 minutes or so—Holmes deemed this "very important" but wouldnt say why he thought so.

Second question: did anyone notice ink stains on Addies hands or clothes?—not a question I was expecting—said I didnt know answer but would make inquiries.

Third question: where does Jonathan Jakes live?—another strange question—Holmes wanted exact address—told him I wasnt sure but could readily find out—Holmes nodded but had no further comment—did say hed send along "some ideas" re case in day or two.

After lunch stopped at Windom Block to look at room where Masterson shot—Holmes made a quick inspection but found little of interest—later I asked Shad what in holy hell was going on—flashed that big Irish grin of his & said, "Mr. Holmes has been thinking some great thoughts upon the matter of the photograph & they may come as a surprise to you"—couldnt get Shad to tell me more—dont know what to make of it all except that Holmes seems obsessed with the picture—missing piece is certainly a big mystery—Boardman Im sure will offer theory of his own when time comes.

Holmes & Shad sat through entire day of testimony—introduced Holmes to Addie after court adjourned—he said nothing about photo—even so it was a very interesting conversation.

———————

15. The Dutch Room was one of Minneapolis's finest restaurants in the early 1900s. Among its attractions was a pipe organ for entertaining diners. The restaurant was located in the National Hotel at 205 Washington Avenue South, just across the street from the Windom Block, scene of Michael Masterson's death.

EXCERPTS FROM THE CROSS-EXAMINATION OF MISS ADELAIDE STRONGWOOD,
Mr. Boardman for the prosecution, January 28, 1904

———

Q: Let us consider the assault which you claim took place on the night of September twenty-sixth in Mr. Masterson's apartment.

A: It is no claim, Mr. Boardman. It is the truth.

Q: We will see about that, won't we? Now, in your account in the *Tribune*, you made very specific note of a "blood-red divan" in the room and even pointed out that Mr. Jonathan Jakes was supposedly wearing a sweater of similar color. Isn't that right?

A: Yes, but I was mistaken, as I have said.

Q: But what a mistake, Miss Strongwood, what a mistake. You singled out that divan in your account, suggesting that Mr. Jakes looked like the devil himself sitting upon it, didn't you?

A: I think you're exaggerating my account, Mr. Boardman.

Q: How so?

A: Well, it was merely something I mentioned. I did not dwell upon the color of the divan.

Q: Curious how you now downplay something that you stressed so strongly in your article, and the reason is that you were caught in a lie, weren't you, Miss Strongwood?

A: It was not a lie. I simply had an incorrect memory.

Q: Oh, I see. It was merely an "incorrect memory," to use your words. Well then, perhaps you can tell us, Miss Strongwood, how many other memories of that night, which you described so vividly in your newspaper article, might be incorrect?

A: None that I know of.

Q: It was just that one bad memory that somehow snuck in on you. Is that right?

A: Yes.

Q: So there couldn't be two or three or maybe a hundred faulty memories in your account?

A: Certainly not.

Q: Well, that is good to know. And yet I am still struck by how you managed to get the single most vivid image in your description of Mr. Masterson's apartment so badly wrong. Come now, we all know why you described that red divan, don't we? You'd seen it before that night, in Michael's apartment, where you in fact were a frequent visitor. Isn't that true?

A: No, it is not.

Q: But you were so drunk that night when you decided to seduce Mr. Jakes that you didn't even notice there was a new divan, did you?

A: That is not true, and you know it, Mr. Boardman.

COURT: Miss Strongwood, I must remind you again that you are not here to debate Mr. Boardman or assess his state of mind. Simply answer his questions and do not take it upon yourself to tell him what he does or does not know.

A: Yes, Your Honor.

———

Q: Miss Strongwood, let me show you Prosecution Exhibit Eleven. It is a report submitted by Inspector Donald Gordon of the Minneapolis Police Department concerning a search he made of Michael Masterson's apartment on November tenth of last year. As you will note, the reports states that the apartment was placed under police lock and seal after Mr. Masterson's death and has remained so to this time. Would you please read the thirteenth line of Inspector Gordon's report, which I have marked for you?

A: You mean, the line you have underlined?

Q: Yes, that one.

A: Very well. It says, "No scrapbook of any kind was found in the apartment."

Q: Interesting, isn't it? You stated in your highly dramatic tale of what happened on the night of September twenty-sixth in Mr. Masterson's apartment that you were overpowered as you bent over to look at a scrapbook. Isn't that correct?

A: It is.

Q: And yet no scrapbook was found in the apartment. How do you account for that fact?

A: I really have no idea, Mr. Boardman. The scrapbook was most certainly there on that terrible night. I can only assume that Michael or perhaps Mr. Jakes removed it at some later time. Where it is now I could not say.

Q: So it's not possible you had another "incorrect memory," to use your own words?

A: No, I saw the scrapbook.

Q: Just as you saw the red divan that was actually light brown. Is that what you're telling us?

A: I have acknowledged my mistake in regard to the divan. I made no such mistake about the scrapbook.

Q: Odd, how all of these inconsistencies keep showing up in your testimony, Miss Strongwood. But I suppose that's what happens when you have to make things up. Hard to keep your story straight, isn't it?

A: The truth, Mr. Boardman, is always a straight story, and that is the story I have told.

————

Q: Let us turn for a moment to Prosecution Exhibit Three, the torn photograph which you have acknowledged shows you in an improperly revealing way. You have testified that the photograph was taken while you were supposedly in a drugged stupor at Mr. Masterson's apartment. Is that correct?

A: That is exactly the point I have tried to make, Mr. Boardman. I would never knowingly have posed for such a lewd photograph.

Q: You are much too decent and upstanding a woman to ever degrade yourself in such fashion. Is that what you are telling us?

A: I am an honorable woman, Mr. Boardman, and I always have been. No honorable woman would ever consent to have such a picture taken.

Q: I see. Well then, let us see just how "honorable" a woman you really are, Miss Strongwood. Let us do so by revisiting the topic of your employment in Chicago last year. Your time in the Windy City, we now know, wasn't entirely a waste, was it? You in fact made a good deal of money there, did you not?

A: I am not sure what you mean by "a good deal of money," Mr. Boardman, but, yes, I made some money in Chicago.

Q: Did you make this money working as a secretary?

A: No.

Q: A clerk?

A: No.

Q: Well then, let us hear about your line of work in Chicago, Miss Strongwood. Let us hear about your time at the Pink Moon.

FIVE

PART FIVE OF "AN ACCOUNT OF MY LIFE AND THE INCIDENT FOR WHICH I Have Been Unjustly Accused of Murder," by Addie Strongwood, *Minneapolis Tribune*, December 18, 1903

So potent had been the anesthetizing agent used to overwhelm my senses that when I awoke the next morning in Michael Masterson's apartment, as though from a long and troubled sleep, I at first had no memory of what had occurred during the night. As my mind began to clear, however, I became aware of a swirl of dim and fleeting phantasmagoria. I saw Michael, grinning like a hyena, taking off his jacket and bending over me. I saw his friend Jakes standing behind him, his mouth twisted into a grim rictus. I saw the blood-red divan and the table where Michael had claimed he wished to show me something. And then I again saw Michael's face, so close to mine that I thought I could feel his breath upon me, and I gave a great shudder.

Far more terrible was what I discovered when my eyes finally opened. I saw that I was naked, on a bed in a small room at the rear of the apartment. My clothes, including my dress, which gave evidence of having been literally torn from my body, lay strewn on the floor. There could be, I realized to my utmost horror, no question as to what had happened in that room while I lay in a drugged and defenseless stupor.

As with all women, I hold my virtue more dear than anything else, and I have guarded it with all of my strength and resolve. Indeed, to me it is as sacred as life itself.

Now, I knew, it was gone, taken violently from me by a man who had once claimed to be my friend and lover. I am not a woman given to easy displays of emotion, but as I lay alone in that dark and ugly room, feeling bereft of all that I hold dear, I could do nothing except cry until my tears became a river of grief.

Is there any woman, after being brutally assaulted by a thief in the night, who could do otherwise?

I cannot say how long I lay crying upon that awful bed of miseries—perhaps I hoped my tears, if allowed to flow long enough, would wash away all that had happened—but at some length I was able to compose myself. Wiping away the last of my tears, I arose and put on my poor tattered clothes as quickly as I could, all the while in the grip of a great anxiety. What if Michael and his minion, Jakes, were still in the apartment and plotting some new outrage against me? I crept up to the bedroom door and looked out into the main chamber, where hours before I had been drugged into unconsciousness. I saw or heard nothing, until I was startled by something rubbing against my foot.

I am not ashamed to say that I jumped back in fear. Only then did I see Michael's tomcat, a large and lean tabby, gazing up at me with a quizzical expression. Catching my breath, I bent down to stroke him, hoping that I would find at that moment a loving and gentle companion. I should have known better. It was Michael's cat, after all, and it had no love for me. Hissing, it bared its small sharp teeth, as though preparing to rip the flesh from my hand, and I was forced to move quickly away. There was a small chair by the bed, and I picked it up so as to protect myself from the vicious little beast, which continued to hiss at me and make other threatening noises. I finally poked at it with the chair and the creature ran out of the room at last. I will state here for the record that I never saw the cat again, and any intimation to the contrary must be regarded as simply one more example in the campaign of lies that has been directed against me.

After a time, I followed the cat out into the main chamber, which gave much evidence of a night of debauchery. On a low table in front of the divan I noticed the ornate hookah Mr. Jakes had been smoking the night before. It emitted a most unpleasant odor that I did not think was tobacco. Next to this strange and hideous apparatus there were several empty bottles of bourbon and gin, as well as an open book displaying disgusting pictures of men and women in sexual congress. I began to feel that I had been lured into the Devil's very own den, by two of his most depraved disciples, and that for all the trials I had endured, I was fortunate simply to be alive.

Still fearful that my assailants might appear at any moment to ravish me further, I went into a small adjoining kitchen and took the biggest butcher knife I could find from one of the drawers. If there was to be another attack, I was resolved to fight to my last breath to save myself. It soon became obvious, however, that both Michael and Mr. Jakes were gone, presumably off somewhere eating a hearty meal after satiating their wicked lust. I put the knife back in its drawer, and then prepared to leave, even as I wondered what to do next. As I was about to let myself out of the apartment, I found a note, on a side table by the door. The note, in Michael's all too recognizable handwriting, consisted of this message: "Hope you enjoyed our splendid little evening together as much as I did, my dearest Addie, but it will be my last with you. As you have said, we cannot go on. Remember to close the door when you leave."

Imagine the agony I felt, reading those cruel and sardonic words from a man for whom I once thought I had entertained the deepest affection! Instead, as the note made all too apparent, I had fallen in love with a perfect monster, a man devoid of even the rudiments of human sentiment. Michael had used me and then discarded me, as though I were one of his poor brothel girls. I was stunned by the note, which sent such a chill through my heart that I almost feared it would stop beating, frozen by the force of Michael's malignant hatred.

Yet as I stood there, still trembling from the terrors of the night, with Michael's mocking note feeling as cold in my hand as death itself, I experienced a revelation that freed me in an instant from the binding chains of shame and disgust. In that shining moment, which truly seemed heaven-sent, I realized it was Michael, not I, who had done a ruinous thing and must face the consequences. He had tried his very best to sully and degrade me, to drag me down to his own bestial level, in the ugly hope that I would lose my will to go on. Indeed, I have no doubt that he fully expected I would meekly walk away and so "close the door" on all of his transgressions. I could not allow that to happen! I decided that instead of closing the door to Michael's wrongdoing, I would open it as forcefully as he had assaulted my womanhood. I would make him pay, and pay dearly, for his misdeeds. I thirsted, not for vengeance, which is a false intoxicant, but for justice, the one true elixir of the soul.

My first thought, naturally, was to report to the police the heinous crime that had been visited upon me. It did not take me long to reject such a plan, for reasons which I am sure will be readily understood. I knew it would be my word against that of a supposedly respectable young man whose family controls one of the biggest industrial fortunes of the city. Does anyone believe that under such circumstances, I would have received a fair hearing? It is far more likely that I would have been vilified as a lying hussy and a low, dishonest woman, and I do not doubt that money would have changed hands before I was escorted out the door and told never to bother the police again with such scandalous allegations.

So, rather than putting my faith in a police department which, as recent events involving Mayor Ames have so strikingly demonstrated, can hardly be relied upon for either competence or honesty, I put my faith in God but also in myself, as we all must do if we are to make our way in the world. Even so, I will admit to feeling a deep sense of trepidation as I contemplated the task before me. I yearned for justice, but I wondered how to obtain it in a city where, like the realm of which the prophet Isaiah wrote long ago, "Judgment is turned away backward, and justice standeth afar off: for truth is fallen in the street."

I suppose it will seem improper to some of you who are reading these words to learn that I decided justice in my case must be measured in the hard currency of dollars and cents. Yet I believed I had no other reasonable choice. My precious virtue was gone, stolen against my will, and I could not have it back, no matter how much I wished it to be so. Nor could I hope that Michael would ever be held accountable in the criminal courts. He was too well insulated by wealth and privilege to face the possibility of spending time behind bars.

The choice I made was not easy, as my heart still ached for a different kind of justice. I wanted the world to know the depths of Michael's cruelty and depravity and yes, dear readers, I wanted him to suffer for his sins. Yet I concluded that I could not allow a mere desire for revenge, however satisfactory it might seem in the short term, to overwhelm my better judgment. My resolve to pursue a monetary settlement grew even stronger once I learned that a child had in all likelihood been conceived as a result of Michael's criminal attack.

Of course, when I made my decision, I was acutely aware that no amount of money, not even the millions amassed by the mighty flour kings of Minneapolis, could ever heal my loss, which was incalculable. Even so, I believed that a substantial payment would serve to penalize the transgressor while providing me with some small measure of solace for the terrible thing Michael had done. Was it venal of me to seek this means of satisfaction? Some may say so, but I will go to my grave believing that I only did what was right and honorable.

The letter I sent to Michael's parents some weeks after Michael's dark deed is now being used as evidence against me. It has been called a "blackmail demand" in the pages of the *Journal*, where all manner of calumnies have been circulated, when in fact it was nothing more than a heartfelt plea for justice.

And while it is true I alluded to the possibility of bringing suit in a court of a law, I did not do so out of any desire to "hold up" the Masterson family, as has been claimed, but rather to let them know that I wished to obtain a reasonable settlement without the painful necessity of going to court.

How I wish now that my honest appeal for justice had met with a positive response! Had the family in fact agreed to my fair terms, I believe Michael would still be alive, for there would have be no need for him to confront and threaten me in the way he did on the fateful night of November 9. Instead, Michael and I would have gone on with our separate lives, and the greater world would today know nothing of what took place between us.

EXCERPTS FROM THE DIRECT TESTIMONY OF MRS. PHILIP (BERNICE) MASTERSON, mother of Michael Masterson, Mr. Boardman for the prosecution, January 20, 1904

Q: Let us talk about the "blackmail letter," as you called it.

[Objection, Mr. Phelps. Prejudicial to describe letter as "blackmail." Conference before the bench. Objection sustained.]

Q: Very well, Your Honor. I have here Prosecution Exhibit Twelve. I will show it to you now, Mrs. Masterson. Is this the letter which you and your husband received from the defendant on November second of last year?

A: Yes.

Q: Please read the letter in its entirety to the jury, if you would.

A: Certainly. "Mr. and Mrs. Masterson: It with a heavy heart but with a profound belief in the righteousness of my cause that I send you this letter. You may find its contents deeply disturbing, but I assure that everything I am writing here is the truth, and I would swear to it without hesitation upon the family Bible that my Dear Mother left me at the time of her death. In the note I left in your hand, Mrs. Masterson, outside Mr. Dayton's store on October twenty-fourth, I said that I feared I might be carrying Michael's child. I regret to inform you that I now know this to be a fact. What I am writing to tell both of you is how I came to be in this situation, which will inevitably produce many desperate consequences unless you can set matters right.

"It would almost be better, I am sure, if I told you that in a moment of weakness I yielded to Michael's importunings and so had relations outside the sacred bonds of matrimony. But the simple fact of the matter is that no such thing happened. Instead, on September twenty-sixth, after telling Michael that I wished to end any further concourse between us, I was lured to his apartment in the Virginia Flats on a pretext. Once inside, I was rendered unconscious by the application of what I now believe to have been a rag soaked with ether and thus left utterly defenseless. In this hapless state, I was assaulted, perhaps more than once, during the long, terrible night that followed. All of this was accomplished, if that is the right word, with the assistance of Mr. Jonathan Jakes. The assault, of which I have no memory, caused me to be with child.

"I realize how shocking this account must be to you, just as it is to me, but I have evidence, if you care to see it, that Michael has in fact acted in a similar way toward other women, and that despite his overtly charming manner, he is a man who will stop at nothing to gratify his lust. I have not reported Michael's crime to the police, in part because of my own shame over what was done to me, but also because I do not wish to create a situation in which the Masterson family name will be exposed to public infamy.

"Nevertheless, I must have justice, as well as means to raise the child that has been so violently implanted in my womb. I am sure you understand my situation, as well as your own, and Michael's. I have thought long and hard upon what course of action to take, and I have determined that a payment of ten thousand dollars[1] would provide me with all that I need to raise the child in the appropriate way. It would also allow me to make a new start in some other part of the world, far from here, so that there would be no question of any continuing effort on my part to seek compensation for Michael's grievous offense.

"I should also tell you that I have been in contact with a prominent lawyer of this city, and he is of the opinion that my case, if brought before a jury, would certainly yield a large settlement. Of course, it would also yield, in the public setting of a courtroom, a great deal of unpleasant publicity, which I naturally would like to avoid, as I am sure you and Michael would as well.

---

1. In 1903, $10,000 was a great deal of money, equivalent to around $300,000 today.

"Please inform me at your earliest convenience if you wish to accept my offer. If I do not hear from you within one week, I will assume you have rejected the offer, and I cannot be responsible for what will happen afterwards.

"Most Respectfully Yours,
Adelaide Strongwood."

Q: What did you and your husband think after reviewing this letter?

A: We were quite stunned. I will also state that we did not believe any of it.

Q: Why was that?

A: Well, what evidence did the girl have to offer? There was none. Even if she was with child, what reason did Philip and I have to believe that poor Michael was the father?

Q: Your husband, I take it, was every bit as upset as you were?

A: More so. He wanted to go to the police at once and report what he regarded as nothing less than a blackmail scheme.

Q: Did he in fact do so?

A: No, not at once. We had to show the letter to Michael first.

Q: And when did you do that?

A: We talked to him the next morning.

Q: That would be November third?

A: Yes.

Q: Did he come over to your home?

A: Yes.

Q: Describe your meeting with him, if you would.

A: Michael was simply beside himself after he read the letter. He said, "Mother dear, there is not a single word, not a single syllable, in this letter that is true."

Q: And you believed him, I take it.

A: Absolutely. Michael has always been a good son to us and perfectly honest.

Q: Mrs. Masterson, you must forgive me for asking this question, as I can only imagine what pain it must cause you, but are you certain Michael was telling you the entire truth about his relationship with Miss Strongwood?

A: You are asking, I suppose, whether I believed him when he said he had never been intimate with her.

Q: Yes, that is what I am asking, in light of the testimony of Mr. Jakes, who stated here under oath that Michael had admitted to him that he had been seduced on one occasion by Miss Strongwood.

A: Michael was a good son, a beautiful son, a wonderful, generous-hearted young man. I do not know all of what happened between him and that girl, but I will believe to my last breath that he would never have assaulted her in the manner she has described. I also believe that she was with many men, for that is what Michael told me, and any of them might have fathered a child, if there really was one. But of course, we don't know that, do we? We don't know how many lies she told to get what she wanted and further her murderous plans.

[Objection, Mr. Phelps. Speculation. Sustained.]

COURT: The witness's last remarks will be disregarded by the jury. Mrs. Masterson, please confine your testimony to what you know directly as opposed to what you may believe. You are entitled to your opinions but you are not entitled to state them here, since they have no bearing on this matter. You may proceed, Counsel.

Q: Thank you, Your Honor. Keeping in mind the court's instructions, tell us please what you and your husband decided to do after going over the letter with Michael.

A: Well, as I said, Philip wished to go the police and bring charges against the girl. He was very adamant. Michael, however, wasn't so sure.

Q: How so?

A: He thought if we went to the police there would be publicity and that this would bring dishonor to the family. Michael was always very concerned in that regard. In any case, Philip asked him what he wished to do, and Michael said he thought that if he could just meet with the girl one more time, he could convince her to drop her blackmail scheme, as he called it.

Q: I see. But I must ask, Mrs. Masterson, how did Michael think he could accomplish such a thing, given the firm and demanding tone of Miss Strongwood's letter?

A: He reminded us that we knew things about her that would be very damaging if they came out. I remember he said, "We must fight fire with fire," or words to that effect.

Q: What did Michael mean when he mentioned these things about Miss Strongwood that he said you all knew?

A: He was talking about the investigation by the Pinkerton man we'd hired.

Q: That would be Mr. Earl Duggers, correct, who testified yesterday?

A: Yes, he found out a good deal about that little tramp.

[Objection, Mr. Phelps. Hearsay, statement of opinion, etc. Sustained.]

Q: We will let Mr. Duggers's words speak for themselves, Mrs. Masterson. In the meantime, let me ask you this: what exactly did Michael propose to do in response to Miss Strongwood's letter demanding ten thousand dollars?

A: As I told you, he said he wished to meet with her as soon as possible. He said he was certain he could handle the situation.

Q: Is that, then, the course of action you, your husband, and Michael agreed upon?

A: Yes.

Q: And did you discuss as well what you would do if Michael proved unsuccessful in his efforts?

A: Yes. We agreed that if Michael couldn't get through to her, we would show the letter to the police.

Q: Even though you knew such a step might result in unflattering publicity for all of you?

A: Yes. Philip said we would simply have to deal with whatever came along but that as far as he was concerned, Miss Strongwood would not receive one dime from us. It was a matter of principle for him.

Q: And for Michael as well, I presume.

A: Oh yes. Michael also believed in standing on principle. He felt Miss Strongwood was trying to drag him into a mud pit of her own making.

Q: Now, did Michael say where he intended to meet with Miss Strongwood?

A: No, but he said he would have to arrange a meeting soon. Philip asked if he should go along with him, but Michael said no, it would be best if he went alone. Oh, how I wish now that we had never let him do so!

———

From the Journal of J. Winston Phelps, January 19, 1903

———

Hope to trot out Mary McDonald saga for jury tomorrow—want to plant idea that Masterson attacked another girl before Addie—of course Boardman will object like crazy—probably wont get far but sometimes smallest seeds yield biggest blooms.

Will also have to be very careful tomorrow when I grill Mrs. Masterson re her no-good son & his relations with Addie—problem is this: young Masterson claimed to Jakes, or so that bag of dung will no doubt testify, that he rogered Addie before Sept 26th—yet dutiful son swore up & down to mama hed never done the deed with Addie—trouble is, if I bring up this discrepancy, jury might well conclude Masterson lied to mama because he & Addie really did dance the hootchy-kootchy—if so, Addies claim to virginity before being ravished goes down the drain & with it possibly our entire case.

Best strategy in this instance is to say nothing—wont mention discrepancy when I cross-examine mama—can only pray my silence will prove golden & jury will not leap to any untoward conclusions—think 12 men good & true are with us so far but hard to say—that fellow Camp who Im sure will be jury foreman stares at Addie constantly—can almost see the old coot licking his chops—hope its just good old-fashioned lust—then again maybe he thinks shes lying her pretty little head off—cant blame him—not so sure myself—shes a strange one, that girl—never had a client like her.

Billy[2] coming over 9 or so—wish he could stay all night but too much work to do.

EXCERPTS FROM THE CROSS-EXAMINATION OF MRS. PHILIP (BERNICE) Masterson, Mr. Phelps for the defense, January 20, 1904

———

Q: Let us turn to the letter you and your husband received from Miss Strongwood. You professed to be shocked by her request for ten thousand dollars, is that correct?

A: Yes.

Q: Why?

A: What do you mean?

———

2. It is not known who "Billy" was. Phelps's journal, however, contains references to quite a few men, identified by first name only, who presumably were lovers.

Q: Well, did you think ten thousand dollars was too much to pay to a woman who had been brutally raped and impregnated by your son? Would five thousand have suited you better? Or perhaps only a few hundred? After all, money is tight these days.

[Objection, Mr. Boardman. Argumentative, badgering the witness. Sustained.]

Q: I withdraw the question, Your Honor. Now, as I recall, you stated during Mr. Boardman's examination that your son Michael was a good son and also an honest young man. Is that right?

A: It is not only right, but true.

Q: I see. He'd never been in any trouble before he met Miss Strongwood?

A: No. He was always a perfect gentleman.

Q: You mean, when it came to his dealings with woman other than prostitutes?

A: I believe he treated all women with respect.

Q: You never heard of any problems he might have encountered in previous relationships?

A: Of course not.

Q: So you and your late husband never, for example, received any letters from young women, within the last year or so, stating that they might have had some difficulty with Michael?

A: I do not recall any such thing.

Q: Really? No letter, say, from a rather desperate young woman in Chicago named Mary McDonald?

[Objection, Mr. Boardman. Defense is on a "fishing expedition." Conference before the bench. Objection overruled.]

COURT: I will allow you to ask this question, Mr. Phelps, but unless some relevant information is soon forthcoming, I will not allow you to go much further down this particular road. The witness is instructed to answer the question.

A: The name is not familiar to me.

Q: You have not answered my question, madam. Didn't you and your husband in fact receive a letter last year from a young woman in Chicago regarding the conduct of your son?

A: Not that I can remember.

Q: I remind you, Mrs. Masterson, that you are under oath.

A: I am perfectly well aware of that, and I have answered your question, in the event you failed to hear me.

Q: What I hear is a woman delivering a bald-faced lie. That is what I hear.

[Objection, Mr. Boardman. Mr. Phelps should be admonished for "improper and outrageous" conduct. Sustained.]

COURT: Mr. Phelps, you know better than to characterize the witness's testimony in such a manner. The jury is instructed to ignore defense counsel's comment. Now, Mr. Phelps, I suggest you begin a new line of inquiry.

Q: My apologies, Your Honor. Mrs. Masterson, didn't you find it odd that while you and your husband wished to go the police in connection with the letter from Miss Strongwood, Michael insisted on seeing her first?

A: I do not understand your question.

Q: All right, let me try again. You have just received a letter from Miss Strongwood stating that your son has brutally raped her, that she is with child, and that she wishes to receive some compensation for her injury and to help her bear the costs of motherhood. You and your husband show the letter to Michael. He protests his innocence. You believe him. But when you propose to go to the police, he demurs. Instead, he says, "Let me talk to the girl. Perhaps I can persuade her not to ask for any money." How do you think he might have accomplished such a thing?

A: I am sure I do not know.

Q: Really, you have no idea? Well, did he say he might apologize to her? So sorry for raping you, now please go away. Is that what you expected him to do?

[Objection, Mr. Boardman. Argumentative. Sustained.]

Q: I have no more questions at this time, Your Honor.

EXCERPTS FROM THE DIRECT TESTIMONY OF MR. JONATHAN JAKES, MR. Boardman for the prosecution, January 25, 1904

———

Q: Now, Mr. Jakes, there is one more matter I need to ask you about. It concerns Mr. Masterson's cat. Something happened to him, did it not?

A: Yes, it was very distressing. He was killed.

Q: When did this happen?

A: I guess it must have been right after that night Miss Strongwood was with me in Michael's apartment.

Q: When exactly did you find the cat dead?

A: Well, I didn't. It was Michael, that next day after we had talked.

Q: You mean it was Michael who found the cat?

A: Yes. He thought at first it might have gotten out but then he found it later that afternoon.

Q: Where did he find the cat?

A: It was under the covers, in his bed.

Q: And what had happened to the animal?

A: Michael said its neck had been broken.

Q: I imagine he was very upset.

A: He was beside himself. He was very fond of the cat.

Q: Did Michael say what he thought had happened to the cat?

[Objection, Mr. Phelps. Hearsay, calls for speculation. Conference before the bench. Sustained.]

Q: Did Michael say that it appeared the cat had met with an unfortunate accident?

A: No, he said someone had broken its neck deliberately.

[Objection, Mr. Boardman. Speculation. Overruled.]

Q: By the way, Mr. Jakes, did you see the cat before you left the apartment that morning?

A: Yes, it was drinking from a bowl of milk I put out in the kitchen.

Q: Did the cat appear healthy?

A: Yes.

Q: No sign of any injury to its neck?

A: No, nothing like that.

Q: No further questions of this witness, Your Honor.

Excerpts from the cross-examination of Mr. Jonathan Jakes, Mr. Phelps for the defense, January 26, 1904

———

Q: I think we all are growing a bit weary of the saga of Balling the cat, Mr. Jakes, so let us try to see if we can allow the animal to rest in peace. Other than your conversation with Michael Masterson, which you have testified to, do you have any direct knowledge as to what might have happened to Balling?

A: I guess not.

Q: You didn't see anyone enter Michael's apartment after you left that morning, did you?

A: No.

Q: Nor did you see anyone break the cat's neck, correct?

A: No, I did not see that.

Q: So for all you know, anyone could have done in the cat, isn't that right?

A: Well, they would have to have gotten into Michael's apartment.

Q: Indeed, they would. Let's see now, who do we know for sure was in the apartment on that Sunday morning? Ah yes, it was you, Mr. Jakes, wasn't it?

A: Well, I don't see—

Q: Isn't it possible that you got angry with the cat for some reason? Maybe it made a mess somewhere, and in a fit of rage—

A: That is a lie. I did no such thing.

Q: So you say, Mr. Jakes, so you say. By the by, after you left the apartment on that memorable Sunday, where did you go?

A: I went to church with my family at St. Mark's.[3]

Q: Well, Mr. Jakes, I am sure the Almighty must have been pleased to see you there after your night's activities. That will be all of this witness, Your Honor.

EXCERPTS FROM THE REDIRECT TESTIMONY OF MR. JONATHAN JAKES, MR. Boardman for the prosecution, January 26, 1904

Q: Mr. Jakes, you have acknowledged in earlier testimony that you and Michael sometimes visited houses of ill repute here in Minneapolis, and also on occasion hired prostitutes for parties, is that correct?

A: Yes.

Q: And do you also admit that the two of you visited brothels in Chicago?

A: A few times, yes.

Q: When was the last time, Mr. Jakes, that you personally visited such an establishment?

A: I believe it would have been sometime in the spring.

Q: Some months ago?

---

3. St. Mark's Cathedral is a large Episcopal church overlooking Loring Park in downtown Minneapolis.

A: Yes.

Q: Have you in fact visited any such establishments since Michael's death, here in Minneapolis or anywhere else, for that matter?

A: No, not a one. I have reformed my life. I realized that what I was doing was wrong and that I must make myself a better man than I have been.

Q: As I understand it, you plan to marry in the fall, isn't that right?

A: Yes. I assure you that I am not the careless young man I once was.

REPORT FROM GEORGE WASHINGTON THOMAS TO J. WINSTON PHELPS, December 13, 1903

Mr. J. Winston Phelps
Temple Court,[4] Suite 602
Minneapolis, Minnesota

Dear Mr. Phelps:

Shad has advised me to send this report directly to you as he wishes to remain "blissfully ignorant" of its contents if he has to testify. Here it is. I have not kept a carbon, so this is the only copy, which you can do with as you see fit.

I spent three days in Chicago last week and talked to several people including Lorna Day, house madam at the Everleigh Club on S. Dearborn St.; Jackie Stuntz, a club "employee"; and Johnny Moore, a "man about town" and numbers runner.

Here is the gist of what I learned: Michael Masterson and Jonathan Jakes visited the Everleigh Club at least twice, once in December of 1902 and again in May of this year. The first time, according to Mrs. Day, nothing unusual happened, tho she did note that they shared the same girl. That is known as

---

4. Temple Court was an eight-story office building at Washington and Hennepin Avenues in downtown Minneapolis. At the time of its completion in 1886 it was among the city's largest office blocks. Phelps was one of many lawyers who maintained offices in the building, which featured a large central atrium. The building was demolished in 1953.

a "double header" in the business and is not uncommon even if it isn't to every man's taste.

The second time was different. There was a ruckus and the two of them were tossed out. Miss Stuntz was the girl they chose and she said that all went "normal" at first but then Michael started slapping her and said she was a bad girl who needed to be disciplined, or some such words. Jakes joined in the "fun," as he called it. The Stuntz girl finally got tired of it and rang the emergency bell. A couple of housemen then came in and told the boys to leave. There was a dustup, but of course the boys had no chance in that fight and were sent flying out the door. Mrs. Day said mistreatment of the girls is not allowed and Michael and Jakes were told they would never be welcome on the premises again. By the by, a night at the Everleigh palace is a $100 affair at least, so the boys were paying dearly for their pleasure.

Now, here is the part you probably don't want to hear, and I have put it on a separate sheet of paper in case you wish to burn it. While I was nosing around the Everleigh I ran into an old acquaintance, Johnny Moore, who used to run a tippling house on Arundel Ave. in St. Paul. That was long before he went down to Chicago. We got to talking and one thing led to another as it will, when Johnny mentioned he has been following Miss Strongwood's case in the Chicago newspapers. That's when he said he knew something about her, when she had been in Chicago. Of course, I was surprised to hear of this and got him to tell the tale.

Here is what he said: He does some numbers work in the Levee for a fellow named Dirk Chalmers, who runs a string of dance halls and saloons. These are top-drawer places with expensive fittings and girls who can make $5 or more a night in tips if they perform up to snuff. Two of his places are in Chicago but he also has them in St. Louis and K.C., or so Johnny said. I should tell you he is reliable and well informed as to the underside of Chicago, where he has made his living for years. Johnny said Miss Strongwood worked in one of Chalmers's places, called the Pink Moon, as a dancer, or so Chalmers told him. Not sure what kind of dancing she did but girls in such places often do other business on the side, as I am sure you are aware. How Chalmers came to mention all of this to Johnny I cannot say, but it is odd if you ask me that they would know so much about Miss Strongwood, who must have made quite an impression.

Of course, if word is out as to the kind of work Miss Strongwood did in Chicago, then that same word may travel to the prosecution in Mpls., in which case I guess you will have some explaining to do as to her reputation. There is another problem which you should know of. Johnny made some inquiries for me (this cost $5, which will be included in my bill) and he swears young Masterson was a known patron of the Pink Moon. This was about when Miss Strongwood was there. Cannot say if they met but it is possible. I am sure you see where this leads as it makes you wonder just how she ended up getting a job at Masterson and DeLaittre in Mpls.

I will gladly answer any other questions you may have as best I can. You know where to reach me.

Yours Truly,
George Washington Thomas

EXCERPTS FROM THE REDIRECT CROSS-EXAMINATION OF MR. JONATHAN JAKES, Mr. Phelps for the defense, January 26, 1904

Q: How pleased I am to hear that you have reformed your ways, Mr. Jakes. I imagine Miss Jackie Stuntz of Chicago must be even more pleased, don't you think?

A: I do not know who you mean.

Q: You don't remember Jackie? Very pretty young woman, employed at the Everleigh in Chicago. Nicest whorehouse in the city, or so it's said. You were there a few times, weren't you?

A: I believe so, yes.

Q: You and Michael, together, sharing an evening of carnal pleasure with Miss Stuntz? You remember, don't you?

A: Not really.

Q: Well, how odd, how very odd. Seems to me that if I and a friend were entertaining a lady at a fancy whorehouse one evening and this entertainment consisted of slapping her around to the point that help had to be called because she feared for her life, well, by gosh, I think I'd remember that.

[Objection, Mr. Boardman. Assumes facts not in evidence, beyond scope of redirect examination. Conference before the bench. Sustained.]

Q: Then let me put it directly to you, Mr. Jakes. Isn't it a fact that you and Michael were physically ejected from the Everleigh last spring and told never to come back because you had been abusing Miss Jackie Stuntz in such a cruel and violent fashion?

A: There was a slight altercation one night, as I recall, but you are exaggerating everything.

Q: What am I exaggerating, sir? Are you saying that the two of you didn't beat up the expensive whore you had hired?

A: I do not recall any such thing.

Q: I imagine Miss Stuntz would remember it all too well.

A: Then perhaps you should call her to testify.

Q: Your Honor—

COURT: Mr. Jakes, the court will provide all the legal rulings and advice needed in this case. You will simply answer the questions put to you.

A: Certainly, Your Honor.

Q: Now, sir, did I exaggerate when I said you and Michael were tossed out of the Everleigh by a couple of the house bruisers? Are you saying this did not occur?

A: As I told you, there was merely a disagreement and we left.

Q: I see. Sorry, fellows, for knocking around one of your girls. We'll be leaving now. Is that how it went?

[Objection, Mr. Boardman. Assuming facts not in evidence, etc. Sustained.]

Q: I withdraw the question, Your Honor. I have had enough of the newly reformed Mr. Jakes. Allow me to wish the best of luck to your bride-to-be, sir. I have no doubt she will need it.

FROM THE JOURNAL OF J. WINSTON PHELPS, JANUARY 18, 1904

10 pm & no end in sight to the cold—Pinkerton man Duggers will spill beans tomorrow re Addie & her dancing adventures in Chicago—probably not much I can do with him—strikes me as a canny fellow & has testified too many times to be rattled.

Boardman will milk dancing angle for all its worth & then some—know all about it, of course, thanks to Wash & his snooping in Chicago—wouldve been nice if Addie had admitted to it right away but shes so full of dodges its hard to know what to believe—she said didnt mention it because she didnt think it was all that important, etc, etc—god what a little maneuverer she is!

No use denying what she did in Chicago—connection with Masterson will be the thing—did she know him there & more important, how well did she know him?—asked her point blank if she met him at Pink Moon—denied it up & down & sideways—if Boardman can put two of them together there & show she was a bought woman, we are as sunk as the Maine.[5]

––––––––

Excerpts from the direct testimony of Mr. Earl Duggers,[6] Pinkerton Agency detective, Mr. Boardman for the prosecution, January 19, 1904

––––––––

Q: Now, Mr. Duggers, you are based in Chicago. Is that correct?

A: Yes.

Q: And on October twenty-seventh of last year, you were assigned the task of looking into the background of Miss Strongwood, the defendant in this case, at the request of Mr. Moody, the attorney for Mr. and Mrs. Philip Masterson. Is that right?

A: Yes, I was given that assignment.

Q: And I take it you have considerable experience in conducting investigations of this kind?

A: Yes, sir, I have been with the Pinkerton Agency for almost twenty years.

Q: What were you asked to find out about Miss Strongwood?

A: The usual sort of things, sir. Where she lived. Where she worked. Who she associated with. Any evidence of moral turpitude.

Q: Now, Mr. Duggers, without going into every detail of your investigation, let us focus on one point in particular. You were able, after several days of investigation, to learn that Miss Strongwood had for some time while in Chicago worked at an establishment known as the Pink Moon. Is that correct?

A: Yes, sir. Mr. Dirk Chalmers, who runs the place, told me all about it.

––––––––

5. The *Maine* was an American battleship that exploded and sank in the harbor at Havana, Cuba, in 1898, an incident that helped precipitate the Spanish–American War.

6. According to *The Trial of Adelaide Strongwood*, Duggers was a "compact man of medium build, with small sharp eyes, sandy hair, and rather vulpine features. Yet on the whole he presented an appearance just anonymous enough to allow him to blend in with any crowd, as a good detective must. Gifted with a dry sense of humor, he proved to be an unflappable and often entertaining witness."

Q: Did you show him a photograph of Miss Strongwood?

A: I did. Young Mr. Masterson had one and it was given to me. When I showed it to Mr. Chalmers, he had no doubt it was her. Said she'd been his best girl and could have made a lot of money if she'd kept at it.

Q: By the way, did Mr. Chalmers know Miss Strongwood by her real name?

A: No, she was going by the name of Alice Smith.

[Objection, Mr. Phelps. Hearsay. Overruled.]

Q: Let us back up a bit, Mr. Duggers. What sort of establishment is the Pink Moon?

A: It's a dance hall, down on South State Street.

Q: Is that an elegant part of Chicago?

A: "Elegant" would not be the word I would use, sir. It is a red-light district, part of what is known as the Levee.

Q: A very disreputable area?

A: You could say that, though some very reputable people go there.

Q: To be entertained?

A: If that is what you wish to call it, yes.

Q: It is an area known for prostitution, correct?

A: I would say that is the great attraction there, certainly for the male portion of the species.

Q: I see. Now, let us return to the matter of the Pink Moon. What sort of work did Miss Strongwood perform in this establishment?

A: Well, sir, what every girl there does. She was a dancer.

Q: How would you describe the dancing that takes place at the Pink Moon? Is it formal ballroom dancing?

A: No, sir, it most definitely is not that, though I suppose a waltz has broken out once or twice.

Q: In point of fact, it is suggestive dancing, is it not?

[Objection, Mr. Phelps. Calls for opinion on part of witness. Conference before the bench. Sustained.]

COURT: Mr. Boardman, perhaps you should lay some foundation before continuing along these lines.

Q: Of course, Your Honor. Mr. Duggers, has your work as a Pinkerton agent taken you into dance halls on more than one occasion?

A: It has.

Q: In fact, are you familiar with many such establishments in Chicago?

A: I am.

Q: And in your experience, how would you rate the Pink Moon? Is it an upper-class establishment or something perhaps less so?

A: I would say that it is fancy enough but it does not have an altogether savory reputation.

[Objection, Mr. Phelps. Opinion. Overruled.]

Q: Be more specific, if you would.

A: Well, sir, it's a rowdy sort of place, as most are in the Levee. The girls who dance at the Pink Moon are usually dressed in what I would call a provocative way.

[Objection, Mr. Phelps. Opinion on part of witness. Overruled.]

Q: How so?

A: They wear short pink skirts and petticoats, their bodices are cut low, and they adopt a teasing manner. It is what the men like.

Q: Not what a respectable woman would wear. Is that what you are saying, Mr. Duggers?

A: Yes.

Q: As someone who is familiar with the dance halls of Chicago, tell us if you would how these establishments work, or perhaps I should say, how they make their money.

A: They sell drinks to the customers, at a very steep price. A dollar or more for a glass of beer is not uncommon.

Q: How are these drinks sold? Is there a bar where the men order what they want?

A: Oh no, sir, it doesn't work like that. They sit at tables and mingle with the girls, who press them hard to buy liquor. The more drinks a girl can sell, the more money she makes.

Q: Very interesting. By girls, you mean the dancers, correct?

A: Yes.

Q: How do the girls inveigle customers to buy them drinks?

A: Sweet-talking them, mostly.

Q: Do they sometimes sit in men's laps?

A: I have seen that.

Q: Perhaps even stroke them on the face?

A: Yes.

Q: Whisper softly in their ear?

[Objection, Mr. Phelps. Irrelevant. Overruled.]

A: Yes, I have seen that, too.

Q: And do especially friendly girls often receive tips from the men?

A: Oh yes, that is what the girls rely upon. I have seen a ten-dollar gold piece handed over more than once.

———

Q: Now, Mr. Duggers, did your investigation reveal how long Miss Strongwood worked at the Pink Moon?

A: Mr. Chalmers told me she was there about a month, from early May to early June.

Q: Did he say how he came to hire her?

A: I didn't ask, but she probably applied.

[Objection, Mr. Phelps. Speculation on part of witness. Sustained.]

Q: You testified earlier that Mr. Chalmers told you Miss Strongwood was his "best girl." Did he explain that statement?

A: Yes, he said she sold more drinks than any of the other girls. She was very popular with the customers. They liked the look of her, and if the men like a girl's looks, then she can do very well for herself.

Q: Now, if a man liked the looks of a girl, as you put it, might he try to do more than buy her a drink?

[Objection, Mr. Phelps. Speculation. Overruled.]

A: He might.

Q: In other words, he might ask to spend the evening with her, for a price?

A: Yes. Anything can happen down in the Levee.

———

Q: Just one more question, and it concerns Mr. Chalmers. Is there, to your knowledge, a reason why he will not be able to testify at this trial?

A: I am afraid he is dead, sir. It was in all of the Chicago papers. He was shot in his apartment on the South Side in early July. Apparently it was the jealous lover of one of his girls.

[Objection, Mr. Phelps. Hearsay. Sustained.]

Q: No further questions of this witness, Your Honor.

EXCERPTS FROM THE CROSS-EXAMINATION OF MR. EARL DUGGERS, MR. PHELPS for the defense, January 19, 1904

————

Q: I have only a few more questions, Mr. Duggers. You have testified at some length regarding Miss Strongwood's brief employment at the Pink Moon Dance Hall in Chicago. Since you have presented yourself as something of an expert on the matter of dance halls, and indeed seem to spend a good deal of your time in them, perhaps you could tell us whether to your knowledge some of the unfortunate young girls who work in such establishments are prostitutes?

A: Some are, yes.

Q: And would it be also fair to say that there are many impoverished young girls who work in dance halls who are not prostitutes?

A: I am sure that is true.

Q: Isn't it also true that girls will often resort to working in such establishments for a short period time out of sheer desperation, to make enough money to stave off the wolf at the door, so to speak, and thereby give themselves an opportunity to find more dignified work?

[Objection, Mr. Boardman. Calls for speculation. Sustained.]

Q: How much money do girls who work at dance halls earn, say, in a week?

A: It depends.

Q: On how many drinks they can sell?

A: Yes.

Q: Would it surprise you that a girl could clear twenty or thirty or even forty dollars a week if she really worked hard?

A: No, but then there is very little that surprises me anymore.

Q: By the way, what is your weekly salary, Mr. Duggers?

A: It varies.

Q: More than forty dollars a week?

A: Not unless I have died and gone to heaven.

Q: Twenty?

A: It could be, yes.

Q: Do you know what a young girl like Miss Strongwood working as an office clerk might earn in a week?

A: I could not say.

Q: Eight to ten dollars perhaps?

A: Perhaps.

Q: Very well, returning now to Miss Strongwood's brief employment at the Pink Moon, did the late Mr. Chalmers ever suggest to you that she went out with any of the men who came to the dance hall?

A: No, he did not say that, but I did not ask.

Q: Let me put it to you this way, sir: Do you have any reason to believe that Miss Strongwood took a job at the Pink Moon for any other reason than to make enough money so that she could establish herself long enough to find a better position?

[Objection, Mr. Boardman. Calls for speculation. Sustained.]

Q: Aside from Miss Strongwood's single month of employment at the Pink Moon, did your investigation reveal anything of note about her life in Chicago?

A: Could you more specific, sir?

Q: Certainly. Did you find any evidence that she was living a conspicuously immoral life? That, for instance, she entertained numerous male friends in her apartment?

A: No.

Q: Where did she live, by the way?

A: In a rooming house well down on Prairie Avenue.

Q: Was this a respectable establishment?

A: Yes, as far as I know.

Q: So, to sum up, Miss Strongwood worked for a period of one month at the Pink Moon in Chicago so as to earn enough money to return to Minneapolis and try to make a good life for herself there, and while she was in Chicago there is no indication she engaged in any sort of immoral or illegal conduct. Is that your testimony, Mr. Duggers?

[Objection, Mr. Boardman. Mischaracterizing witness's testimony. Sustained.]

Q: No further questions.

Excerpts from the direct testimony of Miss Adelaide Strongwood, Mr. Phelps for the defense, January 27, 1904

————

Q: Addie, when you wrote about your experiences in Chicago in the *Minneapolis Tribune,* you never mentioned working at a place called the Pink Moon, did you?

A: No, I did not.

Q: Nor did you mention it when you applied for a job at Masterson, DeLaittre and Sons, isn't that right?

A: That is right. I did not mention it.

Q: Why did you leave out this information?

A: It is very simple. I was embarrassed to admit that I had fallen so low that I had to work in a dance hall to save myself from starvation, or worse.

Q: I imagine that is why you also gave a false name—Alice Smith—to your employers at the Pink Moon?

A: Yes. Knowing what I did about such places, and how working girls there could be molested, I thought it best not to use my real name. Besides, I convinced myself that it was not the real Addie Strongwood who would ever stoop to work at such an establishment, but some other girl who had fallen on desperate times, and so would stand in for me for a while until I could become myself again. I know how strange this must sound, Mr. Phelps, but it is how I truly felt about my situation.

Q: I think we can all understand, Addie. Now, tell us in your own words, if you would, how you came to work at the Pink Moon.

A: Well, as I stated earlier, I'd had no luck finding a job in Chicago and I was down to my last quarter, and I mean that quite literally. I had gone almost two days without eating when I finally unburdened myself to a girl named Jenny at the rooming house where I stayed. She was a very kindly girl and she told me, Addie, you are pretty enough that you could get a job down at one of the dance halls and make a lot of money. Of course, I recoiled at the suggestion—what decent girl would not?—but it is amazing, Mr. Phelps, how persuasive an empty stomach can be. It took me some hours to work up the nerve, but I went with Jenny down to the Pink Moon. She knew Mr. Chalmers there and so—

Q: That would be Mr. Dirk Chalmers, correct?

A: Yes.

Q: Go on.

A: Well, he looked me over in a very leering sort of way, I must say, and said he could hire me and that I could easily make five dollars a night just by getting men to buy drinks.

Q: What did you think of this proposition?

A: I was very near to tears at the thought of it, but I had enough presence of mind to ask him a question, which was if he expected the girls working in his place to do anything besides sell drinks to men. He said his girls could do as they wished but that if I was asking whether I would be required to do anything immoral, the answer was no. "You just sell the boys plenty of liquor, honey," he told me, "and they will be happy and you will be happy and I will be happy."

———

Q: And so, you finally decided to take the job?

A: Yes. I was mortified, of course, to step into one of the costumes they provided, but I steeled myself. I believe that a woman can endure anything if she sets her mind to it, even the most unpleasant and demeaning experiences. I decided that I would endure, and I did.

Q: How long did you work at the Pink Moon?

A: Twenty-two nights in all, for twelve hours a night. Each of those two hundred and sixty-four hours was an agony for me, but I knew I had to keep at it for my own sake.

Q: Why did you quit after twenty-two nights?

A: I had set a goal for myself to earn enough to save one hundred dollars, so that I could then return to Minneapolis and make a decent life for myself. When I had saved that amount, I quit, and it was the happiest day of my life.

Q: Addie, during your time working at the Pink Moon did you ever sell yourself to men?

A: Never, never, never. I would have waded far out into the waters of Lake Michigan and drowned myself before ever consenting to become a bought woman.

———

STRONGWOOD

———

Remarkable scene when court adjourned this afternoon & Holmes came up to see us—Addie of course didnt recognize him in his bohemian disguise, so I did the honors—"Let me introduce to you the one & only Sherlock Holmes," I told Addie as she looked up from her chair—she arose at once to greet Holmes & said how much she admired him & his work—she then surprised even Holmes I think by mentioning Irene Adler[7] & what a great woman she must have been— Holmes replied gallantly that Adler was indeed "an extraordinary woman"—he then fixed his probing eyes on Addie & asked if she too was "extraordinary"— she held his gaze, which could wither most men, for what seemed like a very long time—finally, she said in a quiet voice, "I hope to become so, Mr. Holmes, if only the jury will do what is right in this unfortunate matter"—to which Holmes replied, "I am sure the jury will reach the correct verdict."

Addie then asked Holmes outright what he thought of her case—"There is of course a missing piece at the heart of it," he said, "and when that piece is found, as surely it will be, we shall all know the truth. Don't you agree, Miss Strongwood?"—"I believe you are right, Mr. Holmes," she replied, "though much will depend, as I am sure you would agree, on when that piece is found."

They locked gazes once again & I felt as tho I was witnessing some strange & intense ritual, the meaning of which no outsider could grasp—spell soon broken, however, when bailiff tapped Addie on shoulder & told her she must return to her cell—Addie nodded & said to Holmes, "Thank you for coming to see me. I am pleased to have so mighty a champion of justice in my corner"— then the matron led Addie away.

"What do you think of my client?" I asked Holmes after Addie left—he gave a slight smile & said, "She is that rare young woman who knows her mind as well as her heart, and I do not doubt that she will one day attain her goal of being quite extraordinary, in one way or another. However, I would advise the man who marries her, if she does not go to prison first, to be very, very careful."

———

7. Irene Adler, always referred to by Holmes as *the* woman, was featured in one of Dr. Watson's most famous stories, "A Scandal in Bohemia," published in 1891. In the story, she outwits Holmes, who tries unsuccessfully to retrieve a potentially compromising photograph in her possession.

Now almost midnight & time for bed, tho sleep is elusive when so many questions whirl in the air—will finish up with Addie tomorrow & then see what damage that bastard Boardman can do.

EXCERPTS FROM THE DIRECT TESTIMONY OF MISS ADELAIDE STRONGWOOD, Mr. Phelps for the defense, January 28, 1904

———

Q: Addie, now that you have taken us through the wrenching events of September twenty-sixth in Michael Masterson's apartment, please tell the jury why you did not immediately go to the police to report this violation upon your person?

A: Well, as I wrote in the *Tribune,* I saw no possibility that the police would believe me, given how influential the Masterson family is in this city. I am sure Michael would have lied about it, just as his mealy little friend, Mr. Jakes, has now done in this courtroom—

[Objection, Mr. Phelps. Witness should be cautioned. Sustained.]

COURT: Miss Strongwood, your editorializing is not acceptable. The jury will be the judge of the witnesses who have been heard here. Do you understand what I am telling you?

A: I do, Your Honor.

COURT: Very well, but it must not happen again. You may proceed, Mr. Phelps.

Q: Thank you. Now, Addie, as you were saying, you believed the police would never bring charges against your tormentors. Is that right?

A: Yes, it would be the word of a poor working girl against that of two supposedly fine young men of excellent bloodlines. I know how the world works, Mr. Phelps. I know all too well. But I do believe in justice, as strongly as I believe in anything, and I knew that justice in my case could only come of my own efforts to obtain it.

Q: And that is why you ultimately decided to write to Mr. and Mrs. Masterson and ask them for ten thousand dollars in payment for the crimes against you?

A: Yes, and to help raise the child.

Q: But you never heard a single word back from them, did you?

A: Never.

Q: That must have been very disappointing.

A: Yes, it was. I began to believe that they simply could not see me, that I was as unreal to them as those little wiggling creatures visible only under the lens of a microscope. I did not exist for them, and so they could not concern themselves with me or my cry for justice.

Q: You must have felt very bereft.

A: Oh, Mr. Phelps, you cannot imagine how alone and abandoned I felt after what had been done to me. I will confess that for a few days I thought of throwing myself over the Hennepin Avenue Bridge and so down to the mighty falls and certain oblivion. But I did not do it.

Q: May I ask what held you back, Addie?

A: Why, it was the child within me, Mr. Phelps. What had it done to deserve such a fate? Nothing, of course, and that is why I decided that I had to fight on, no matter how poor my prospects seemed.

————

Q: It was not blackmail or hush money you sought, was it, Addie?

A: Absolutely not. The money to me was justice—not complete justice or even very satisfactory justice—but all that I thought I could secure for myself, given my circumstances as opposed to theirs.

Q: At the end of your letter, Addie, you mentioned that if the Mastersons decided against paying you what you believed you were owed, you could, and I quote, "not be responsible" for what might happen next. What did you mean by that?

A: I meant only that I would have to find another way to achieve justice. To be very honest, I wasn't certain what I might do, except perhaps take my story to the newspapers and hope I could receive a friendly and honest hearing there.

————

EXCERPTS FROM THE CROSS-EXAMINATION OF MISS ADELAIDE STRONGWOOD, Mr. Boardman for the prosecution, January 28, 1904

————

Q: Well, Miss Strongwood, here we go again, don't we? The Pink Moon. Just another part of your story that you somehow neglected to tell us about in your articles for the *Tribune*. Quite an oversight, don't you think?

A: I have explained why I did not mention it.

Q: Ah yes, you were just too embarrassed, or so you told us, and to hide your shame even gave yourself an alias—Alice Smith. Did lying about your own name bother you, Miss Strongwood, or was it just another part of the big con game you've been playing for quite a while now?

A: I am just a poor working girl who found herself in terrible circumstances and did what she needed to do to survive. If that is a confidence game, Mr. Boardman, then I will readily plead guilty.

Q: Oh please, spare us the poor sister story. You now tell us you were embarrassed by your job as a paid tart in Chicago—

[Objection, Mr. Phelps. Prosecution has resorted to name-calling. Sustained.]

Q: My apologies to the witness. Let me rephrase the question: You have stated, Miss Strongwood, that you are embarrassed to recall your employment in a dance hall, but that you had no other choice but to take the job. Is that correct?

A: Yes.

Q: No other choice. I wonder about that. In a city full of job opportunities for a bright girl such as yourself you simply couldn't find anyplace to work except in a dance hall in one of the most notorious red-light districts in all of America. Isn't the real truth, Miss Strongwood, that you took that job at the Pink Moon because you liked the idea of making a lot of money just by flirting with men? And you not only liked the job, you were very, very good at it.

A: No, that is not true. I hated every minute of my time there.

Q: Ah, I see, and you hated it so much that you managed to spend twenty-two nights there, by your own admission, raking in five dollars a night or more just by being a friendly girl to all those poor, lonely men. Tell us, Miss Strongwood, just how friendly were you?

[Objection, Mr. Phelps. Vague. Sustained.]

Q: Very well, let us be more specific. Did you sit in men's laps?

A: I did not.

Q: Did you rub men on the cheek and tell them how nice you would be to them if they'd just buy a drink?

A: No.

Q: You never did that?

A: Never.

Q: Did you dance with men?

A: Sometimes. We were required to.

Q: Ah, so there you were, dressed in your skimpy little pink outfit, a stranger's arm around your waist, merrily dancing away the night, all the while urging him to buy more liquor. Quite a pretty picture, isn't it?

[Objection, Mr. Phelps. Irrelevant, lurid, improper, etc. Overruled but Mr. Boardman cautioned.]

COURT: Mr. Boardman, I am allowing you the usual leeway for cross-examination, but do not think that the court's patience is unlimited. The witness may answer the question.

A: I agree, Mr. Boardman, it was not a pretty picture, but if you are a poor girl in a harsh world, then life is not always a pretty picture and never will be. I regret what I was forced to do, but I cannot apologize for wishing to live.

Q: You have told us you made an average of about five dollars per night while working at the Pink Moon. Is that correct?

A: Yes.

Q: How many drinks did you sell in a night to earn such high wages? Fifty? A hundred?

A: I am not certain. Every night was different.

Q: But fifty would not be out of the question, would it?

A: On a busy night, no.

Q: And the money you made came largely from tips from the men, did it not?

A: Yes.

Q: I am curious how you earned these tips, since you have told us you didn't sit in men's laps or stroke their cheeks or dance enthusiastically with them. Indeed, you make it sound as though you were cool and distant toward your customers. The ice queen of Chicago, I should say. And yet these men showered you with gratuities. Was it just out of the generosity of their hearts that they did so?

A: I cannot say what their motives were.

———

Q: Miss Strongwood, while you were entertaining all of your customers at the Pink Moon, did you ever have occasion to meet Michael Masterson there?

A: No.

Q: You are sure?

A: I have said so.

Q: So if I were to show you a matchbox found in Mr. Masterson's apartment, a matchbox imprinted with the name "Pink Moon Dance Hall, Chicago," what would you say to that?

MR. PHELPS: Your Honor, I must object and object strenuously. This is absolutely outrageous. There is no such matchbox in evidence and Mr. Boardman knows it. He is simply making something up in a pathetic attempt to sway the jury.

MR. BOARDMAN: I am prepared to make an offer of proof regarding this matchbox, Your Honor, and I resent Mr. Phelps's unwarranted attack upon my character.

[Conference before the bench.]

COURT: There being no persuasive offer of proof, the jury is instructed to disregard Mr. Boardman's comments regarding a supposed matchbox. For purposes of this trial, no such piece of evidence exists and the jury must not assume that it does. Mr. Boardman, you are walking a very fine line here and the court strongly advises you not to approach that line again.

Q: I understand, Your Honor.

———

FROM THE JOURNAL OF J. WINSTON PHELPS, JANUARY 28, 1904

9:30 pm—damnedest thing delivered to my doorstep in brown envelope this evening, courtesy of Sherlock Holmes—photo of Addie taken in courtroom yesterday when she testified wearing dark gray sweater—how Holmes managed it I cant say as Elliott allows no cameras in courtroom—note from Holmes said I might find photo "instructive" but didn't elaborate—photo appears to be exactly the same size as torn picture of Addie—also has similar look in terms of grain, contrast, type of paper, & even beveled corners—not sure what Holmes is up to—called Shad for advice after dinner—told me Holmes would explain everything in due time—then Shad delivered surprise of his own—said he & Holmes are sending Wash on a "fishing expedition" to the Rappahannock[8] to see what he can find—told him if Wash gets caught there will be hell to pay—Shad just laughed & said Wash is the slippery eel that always wriggles free—hope to god hes right!

———

Boardman did quite a job on jury today with Pink Moon matchbox supposedly found in Mastersons apartment—knew hed never get it into evidence due to fact coppers "magically" discovered it only two days ago—too much of a deus ex machina even for Elliott to swallow—have to believe it was a plant but then again who can doubt coppers are just as stupid & careless as they seem to be & overlooked it first time around?—damn curious thing, tho, no matter what Addie says.

———

Excerpts from the cross-examination of Miss Adelaide Strongwood, Mr. Boardman for the prosecution, January 29, 1904

Q: I would like you to explain something to me, Miss Strongwood.

A: I am always happy, Mr. Boardman, to clarify anything that confuses you.

Q: Why, thank you. If your offer is sincere, then we just might get to the truth of this matter. Now, here is the point I am puzzling over. You have told the jury, at great length, about the supposed attack upon your person made by Michael Masterson and Jonathan Jakes, an attack Mr. Jakes denies. Mr. Masterson, of course, cannot deny it because he is dead. Now, after this alleged assault, you have said that Mr. Masterson left a message for you. Is that right?

A: Yes.

Q: Where is that message, Miss Strongwood? I am sure the jury would like to see it.

A: I destroyed it.

———

8. This is a reference to the Rappahannock (also known as the Rappanock) Apartments, which still stand at Ninth Street and Portland Avenue South in downtown Minneapolis. Other references in Phelps's journal indicate that Jonathan Jakes lived in the apartments and that Phelps had shared this information with Rafferty and Holmes, per Holmes's request. The nature of the "fishing expedition" undertaken by Wash Thomas will be made clear in a later chapter.

Q: Destroyed it? How strange. Why would you do such a thing? Surely, it must have occurred to you that this note would be significant evidence of the assault against you.

A: I can only respond that I was quite naturally upset over what had been done to me, and so I tore the message up and threw it away. I simply could not bear to look at it anymore. I can see now that it was a mistake. I did not think the situation through as I should have.

Q: Well now, that is surprising, since you strike me, Miss Strongwood, as a girl who thinks everything through.

A: I had been brutally attacked and violated, in case you have forgotten, Mr. Boardman. Clarity of mind does not come easily after such an experience.

Q: And is that also why you failed to go immediately to the police?

A: No, I thought about going to the police but decided against it, as I have explained previously.

Q: Yes, so you told Mr. Phelps. But did it not occur to you that by making a complaint, even if you feared it might not be upheld, you would at least have some official documentation as to what had happened to you? Documentation, I might add, that would certainly have been of great value to you in the event you decided to pursue any kind of claim against Michael Masterson.

A: As I have said, I had no reason to believe the police would be of any help to me. Surely you of all people, Mr. Boardman, must understand why not everyone in the great city of Minneapolis has confidence in their police department.

Q: Isn't the real reason you failed to go to the police much more simple? Isn't the real reason that there was no attack upon you, as you have described it?

A: I have told the truth, Mr. Boardman.

Q: Have you? Then where is the proof, Miss Strongwood? Mr. Jakes, the only other living person present at the supposed attack, has vigorously denied it. The note you say Michael Masterson wrote to you does not exist. You filed no report with the police. You in fact made no mention of this attack to anyone until, more than a month later, you mailed a letter to Mr. and Mrs. Philip Masterson demanding that they pay you ten thousand dollars for the privilege of your silence. It was all a big scheme, wasn't it, Miss Strongwood, a big scheme to enrich you by making a phony claim that you had been assaulted and impregnated by the man who rejected you? And when your scheme failed, you killed that man in cold blood, didn't you, because he would not pay?

A: No, there is not one ounce of truth in what you say, Mr. Boardman, not one ounce. I have spoken the truth here and will continue to speak the truth as I know it, no matter how much you or anyone else try to twist my words. I have come to this courtroom to fight for justice and I will not stop fighting until I have it.

———

Q: All right, Miss Strongwood, let us talk at some length about Mrs. Violet Cutter, the well-known abortionist. You know her, do you not?

A: No, I know nothing of her.

———

EXCERPTS FROM A LETTER FROM SHERLOCK HOLMES TO SHADWELL RAFFERTY, January 31, 1904

Cook House
Rochester, Minnesota

My Dear Rafferty:

Who would have thought just a few months ago that Dr. Watson and yours truly would once again be in Minnesota, not to operate in our usual fashion but instead—you must pardon my little joke—to be operated upon? Yet it has all been worth the long trip, and Dr. Watson, who is now looking better than he has in a very long time, sends along his regards. He is healing nicely after his surgery and the terrible pains that once assailed him are a thing of the past. It is wonderful to see him with his old energy and spirit returning, even as he grows ever more querulous regarding his prolonged confinement. The doctors Mayo are indeed a most remarkable duo, and I should not be surprised if their skill and enterprise will one day lead to this dreary little prairie town becoming a far greater Mecca than it already is for the ill and troubled of this world.

Unless there is some unexpected relapse in the doctor's condition, we are thinking now that we shall leave here not long after the first of February and go directly to Chicago, then on to New York and finally home to London at last.

However, I entreat you and Mr. Thomas to come down for a last visit to Rochester when you can. As always, we will have much to talk about.

It was a great pleasure to see you, the estimable Mr. Thomas and your friend Mr. Phelps in Minneapolis. As you well know, I found the trial of Miss Strongwood to be of great interest. My brief encounter with her was also most instructive. She strikes me as quite remarkable and, as you once put it, more than a match for the scheming men of this world. Since we will be leaving soon, I doubt that I shall ever have the opportunity to talk with her at length, which is a pity, since there is much about her I should like to know. It is always fascinating to observe how a powerful mind of her type can grow out of what would seem to be barren ground, and I suspect she is as much a surprise to herself as she is to others.

As to the circumstances of her case, you are well aware of what I have been thinking, especially regarding the torn photograph. Even so, I wish to set it all down on paper now so that if Dr. Watson ever decides to turn his busy pen to the matter he will have a solid record upon which to build his usual fancies. I should add here that you may feel perfectly free to convey this letter to Mr. Phelps, but I believe it would be best to do so after Miss Strongwood's trial so as not to cloud his mind with information that may not in fact prove useful to him in defending his client.

I am aware that the photograph of Miss Strongwood could in the end prove to be one of those accidental features of a case that has no purpose other than to bedevil the detective. Indeed, I can already hear your objections, my dear Rafferty. That poor fool Holmes is about to embark on one of his famously long expeditions in search of great meaning in small things, and you will no doubt cite as a prime example the unfortunate business of Mr. Harlan's grey socks.[9] Be that as it may, I am of the strong opinion that the photograph of Miss Strongwood is *the* essential piece of evidence in this case and that its presence in Mr. Masterson's hand at the time of his demise will, if properly understood, tell us how and why he died. Once Mr. Thomas undertakes the "fishing expedition" we have discussed, I have no doubt that my theories will be confirmed.

---

9. This comment apparently refers to a case in which Holmes was led astray by making too much of a certain piece of evidence. The case of the socks is not mentioned in any of Dr. Watson's writings, nor in any of Rafferty's notes, so there is no way of knowing when and where it took place.

SIX

PART SIX OF "AN ACCOUNT OF MY LIFE AND THE INCIDENT FOR WHICH I HAVE Been Unjustly Accused of Murder," by Addie Strongwood, *Minneapolis Tribune*, December 19, 1903

Of all the regrets I have accumulated in connection with the events of the past year, the greatest centers upon the child that was the unfortunate consequence of Michael Masterson's act of violation. When I became aware that I was carrying the child, I naturally felt as though yet another burden had been placed upon me by fate's relentless hand. Yet, contrary to what has been written elsewhere, I never sought to "rid" myself of the child, who after all had no choice in springing to life in my womb. Nor did I ever ask to avail myself of the services of Mrs. Violet Cutter, whose lies are as foul and fetid as Satan's very breath. Truly, she is like the wicked man of whom the Psalms speak: "His mouth is full of cursing and deceit and fraud: under his tongue is mischief and vanity."

Despite her unsavory and duplicitous character, this pathetic old woman has been held up by the *Journal* as the most reliable of witnesses, a veritable paragon of honesty! Her story, however, will not survive long under the rigors of cross-examination, truth's great solvent, and she will leave the courtroom exposed as a complete and shameless fraud.

Mrs. Cutter's cruel and deceitful statements have so turned sentiment against me that I fear many readers will not countenance that I fully intended to raise the child on my own, no matter how painful the circumstances of its conception had been. Indeed, I decided from the very moment I became aware the child was within me that I would not, under any circumstances, give it up for adoption, as is so often the course of action followed in such matters. Yet it was not to be. Once again fate intervened, and the precious little vessel I was carrying was lost to me, through no action of my own, before it could ever come fully formed into this world. Oh, how my heart aches for that unborn child, and how I dream of what might have been!

I must now begin the final part of my story and the events that immediately preceded the tragedy at the Windom Block. The newspapers of Minneapolis have already published all manner of accounts of those days, most of them so riddled with lies that the truth has become a corpse, and I therefore feel compelled to do all that I can to set the record straight.

As I have written previously, I made an overture to Mr. and Mrs. Philip Masterson early last month, asking them to help support me and the child that was the product of their son's act of ravishment. The Mastersons, alas, were deaf to my sincere plea, and after nearly a week had gone by with no response to my letter, I wondered what to do next. I considered hiring a lawyer to represent my interests, but a few quick inquiries made it apparent that I had too little money to do so. After much further thought, I determined that my best course would be to tell my story to the newspapers, in which I put perhaps a naive degree of faith, in the hope that public sentiment might compel the Mastersons to treat me fairly.

Before I could do so, however, I received a telephone call on the afternoon of Saturday, November 7, that came as both a great shock and a small glimmer of hope. The caller, of course, was Michael, and he stated without preamble that he and his parents had agreed on what he called a "settlement" to my case.

The sound of his voice, even though it had a faint and distant quality over the telephone, so alarmed me, and brought back such excruciating memories, that it took all of my presence of mind not to hang up at once. But I knew I must talk to him, for my sake and that of the child.

"Very well," I said, "tell me what this settlement is."

"It is very simple," he said, speaking as though he were passing on instructions to a secretary. "We will pay you one thousand dollars and not a penny more, and you in turn will agree not to ask for any additional money, ever. You will also agree, on penalty of legal action, not to publicize this matter in any way, or your payment will be forfeited. You will further agree to leave the city of Minneapolis and never return. Take it or leave it."

One thousand dollars for all of my suffering and pain! How little Michael thought of me and how easily he believed I could be brushed away, like a speck of dirt on one of his clean white shirts! I am sure he believed that his offer, a mere pittance from his majestic point of view, would be sufficient to send me on my way. Strange, is it not, how in this world our lives are ledgers, and we thrive or fail depending upon which side we are fortunate enough to occupy! I will not deny, dear readers, that the coldhearted settlement offered by Michael gave me pause, even though it was far less than I knew I would need to raise a child. Yet what of the price of my violation? Michael made no mention of that, and I had no indication that he cared about it in any event.

"Well," he demanded, growing impatient at my silence, "what will it be?"

"No," I said, mustering up my firmest voice. "I will not be gotten rid of that easily. I am owed more for my suffering and your cruelty."

"Why you little ——," he said, using a word I cannot repeat. "You'll never see a thousand dollars again in your miserable little life."

"Perhaps not, but I will see justice, by one means or another. I promise you that."

Quivering with indignation, I hung up even as Michael uttered another vile obscenity.

I will not gainsay that I felt a small twinge of regret about turning down the settlement, for I knew full well how much of a difference in the circumstances of my life a thousand dollars would make. Yet I also felt, in a certain way, vindicated. Michael and his family wished to treat me as nothing more than a minor annoyance, an irritating pest to be removed from their lives. Now, they had learned that however humble my circumstances, I would not be bullied by their money or their power. I would fight on.

Nonetheless, I still faced the problem of how to proceed in my attempt to secure justice. As it turned out, however, I did not have long to consider my next course of action. The very next day, I received another telephone call at my boardinghouse. It was from a man who identified himself as Charles Warren and said he was an attorney for the Masterson family.

"What is it you want?" I asked the caller.

"Michael Masterson asked me to get in touch with you. As I understand it, you had a conversation with him yesterday regarding possible settlement of a certain matter but that you were unable to come to terms. Is that correct?"

I said it was.

The caller continued: "I have been instructed to tell you, Miss Strongwood, that I am authorized to negotiate further on behalf of Mr. Masterson in hopes of resolving the matter. I am confident that if we can sit down and talk, we can come to terms suitable to both parties."

Naturally, I was surprised by this turn of events, given Michael's abrupt and vicious manner when he spoke to me on the telephone.

"Am I to assume something has caused a change of heart on Michael's part?" I asked.

"I really cannot say," the caller responded. "All I can tell you is that Mr. Masterson is willing to continue negotiations, but from this point forward they must go through me."

"All right," I said, despite a vague sense of unease settling into the pit of my stomach. "I am willing to talk. Where do you wish to meet?"

"I am on the top floor of the Windom Block, on Washington Avenue at Second Avenue South. Do you know it?"

I said I could find the building with no trouble.

"Very good. My offices are at the rear, suite 413. You won't see any signs, as we are only temporary occupants and will soon relocate. Just knock on the door and you will find me. Would eight o'clock tomorrow night suit you?"

"That is rather late," I said.

"Yes, I know, but as I am in the midst of an important case, it is the only time I have."

I said I would be there.

"Then I will see you at the appointed hour. I look forward to meeting you, Miss Strongwood. Let us hope our meeting will prove advantageous to both of us."

I hung up the phone, marveling that the justice I so longed for might yet be at hand. But as the day went on, the sense of unease I'd felt talking with Mr. Warren on the telephone began to deepen. I cannot explain it or account for it in any way, except to say that I have long believed there are more than five senses and that mysterious forces are at work in the world. Some tremor of doubt was registering deep inside me, and it would not go away.

My sleep was uneasy that night. I remember dreaming that I had entered a large building with long, blank corridors lined with dark marble walls and bright red doors that could not be opened. Light from some mysterious source filtered into these corridors; however, I saw no windows. Every time I turned down a new hallway, the same scene presented itself, and I began to believe I might never escape. When I awoke, at six in the morning, an idea had crept into my head and there was no evicting it. I knew that I must visit the public library.

I was at the front door of the library on Hennepin[1] when it opened at ten o'clock. Once I gained admission, I rushed up to the reference room and found the latest *Polk's Directory*, which includes a list of all the lawyers practicing in the city of Minneapolis. I found no listing for Charles Warren and no law offices of any kind in the Windom Block.

What was I to make of this startling revelation? If there was no Charles Warren, then who had called me and what was this person's real purpose? Dark suspicions soon gathered like storm clouds at the back of my mind, and I began to fear that Michael was engaged in some new plot against me. What were his intentions? I wondered. Who else was plotting with him? How might I outplot the plotters? I know now that what I did next is a thing I would have been better not doing. My defense is that I believed there would be no end to Michael's machinations unless I could somehow defeat them and thereby convince him that he must at last provide the justice I desperately desired.

So it was that I decided that I would go to the Windom Block, only well before the appointed hour of my meeting with the phantom lawyer, Mr. Warren. I would go there to watch and listen and try to catch Michael at his devious game. And yes, dear readers, I took along my derringer, fully loaded, for I did not know what evils might await me.

ARTICLE IN THE *MINNEAPOLIS TIMES*, NOVEMBER 27, 1901

The police under Chief Ames[2] have once again raided the quarters of Mrs. Violet Cutter, the midwife who has long been suspected of performing operations on desperate young women. And once again, it appears they have little to show for their work.

"We are devoted to putting a stop to her barbaric practices," said the Chief, who summoned reporters to the house at 1905 Eighth St. S., where Mrs. Cutter is said to maintain a basement operating room.

---

1. In 1903 the Minneapolis Public Library was located in a handsome brownstone building, now long gone, at Tenth Street and Hennepin Avenue.
2. Frederick Ames was appointed chief of police in 1900 by his brother, Albert A. ("Doc") Ames, who was elected mayor of Minneapolis that year. Frederick Ames ran the department in such a corrupt manner that he was removed as chief in 1902. He was later sent to prison after being convicted of various crimes.

However, the dim basement to which the Chief led reporters hardly seemed to qualify as an operating theater, lacking as it did any kind of surgical equipment or even a table.

"We know what Mrs. Cutter is doing here," the Chief insisted, "but it is likely she was tipped off regarding our intentions by some irresponsible party. Rest assured, we will not allow her vile work to continue. It is an outrage against the good people of Minneapolis."

Mrs. Cutter, who was not taken into custody, stated later that the Chief was on a "witch hunt" and that she has never performed operations or done anything illegal. "I simply assist young woman who find themselves in a family way but who lack the money to see a doctor. I do not know why I should be persecuted because of that."

The raid yesterday was at least the third conducted by police at her home over the past few years. In each instance, however, insufficient evidence was found to bring charges against Mrs. Cutter.

EXCERPTS FROM AN ARTICLE IN THE *MINNEAPOLIS JOURNAL*, DECEMBER 3, 1903

A shocking revelation has occurred in the case of Miss Adelaide Strongwood, who will go on trial in January on charges of murdering her lover, Michael Masterson. The revelation was provided by Mrs. Violet Cutter, a well-known midwife in this city, who stated in an interview with the *Journal* that she was asked to operate on Miss Strongwood to abort a child but refused to do so.

"I received a telephone call late in October from a woman who identified herself as Miss Adelaide Strongwood. She informed me that she was with child but did not wish to give birth, for reasons which she was sure I would understand. She said she had made a mistake and needed to correct it. I recall those words very precisely. She then asked me how much it would cost to 'rid herself' of the child, as she put it. I told her that I was not in that sort of business."

Mrs. Cutter went on to state that Miss Strongwood seemed "very desperate" and pleaded with her to be of assistance. "I told her that I could certainly be of help to her when the time came to deliver the child, and that I would be willing to visit with her at some time before the birth to see to her health. I then asked her when the child was due, and she replied: 'It does not matter, for the child will never be born.'"

Said Mrs. Cutter, "I told the poor girl not to think in such a way, but she would not hear of it and ended the call before I could offer her any useful advice. I felt very sorry for her, as she sounded as though she was in a very distressed state of mind."

Mrs. Cutter added that she never heard from Miss Strongwood again and does not know what happened to her unborn child.

———

EXCERPTS FROM THE DIRECT TESTIMONY OF MRS. VIOLET CUTTER,[3] MR. Boardman for the prosecution, January 22, 1904

———

Q: Tell us, Mrs. Cutter, exactly when you received the telephone call from Miss Strongwood?

[Objection, Mr. Phelps. Caller identified herself as Miss Strongwood but there is no evidence that she actually made the call. Conference before the bench.]

COURT: Why don't you rephrase the question, Mr. Boardman?

Q: Certainly. When did you receive a call from a young woman identifying herself as Miss Strongwood?

A: It was the last week in October, as best I can remember.

Q: But you're not sure of the exact date?

A: No, it has been awhile, but I think it was toward the end of the week, October thirteenth or thereabouts. Yes, I am pretty sure that is when it was.

Q: Tell us, please, what the caller said.

A: Well, she said she was in a family way and needed to get rid of her child, but I told her I couldn't—

Q: One moment, Mrs. Cutter. Do you recall specifically that the caller said she wished to "get rid" of her unborn child?

———

3. Here is how Mrs. Cutter was described in *The Trial of Adelaide Strongwood*: "She is a very large but short woman, perhaps sixty years of age, with snow-white hair, a broad face well-incised with wrinkles, and shrewd dark eyes, deeply set. Her manner on the witness stand was conspicuously odd, for she never looked directly at her questioner or at the jury, her eyes instead darting constantly from one corner of the courtroom to another. In much the same way, her answers to questions were often quite vague, perhaps out of fear of implicating herself in the illegal practices of which she has been so often accused."

A: Yes, or something close to that.

Q: All right. Go on.

A: There wasn't much else. I told her I wasn't in that kind of business, and that I was a respectable woman and was surprised she would think otherwise. As I recall, I also told her I could be of some help as a midwife if that is what she wanted. That was all there was to it.

Q: But didn't you also tell a reporter for the *Journal* last month that the caller stated that her child would never be born?

A: Oh yes, I guess she did. I forgot about that.

Q: What did you think of that remarkable statement: a mother telling you she would not allow the child growing in her womb to be born?

[Objection, Mr. Phelps. Calls for opinion on part of witness, irrelevant, etc. Sustained.]

Q: But you are certain that the caller made such a statement. Is that right?

A: Yes.

Q: And then the caller hung up?

A: Yes.

Q: And you never talked with her again?

A: That's right. It was the first and last time I ever heard from her.

———

FROM THE JOURNAL OF J. WINSTON PHELPS, JANUARY 21, 1904

———

Mrs. Cutter likely on stand tomorrow—will say Addie called her re baby & I will say she didnt & then what?—ha!—have a secret weapon, thanks to our little birdie[4]—Boardman in for a rude surprise—cant wait to spring it.

———

4. It appears likely that "the little birdie" mentioned here was a source Phelps had somewhere in the Hennepin County courthouse, possibly even in Frederick Boardman's office.

EXCERPTS FROM THE CROSS-EXAMINATION OF MRS. VIOLET CUTTER, MR. Phelps for the defense, January 22, 1904

———

Q: You have testified regarding a telephone call you said you received in late October from a person identifying herself as Adelaide Strongwood. Now, supposing for a minute that you did indeed receive such a call, do you know for a fact that the caller was indeed Miss Strongwood?

A: Well, she said she was.

Q: We know that. But you didn't know that, did you? All you knew is that on the other end of the line was the voice of a person claiming to be Miss Strongwood, correct?

A: I suppose you could say that.

Q: What did the voice sound like?

A: What do you mean?

Q: Well, was it clear toned, high, loud, nasal? What did the voice sound like?

A: Well, you know how voices sound on the telephone. It is hard to say.

Q: Because the voice you heard over the line wasn't all that clear, was it?

A: I don't know how clear it was.

Q: With the permission of the court, I would like Addie to stand up and say, "Good afternoon, Mrs. Cutter, how are you today?"

[Objection, Mr. Boardman. Improper and irrelevant. Conference before the bench. Overruled.]

Q: Go ahead, Addie, please address the witness.

DEFENDANT: Good afternoon, Mrs. Cutter, how are you doing today?

Q: Thank you, Addie. Now, Mrs. Cutter, is that the voice you heard on the phone?

A: It could be.

Q: Really? But if it could be, it also could not be Addie's voice, correct?

[Objection, Mr. Boardman. Leading question. Overruled.]

A: I guess you could say that.

Q: No, it is what you say that matters, Mrs. Cutter. And what you are saying is that you can't identify the voice you supposedly heard on the telephone as being that of my client. Isn't that right?

A: No, I cannot be sure.

Q: All right, but the real truth, is it not, is that you can't identify the voice because there was in fact no such call in the first place?

A: That is not true. There was a call.

Q: And you would never lie about such an important matter, would you?

A: No.

Q: We will see about that. I have here a document obtained on July sixteenth, 1902, following a search of the offices of one Frederick Ames, then the police chief of the city of Minneapolis? Does his name ring a bell?

[Objection, Mr. Boardman. Document not evidence, irrelevant and immaterial, etc. Offer of proof made by Mr. Phelps. Conference before the bench. Recess. Offering of proof accepted after hearing. Trial resumed.]

COURT: You may make inquiries about the document, Mr. Phelps, but only along the lines that have been agreed to.

Q: Thank you, Your Honor. Mrs. Cutter, I will show this ledger sheet, which was maintained in the personal files of Frederick Ames, the former police chief of Minneapolis, and which has now been listed as Defense Exhibit Eleven. Please take a moment to look at it.

A: All right.

Q: Have you gone over it?

A: Yes.

Q: Does it show various names and payments, organized on a monthly basis?

A: That is what it looks like, though I am no bookkeeper.

Q: We know. You are in another line of work. Be that as it may, does your name appear on this ledger sheet?

A: Yes.

Q: How many times?

A: Looks like twice. No, wait, four times.

Q: That is right, four times. Once in the month of January of 1902, once in February, again in March, and yet again in April. Is that correct?

A: Yes.

Q: Now, what is the amount of money listed in each case beside your name?

A: Twenty-five dollars.

Q: And four times twenty-five makes one hundred. Tell us, if you would, Mrs. Cutter, why you paid one hundred dollars directly into the private account of the most corrupt police chief in the history of this city? I assume it is not because you thought him a splendid fellow.

A: It was just business.

Q: The business of bribing a public official. That is what it was, wasn't it?

A: I don't know what you would call it. The police wanted money from me every month, so I paid it.

Q: And why did the police want money from you if, as you say, you are merely a midwife serving the poor mothers of Minneapolis?

A: I am sure I cannot say. Everybody paid the police back then.

Q: Every crook paid the police, isn't that what you mean, and you were one of them, weren't you? Operating on women in your basement to end their pregnancies. That is your line of work, isn't it? But it's illegal, so you needed police protection, at a cost of twenty-five dollars per month.

[Objection, Mr. Boardman. Irrelevant. Overruled.]

A: You are just making things up.

Q: Are these entries in Chief Ames's ledger book "made up," as you put it?

A: I made payments, but everyone did at the time. I told you, it was just business.

Q: I see. Just business. But what a deceptive business it was! Let me show you something else, Mrs. Cutter. Here it is: Defense Exhibit Seven, an article from the *Minneapolis Times* dated November twenty-seventh, 1901. Have a look at it. It's quite interesting. It tells all about a supposed raid at your house by Chief Ames and his eminently honest coppers, a raid in which they found no evidence of wrongdoing on your part because, lo and behold, miracle of miracles, someone had tipped you off about the police raid. Whoever could it have been? Any ideas, Mrs. Cutter?

A: They found nothing because there was nothing to find.

Q: Or was it because you were paying them to find nothing?

A: I deny it.

Q: Of course you do because you have no regard for the truth, Mrs. Cutter, and you never have. Lying is your game. That raid at your house was nothing but a giant charade from the start, wasn't it?

A: It seemed real enough to me.

Q: Oh, I doubt that. It was a show in which everyone played a role. Chief Ames was the moral crusader striving to free the community of sin, you were the poor innocent midwife being persecuted, and after the show was over and the gentlemen of the press had gone away, it was back to business as usual with you and the girls you operate on. It was all a big lie, Mrs. Cutter, wasn't it? A big whopping lie, just like your story about receiving a phone call from Addie.

A: No, I received the call, just as I said.

Q: Ha! Who paid you to report this phantom call? The Mastersons perhaps? How much did it cost to buy you, Mrs. Cutter? Fifty dollars, I should think, would have done the trick.

[Objection, Mr. Boardman. Defense counsel engaging in outrageous accusations, etc. Sustained.]

Q: I withdraw the question, Your Honor. Very, well, Mrs. Cutter, let me ask you this: How did you come to report this supposed telephone call to the authorities?

A: I read about Miss Strongwood in the newspapers and remembered her call. So I went to the police and told them about it.

Q: What an upstanding citizen you are, Mrs. Cutter. A friend of the police, a champion of justice.

[Objection, Mr. Boardman. Disparaging the witness. Sustained.]

COURT: Your commentary is unnecessary, Mr. Phelps, and must not continue. Now, ask a question if you have one.

Q: Certainly. Given all of your, shall we say, interesting experiences with the police of Minneapolis, what caused your urge to volunteer information out of the blue about Addie? I should think you would have washed your hands of the police by now.

A: I was simply trying to be a good citizen, as I have always been. I do not see why I should be criticized for that.

Q: You wanted the truth to come out. Is that it?

A: Yes.

Q: And who better to tell the truth to the police than a woman who was accustomed to bribing them on a regular basis. Is that what you are telling us?

[Objection, Mr. Boardman. Argumentative. Sustained.]

Q: That is all I have of this witness, Your Honor.

EXCERPTS FROM THE REDIRECT TESTIMONY OF MRS. VIOLET CUTTER, MR. Boardman for the prosecution, January 22, 1904

———

Q: Mrs. Cutter, did anyone pay you to perjure yourself in this courtroom by testifying to a telephone conversation that did not in fact take place?

A: No, I told the truth. That girl who said she was Miss Strongwood called me, just as I told you.

EXCERPTS FROM AN ARTICLE IN THE *MINNEAPOLIS TRIBUNE*, NOVEMBER 13, 1903

Frank Kendall, a well-known pool hall operator in St. Paul, has been brought in for questioning in connection with the shooting death of Michael Masterson by his one-time lover, Adelaide Strongwood. It is not known why the police thought it necessary to question Kendall, whose establishment on Wabasha St. has long been a favorite gathering place for the lower specimens of life in the Saintly City.

Inspector Robert McCall of the police would not state why Kendall got a grilling, nor did the pool hall operator himself have anything to say to a *Tribune* reporter after being released from custody last night.

It is rumored, however, that Kendall had ties to Masterson, the wealthy young industrialist who was shot dead by Miss Strongwood in the Windom Block Monday night. Miss Strongwood has claimed self-defense.

EXCERPTS FROM THE DIRECT TESTIMONY OF MR. FRANK KENDALL,[5] POOL HALL proprietor, Mr. Boardman for the prosecution, January 25, 1904

Q: Mr. Kendall, you operate a billiard hall in St. Paul at 450 Wabasha Street, is that correct?

A: Yes.

Q: What sort of customers frequent your establishment?

----

5. According to the *Minneapolis Journal*, Kendall was "a tall, dapper man, about 45 years of age, with several large gold rings on his fingers and the wary eyes of a gambler. His well-known criminal connections gave defense counsel Phelps much to talk about but Kendall also provided testimony of benefit to prosecutor Boardman."

A: Working men, mostly, but the occasional swell comes sauntering in to mix with the hoi polloi and pretend to be a regular fellow. You know the type. But we welcome one and all.

Q: Was Michael Masterson one of those "swells" you have just described?

A: Well, I guess you could say so. Mikey had plenty of money, that's for sure, but he was an all right fellow in my estimation. Knew how to play, too. The boys liked him well enough and so did I. He wasn't stuck-up like most swells.

Q: Do you know why Mr. Masterson went all the way to downtown St. Paul to play billiards?

A: I guess he'd heard that we have the best players around and wanted to see for himself. He was one of the best himself so he liked to go up against good players.

Q: How often did he play billiards at your place?

A: Oh, I would probably see him once or twice a month, usually with Jake.

Q: His friend Jonathan Jakes?

A: Yes.

Q: Let us turn to the events of November fourth of last year. Did you see Mr. Masterson that day?

A: Yes, he came in about nine o'clock and said he wanted to talk about something. Said it was urgent.

Q: How do you happen to remember the exact date of this encounter?

A: Well, the coppers asked me about it and I just kind of went back in my head and figured out when it must have been.

Q: All right. Now, what did you and Mr. Masterson have a talk about that evening?

A: He told me he was having problems with a girl named Addie Strongwood he threw over and now she wanted money from him even though he did nothing to her. I told him he wasn't the first rich man to be in that situation and paying up was likely the best thing to do.

Q: What did Mr. Masterson have to say about that?

A: He said he was willing to pay her well enough but that what she wanted was highway robbery and he couldn't stand for it.

Q: What else did he tell you?

A: He said he was afraid she might try to kill him.

Q: What was the basis for this fear?

A: Well, he said she had a gun, or so she told him, and she might try to use it. He said she was the kind of woman who could shoot a man down and not lose a minute's sleep over it.

Q: Did Mr. Masterson say when Miss Strongwood had told him about having a gun in her possession?

A: As I remember, he said she called him one night and made all sorts of wild threats about what she would do because he threw her over.

Q: Did Mr. Masterson seem genuinely frightened to you?

[Objection, Mr. Phelps. Speculation. Overruled.]

A: Yes, he looked scared.

———

Q: Now, did Mr. Masterson at some point during this conversation ask you to do him a favor?

A: Yes. He wanted to know if I could act as his assistant for a few days on account of how much he feared Miss Strongwood. He thought maybe I could stop her from doing anything crazy, if it came to that.

Q: Why did you suppose he asked such a thing of you, as opposed to say, the police?

A: He didn't think the police could do anything for him. He thought I was a man who knew how to handle himself in a spot and could protect him until he made some sort of deal with Miss Strongwood.

Q: Did he offer to pay you for your services?

A: Ten dollars a day.

Q: A nice sum of money.

A: Yes.

Q: And did you take him up on his offer?

A: In a way. I told him I was awfully busy but that I could help him out the next week if he wanted me to.

Q: What did he say to that?

A: He said he wished I could help him sooner but that the next week would have to do.

Q: Did he say anything else?

A: Just that he had taken a room in the Vendome Hotel[6] for a few days, in case Miss Strongwood came looking for him in his apartment. He thought he would be safe there.

———

Q: Did you talk again with Mr. Masterson later in the week?

A: Yes. He called me on Saturday—

Q: Do you mean Saturday, November seventh?

A: Right.

Q: What did he tell you?

A: He said he was going to meet with the Strongwood girl on Monday night and wanted to know if I could be there with him.

Q: Did he say where this meeting would take place?

A: Yes, he said it would be in the Windom Block in downtown Minneapolis.

Q: Did he say why the meeting would be there?

A: No, not that I recall.

Q: Did he tell you how the meeting came about?

A: I'm not sure what you mean.

Q: I mean this: Did Mr. Masterson tell you whether it was he or Miss Strongwood who initiated the meeting at the Windom Block?

A: I don't think he said one way or the other.

Q: All right. Now, what did you tell Mr. Masterson?

A: I told him I couldn't meet him on Monday night because I had something else I had to do.

Q: How did he respond to this news?

A: He wasn't happy. He said he really didn't want to meet the girl alone.

Q: He was truly frightened of her, wasn't he?

[Objection, Mr. Phelps. Leading question, speculation, etc. Overruled.]

A: It sure sounded that way.

Q: What happened next in your conversation with Mr. Masterson?

A: Well, I told him that I knew somebody who could maybe help him out.

Q: And who was that?

A: Joe Mugliano.

———

6. The Vendome Hotel was located on Fourth Street between Hennepin and Nicollet Avenues in downtown Minneapolis. The hotel, crowned by a carved replica of the Statue of Liberty's head, was torn down in about 1960.

———

Q: Mr. Kendall, did Mr. Masterson ever ask you to harm Miss Strongwood in any way or to hire someone to do so?

A: No.

Q: Did he pay you any money for such a purpose?

A: No.

Q: Did you ever call Miss Strongwood pretending to be a lawyer named Charles Warren?

A: No.

Q: Did you occupy a vacant office in the Windom Block on Washington Avenue in downtown Minneapolis on November ninth of last year?

A: No.

Q: Have you, in fact, ever been in the Windom Block for any reason?

A: Not that I know of.

Q: Have you told the jury the truth as you know it in every particular?

A: I have.

Q: No further questions, Your Honor.

FROM THE JOURNAL OF J. WINSTON PHELPS, DECEMBER 20, 1903

6 pm—dreary Sunday—read Addies last piece in Tribune—wish she had kept quiet & let me do the talking but no such luck—she cannot be stopped once shes set her mind on something.

———

Talked to Shad this pm re Frank Kendall, whom Boardman will surely call as a witness—Shad said Kendalls a known hoodlum & fixer, as per long criminal record in St. Paul—said hed know how to get a person killed for right price & that he knows "Muggy" aka Joseph Mugliano—probably sent him to Windom Block to threaten Addie & maybe even kill her—Shad said Wash knows all about Mugliano & will send info when he can.

———

LETTER FROM GEORGE WASHINGTON THOMAS TO J. WINSTON PHELPS, December 27, 1903

Mr. Phelps:

Shad asked me to write up some notes for you re Joe Mugliano, whose name has come up, as I understand, in the Strongwood case. Joe is well known to us, and you should be aware that he is considered one of the most dangerous men in St. Paul. His official line of work is barbering. He has a small shop on Selby Ave., but it is doubtful he spends much time there. His real business is running a tippling house at Thomas and Western up in Frogtown.[7] The joint is known to be a favorite gathering place for criminals of all stripes and colors. If you are looking to get something of a criminal nature done in St. Paul, then Joe's place is where you would go to find what you need. He pays the coppers $10 a month for protection, tho they raid it every year or so just for appearances' sake.

It has long been rumored that Joe has killed several people for money, but the coppers have never been able to prove that against him. If he was sent over to deal with Miss Strongwood, as you suspect, then he was probably hired to kill her since he is hardly known for his negotiating ability. I am including a copy of his criminal record for your inspection; as you will see, he was sent up for manslaughter in 1895. He has also done some strong-arm business for local gamblers. If you do get him on the stand, he will not admit to anything and you will have a hard time with him all around as he does not much care for lawyers. Let us know if there is anything else we can do.

Sincerely Yours,
George Washington Thomas

EXCERPTS FROM THE CROSS-EXAMINATION OF MR. FRANK KENDALL, MR. Phelps for the defense, January 25, 1904

---

7. Frogtown is a working-class neighborhood in St. Paul just northwest of the downtown area.

Q: It's your story that Michael Masterson came to you, the operator of a billiard hall much frequented by the criminal element of St. Paul, and wanted you to protect him for a few days from a one-hundred-pound woman. Is that right?

A: I don't know how much the girl weighs.

[Laughter in the courtroom. Spectators admonished.]

Q: Well, I don't believe we need to bring in a scale, but touché, Mr. Kendall, touché. In any case, Mr. Masterson asked for your protection.

A: Yes.

Q: Isn't it a fact that he asked for much more than that? Isn't the real truth that he hired you to fix his problem by arranging for Addie to be killed?

A: No. I don't know where you got that idea but there is nothing to it.

Q: A fantasy on my part?

A: Sounds like it.

Q: And what about your arrest record, Mr. Kendall? Is that, too, a fantasy?

A: You know it is not.

Q: In fact, your career in St. Paul has resulted in quite a few arrests. I have here Defense Exhibit Eight, which is a copy of your police record. Let's see now. Why, it shows no fewer than eight arrests. Disorderly conduct, illegal gambling, theft by swindle, attempted bribery and, my oh my, Mr. Kendall, look at this: You were charged back in 1899 with solicitation of murder for trying to have a man killed. You have had quite a career across the river, haven't you?

A: Not a single one of those charges stuck, as I am sure you know. They were all trumped up by the police because I would not pay them off.

Q: So you say. But this long list would certainly suggest that you are just the kind of man with underworld connections who could take care of a problem for someone with no questions asked. That's what you did in Addie's case. You made arrangements with Michael Masterson to have her killed in cold blood.

A: I did no such thing.

———

Q: Let us talk for a bit about a man named Joseph Mugliano, also known as Muggy. You know him, don't you?

A: Yes. He stops by my place sometimes.

Q: What sort of fellow is he?

A: Just a fellow. I don't really know him that well.

Q: And yet you recommended him to Mr. Masterson, did you not?

A: I just said he might be able to help out if he needed a fellow who could handle himself.

Q: I see. Would it surprise you to learn that Mr. Mugliano once served six years at the state prison in Stillwater on a charge of manslaughter?

A: There is very little that surprises me.

Q: I can only imagine. Now, Mr. Kendall, if you were looking to have someone killed, Mr. Mugliano would be the man for the job, wouldn't he?

[Objection, Mr. Boardman. Calls for speculation. Sustained.]

Q: I withdraw the question, Your Honor.

————

Excerpts from the direct testimony of Miss Adelaide Strongwood, Mr. Phelps for the defense, January 28, 1904

Q: Addie, let us talk about Mrs. Violet Cutter. Have you ever met her?

A: No. I saw her for the first time here in this courtroom.

Q: You have heard her testimony that a woman identifying herself as Addie Strongwood telephoned late last October and inquired about ending the life of the child in her womb? Did you make that call, Addie?

A: I most certainly did not. I did not even know of the woman's existence until I read of her a few weeks ago in the newspapers.

Q: Your intent was always to give birth to the child. Isn't that right?

A: Yes. I would never have deprived an innocent child of an opportunity to live.

Q: Now, Addie, I must ask you what happened to the child.

A: I find it hard to speak of.[8]

Q: I understand, but it is a matter we must discuss. You had a miscarriage. Is that correct?

————

8. At this point, according to *The Trial of Adelaide Strongwood*, "the defendant shed visible tears for the first and only time during her trial."

A: Yes, it all happened so very fast. I felt extremely ill one morning and then, well, I do not wish to say more. I lost the baby.

Q: When did this happen?

A: November fifth.

Q: Just a few days after you had written your letter to Mr. and Mrs. Masterson.

A: Yes.

Q: Did your miscarriage occur spontaneously?

A: If you mean, did I do anything to cause the miscarriage, the answer is no.

Q: It happened through no agency of your own?

A: Yes. It was one of the saddest days of my life.

———

Q: Now, after Michael Masterson called you on November seventh and offered you a settlement of one thousand dollars, you thought about it but quickly decided to reject his offer. Is that correct?

A: Yes. I know how strange this must sound, but I could not bring myself to accept such a sum. I believed in view of all that had happened to me that I deserved a more honorable and generous settlement. It wasn't a matter of greed. It was matter of justice, or at least whatever small degree of justice money could provide.

Q: When Michael called, did you tell him that you had lost the baby?

A: I did not. I feared that if I did so, he would offer not a single penny in settlement of his crimes against me. But if he had been willing to talk honestly with me, I certainly would have asked for less than the ten thousand dollars I originally sought, when I believed I would have to bear the cost of raising a child on my own.

Q: But Michael would not talk with you.

A: He would not. Instead, he hired someone to kill me.

———

AFFIDAVIT OF MISS ELLEN MORSE, DECEMBER 16, 1903

Miss Ellen Morse, being of full age and sound mind, upon her oath hereby deposes:

1. I am twenty-three years of age and a resident of the city of Buffalo, New York, where my father, George Morse, owns a company which manufactures tools used in the milling industry.

2. From November 4 to November 8, 1903, I was in the city of Minneapolis, Minnesota, with my parents to visit friends, among them Mr. and Mrs. Philip Masterson and their son, Michael Masterson.

3. On the afternoon of November 7, 1903, I was escorted by Michael Masterson to a matinee performance of "The Mummy and the Humming Bird," a play starring Paul Gilmore, at the Metropolitan Opera House at 320 First Avenue South,[9] said show commencing at one o'clock and continuing until three o'clock.

4. After the show, I went with Michael Masterson to Mr. Walker's art gallery[10] on Hennepin Avenue, where we remained for more than an hour.

5. Upon leaving the art gallery at approximately five o'clock in the afternoon, I returned with Michael Masterson to the West Hotel, at Fifth Street and Hennepin Avenue, where my parents were staying.

6. During the whole of my time with Michael Masterson on the afternoon of November 7, 1903, I did not observe him using a telephone, and I believe I would have noticed him using a telephone had he done so.

Further the affiant sayeth not.

EXCERPTS FROM THE CROSS-EXAMINATION OF MISS ADELAIDE STRONGWOOD, Mr. Boardman for the prosecution, January 28, 1904

Q: So it is your claim that you do not know Mrs. Violet Cutter. You saw her for the first time here in court. Is that right?

---

9. *The Mummy and the Hummingbird,* written by Isaac Henderson and first performed in 1901, was a popular play about a scientist and his neglected wife. It was made into a movie in 1915. Paul Gilmore (1873–1962) was a well-known stage actor of the period and also performed in movies. In 1948 Gilmore and his daughter established the Gilmore Comedy Theater in Duluth, which operated well into the 1950s. The Metropolitan Opera House opened at 320 First Avenue South (now Marquette Avenue) in 1894 and was long considered one of Minneapolis's most fashionable theatrical venues. After a stint as a movie theater, it was demolished in 1937.

10. Thomas Walker, founder of what is now the Walker Art Center, originally displayed his art collection in galleries in his home at 803 Hennepin Avenue in downtown Minneapolis. His home was later torn down to make way for the State Theater, which still occupies the site.

A: Yes.

Q: Never called her on the telephone?

A: Never.

Q: We will come back to Mrs. Cutter in due time. Now, you have said that you were with child for a period of some weeks last fall. Is that right?

A: Yes.

Q: A child you claim was sired by Michael Masterson?

A: When he drugged and assaulted me, yes.

Q: Couldn't have been somebody else's child?

A: I do not see how.

Q: Well, what about Jonathan Jakes? You were intimate with him, were you not?

A: Not to my knowledge, unless he had his way with me when Michael did. I certainly did not seduce him, as is his vile claim.

Q: But you've had plenty of other lovers, haven't you, Miss Strongwood, or have you forgotten what your friend, Catherine Malone, said about you on December thirtieth in the *Minneapolis Journal*?

MR. PHELPS: Stop, sir, stop right there. Your Honor, this is outrageous. Mr. Boardman knows full well that any statements supposedly made by Catherine Malone are inadmissible in this case. I ask that his question be stricken from the record and that he be severely censured for his behavior.

[Lengthy conference before the bench.]

COURT: Ladies and gentlemen of the jury, you are to disregard Mr. Boardman's last question regarding the statements of a woman named Catherine Malone in the *Minneapolis Journal*. Any statements she may have made to that newspaper cannot be used as evidence in these proceedings and you must not consider them in reaching your verdict. Mr. Boardman, you will upon pain of contempt make no further references to Catherine Malone or anything she may have said. Is that very clear?

MR. BOARDMAN: It is, Your Honor.

———

EXCERPTS FROM AN ARTICLE IN THE *MINNEAPOLIS JOURNAL*, DECEMBER 30, 1903

"She was a regular tart who talked all the time about the young men she was seeing and all of us girls thought she was the loosest woman we had ever seen." These unflattering words were used by a former coworker to describe Adelaide Strongwood, who stands accused of murdering Michael Masterson, heir to one of the city's largest industrial fortunes.

Miss Strongwood, who is charged with first-degree murder in the case, has depicted herself in a series of recent articles in the *Tribune* as an innocent victim of young Masterson's wiles and has claimed that she shot him on Nov. 9 in the Windom Block purely as a matter of self-defense.

But Catherine Malone, who worked for a time with Miss Strongwood in the offices of Masterson, DeLaittre & Sons, painted a far different picture of the defendant in an exclusive interview with a *Journal* reporter.

"None of the girls in the office liked her," Miss Malone said. "She always acted very cool and aloof, except when she talked about all the men she had chasing her. Many of us found her remarks quite distasteful, but she did not seem to care. She knew she was very beautiful, and of course all the young men flirted with her, but she would laugh when she talked about them and tell us she liked to play them all along.

"I remember one time in particular when she told us she went to one of the men's apartment and spent most of the evening there. We were all shocked but she did not seem the least bit concerned and said we didn't know how to have fun."

Miss Malone said that Miss Strongwood's behavior changed markedly after she met Michael Masterson. "It was Michael, Michael, Michael, all the time. It was all she could talk about and she said she would land him just like a big fish and then she would be rich and she wouldn't have to be around girls like us anymore."

Miss Malone added, "I have read what she wrote in the *Tribune*, and I doubt there is much truth in it. Addie is a very clever girl and very good with words, but we all knew that she would do anything to get what she wanted. You did not want to turn your back on her for a second. That is how all of us girls felt about her. We are all very sorry about what happened to poor Michael, as he was a very nice young man, and it is too bad that he got tied up with somebody like her."

FROM THE JOURNAL OF J. WINSTON PHELPS, JANUARY 13, 1904

Good news!—Malone girl who spouted off in Journal re Addie has vanished to points unknown—little chance Boardman will be able to find her before trial starts—Addie says girl is big liar anyway & made up everything she told the newspaper, etc.

EXCERPTS FROM THE CROSS-EXAMINATION OF MISS ADELAIDE STRONGWOOD, Mr. Boardman for the prosecution, January 28, 1904

Q: Now, as to the child, did you reveal to anyone that you were in a family way?

A: No. I saw no reason to make my situation known to the world.

Q: You didn't mention it to a girlfriend or some other confidant?

A: No.

Q: Did you consult with a physician?

A: I had no money to do so.

Q: And were you showing, to use the common term?

A: Not that I was aware of.

Q: So it was your secret?

A: Yes, until the secret could no longer be hidden.

Q: And you were reaching that point, weren't you, when you called Mrs. Cutter?

A: I never called her.

Q: Ah, I see. So it had to be someone impersonating you, correct?

A: I cannot say. I know only that Mrs. Cutter claims to have received a telephone call from someone using my name.

Q: Let me guess. I wager you will now tell us that it was all a lie. Just another lie directed at poor Addie Strongwood. Is that it?

[Objection, Mr. Phelps. Counsel is answering his own question. Sustained.]

Q: I withdraw the question. Let me ask you this: If, as you seem to suggest, Mrs. Cutter made up the story about someone named Addie Strongwood calling her, what earthly reason would she have had for doing so?

[Objection, Mr. Phelps. Calls for speculation. Conference before the bench. Overruled.]

COURT: The witness may answer the question.

A: I am sure I do not know, except that she perhaps owed a favor to the police.

Q: So the police put her up to it?

A: I do not think that impossible in light of what has happened in this city in recent years.

Q: Ah, there's a conspiracy, is that it? Mrs. Cutter, the police, all those people supposedly lying about what you've said and done. They are all plotting against you.

A: I do not recall ever saying such a thing, nor do I believe it. But if you think a poor girl such as myself is in an even fight when so much money and influence are directed against her, then you are not living in the world in which I live, Mr. Boardman.

Q: You have testified that your baby was lost due to a miscarriage just two days before Michael Masterson supposedly called you with the offer of a thousand-dollar settlement. Is that correct?

A: Yes.

Q: Interesting how the timing worked out, isn't it?

A: I do not know what you mean.

Q: Well, actually having to raise a baby, that would have been most inconvenient for you, would it not? But as you were expecting a plump payment from Michael, how much easier to simply rid yourself of that nettlesome child and then announce at some later time that you had suffered a miscarriage. That was your little game, wasn't it, Miss Strongwood?

A: I can scarcely imagine anything so diabolical, Mr. Boardman, and I most certainly did not "rid myself" of the child. That is a cruel lie.

Q: Is it? Tell me, where did this spontaneous miscarriage occur, Miss Strongwood?

A: In my room at Mrs. Jacobson's boardinghouse on Chicago Avenue.

Q: It must have been quite a frightening and painful experience, and yet you
called in no one to help. Why not?

A: I do not know who in such a situation could have been of help, and as I said,
it all happened very quickly.

Q: No aftereffects, no spasms, no loss of blood, just the baby suddenly gone. Is
that how you would describe what happened?

A: I could describe to you in much greater detail exactly what happened to me,
if that is your wish.

Q: You did not answer my question.

A: There was blood, Mr. Boardman. It was not a pleasant experience, as any
woman who has suffered such a fate could tell you.

————

Q: Let us talk about the telephone call you supposedly received from Michael
Masterson on November seventh. What time did you receive this call?

A: I believe it was late in the afternoon or perhaps early evening.

Q: I see. I call your attention to Prosecution Exhibit Seven, which includes an
article you wrote for the *Minneapolis Tribune* on December 19, 1903. In this
article, you state that you received the call from Michael "on the afternoon
of November seventh." Isn't that right?

A: Yes, that is what I said.

Q: But now you speak of "early evening" as possibly the time you received the
call. Which is it going to be, Miss Strongwood, afternoon or evening?

A: To be perfectly honest with you, Mr. Boardman, I am not certain. I initially
recalled it as being in the afternoon, but it is possible it was later.

Q: Ah, another of those little memory lapses you occasionally suffer from. Is
that it?

A: I make no claims to perfection.

Q: Let me show you now Prosecution Exhibit Thirteen, which is an affidavit
given by Miss Ellen Morse. You have seen this affidavit, have you not, in
which Miss Morse states that Michael Masterson could not have made a telephone call to you or anyone else on the afternoon of November seventh?

A: I have.

Q: And now, after being confronted with the inconvenient facts of this affidavit, you've found it necessary to change your story, haven't you?

A: No, I have not changed my story. I have simply admitted the possibility of error on my part. For the record, Mr. Boardman, despite what is contained in the affidavit, my best memory is that the call from Michael came sometime in the late afternoon. But as I said, I am willing to admit that I may be wrong.

Q: How generous of you. Nothing like some contradictory evidence to bring on claims of memory lapse, is there?

[Objection, Mr. Phelps. Argumentative. Overruled.]

A: I do not see it that way, Mr. Boardman. I can only state facts as I find them to the best of my recollection, and that is I what I am doing now.

Q: So Miss Morse must be lying then?

A: No, I am sure she is stating the situation as she remembers it. I am doing the same.

Q: Now, did you mention this alleged call from Mr. Masterson to anyone else?

A: No, not that I recall.

Q: So it's just your word again. Isn't it?

A: I can only tell you what I know, Mr. Boardman. Michael called me, just as I have said.

Q: And offered you one thousand dollars?

A: Yes.

Q: But you wanted more, didn't you?

A: I believed I was entitled to more in light of all that I endured at his hands.

Q: Ten thousand dollars, that's what you were asking for, wasn't it, to help raise the baby he supposedly had fathered? Oh, wait a minute. The baby suddenly was "gone," as you so delicately put it, but no matter. You still wanted that ten thousand dollars, didn't you?

A: No, that is not what I would have asked for if Michael had been willing to talk with me and come to a fair agreement.

Q: Ah, so your price would have come down, because you no longer had that baby?

A: That would have been a consideration, yes.

Q: How nice of you to offer a discount. And yet you have stated, have you not, that you never told Michael you were no longer with child?

A: That is correct. I did not tell him.

Q: You did not tell him. And the reason is obvious. You knew your little black-mail scheme might fall apart if Michael and his family discovered that there was no baby in need of support. The truth is, Michael never fathered your baby, just as he never raped you, just as he never made a promise to marry you. You lie and you lie and you lie, don't you, Miss Strongwood?

[Objection, Mr. Phelps. Badgering the witness, speculation , etc. Overruled.]

A: I have spoken the truth, Mr. Boardman. Michael was the prince of liars, not I.

———

Q: You also testified regarding a telephone call from a man who identified him-self as a lawyer named Charles Warren.

A: Yes.

Q: Did anyone happen to overhear this call?

A: Not that I am aware of.

Q: Did you tell anyone about the call?

A: No.

Q: Once again, it's just your word, isn't it, that there was such a call?

A: If you could find whoever purported to be Mr. Warren, he could confirm it.

Q: But, of course, we don't know the identity of this mysterious caller, do we?

A: I cannot speak for you, Mr. Boardman. All I can say is that I do not know who made the call.

Q: Now, after you supposedly received this call, you've testified, you went out and played Sherlock Holmes.[11] You marched right over to the library and checked for Mr. Warren's name in the city directory and couldn't find it, correct?

A: Yes.

Q: Convenient, isn't it, how you've constructed an elaborate story on the basis of a telephone call from a person who doesn't really exist? Hard to verify something like that, isn't it?

A: I cannot help that fact, Mr. Boardman. I can only tell you the full and com-plete truth as I know it.

———

11. Boardman, like everyone else in Minnesota who read the newspapers, would have known that Holmes and Dr. Watson were in Rochester at the time of the trial. It's not clear, however, whether Boardman knew of Holmes's visits to the courtroom or of his investigation into the photograph of Addie Strong-wood. But Boardman, at the least, must have suspected that Holmes had taken an interest in the case.

Q: And after this call from the nonexistent Mr. Warren, you nonetheless decided to go to the Windom Block to meet with a phantom. A strange thing to do, don't you agree?

A: No, I do not see it that way. I assumed Michael was somehow behind the call and I wanted to find out more so that I would not fall into another of his traps.

Q: And you took your derringer along, didn't you?

A: Yes.

Q: Did you have to load it first? Put in the two bullets?

A: I believe it was already loaded.

Q: Ready for action?

A: If need be, yes, but I did not think I would ever have to use it. I only wished to have some protection for myself.

Q: Isn't the real truth, Miss Strongwood, that it was Michael who needed protection from you?

A: No, I would not put it that way.

Q: But Michael is the one who's dead, isn't he?

A: Yes, and I will always regret that.

———

Q: I am struck, Miss Strongwood, by how little emotion you have displayed thus far in describing all of the allegedly horrific events that have occurred in your life over the past year. Hardly a tear shed, or a wounded look, or the slightest quivering in your voice. It is almost as if you have been telling us a story about someone else, or that you are acting a great role upon the stage.

A: I assure you, that is not the case.

Q: Most women, I should think, would show their feelings under such circumstances, but you are as cold as a rock, aren't you?

A: I am no rock, but I do not believe there is any benefit to be gained in this world by acting the part of a weak sister. If I were a man and were weeping here before you now, you would think me spineless, but you expect that as a woman I must do so in order to convince you of the depth of my feelings. Believe me, Mr. Boardman, I have shed more tears than you can ever hope to know, but in this ordeal I know I must be strong. I do not apologize for that.

Q: Oh, I doubt anyone would take you for a weak sister, Miss Strongwood. I doubt that very much.

STRONGWOOD

Excerpts from a letter from Sherlock Holmes to Shadwell Rafferty, January 31, 1904

The singular feature of the photograph is that it does not show Miss Strongwood's face, that portion of it having been torn away. Four questions immediately arise from this circumstance: Who removed her face from the photograph, when did this happen, why was it done, and what happened to the missing piece of the picture? The answers to these questions depend, in turn, on a determination as to when, under what conditions, and by what sort of camera the photograph was taken, notwithstanding Miss Strongwood's claims in this regard.

As you know, I have already determined what type of camera was used to take the revealing photograph of Miss Strongwood. Indeed, once I examined the photograph with the help of Mr. Phelps, I knew at once that it could only have been taken with a handy little device, made by the Magic Production Co.[12] of New York, that no good detective—including yours truly—should be without.

---

12. The Magic Production Company was a New York firm, apparently founded in the 1880s, that produced toys, optical novelties, an early cigarette lighter called the "magic pocket lamp," and, beginning in the 1890s, subminiature cameras.

SEVEN

PART SEVEN OF "AN ACCOUNT OF MY LIFE AND THE INCIDENT FOR WHICH I Have Been Unjustly Accused of Murder," by Addie Strongwood, *Minneapolis Tribune*, December 20, 1903

Today marks my twenty-second birthday, as well as the forty-first day of my confinement inside the bleak walls of the Hennepin County jail. How I wonder at the turn my life has taken and the awful circumstances that led to the charges brought against me! Had I the power to undo all that happened since I first met Michael Masterson, I would in an instant do so, and I would gladly substitute the quiet anonymity of my previous life for the storm of notoriety in which I now find myself enveloped. But as you know, dear readers, time stamps us all and the mark of it cannot be erased.

So it is that I must now turn to the final events of November 9, 1903. Almost everything that happened on that cold and wet night is now lodged in my memory like some obdurate stone impervious to erosion. As I left my room at Mrs. Jacobson's boardinghouse, bound for the offices of the man who claimed to be the lawyer Charles Warren, I knew that I must exercise the greatest caution so as not to fall prey to some new outrage. I was convinced—rightly, as it turned out—that the meeting to which I had been summoned had no legitimate purpose, and that Michael had set in motion some pernicious scheme by which I was to be silenced, perhaps for all eternity. Yet I went forward with faith in the Almighty and a firm belief that I was safe in His sheltering arms, for the Holy Book tell us, "The Lord knoweth the way of the righteous: but the way of the ungodly shall perish."

It was a few minutes before eight o'clock when I reached the Windom Block, a gloomy old place of commerce on Washington Avenue. Signs of all kinds bedecked the building's soot-stained walls, including one for a corner saloon that appeared to be well stocked with raucous customers. I walked down to the building's main entrance on Second Avenue and then into a small lobby paneled in dark wood. I studied the building directory, but as the phantom Warren had warned me, I saw no indication of a law firm among the tenants.

The building's sole elevator did not appear to be operating, so I climbed a narrow flight of stairs to the fourth floor, where I found a broad hallway, dimly lit by gas lamps. Office doors with frosted glass windows and transoms lined this dingy corridor, but as I stepped forward it soon became apparent that most of the tenants were gone for the day. I passed by the offices of a real estate company and an insurance broker, but neither gave evidence of lights burning within. At the far end of the hall, however, I saw an office—undoubtedly the one occupied by the mysterious Mr. Warren—that emitted a faint glow.

My heart was beating at a fearsome rate as I crept down the hallway toward the lighted office, which was number 413. Stenciled upon its door, in faint lettering, were the words "C. A. Pillsbury & Co." I knew that the immense flour milling concern must have long ago moved to larger and more elaborate quarters, but it seemed strange to me that no effort had been made to remove this antiquated lettering. Although Warren, or whoever he was, had told me to knock on the door, I in fact had no intention of going inside, for I was all but certain that a trap had been laid for me there. Instead, I looked for a place to secrete myself, and I soon found it—a janitor's closet a few steps down from the office door. I slipped into the closet, which was so small and so crowded with equipment that I was forced to stand with one foot balanced precariously on a bucket, and waited in the darkness, with the door slightly ajar so that I could peek out into the hallway.

My hope was that from this position I could overhear any conversation in the office, for I believed that Michael himself might be there, along with his accomplice, Warren. If I could learn of their plans, or so I believed, I might gain some useful leverage in my efforts to secure what was rightfully mine. And, of course, I might also be in a better position to save my own life should Michael or one of his minions make an attempt upon it. Such were my thoughts as I stood in that tiny closet, waiting to hear men speak of dark things.

At first, all was silence on the other side of the wall, save for the occasional creaking of floorboards, as though someone were pacing back and forth inside. After what seemed like an interminable wait, I heard the sound of a door being flung open from somewhere within the office, followed by rapid footsteps.

Then I heard, at last, voices. The thickness of the wall separating me from the office was such that I could make out only occasional words.

"She's late...what do you think?...how would I know?...maybe something scared her...damn it!...she's not coming...have to try again...all right...you know where to find me."

I could not identify the voices, but I thought there were two of them, and that both speakers were men. I knew at that moment that I had been right and that some awful fate would have been in store for me had I followed the instructions of the supposed lawyer Warren and gone into the office.

After several minutes, the voices stopped, and my expectation was that the men would leave, after which I could do the same. I heard the office door open and peered out from my hiding place, hoping to see both men depart. Instead, I saw only one man, whom I did not recognize, step out into the hallway. He was large and rumpled and wore a brown suit. Pausing for a moment to light a cigar, he reached into his pocket for a match, and as he did so I saw the ivory handle of a pistol tucked into the waistband of his trousers. The man, whose face was stony and cruel, suddenly turned to look in my direction, and for an instant I feared that he saw me. I felt suddenly faint, as though foreseeing my own death. But just as I thought I might involuntarily cry out in fright, the man, whom I now know to have been the notorious hoodlum Joe Mugliano, turned away and walked off down the hallway toward the stairs. Only when I heard his descending footsteps did I allow myself to breathe.

Yet I knew that one more man, possibly Michael himself, remained in the office, and I considered what to do next. I thought it best to wait, assuming that the second man would leave momentarily. I waited and I waited and I waited, for what felt like an agonizing eternity, all the while growing ever more uncomfortable in my cramped quarters because my left foot, which rested upon the bucket, had begun to go numb. Fearing I might tumble over unless I found a better position, I lifted my foot off the bucket, only to lose my balance. I inadvertently leaned against a mop that had been stored inside the bucket, and before I could grab it, the mop fell out, knocking over the bucket as it did so. All of this bumbling created such a racket that I knew the occupant of the office would hear it.

Seeing no choice now but to flee, I ran from the closet just as the office door flung open. Michael!

"My God!" he shouted. "You little sneak!"

I tried to go around, but he grabbed my arm and pulled me toward him.

"Let me go, let me go!" I screamed, praying that someone might hear my cry for help. No one did.

"Quiet," he hissed, "or I will cut your pretty little throat," and it was only then that I realized he held a small knife to my neck. "I mean it. One false move and you are done for. Do not make another sound."

I knew he was as good as his word. "All right," I said. "I will be quiet."

With the knife still at my throat, he pulled me into the office and shut the door. The office was empty save for a desk, a chair, and a stool. A single gas jet provided what feeble light there was.

Michael dragged me over to the desk, where there was a sheet of fine linen paper and a fountain pen. He forced me to sit in the chair, the knife still pressed against my flesh, promising instant death.

"Now then, since you have been so good as to appear after all, let me show you something," he said, reaching into his coat pocket. He then laid before me the photograph of a naked woman, but with the portion showing her face torn away.

"Quite fetching, isn't she?" he sneered. "I imagine you recognize her all too well."

Only then did I realize, to my utmost shock, that I was the woman in the picture! I immediately surmised that Michael must have taken the photograph while I lay drugged and unconscious in his apartment.

Michael saw the appalled look on my face. "Ah, so now you see where the situation stands. I tore your ugly face off because I was tired of looking at it, but I can always put it back. Imagine, Addie, what the world will think of you once they see what a little whore you are."

"You are despicable," I said.

"Careful, my dear, careful," he said, pressing the knife more firmly against my neck. "You must speak kindly of me or there will be consequences. Now, take notice of the pen and paper on the desk. They are there for a reason. It is time for you to write a letter."

"What do you mean?" I asked.

"You are going to absolve me of any responsibility of fathering your child, if in fact you actually have one, and you are also going to state that you have no monetary claims against me or my family."

"Or you will blackmail me with the photograph, is that it?"

"Perhaps. Or maybe, Addie, if you don't cooperate, I will just have to kill you right here and now. How would you like that?"

I cannot say how under such desperate circumstances I was able to retain some measure of reason. Michael sounded quite mad, and I knew I dared not feed that madness by arguing. I said, "Very well, I will do as you wish. But tell me this: If I prepare this document and sign it as you have asked, can you assure me that you will do me no further harm?"

"Why, of course, my dear Addie. You will be able to prove nothing against me, and we shall at last be done with one another. It is all very simple. Now, start writing:

'I, Addie Strongwood, do hereby declare of my own free will the following…'"

I began to write, but after I had put down my name, I felt a surge of fear run down my spine with the force of an electrical charge. I sensed that no matter what I did, I was in mortal danger. "If this is all to end as you say," I asked, "then why did you hire a thug with a pistol in his waistband to ambush me here?"

"You ask too many questions. Just keep on writing like a good girl."

Now came the elemental moment—life or death. Michael had lied to me a hundred times before and I knew he was lying now. I would write what he asked, he would backdate it to prove I had given up any claims against him, and then he would kill me, my demise to be a mystery without a solution. It would be said no one knew why I had gone to a vacant office in the Windom Block. Perhaps it was an assignation or a meeting with some criminal confederate. No matter. There had been an argument and my throat had been slit. The police would investigate for a day or two, the usual suspects would be assembled in most perfunctory fashion, and that would be the end of it, for it would be assumed that the greedy blackmailer had simply gotten her just deserts at the hands of some unknown killer. And if necessary, plenty of money could be spread around like manure to fertilize the big lie.

How could I allow my life to end in such a horrible and unjust way without at least putting up a fight? I determined at that moment that if I were indeed to die, I would at least do so with something like a soldier's courage.

"Quit stalling," Michael said, reaching over my shoulder to grab my hand. As he did so, I braced my legs against the base of the desk and pushed back with all of my strength. The chair moved swiftly on its casters, and as I thrust myself back, I knocked Michael to one side. Then I felt the chair tip over, even as I was reaching in the pocket of my coat for the gun I had taken with me. By the time I fell to the floor, the gun was in my hand, and I turned to face Michael, who had stumbled back to his feet.

"Come no closer," I said. "I will shoot you if I must."

I will never forget the look on Michael's face, which expressed a fury so deep and ungovernable that it might have been that of the Great Satan himself at the moment of his exile from heaven.

"You stupid little wench," he said. "Do you even know how to use that thing?"

I lifted myself back onto my feet. "You must leave right now," I said, "for your own sake as well as mine."

Michael still held the knife, but to my surprise he slowly folded it up and put it back into his jacket pocket. "I won't need this," he said, all the while staring at me with a look of fierce and unyielding hatred. "I will hurt you before I kill you."

Then it ended, so quickly that I can barely make sense of what happened. He lunged toward me, his hands reaching for my neck to squeeze the last breath of life from me. Stepping back, I fired both barrels of my derringer. I saw a red stain bloom on his chest and he fell forward on the floor. He did not move after that.

"Oh, Michael!" I cried. "What have you done?"

All of the emotion that had been building in me like steam in a boiler now burst forth. I dropped the gun, fell to my knees, and began sobbing uncontrollably. I cannot say how long I wept, for time seemed to have ended. I soon regained my senses, however, and realized that I must seek help for Michael in the hope that his life might be saved. Still consumed with grief and horror, I rushed to the door. But as I started to open it, I saw, to my dismay, a man standing at the far end of the hallway, and I felt a sudden surge of panic. Had Michael brought along a second accomplice? I quickly shut the door, fearing that I might yet be murdered.

Of course, I now know that it was Mr. Wangstad, the elevator repairman, who stood in the hallway, but I did not know it then. I waited for several long minutes in the office, terrified as to what might happen next. It was only when I heard a policeman announcing his presence that I felt safe at last. I immediately went out into the hallway and told the officer that I had shot Michael and that

I feared he was dead. After that came long hours of interrogation before I was taken away.

Since that night at the Windom Block, I have spent all of my days and nights in the Hennepin County jail, ever hopeful that in the end I will see the pure flame of justice shine as bright as the sun before my eyes. During my long incarceration, I have been reading, in addition to the Holy Bible that is my most comforting companion, one of Mr. Dickens's great epics, the book called *Bleak House*. As I have followed the windings of its plot through the vast maze of the English legal system, I have wondered what my own fate will be in the courts of Hennepin County, Minnesota. I can make no prediction, for like Esther Summerson, the heroine of *Bleak House*, I am prostrate before the law and its intricate workings. Even so, I can promise you, dear readers, that when my day comes before the tribunal, I will speak the whole truth and nothing but the truth and I will speak it without hesitation or apology. In the meantime, I await my hour of judgment with a calm and patient heart.

EXCERPTS FROM AN ARTICLE IN THE *MINNEAPOLIS TIMES*, JANUARY 27, 1904

The final chapter in what has been one of the most riveting spectacles in the history of the courts here will begin today as Miss Adelaide Strongwood, charged with the murder of Michael Masterson, takes the witness stand in her own defense.

People began lining up before dawn on Fourth Street outside the new courthouse in hope of securing a seat to hear Miss Strongwood's testimony, which is likely to include many intimate details of her relationship with Masterson, her one-time beau.

One woman, who arrived at three o'clock in the morning and was second in line, sold her place a few hours later to a local society matron for the sum of $10, and it is reliably reported that similar transactions occurred as the line swelled to several hundred people.

The trial, which began Jan. 11, has already played to a full house every day in the large courtroom on the third floor of the courthouse, which seats about 100 spectators.

J. Winston Phelps, Miss Strongwood's attorney, stated to the *Times* yesterday that his client is "fully prepared to testify" and that she is "remarkably free of nervous anticipation." He added, "She is an extraordinary girl, and she is eager to give a true and correct account of what happened between her and Mr. Masterson. I believe the jury will have no doubt as to her innocence once they hear her story."

It is expected Miss Strongwood's direct testimony will take up all of today's court session and extend into tomorrow morning, after which Prosecutor Frederick Boardman will conduct what is likely to be a vigorous and challenging cross-examination.

Boardman would not comment regarding his line of attack other than to say he will "certainly have a few questions" for Miss Strongwood, who has claimed she killed Masterson in self-defense. Boardman, however, has thus far attempted to depict her not as a violated woman, as Miss Strongwood contends, but as scheming blackmailer who murdered Masterson, scion of an industrial fortune, in cold blood.

EXCERPTS FROM THE DIRECT TESTIMONY OF MISS ADELAIDE STRONGWOOD, Mr. Phelps for the defense, January 28, 1904

———

Q: I am sure, Addie, that some people will wonder why you went to the Windom Block at eight o'clock on a Monday night even though you knew the person you were supposed to meet, who claimed to be a lawyer by the name of Charles Warren, was in fact not that person. Indeed, you yourself have stated in the last of the articles you wrote for the *Tribune* that you believed you might be walking into a trap. Why then did you go?

A: For the simple reason that I saw no other way to fully comprehend, and thereby perhaps foil the plot against me. You must understand that given what I knew of Michael, his hatred for me and his violent temperament, that I was very much in fear of my life. Indeed, I believed that the man waiting for me in the Windom Block was in all likelihood a paid assassin, and that is why I took the gun with me. But if I hadn't gone to the Windom Block that night, then what? Was I simply to sit and wait for the assassin to break into my room one night and kill me, or spring out from a dark alley as I walked home and shoot me down? Fear is what sent me to the Windom Block, not any desire to confront Michael.

Q: You hoped you could learn something, in other words, perhaps even the identity of the assassin?

A: Exactly. That is why I hid in the closet and listened so intently to what was said in room four thirteen. Knowledge, as the philosopher tells us, is power, and I hoped that by learning more about what was being plotted against me I might ultimately have the power to stop it.

Q: All right, tell the jury, if you would, exactly what you heard.

Q: Now, after the conversation stopped, you assumed that the men you had heard would leave. Is that correct?

A: Yes. It was obvious that they were not the real occupants of the office and that they were simply using it as a place where they could meet in secret.

Q: And perhaps murder you?

A: That is what I believed.

Q: But only one of the men left immediately, as it turned out. Who was that man?

A: Joseph Mugliano.

Q: The same man you saw testify here Tuesday?

A: Yes, the same man.

EXCERPTS FROM THE DIRECT TESTIMONY OF MR. JOSEPH MUGLIANO,[1] MR. Boardman for the prosecution, January 26, 1904

Q: Mr. Mugliano, do you know a man named Frank Kendall?

A: Yes, I have met him a few times.

Q: Did you ever do any work for him?

---

1. *The Trial of Adelaide Strongwood* described Mugliano as "a burly, hot-tempered man whose criminal nature was quite apparent to all....Although he repeatedly denied playing any role in the case, his bellicose demeanor, shifty eyes and crude manner did not leave a good impression with the jury."

A: Well, he was having some trouble with grifters at his place and I helped him out a few times.

Q: How exactly did you help him?

A: Threw the bums out.

Q: Did you do so in a violent manner.

A: Naw, I don't work that way. I just told them that Frank ran an honest joint and they weren't welcome. They got the message.

Q: Now, turning your attention to November seventh of last year, did Mr. Kendall contact you in connection with a matter regarding the defendant in this case, Miss Adelaide Strongwood?

A: Yeah, he said he knew a fellow who had a girl hitting him up for money and she was getting kind of crazy. He said this fellow wanted somebody to be with him when he met with her.

Q: To intervene in case there was trouble?

A: That's right.

Q: Who was this "fellow," as you call him?

A: Michael Masterson. That's who Frank told me it was.

Q: Had you ever met Mr. Masterson before?

A: No, never heard of him.

Q: And did Mr. Kendall also tell you the name of the girl involved?

A: Yeah, it was Addie Strongwood.

Q: Had you ever met her before?

A: Nope.

Q: All right, what else did Mr. Kendall tell you?

A: He said this Masterson fellow was going to meet the girl Monday night and that he would pay me ten dollars to be there just in case.

Q: That would be Monday, November ninth, is that correct?

A: Yeah.

Q: Did you accept the offer?

A: Sure. It looked like an easy ten bucks.

Q: At any point during your conversation with Mr. Kendall did he tell you that your job was to murder Miss Strongwood?

A: Who told you that? It's ridiculous. I don't go around killing people.

Q: You're not a paid assassin?

A: That's a crazy idea if I ever heard one. I would never do a thing like that.

————

Q: Now, on November ninth did you go the Windom Block here in downtown Minneapolis sometime before eight o'clock to meet with Michael Masterson?

A: Yeah, I got there about seven thirty and went up to room four thirteen. That's where Frank told me to meet him.

Q: And was Mr. Masterson there?

A: He was.

Q: Describe your meeting with him, if you would.

A: Well, he just shook my hand and said he was glad I was there because he was very worried about this girl.

Q: Did he look worried to you?

[Objection, Mr. Phelps. Calls for speculation. Overruled.]

A: He was kind of jumpy, I guess you could say.

Q: Did Mr. Masterson say why he was worried?

A: No. All he said was that I was to keep an eye on the girl in case she tried something. He said I should put the fear of God in her if that is what it took.

Q: Very well. Now, let me ask you this: In all the time you were with Mr. Masterson, did he ever say he wished to have Miss Strongwood killed or harmed in any way?

A: Are you kidding? It was more like he thought she might kill him.

[Objection, Mr. Phelps. Speculation. Conference before the bench. Sustained.]

————

Q: Now, what instructions did Mr. Masterson give you?

A: He told me to wait in the office until the girl arrived. When she did, I was to tell her that I was a friend of his and was just making sure everything was on the up-and-up.

Q: And where was Mr. Masterson going to be?

A: He was waiting in an office next door that connected to the one we were in. As soon as I gave him the all clear, he said he'd come in and talk to the girl.

Q: By the way, did Mr. Masterson tell you that you were to pose as a man named Charles Warren?

A: No, he didn't say nothing like that.

Q: So you didn't call Miss Strongwood, using that name, and arrange to meet her at the Windom Block?

A: No, I never called her.

Q: Did Mr. Masterson say why the Windom Block had been chosen as the place for his meeting with Miss Strongwood?

A: I got the impression she wanted to meet him there.

[Objection, Mr. Phelps. Vague, speculation, etc. Sustained.]

———

Q: How long did you wait for Miss Strongwood to arrive?

A: It was close to nine o'clock.

Q: But you never saw her?

A: Nope.

Q: Never heard anyone approach the office?

A: I didn't hear nothing.

Q: Did you talk with Mr. Masterson while you were waiting?

A: Not that I remember. He was in the other room. I just sat there.

Q: What happened at around nine o'clock?

A: Mr. Masterson came into the office. He gave me the ten dollars he owed me and said I might as well go.

Q: When was this?

A: Couldn't have been much after nine.

Q: Did Mr. Masterson leave with you?

A: No. He said he had some things to think about.

Q: Did he say what he wished to "think about," as you have put it?

A: He didn't tell me and I didn't ask. None of my business.

Q: Did he say anything else before you left?

A: Just that he might call me again to help him out because he figured the girl was up to something now that she'd skipped the meeting.

Q: That was all he said?

A: Yeah, that was it.

Q: And then you left?

A: Right. Like I said, it was an easy ten bucks.

———

Q: Do you own a pearl-handled pistol, Mr. Mugliano?

A: I don't fool around with guns. They're too dangerous.

Q: So you didn't have one with you on the night of November ninth at the Windom Block?

A: Not a chance.

———

FROM THE JOURNAL OF J. WINSTON PHELPS, JANUARY 25, 1904

———

Looks as tho Muggy, aka Joe Mugliano, will testify tomorrow—will lie of course as people of his ilk always do—my job will be to pound at him as best I can—dont think jury will find him convincing as he looks like a cheap thug but who can say?—been at this business too long to think anybody can ever make sense of a jury.

———

EXCERPTS FROM THE CROSS-EXAMINATION OF MR. JOSEPH MUGLIANO, MR. Phelps for the defense, January 26, 1904

———

Q: Would it be fair to say, Mr. Mugliano, that you are a professional hoodlum?

A: No. I work just like everybody else.

Q: Ah, that's right. You run a tippling house, as I recall.

A: So the cops say, but it ain't true.

Q: What is your line of work then? Surgery? The teaching of mathematics at one of our local colleges? Or are you a captain of industry?

[Objection, Mr. Boardman. Mocking the witness. Sustained.]

Q: Again, what is your line of work?

A: I'm a barber.

Q: I see. But you do other types of work, do you not?

A: I tend bar sometimes, do odd jobs, that sort of thing.

Q: What sort of odd jobs?

A: Helping people out with this and that.

Q: How admirably imprecise of you. I presume you do these odd jobs in your spare time, while you're not busy reading poetry or tending to your flower garden. Come now, Mr. Mugliano, isn't it a fact you're a thug for hire, a strong-arm man?

A: I resent that.

Q: Well, sir, pardon me if I have upset your delicate sensibilities. I have here Defense Exhibit Nine, which is the arrest record of one Joseph Mugliano as dutifully maintained by the police of St. Paul. My, my, my, Mr. Mugliano, this document would suggest you have not been an entirely upstanding citizen. Let's see. Suspicion of armed robbery. Assault with a dangerous weapon. Frequenting a bawdy house. Loitering with intent. My goodness, sir, I count fourteen different charges in all.

A: All lies. The coppers have it out for me because I won't play their game.

Q: You are, in other words, a victim of one injustice after another. Is that what you're telling us?

A: I've got nothing more to say about it.

Q: Spoken like a true gentleman. So you are not, despite all of your unhappy interactions with the police, the sort of man who might be hired, say, to kill someone?

A: That is a god———ed lie and you know it.

COURT: Mr. Mugliano, you will refrain from using such language in this courtroom.

WITNESS: Sorry.

Q: Would it also be a lie to state that, in addition to all of your difficulties across the river, you were convicted of manslaughter back in 1895, here in Hennepin County? You killed a man with a knife in a saloon over on University Avenue Northeast, isn't that right?

A: It was self-defense.

Q: I see. The courts were mistaken, then, in sentencing you to more than six years in prison?

A: It was not a fair shake. That's all I'll say.

———

Q: Now, you have told a nice tale of how you were hired to guard poor Michael Masterson, who claimed to be in fear of Miss Strongwood. Had you ever done work like this before?

A: Not that I recall.

Q: And apparently it didn't seem at all odd to you that you were being asked to go to a vacant, dimly lit office, meet a man there you did not know, and then supposedly protect him from a small woman who was threatening him in some vague and unspecified manner? Just business as usual for a bruiser such as yourself. Is that what you are telling us?

A: It wasn't the usual sort of thing, but like I said, it looked like easy money to me, so why not? That's how I saw it.

———

Q: I show you now Defense Exhibit Ten. Would you take a look at it?

A: All right.

Q: What is written on this scrap of paper?

A: I'm not sure. I don't read so good.

Q: Well then, let me read it for you: It says, "Muggy, Thomas Western, 1 a.m. Tuesday, red barrel." Now, you are sometimes called Muggy, are you not?

A: Yeah. Is there something wrong with that?

Q: Nothing wrong at all. It is a most colorful appellation. And is it also true that you live in a house at the corner of Thomas and Western Avenues in St. Paul?

A: Yeah, I live there.

Q: And, if I am not mistaken, since I had someone take a look the other day, there is a rusted red barrel in the backyard of your domicile. Is that correct?

A: There could be.

Q: Well, then, this is quite a little mystery, isn't it? Why would Michael Masterson, a young gentleman from one of the wealthiest families in Minneapolis, carry a slip of paper in his pocket indicating that he was to make note of a red barrel in the backyard of your house in St. Paul at one o'clock in the morning?

A: Couldn't say.

Q: Not even the merest hint of any idea?

A: Nope.

Q: Do you suppose this note might have been instructions as to where to and when to drop something off?

A: How would I know?

Q: Well, since the barrel is behind your home, who better to know than you, Mr. Mugliano? In point of fact, didn't you instruct Mr. Masterson to place some money in that barrel at the appointed hour, money you were to receive for killing Addie?

A: That's the stupidest thing I ever heard.

Q: Really? So the mere suggestion that a convicted killer such as yourself might be paid to kill again, why that is complete nonsense. Is that what you are saying?

A: I wasn't hired to kill nobody and all I ever got from Masterson was ten dollars, just like I said.

———————

Q: In your direct testimony, you stated that you had the "impression" that Addie arranged for the meeting at the Windom Block. Is that right?

A: Yeah, that's what I said.

Q: What gave you this "impression," as you call it?

A: I don't know. Maybe it was something that Masterson fellow said. I really can't remember.

Q: Of course you can't, because in point of fact Mr. Masterson never said any such thing, did he? You and your friend Kendall conspired to set up the meeting. Isn't that right? Tell me, which one of you played the role of Charles Warren, the nonexistent lawyer? Was it you, Mr. Mugliano, or your pal, Mr. Kendall?

A: You're not making any sense. I didn't set up nothing.

———————

Q: Now, when you met Mr. Masterson in the Windom Block, he simply confirmed the bizarre arrangement to which you've testified. Is that correct?

A: What do you mean by that?

Q: Let me put it this way: Your job was simply to watch Addie in case she tried something and maybe even put the fear of God in her. Is that right?

A: That's what he said.

Q: What did he say you were to do if she did indeed "try something," as you've so eloquently put it? Wrestle her to the ground? Knock her out with a punch? Poke her in the eye? Slit her throat? What was your strategy to be, Mr. Mugliano, when it came to putting the fear of God in Addie?

A: You're crazy saying things like that.

Q: Am I? Well, you weren't there just to be a passive observer, were you? Men of your kind are brought into a situation to be physically intimidating, isn't that right?

A: Like I said, he just wanted me to be there in case there was trouble.

Q: I see. Maybe just slap some sense into her?

A: I don't go around slapping people.

Q: Murdering them with a knife, maybe, but no slapping. Is that it?

[Objection, Mr. Boardman. Argumentative. Sustained.]

Q: And all of your fine services were to be had for a mere ten dollars?

A: That's a lot of money to me.

Q: But not nearly as much as you really hoped to earn for your night's work. Is it? Come now, Mr. Mugliano, let's drop this ridiculous story you've been telling us and talk about what really happened in the Windom Block. The truth is, you went there on the night of November ninth, with a gun in your waistband, for the purpose of murdering Addie Strongwood, an assassination ordered and paid for by Michael Masterson and his go-between, Frank Kendall. Isn't that what really happened?

A: No, it ain't.

Q: And you would have shot her down without so much as a second thought, wouldn't you, just like you killed that man eight years ago.

A: That's a lie.

Q: What did Mr. Masterson pay you? A hundred dollars? Five hundred? A thousand? How much was he going to leave in that barrel? What was your price for cold-blooded murder?

A: You don't know what you're talking about.

Q: I know a liar and a hired gunman when I see one.

[Objection, Mr. Boardman. Defense counsel is testifying. Sustained.]

Q: No further questions at this time.

———

Q: Addie, we have now gone over all the details of the night of November ninth, leading to the moment when you shot Michael Masterson. We have seen how you were lured to a vacant office, how you overheard two men talking there, how you tried to escape but were then cornered by Mr. Masterson at the point of a knife, how he threatened to blackmail you with the photograph he'd surreptitiously taken, and how he finally forced you to begin writing a recantation of your all-too-valid claims against him. As you sat at that desk, Addie, in that lonely office where no one could hear your screams or come to your aid, did you believe Michael Masterson intended not only to blackmail you but to kill you as well?

A: I did, with all my heart.

Q: And that was when you decided upon a desperate expedient?

A: Yes.

Q: You braced you legs against the desk.

A: Yes.

Q: You pushed back with every ounce of strength in your body.

A: Yes.

Q: You temporarily freed yourself from his death grip.

A: Yes.

Q: You fell to the floor as the chair tipped over.

A: Yes.

Q: You reached for the derringer in the pocket of your coat, the gun you knew was your only defense against the cruel and remorseless man who intended to kill you.

A: Yes.

Q: You got back up on your feet.

A: Yes.

Q: You aimed the gun at Michael, who was also back on his feet and standing just a few feet from you.

A: Yes.

Q: But at that moment, you didn't fire the gun in your hand, did you?

A: No.

Q: You were terribly frightened, weren't you?

A: More frightened than I had ever been in my life.

Q: But you did not fire the gun. You did not fire the gun. Why not, Addie? Why did you not at that instant, having endured all of the violence and evil that Michael had inflicted upon you, why in God's name did you not fire your gun?

A: Because I did not wish to kill Michael. I only wished to stop him from killing me.

Q: So you told him to leave, didn't you?

A: Yes. I all but pleaded with him to do so for his own sake.

Q: And what was his response?

A: It was the most horrible thing I have ever seen. He folded up the knife he was holding and put it, very slowly, into his pocket, all the while staring at me with a look of such burning malevolence that I could almost feel the heat of it on my face. Then he said, "I will hurt you before I kill you." Were more terrible words ever spoken? My heart at that moment all but failed me.

Q: And then what happened?

A: He gave out a wild cry and lunged at me, like some beast of the jungle about to devour its prey.

Q: And you fired your gun?

A: Yes, but I was hardly conscious of doing it.

Q: You fired both barrels?

A: Yes, I must have.

Q: And one shot struck Michael in the heart?

A: Yes.

Q: Did you aim for his heart?

A: I aimed not at all. There was a beast about to kill me. I simply fired in hopes of stopping it. How I wish Michael had left as I begged him to do. It is all so sad. None of this had to happen.

———

Q: Now, when the police arrived, did you tell them the full truth of what happened?

A: Yes.

Q: You didn't deny that you had shot Michael?

A: It was the truth. I could not deny it.

Q: You told them from the very start that you had acted in self-defense, didn't you?

A: Yes.

Q: Your story hasn't changed in any significant respect since that time, has it?

A: No. I have always told the truth as best I can remember it.

Q: And you have told the truth here today?

A: Yes. I believe that the truth is the most powerful thing in the world.

Q: No further questions, Your Honor.

A LETTER[2] FROM MINNEAPOLIS POLICE INSPECTOR ROBERT McCALL TO Frederick Boardman, November 27, 1903

Dear Mr. Boardman:

I have been asked to apprise you of the possibility of obtaining a confession from Miss Adelaide Strongwood, who is now charged with the first-degree murder of Michael Masterson on November 9 of this year. It is my understanding that you have offered to allow her to plead to a lesser charge of second-degree murder in Mr. Masterson's death provided that she admits to her crime.

I have spent more than twenty hours interviewing this girl and have used every means at my disposal to trip her up and find some way to force her into confessing her guilt. Insp. Donald Gordon, who as you know is an especially skilled interrogator, has assisted in many of these interviews, most of which have been without her lawyer present.

I can only tell you this: Miss Strongwood is surely the cleverest girl I have ever come across and it is all but impossible to back her into a corner. She possesses an iron will and appears to have no fear of the police or of anyone else for that matter. I do not think she will admit to her crime under any circumstances, no matter how much pressure is applied, and I am given to believe by everything she says that she intends to go to court and try to win her freedom there.

Of course, I wish I could give you better news, but I must be honest. You will be in for a time of it with her. Naturally, we will provide you with all of the incriminating evidence that we can, but I would not hold out any hope that

---

2. A mimeographed copy of this letter was found in the papers of J. Winston Phelps. It is possible the letter was turned over to Phelps as part of the prosecution's evidence in the case. It is also possible that Phelps, who apparently had a source in Boardman's office, obtained the letter by extralegal means.

she will ever confess to wrongdoing in this matter and so be willing to enter a guilty plea.

Sincerely,
Robert McCall

FROM THE JOURNAL OF J. WINSTON PHELPS, JANUARY 28, 1904

————

Curious what Boardman will have to say about naked photo of Addie—no doubt he doesnt believe her version of how it came to be torn—not sure I do either—Holmes has doubts too from what Shad tells me—Boardman will also harp on phone call Addie got from mysterious Charles Warren (sure it was really Kendall) & try to prove she made it up—he went after telephone records but there was some problem (our lucky day!)—so as usual will come down to Addie & her word—pray the jury will take her side.

————

EXCERPTS FROM THE CROSS-EXAMINATION OF MISS ADELAIDE STRONGWOOD, Mr. Boardman for the prosecution, January 29, 1904

————

Q: So, let me see if I have your story straight. You are convinced that the evil, scheming Michael Masterson has set in motion an intricate plan to lure you to a vacant office in the dark of night and murder you in cold blood because you want ten thousand dollars from him to raise a child no one knows about except you. Yet even though you believe death awaits you, plucky girl that you are, you go to the Windom Block anyway, a loaded derringer in your coat pocket, and hide in a janitor's closet while Michael and his henchman plot your demise. Ah, but the henchman departs, leaving you to face Michael alone. And only after he springs at you like a beast do you most reluctantly take out your derringer and, no doubt with your eyes closed, fire at him and, by the grace of God, manage to put a bullet right through his heart.

[Objection, Mr. Phelps. The prosecutor has not asked a question.]

COURT: Please get on with it, if you would, Mr. Boardman.

Q: Sounds like a tale right out of a cheap novel, doesn't it, Miss Strongwood? And it sounds that way because it is in fact all a work of fiction. Isn't it?

A: No, it is the truth.

Q: Do you really expect us to believe that?

[Objection, Mr. Phelps. Argumentative. Sustained.]

———

Q: All right, let's take a closer look at your story, Miss Strongwood. You say you were lured to the Windom Block by Mr. Masterson. In fact, wasn't it the other way around? It was you who importuned Mr. Masterson, who insisted on a meeting. He came to that vacant office because you told him to. Isn't that right?

A: I did no such thing.

Q: Is that so? Tell me, before November ninth of this year, had you ever been in the Windom Block?

A: It is possible, I suppose. I have been in quite a few downtown buildings looking for work and the like.

Q: But you don't specifically remember being in the Windom Block?

A: As I said, it is possible.

Q: But surely you must remember one way or the other. It is quite a distinctive building, is it not?

A: I do not generally notice such things.

Q: Miss Strongwood, I am inclined to think that there is very little you fail to notice. Let me show this affidavit, just obtained this morning, from a Miss Emily Litton of the Robertson Secretarial Agency in room four ten of the Windom Block. It states—

[Objection, Mr. Phelps. Document not admitted into evidence, "blindsiding" defense, etc. Conference before the bench. Court adjourned for one hour, then reconvened.]

COURT: An affidavit by Miss Emily Litton of the Robertson Secretarial Agency has been offered as evidence in this case. The affidavit has been accepted by the court and will hereafter be admitted into evidence as Prosecution Exhibit Eighteen. Miss Litton is not able to testify in person because of illness. Since the affidavit has been submitted at such a late stage in these proceedings, I have ruled that Mr. Phelps will be given the opportunity to conduct a redirect examination of his client on the topic of the affidavit. You may proceed, Mr. Boardman.

Q: Thank you. Miss Strongwood, please read the affidavit in question to the jury.

A: As you wish. "I, Emily Litton, being of full age and sound mind, upon her oath hereby deposes: I am a clerk for the Robertson Secretarial Agency, with offices in suite number four ten of the Windom Block in the city of Minneapolis, Minnesota. On or about October second, 1903, a woman identifying herself to me as Adelaide Strongwood entered the offices of the Robertson Secretarial Agency and made inquiries regarding possible employment. I instructed her to fill out a form giving her full particulars as well as the specific type of employment she was seeking. She filled out the appropriate form, after which I told her that we would notify her if any suitable positions became available. Miss Strongwood then left the office. Further the affiant sayeth not."

Q: So you were on the fourth floor of the Windom Block well before November ninth, weren't you?

A: I can hardly deny it in view of this affidavit.

Q: No, you hardly can. Now, you stated in your account in the *Tribune* that you passed two offices on your way to room four thirteen in the Windom Block on the night of November ninth. Yet in your account you somehow failed to mention that you had also gone by the large and prominent offices of the Robertson Secretarial Agency, which you had visited barely a month before. You also neglected to make note of this salient fact in your direct testimony yesterday, didn't you?

A: You are correct, Mr. Boardman. I did not mention it.

Q: A mere oversight on your part? Another lapse in your otherwise flawless memory?

A: I will be honest. I cannot account for it. I do indeed pride myself on possessing a good memory, but in this instance it failed me. I can only surmise that such was my state of mind on that night that I could only think of what awaited me in room four thirteen and nothing else, and so I passed by the secretarial agency, saw the name on the door, and yet it somehow failed to register in my memory as it normally would. In my defense, I will state that once I was thrown out of work by the Masterson family, I made visits to innumerable offices here in Minneapolis in search of work and I cannot remember all of them.

Q: Bravo, Miss Strongwood, bravo. How fluently you have tried to cover up your mistake.

[Objection, Mr. Phelps. Mocking the witness, offering an opinion, immaterial, etc. Sustained.]

Q: But the fact of the matter, Miss Strongwood, is that you cannot disguise the truth, despite your avowals of undying devotion to it. The real truth is that you were very familiar with the fourth floor of the Windom Block and that you knew it would be vacant that night. You therefore decided it would be an ideal place to confront Michael in private and demand that he pay your ransom. You lured poor Michael into your den, didn't you, and then you killed him because he would not pay up?

A: There is not a single shred of truth in anything you have said, Mr. Boardman. As I have stated, I received a telephone call instructing me to go to the Windom Block. I did not set a trap. The trap was set for me.

Q: Ah, yes, let us talk for a minute about that telephone call you supposedly received from someone named Charles Warren. When exactly did you get the call?

A: It was on November eighth.

Q: What time?

A: In the evening, I believe.

Q: Five o'clock? Six o'clock? Ten o'clock?

A: It was after supper, which is at six o'clock, but certainly before ten. I am in bed by then.

Q: And this call came to you at your rooming house at 2701 Chicago Avenue South, is that right?

A: Yes.

Q: How many telephones are there in the house?

A: Only one that I know of.

Q: Where is it located?

A: In the main hall, downstairs.

Q: Who customarily answers the phone?

A: Usually, it is Mrs. Jacobson.

Q: The woman who runs the boardinghouse?

A: Yes.

Q: Now, you heard Mrs. Jacobson's earlier testimony, did you not?[3]

A: Yes.

Q: She stated that she was there that evening and that there was no phone call for you, didn't she?

A: Yes, that is what she said, but she was wrong. Mrs. Jacobson is a dear woman who has been very kind to me, but I have found on occasion that her memory is not as sharp as it might be.

Q: Ah, I see. Just another in the long list of people whose memory of events seems to diverge from your own. The fact is, there was no call, was there?

A: There most certainly was.

Q: Only because you say there was. Where is the proof of it?

A: I had no idea, Mr. Boardman, that I would be required to prove its existence. How could I have done so?

Q: Did you mention the call to anyone?

A: I do not believe so.

Q: You see my point, don't you? The call, like so many features of your fantastic story, is without any kind of independent verification.

A: Well, then, perhaps you are prepared to prove that I did not receive the call. I eagerly await this demonstration.

Q: Ah, you wish me to prove that nothing is nothing, is that it? I decline your offer, Miss Strongwood. Now, let us turn back to what happened at the Windom Block.

———

Q: It is quite a dramatic story that you've told, but it isn't the real story, is it?

A: It is the real story as far as I am concerned.

Q: Let me offer another version. You creep down the hallway toward room four thirteen, but wait, you hear voices, or at least you claim to. And you think to yourself, what if Michael Masterson has brought someone along with him? Your grand plan is suddenly in jeopardy. So you hide yourself in the closet until Mr. Mugliano leaves. Now you have your chance. Now you have Michael all to yourself. And so, Miss Strongwood, you pounce. You pounce on that poor man like a lioness attacking its unfortunate prey.

---

3. Hilda Jacobson testified that she could not recall answering a telephone call for Addie Strongwood on the evening of November 8, although she admitted on cross-examination that her memory "might not be perfect."

A: I assure you that it was the other way around. Michael attacked me.

Q: Is that so? I wonder. Do you know what I think, Miss Strongwood? I think you are the wild beast in this affair, not Michael. You are the hunter, aren't you, looking for rich men you can manipulate for your own greedy purposes?

A: You have accused me of fiction, Mr. Boardman, but it seems to me you are the one with real talent in that regard.

Q: No, I am merely a man who sees through your endless deceptions. The fact of the matter is that Michael refused to pay the ransom you sought. Not only that, but he had an ace up his sleeve, didn't he?

A: I don't know what you mean.

Q: Of course you know what I mean. The photograph, Miss Strongwood, the photograph of you stark naked, in Michael's bed. It must have come as quite a shock to you.

A: I have already said that it did. I was appalled that Michael would have taken a picture even as he ravished me against my will.

Q: Yes, that is your story, isn't it? But then there's the matter of the missing face—your face, Miss Strongwood. It was torn right off the picture. You claim that it was Michael who tore the face away, presumably in a fit of anger. Is that right?

A: That is what he told me.

Q: And he is not here to testify to the contrary, is he? But what if that photograph showed you with your eyes wide open and perhaps a smile on your face? What if it was taken not when you were drugged and asleep but when you were in fact enjoying an evening of carnal pleasure with the man you had just seduced? Imagine how damaging such a picture would have been to your relentless campaign of extortion, based as it was on the claim that Michael had raped and impregnated you.

[Objection, Mr. Phelps. Speculation. Overruled.]

Q: You tore that picture, didn't you, after you had shot Michael down in cold blood?

A: I did not.

Q: You couldn't quite get it out of his hand, could you? Poor man, he had it in a death grip. But you knew what damage that picture would do if it ever saw the light of day. So you simply ripped away the part showing your face. Ah, what a clever girl you are, Addie, what a clever girl, but maybe too clever in the end for your own good.

[Objection, Mr. Phelps. Prosecutor is testifying, etc. Overruled.]

A: I do not think of myself as clever, Mr. Boardman, and I certainly did not tear that photograph as you have alleged. The only thing I did that terrible night was to fight for my life so that I could prevent a vicious man from murdering me. That is the fact of the matter.

Q: Is it? I submit, Miss Strongwood, that the fact of the matter is that you shot Michael Masterson because he finally decided to reject your blackmail scheme. Not only that, but he showed you a picture of your lovemaking, a picture that you obviously were unaware of, and it made you enraged because you saw that all of your scheming might come to naught. So you shot him straight through the heart and then you watched, with steely calm, as the very lifeblood flowed out of his body. The fact of the matter is that you have no heart or conscience and that you sent Michael Masterson to his grave without compunction or remorse. Now is your chance, Miss Strongwood. For once in your life, speak the truth.

A: I have spoken the truth, but I will speak it again now for all to hear. As I have maintained from the very beginning of this tragic affair, I acted in self-defense and you may be assured that I would do so again in similar circumstances.

———

Q: Now, you stated in the *Tribune* that after shooting Michael, you cried copious tears before regaining your composure, after which you looked out the office door, only to see Mr. Wangstad, the elevator repairman, at the far end of the hall. Is that correct?

A: Yes, except that as I said, I did not know at the time that it was Mr. Wangstad.

Q: Now, I am curious about the tears you claim to have shed after Mr. Masterson's death. I believe you said in your *Tribune* article that you were "sobbing uncontrollably." Isn't that right?

A: Yes, that is what I wrote.

Q: Yet Mr. Wangstad testified that he heard no sobbing or crying after the shots were fired. Strange, isn't it, that he didn't hear your terrible weeping and wailing?

A: I cannot say how loud my crying was. It is entirely possible that Mr. Wangstad would not have heard me, since the door to the office was closed.

Q: Isn't it far more likely, Miss Strongwood, that you didn't shed any tears at all? Indeed, I submit that when you looked out the door after shooting Michael

Masterson, you simply wanted to make sure the coast was clear so you could make your getaway. But it wasn't, was it? Mr. Wangstad had inconveniently appeared on the scene. And that meant you had to act quickly to cover your tracks. I can picture you in that office, bent over Mr. Masterson's body, frantically trying to remove the damning photograph from his hand before the police arrived. But his death grip was so powerful that the best you could do was tear away a part of it. Isn't that the real truth, Miss Strongwood?

A: No, it most certainly is not. As I have said, I was devastated by what had happened. I was hardly in any condition to undertake the sort of cover-up that you have alleged.

Q: Is that so? And yet we have heard from both Mr. Wangstad and Officer Sweeney,[4] have we not, that your eyes were dry and your manner utterly composed when you talked with them and told them you had shot Mr. Masterson? It is nothing short of amazing how quickly you went from what you have described as a flood of tears to such complete command of your emotions.

A: I only did what I had to do, Mr. Boardman. I knew, as I came out of that office, that I could not allow my emotions to overtake me.

Q: Somehow, Miss Strongwood, I doubt that emotions have ever overtaken you.

———

Q: You have stated repeatedly, have you not, that you lived in fear of Michael Masterson?

A: Yes.

Q: But he had no fear of you?

A: He had nothing to fear from me except that I was prepared to speak the truth about what he had done.

Q: Is that a fact? Why, then, do you suppose that a few days before you killed him, Michael Masterson moved into the Vendome Hotel, even though he had a perfectly fine apartment less than a mile away?

A: I am sure I could not say.

Q: He was deathly afraid of you, wasn't he?

---

4. Officer Michael Sweeney's testimony echoed that of Wangstad. He stated that "Miss Strongwood was very matter-of-fact in describing what she had just done. She didn't seem flustered at all."

A: No, as I have said, it was I who feared him.

Q: And yet there he was, hiding out at the Vendome, and so frightened of your threats and your scheming that he'd only agree to meet you if he had a big, tough man along with him, just in case. But you outsmarted him, didn't you?

A: I do not know if that is true. I could easily have been murdered.

Q: Oh, it is true, as true as anything I know. You've outsmarted just about everybody, haven't you? Michael. His parents. The police. And I imagine you think you can outsmart this jury as well.

[Objection, Mr. Phelps. Speculation. Overruled.]

A: No, my hope is simply that the jury will see the truth in all that I have said here.

Q: I, too, am also confident that the jury will see the truth about you, Miss Strongwood. I have nothing further of this witness, Your Honor.

COURT: Do you wish to conduct a redirect examination, Mr. Phelps?

MR. PHELPS: Yes, I have just a few questions.

Q: Addie, you have testified that after shooting Michael Masterson, you left the office and immediately encountered Officer Sweeney and Mr. Wangstad. Is that correct?

A: Yes.

Q: And you were detained by Officer Sweeney until other police arrived?

A: Yes.

Q: Were you ever out of Officer Sweeney's view or that of other authorities until such time as you were formally arrested and taken away to the Hennepin County jail?

A: No. They kept a very close watch on me.

Q: And were you subjected to a search of your person after your arrest?

A: Yes, I was asked to empty my coat pockets and to remove my shoes.

Q: And at the jail, was a more thorough search undertaken by a matron there?

A: Yes.

Q: If fact, you were forced to remove all of your clothes. Isn't that right?

A: Yes.

Q: Even your bodily functions were subsequently monitored, were they not, to see if you had swallowed anything out of the ordinary?

A: I am embarrassed to say that such was the case.

Q: But despite all of these efforts by the authorities, the missing portion of the photograph was never found, was it, thereby lending credence to your testimony that Michael Masterson tore your face from the picture out of sheer spite?

[Objection, Mr. Boardman. Calls for conclusion on part of witness. Sustained.]

Q: I have nothing further, Your Honor.

COURT: Then court will adjourn until ten o'clock Monday morning, when the jury will hear final arguments.

FROM THE JOURNAL OF J. WINSTON PHELPS, JANUARY 29, 1904

7:30 pm—coldest night yet, heading for -25—well, its done at last, except for the finals, jury instructions, etc—cant say Im brimming with confidence but not pessimistic either—many, many things in this case dont add up one way or another & people who have never seen a trial find this amazing—yet it is *always* so & most trials come down to figuring out who is telling biggest lies.

Which brings me to my client—damn that girl!—not a word to me about being in Windom Block before big event—"Why didnt you say so, my dear?" I asked & she said, "Oh, I forgot"—ha, ha & ha!—but how she finessed it was a thing of wonder & beauty—quick as cat on her feet & so good at deflecting Boardman—god help me for saying so but she should be a lawyer.

Boardman is an ass but after this is done I will buy him a drink & commiserate re Addie—unless, of course, I lose—then he will be buying.

———

Shad called at 830 & said hes expecting letter from Holmes any day now re the case—interesting to think that even greatest detective of all seems fascinated by our little Addie.

———

EXCERPTS FROM A LETTER FROM SHERLOCK HOLMES TO SHADWELL RAFFERTY, January 31, 1904

———

The device is a very small camera, called the Photoret,[5] which is designed to resemble a pocket watch. I acquired one some years ago while in New York and have kept it with me ever since, as I find it quite useful. Indeed, I have come to employ it in so many interesting circumstances that Dr. Watson has, on more than one occasion, accused me of ungentlemanly behaviour. But as we both know, a good detective is rarely a perfect gentleman. In any event, when I saw the photograph of Miss Strongwood, which is square in format and has beveled corners, I suspected at once that it was an enlargement made from a Photoret snapshot.

I have since taken several new pictures with my Photoret, among them three snapshots of Miss Strongwood on the witnesses stand. I did so in order to reassure myself that photographs can be taken secretly with the camera even in the most public of situations. The experiment proved to be a success, as no one in the courtroom appeared aware that I was doing anything other than consulting my watch. Incidentally, I sent one of the snapshots to Mr. Phelps, who was no doubt mystified by it. Please tell him that I intend no harm to his case and that I am content to let the jury determine Miss Strongwood's guilt or innocence.

We know, thanks to Mr. Thomas's efforts, that Jonathan Jakes owns a Photoret and also has a small darkroom in which to develop the pictures.[6] The fact that the photograph of Miss Strongwood was taken with a Photoret strongly suggests that it was made in a surreptitious manner, either by Mr. Masterson or by Jakes. We know from Mr. Jakes's testimony that both men possessed standard Kodak cameras, so it is logical to assume that they used the Photoret solely for the purpose of taking pictures secretly, presumably during their many amorous exploits. It is likely that Mr. Jakes has in his possession numerous photographs of a scandalous nature obtained with the camera. Unfortunately, Mr. Thomas was unable to find any such pictures during his little expedition,

---

5. The Photoret camera, made by the Magic Introduction Company from 1894 to 1901, was among the smallest cameras of its time. Disguised as a pocket watch, it could take six half-inch square photographs on a round sheet of film. The camera cost $2.50 and was widely advertised for its ease of use.

6. This reference leaves no doubt that Wash Thomas was enlisted by Rafferty and Holmes to break into Jonathan Jakes's apartment to look for a Photoret camera and other evidence. Both Holmes and Rafferty occasionally resorted to burglary as a means of gathering evidence. One of Holmes's most notable burglaries occurred in 1899, when he broke into the safe of a blackmailer, a story told by Dr. Watson in "The Adventure of Charles Augustus Milverton." Thomas would have had no trouble breaking into Jakes's apartment, since he was an expert locksmith, as noted in *The Magic Bullet*.

which leads me to believe that Mr. Jakes has taken great pains to hide them away, since they constitute the ultimate proof of his and Mr. Masterson's utterly dissolute character.

Now, having dispensed with all of these preliminaries, let me tell you what I think happened on the night Mr. Masterson was killed.

———

EIGHT

———

As might be expected in a case of such consequence, the final arguments were highly anticipated, and the courtroom was filled to overflowing when, on the morning of February 1, Frederick Boardman gave the prosecution's summation. Although Mr. Boardman claimed center stage, Miss Strongwood, as always, drew her fair share of attention from the spectators. Dressed in a brown wool gabardine skirt and lace-trimmed white blouse, she sat perfectly straight in her chair, her folded hands resting on the defense table. Now and then she adjusted her long black hair, which was bundled atop her head and tied with a white ribbon, but otherwise gave no indication of nervousness. She appeared to nod slightly in the prosecutor's direction as he rose from his chair and looked directly at him as he delivered his arguments over the span of nearly three hours.

He began by reviewing, in a very meticulous manner, all of the evidence that he contended must point directly to Miss Strongwood's guilt. Time and again, his theme was that the defendant, despite what he called "her fancy way with words," was a woman given to "deceit and calculation," and that Michael Masterson was "caught in her web of intrigue as surely as the poor fly struggles to escape the wily spider."

Among the points he emphasized were these:

That Miss Strongwood had lied about stealing two silver spoons from the Van Dusen residence, an act he said demonstrated her "corrupt nature."

That she had lied about her work as "a paid seducer of men in a disreputable Chicago dance hall."

That she had lied about her first meeting with Michael Masterson, which in fact must have occurred in Chicago, and that it was "she who pursued him, and not the other way around."

That her claim to having been ravished under the influence of drugs by Mr. Masterson was a "fabrication of the first order" designed to disguise her "drunken seduction" of his best friend, Jonathan Jakes.

That there was "not a single scintilla of proof" she had been impregnated by Mr. Masterson.

That the $10,000 she sought to gain from the Masterson family was "extortion pure and simple and could reasonably be viewed in no other light."

That she had been "deliberately deceitful" in failing to mention that sometime before Mr. Masterson's death, she "had visited the very same floor of the Windom Block where she killed him."

That there could be little doubt that she "lured him there for the purpose of making him pay the ransom she demanded. When he refused to do so, and instead threatened to make public a revealing photograph of her taken during one of their lovemaking sessions, she shot him dead, with a gun she had brought with her for that express purpose, after which she tore her face from the picture to disguise what it really showed."

Mr. Boardman also argued that the defense's effort to depict Mr. Masterson as a "brutal user of woman" was without merit. "When in doubt, attack the victim. That was the defense's strategy," he said, adding, "Mr. Masterson was by no means perfect—who among us is?—and while it cannot be denied that he sometimes visited brothels, he was hardly alone in that regard, and we should not judge him too harshly for possessing the animal spirits so typical of young men."

In his final peroration, spoken with considerable passion, Mr. Boardman said, "This is not a complicated matter, despite the attempts of the defense to make it so. We know who shot and killed Michael Masterson on the evening of November ninth in room four thirteen of the Windom Block, for Miss Strongwood has openly admitted doing so. Keep these simple facts in mind. She brought the gun to the Windom Block. She waited until the man Mr. Masterson had hired to protect him was gone. She entered that room, fully prepared to extract the final fruit of her wiles.

"Imagine the scene, not through her eyes, but through those of Michael Masterson, who can no longer speak for himself and who now cries out to us from the grave for justice. He is apprehensive and nervous. He has been called to a meeting with a woman whom he thought he loved but who instead turned out to be after nothing but his money and who cannot accept the fact that he has done the sensible thing and spurned her. She enters the room, a deadly weapon in her pocket. Her efforts to win a ransom of ten thousand dollars have thus far failed, and she is no mood to be denied.

"Michael Masterson wishes to be done with Miss Strongwood at last. Indeed, his parents stand ready to lodge a formal complaint against her. He tells her that she must give up her claim, and shows her the revealing photograph. This infuriates her. She has plotted and plotted and plotted to gain the fortune that is the great goal of her life, and now it will be denied to her. She takes the pistol from her pocket and levels it at Michael's breast. 'No,' he says, 'please, no,' and then she fires, not once, but twice, and Michael, a young man of twenty-six years just reaching the prime of his life, falls dead to the floor.

"Afterward, she has just enough time before the police arrive to complete her great cover-up. She rips away part of the photograph that is clenched in his hand and finds a way to dispose of it. She writes a few words on a sheet of paper so that she can claim Michael forced her to do so. Then, she walks calmly out into the hallway to meet Officer Sweeney and begin telling her deceitful tale.

"Members of the jury, it is up to you now to deliver justice to Michael Masterson and his family. You must be the last line of defense against the lies, one after another after another after another, that Miss Strongwood has spoken here. She is not a woman wronged. She is a woman who has done wrong, who has committed cold-blooded murder in the first degree. Do not be fooled. Do not let her get away with it. Tell her, by your verdict, that you have seen through her lies and into her black heart. Tell her that she is not mightier than the law. Tell her that she must, at last, pay for her terrible crime."

―――――――

It was just after one thirty in the afternoon when J. Winston Phelps rose to offer his final summation. He smiled at his client, who returned this favor with a slight smile of her own, and then positioned himself directly in front of the jury box. Long known for his spellbinding oratorical skills, he did not disappoint, and some jurors appeared all but mesmerized as he delivered his final defense of Miss Strongwood.

He first reviewed key points made by the prosecution, and rebutted them one by one, arguing that in every instance his client's account of what happened was far more persuasive than what he termed "Mr. Boardman's fanciful reconstructions of reality." Again and again, he hammered home the idea that there was "no proof" of any of the claims made against Miss Strongwood, whether it be her alleged theft of spoons from the Van Dusen mansion or her supposed seduction of Jonathan Jakes or the claim that she had enticed Michael Masterson to the Windom Block. The prosecution's case, Mr. Phelps averred, "is nothing but a house of cards, built upon the slippery footings of innuendo and speculation, and it cannot withstand even the slightest gust of truth."

The bulk of Mr. Phelps's argument, however, was devoted to depicting Michael Masterson as a "violent and dangerous young man known for his reprehensible conduct toward women." Said Mr. Phelps, "The real villain in this case, the person whose offenses turn the stomach and chill the heart, is not Addie Strongwood. She is merely a girl who had the temerity to fight for her life against a monster, and that is what Michael Masterson was, make no mistake about it."

Warming to his topic, Mr. Phelps continued: "Mr. Masterson was not a man merely exercising his 'animal spirits,' as the prosecution has so colorfully put it. No, this was a man, as we have learned from his very own words in the letter he sent to his cousin, Theodore, who took up with women for one purpose, and one purpose alone: the ace of spades, as he called it. Members of the jury, you are all men of the world and you know what that term means. And you know as well the kind of man who has no respect for the fair sex, no sense of decency. The kind of man who lies and cheats and even resorts to outright rape to secure what he desires. The kind of man who takes a photograph of his naked, helpless victim as a foul reminder of his awful deeds. Michael Masterson was just such a man, as the record before you so convincingly demonstrates, and Addie Strongwood, I am sure he believed, would simply be another of his victims.

"But she did not turn out to be the average sort of girl, did she? No, she was, and is, a girl possessing tremendous resolve, high intelligence, and an unwavering belief in justice. So after Michael Masterson had used her and abused her and lied to her in every way that a man can lie to a woman, she determined to do the one thing he did not expect: she fought back. She demanded justice, and yes, she took the fight to his family, to his mother and father. She asked for money, because she believed it was the only remedy available to her, given the stench of corruption that still lingers over the police department of this city. Was she wrong to ask money of the Mastersons, to demand that their son quite literally pay for his depredations against her? I think not. I most assuredly think not."

———

"Now, jurors, Addie Strongwood's fate is in your hands. You must decide whether she goes free or spends the rest of her days behind bars or even must face the hangman's noose. Look at her, sitting there in her plain skirt and blouse. Think of all you have heard at this trial and how, time and again, despite the most probing challenges by the prosecution, she has been utterly steadfast in her testimony. She has not shirked, she has not evaded, she has not put on airs or tried to be anything but what she is: a very fine and gifted young woman who was forced to take another life in order to preserve her own. That is no crime and never can be, before the eyes of man or the eyes of God.

"It is not Michael Masterson who cries out for justice here; his fate is now in the hands of the greatest of all judges. No, it is Addie who cries out for justice, and I ask you, I implore you, to give her that which she truly deserves. Acquit her of this crime, restore to her her freedom and her life, and I have no doubt she will do much good in this world before her own time comes to an end. Members of the jury, do not hesitate or waver in your duty. Strike a blow for the truth, strike a blow for justice, do what you know in your hearts is right. Acquit Addie Strongwood!"

As it was half past four by the time Mr. Phelps finished his argument, Judge Elliott recessed court until the next morning, when he gave his final instructions to the jury.

———

EXCERPTS FROM AN ARTICLE IN THE *MINNEAPOLIS JOURNAL*, FEBRUARY 2, 1904

The jury in the Strongwood murder case began its deliberations at eleven o'clock this morning after receiving final instructions from District Judge Charles Elliott. The twelve men who will determine the fate of Miss Adelaide Strongwood, accused of murdering Michael Masterson, will have but two choices. They must either decide she is guilty of murder in the first degree or they must clear her of the charge and set her free.

Lesser charges of second-degree murder and manslaughter were included in the original indictment against Miss Strongwood but they were dropped at her own behest, according to her attorney, J. W. Phelps, who said his client believes she bears no guilt whatsoever in the matter and therefore refused to negotiate a plea to a lesser offense.

"We are confident that the jury will acquit her," Mr. Phelps said after leaving court. He declined to speculate how long deliberations might take, noting that "every jury is different, as is every case, and so predictions in matters like this are really quite worthless."

Hennepin County District Attorney Frederick Boardman, who prosecuted Miss Strongwood, said he will have no further statements for the press until a verdict is returned.

Courthouse observers believe that because of the length and complexity of Miss Strongwood's trial, which began on January 11, the jury might well require several days to sort through all of the evidence before finally arriving at a verdict.

———

FROM THE JOURNAL OF J. WINSTON PHELPS, FEBRUARY 2, 1904

———

All up to the jury now—what a case this has been!—if appeals to the almighty werent such a fools game, would be planted at this moment on a kneeler at Immaculate Conception[1] begging for divine mercy—Addie may need it, tho I gave her the best defense money can buy.

———

Looked at jurors as they were getting Elliotts instructions but all had on their best poker faces—Col. Camp will be the key—he has a military mans commanding presence & is sure to be elected foreman—can only hope he understands "beyond a reasonable doubt" & all that entails as there are plenty of

---

1. The Church of the Immaculate Conception was a Roman Catholic church at Third Street and Third Avenue North in what is now the warehouse district of downtown Minneapolis. Built in 1872, it was demolished in 1922, a few years after completion of the much larger Basilica of St. Mary.

doubts in this business, beginning with Addie herself—will probably go to deathbed not sure what she did or did not do.

Shad tells me Holmes has reached interesting conclusion re case—but wont share it with me until after jury renders verdict—damn that fat Irishman!

EXCERPTS FROM AN ARTICLE IN THE *MINNEAPOLIS TRIBUNE*, FEBRUARY 5, 1904

Yet another full day of deliberations went by Thursday with nothing heard from the jury that will determine the fate of Miss Adelaide Strongwood. Thus far, the jury has sent no message to District Judge Charles Elliott, who presided over Miss Strongwood's murder trail, and some within the legal community are speculating that the jury may be at an impasse.

Prosecutor Frederick Boardman has maintained a Delphic silence since the case went to the jury Tuesday morning, and his office today again refused to make any comment.

Meanwhile, Miss Strongwood's attorney, J. Winston Phelps, continues to profess the belief that his client will be exonerated. "I would not read too much into the length of the deliberations," he told the *Tribune* exclusively this morning. "The jurors have much evidence to review and it appears they are doing a good job of it. I remain confident that they will come to the right decision in the end."

EXCERPTS FROM AN ARTICLE IN AN EXTRA EDITION OF THE *MINNEAPOLIS JOURNAL*, February 5, 1904

It would be hard to imagine a more dramatic scene than that which unfolded late Friday afternoon in Judge Elliott's courtroom.

The word that a verdict had been reached was conveyed to the judge just after 4 p.m. Almost immediately, his courtroom on the third floor of the city and county building, which had been silent as a tomb since Miss Strongwood's trial, began filling with spectators, as though a floodgate had suddenly been opened. Within fifteen minutes of the announcement, the courtroom was so full that the bailiffs began turning people away.

Among those in attendance were Mrs. Philip Masterson, mother of Michael Masterson; Jonathan Jakes, Mr. Masterson's best friend, whose testimony had produced some of the most controversial and shocking moments of the trial; and several other friends of the deceased.

Meanwhile, reporters from all of the local dailies, as well as several representing newspapers in New York, Chicago, and elsewhere, crowded into the row reserved for the press, eager to hear the verdict and send out the news to the world.

Prosecutor Frederick Boardman was among the first to reach the courtroom, but it took nearly a half hour before Miss Strongwood's attorney, J. W. Phelps, who had been getting a haircut in a nearby barbershop, finally arrived. He appeared tense and somber, and unlike his usual manner, he said nothing to reporters.

Judge Elliott reconvened court at precisely 4:44 p.m. and then asked the bailiff to call in the jury.

It has long been observed that the countenance of jurors as they prepare to render their verdict can tell much about what that verdict will be. Jurors who are smiling or who otherwise appear to be in a good mood are most likely to acquit the defendant, whereas grim and drawn faces usually presage a conviction upon the charges.

Yet as the twelve jurors filed into the box and took their seats, it was hard to detect any overriding sentiment on their faces. They appeared cool and businesslike, neither smiling nor excessively stern, and all of them made a point of looking at the judge rather than at Miss Strongwood, who as always was a perfect picture of composure.

"Gentlemen of the jury, do you have a verdict?" Judge Elliott asked.

Col. J. R. Camp, the jury's foreman, rose from his chair, his posture supremely erect as befitting his long service in the military, and said in a firm and unwavering voice, "We do, Your Honor."

"Please hand your verdict to the bailiff," Judge Elliott instructed.

Bailiff Walter Niff, who has stood guard at many trials over his long career in the Hennepin County courts, retrieved the verdict form, a single sheet of paper, from Col. Camp and then walked a few steps back to the bench and handed it to Judge Elliott.

The atmosphere in the courtroom was now electric, as though everyone had been touched by a live wire. Curiously, the one person who seemed immune to this state of high tension was the defendant herself, who still gave not the slightest evidence of any emotion. Instead, she sat ramrod straight next to Mr. Phelps, her eyes affixed upon Judge Elliott as he studied the verdict.

After what seemed like a small eternity, though in fact it was a matter of but a few seconds, the judge turned to the jury and said, "Is this a verdict upon which you are all agreed?"

"It is," Col. Camp said.

"Very well," said the judge before turning his attention to Miss Strongwood. "Will the defendant please rise."

Her face betraying no sign of anxiety or apprehension, Miss Strongwood rose from her chair, her eyes still focused directly upon the judge.

"The verdict is as follows," Judge Elliott said, his words ringing through the hushed courtroom. "We the jury in the above-mentioned case, find the defendant, Adelaide Strongwood, NOT GUILTY of the charge of first-degree murder."

The reaction to this stunning news was immediate and varied. Miss Strongwood, for the first time during her long ordeal before the bar, permitted herself a broad smile as she was enveloped in the arms of Mr. Phelps, who appeared to be more excited than his client by the verdict.

"By God, we did it!" Mr. Phelps shouted, all but crushing Miss Strongwood in a bear hug.

Far different was the reaction of Mrs. Masterson, who shook her head in disgust and began at once to push her way through the crowd of spectators in order to leave the courtroom.

Mr. Boardman was more subdued, dropping his head for a moment as the verdict was announced, and then slumping back in his chair.

Judge Elliott gaveled the courtroom back to order before speaking his final words of the trial.

"The court wishes to thank the jury for its faithful service. Miss Strongwood, you are to be released from custody immediately. There being no further business before it, this court is hereby adjourned."

Hardly had the judge retreated to his chambers than reporters gathered around Miss Strongwood, peppering her with questions.

Was she surprised by the verdict? "I was not surprised. I believed from the very beginning that I would in the end obtain justice. Now I have done so, and I am very grateful to the jury."

Was there a turning point in the case that led to the jury deciding in her favor? "I cannot say with any certainty, but I believe my own testimony was convincing to the jury. A chance to tell my story was all that I ever asked."

Did she feel completely vindicated by the verdict? "Yes, but I also know some people will always think me guilty of the crime, no matter what the jury has done. But I can do nothing about such feelings. I can only state, as I always have, that I deeply regret the death of Michael Masterson and fervently wish that he had not forced me to defend my life at the cost of his."

What are her plans now that she is a free woman? "I have given the matter some thought and I believe it would be best for me to leave Minneapolis and try to make a new life elsewhere. I do not see a future for me here."

———

Prosecutor Boardman received the verdict with his characteristic aplomb. "I believe we had a good case when the grand jury handed down its indictment and I still believe that to be true," he said. "But the jury has now made its decision, and I accept its verdict, as I must."

Mrs. Philip Masterson, who rushed from the courtroom after the verdict was read, could not be reached for immediate comment. However, Michael Masterson's friend, Jonathan Jakes, said he believed the jury had made "a terrible mistake" as a result of being "taken in by Miss Strongwood's lies. No verdict will ever convince me that she is anything but a murderer."

———

FROM THE JOURNAL OF J. WINSTON PHELPS, FEBRUARY 5, 1904

———

Much celebrating after verdict—only person not showing great excitement was Addie herself—said she expected verdict all along—asked her what she'd have done had jury found her guilty—she just smiled in very peculiar way & said that could never have happened—lord, is it possible she bribed a juror?—dont see how but suppose I will never know.

Of course verdict doesn't really settle case—many people Im sure believe she murdered young Masterson in cold blood & got away with it—cant say I really know what happened one way or other—if I could read Addie as most people can be read Id have the answer but dont think its possible with her—she seems to move on a different plane from the rest of us & at a different speed, as tho time for her is so wide & deep she can see where we are going before we get there & so act accordingly—entirely possible, I think, that all was orchestrated by her, but who can say?—would like to know what jurors thought & will try to speak with them if press doesnt.

————

Shad called just after 8 pm & offered congrats—said a free dinner awaits me at the Ryan[2]—talked for an hour about Addie—Shad says he has letter from Holmes he wants to show me—promises it will answer "many questions"— also told me Holmes & Dr. Watson, who is recovering well from his surgery, have left for England—Shad sounded wistful & said he wasnt sure hed ever see them again—told him you never can tell.

————

EXCERPTS FROM AN ARTICLE IN THE *MINNEAPOLIS TRIBUNE*, FEBRUARY 7, 1904

Col. J. R. Camp,[3] foreman of the jury that on Friday acquitted Miss Adelaide Strongwood of murdering Michael Masterson, spoke for the first time to the press yesterday, and his comments included a number of startling revelations, most notably that the jury very nearly reached an impasse that could have resulted in a mistrial.

"The first vote we took, which was on Tuesday night, was six and six between conviction and acquittal," said Col. Camp, who stated that he had

————

2. The Ryan Hotel at Sixth and Robert Streets in downtown St. Paul was the city's largest hotel when it was built in 1885. Shadwell Rafferty's saloon was located on the hotel's first floor. The Ryan was razed in 1962.

3. Little is known about Col. J. R. Camp's military career, but by the time of Addie Strongwood's trial he was well established as an author of juvenile literature. He is perhaps best remembered for his 1902 adventure saga, *A Boy's Life in Old Santa Fe*, which was very popular in its day.

been empowered to speak for the entire jury but would not reveal the votes or inclinations of any individual jurors during the long deliberations.

Col. Camp said jurors who initially favored a guilty verdict believed there were too many "holes," as he called them, in Miss Strongwood's version of events to make her a credible witness. "Her failure to mention her work in that dance hall in Chicago certainly played against her, as did the fact that she had been to the Windom Block prior to her fatal encounter with Mr. Masterson. It was also felt that the ten thousand dollars she asked from the Masterson family was, if not blackmail, very close to it."

But those jurors who from the outset favored acquittal believed that there was "overwhelming evidence as to Mr. Masterson's villainy," as Col. Camp put it,"and that while there were some inconsistencies in Miss Strongwood's testimony, they were hardly sufficient to prove her a murderer."

After the initial vote and his election as foreman, Col. Camp said, he determined to lead the jury through a "thorough review of all the evidence" in the hope that a unanimous verdict might ultimately result.

"We did so," he said, and by the end of the day on Wednesday, another straw vote revealed that the jury had shifted to eight in favor of acquittal and four still calling for conviction. He added: "That photograph of Miss Strongwood found in Mr. Masterson's hand was a sticking point with the four jurors, who believed Miss Strongwood must have removed her face from it in order to disguise something. But the others argued that if she was lying, then why wasn't the missing piece of the picture ever found?"

Col. Camp said he was "not certain as to what ultimately changed the minds of the four jurors," but noted that at least one of them "spoke of the letter which Mr. Masterson had sent to his cousin as a particularly strong piece of evidence as to his vile intentions regarding Miss Strongwood."

———

By Thursday night, after many hours of deliberation, the jury had "reached a crisis point," Col. Camp said. "The vote at that point was eleven to one for acquittal, but the juror holding out held a very strong opinion as to Miss Strongwood's guilt and I was by no means certain he would ever change his mind. We retired for the night at eight o'clock and I told my fellow jurors that if we could not reach a unanimous verdict by the end of the day Friday, we would have to tell Judge Elliott that we were hopelessly deadlocked.

"I also urged the recalcitrant juror to think long and hard upon the issue of reasonable doubt, and told him that he did not have to believe in his heart of hearts that Miss Strongwood was innocent in order to acquit her. I said we were not in the business of establishing Miss Strongwood's innocence but only in determining whether there was sufficient evidence to prove beyond any reasonable doubt that she had committed the crime of first-degree murder.

"I think it was that argument which finally won the day," Col. Camp stated. "As we continued to review the evidence on Friday morning, the holdout finally admitted, begrudgingly, that he could not be entirely certain that Miss Strongwood was guilty even though he very much believed that she was. Once this admission had been gained, it took but a little more persuading to reach our verdict."

Asked whether he thought Miss Strongwood was indeed innocent, Col. Camp said, "I can only reiterate to you what I said to the juror who was holding out. Our choice in the matter was guilty or not guilty, and we believed there were enough doubts regarding the prosecution's case that we could not render a guilty verdict. I will leave it to you to interpret that statement however you wish."

————

EXCERPTS FROM A LETTER FROM SHERLOCK HOLMES TO SHADWELL RAFFERTY, January 31, 1904

————

Given that a miniature, easily disguised camera was used to take the photograph of Miss Strongwood, I believe it is safe to conclude that she did not in fact know of the picture's existence until Mr. Masterson showed it to her that night at the Windom Block. I further believe that Mr. Boardman was correct in asserting that the revelation of this compromising photograph must have enraged Miss Strongwood. When she saw the picture, which in all likelihood demonstrates that she was not drugged or asleep in her naked state, she understood at once that it would be a devastating blow to her efforts to obtain money from Mr. Masterson for his alleged wrongdoing. So it was that she tore away her face from the picture.

Miss Strongwood's story, of course, is that Mr. Masterson ripped her face from the picture before arriving at the Windom Block. I find this highly unlikely, for the simple reason that if the photograph were indeed Mr. Masterson's last line of defense against a blackmail scheme, he would hardly have mutilated it in a way that left doubt as to what it actually depicted. To have done so would have been utterly irrational on his part. No, it must have been Miss Strongwood who tore the photograph, presumably after she had shot Mr. Masterson.

I should add here that I have no doubt that Mr. Masterson was a vile young rake who used woman badly, but whether he and Mr. Jakes did indeed drug and rape Miss Strongwood I cannot say with any certainty. All the photograph will tell us is whether, at some point, Miss Strongwood may have engaged in consenting intimate behavior with Mr. Masterson. If she did so, then her entire story is based upon a colossal lie as to the real nature of her character.

I imagine you are wondering, my dear Rafferty, what the missing portion of the photograph will show, assuming my theory is correct. There are several possibilities. Perhaps Miss Strongwood will display a fetching smile that suggests she was not being ravished against her will. Perhaps she will be wearing the sort of expensive jewelry that bespeaks of a kept woman. Or perhaps something in the background of the picture, near her face, will contradict her account as to where and when the photograph was taken.

In any event, the answer will be known only if the missing part of the photograph can be found. Is that even possible, you may ask? After all, the police made a thorough search of the office and its surroundings and found no trace of it. They searched Miss Strongwood's person to the point of removing all of her clothes. Again, nothing. They also allowed for the possibility that she had swallowed the evidence, but this, too, yielded nothing of value.

So where might the missing piece be? I have thought long and hard upon the matter, and I have concluded that Mr. Poe and his purloined letter[4] may point us in the right direction. Now, here is what I would like you to ask Mr. Phelps to do once the trial is over...

---

4. "The Purloined Letter" is a famous short story by Edgar Allan Poe, first published in 1845. It features the French detective C. Auguste Dupin and concerns a stolen letter that is cleverly hidden in plain sight.

FROM THE JOURNAL OF J. WINSTON PHELPS, FEBRUARY 6, 1904

8 pm—Shad came over this afternoon bearing a most remarkable letter from Holmes—no need to repeat contents here except to say Holmes wants me to go to police property room & examine one of the prosecution exhibits at Addie's trial—will have to wait until Monday to do so—if Holmes is right it will be an amazing discovery & maybe I will have some answers after all.

———

FROM THE JOURNAL OF J. WINSTON PHELPS, FEBRUARY 8, 1904

930 pm—I am in disbelief or maybe not but in either case I will never doubt the genius of Sherlock Holmes—as per his request went to police property room in courthouse this am & asked to see fountain pen taken from office in Windom Block where Addie shot Masterson—standard Waterman Ideal pen[5] with #16 nib—worked fine when I tried it out—after guard left took off nib & opened ink reservoir—drained out ink & found small piece of paper rolled up inside—covered with ink of course but could tell it was photographic paper— removed it & put in it my pocket with no one the wiser.

Could hardly wait to see what paper showed so took it posthaste to discreet friend who is in photo business & has darkroom, enlarger, chemicals, etc—he was able to clean off ink & enlarge image—no doubt its missing piece of photo, just as Holmes predicted in his letter!—Holmes believes Addie tore her face from photo because she was unable to pry entire picture from Mastersons hand after shooting him—she knew if police found full photo her story would be ruined, or so Holmes says—ergo, she had to figure out where to hide torn piece—knew she didn't have much time because she peeked out door & saw elevator man Wangstad in hall—she glanced at Mastersons pen & had bright idea of hiding photo piece in reservoir—wrote her name on paper to make sure pen still worked, so no one would suspect she had tampered with it—then

———

5. Like most fountain pens of its time, the Waterman Ideal was refilled by removing the nib to expose the ink reservoir. An eyedropper was then used to resupply the reservoir with ink.

walked out in hallway & started telling her tale, cool as ever—god what a clever creature she is!

My friend cleaned & enlarged piece of photo in no time—shows Addies face & neck as clear as can be—she is looking at camera with Giaconda smile & wearing diamond necklace with pendant in shape of letter "E"—couldnt figure out at first what that meant, so called Shad—he told me Everleigh sisters brothel in Chicago provided just such a necklace to their costliest concubines—imagine that!

Took torn piece of photo & enlargement home & put them in safe place—my photographer friend promised to tell no one what he had seen—I know his word is good—gave him $20 for his trouble.

Guess there can be no doubt now that Addie first met Masterson in Chicago & he arranged to bring her back to Mpls to work in family business—then everything went to hell between them & so dance of death began—wonder why Masterson didnt expose Addies lies early on & end relationship before he got in too deep—can only assume she had something on him (maybe re his delight in beating up whores), so he had to keep quiet or face ugly consequences—but something finally pushed him to the edge & he confronted Addie—probably threatened to tell all re her unsavory past in Chicago — then there was a fight & maybe she did shoot in self-defense as Masterson was certainly a nasty customer—or maybe it was cold-blooded murder after all.

Dont suppose world will care either way in the end—whole business will be forgotten soon enough—ah, tempus fugit, vanity of vanities, & all of that—will keep my little picture of Addies face,[6] tho—will never forget her, no matter where she ends up, but pretty sure she wont die a poor woman.

EXCERPTS FROM AN ARTICLE IN THE *MINNEAPOLIS TRIBUNE*, MARCH 13, 1904[7]

Miss Adelaide Strongwood, who just over a month ago was acquitted of murder in one of the most celebrated cases in the history of Minneapolis, is

---

6. The nude photograph of Addie Strongwood and the portion of it Phelps recovered from the fountain pen are not in Phelps's papers or in any surviving court records, and it is likely both have been lost.
7. This newspaper story, and the five others that follow, were found in a scrapbook maintained by J. Winston Phelps. The scrapbook, like all of Phelps's papers, is at the Hennepin History Museum in Minneapolis.

now in New York City, and may soon make a motion picture with the American Mutoscope and Biograph Co.[8] The *Tribune* learned of this surprising development from J. Winston Phelps, the attorney who represented Miss Strongwood and won her acquittal on charges of murdering Michael Masterson.

"It seems that one of the principals of the company had followed Miss Strongwood's case in the newspapers in New York," said Phelps, "and he decided it would make for a good story film of the kind that is becoming all the rage these days, especially since the release of Mr. Thomas Edison's fire picture."[9] The attorney identified the principal of the company as Mark Grantham, regarded as an up-and-coming talent in the motion-picture business. "I told him that Miss Strongwood is an extraordinary young woman and that he should meet her for himself. He agreed and paid for a train ticket for her to New York."

Phelps said he has not talked with Miss Strongwood for some time now, but that she "must have made quite an impression" with Grantham, as he has offered her a contract to play in the film, which is to be released next year under the title of "A Woman Wronged."

"I am sure the local nickelodeons will do a great business when the film comes out," Phelps said, adding that he is heartened to learn that his former client is achieving "some well-deserved success."

EXCERPTS FROM AN ARTICLE IN THE *MINNEAPOLIS JOURNAL*, NOVEMBER 7, 1904

In what can only be regarded as a supreme irony, a new film made by the Biograph Co. of New York in which Miss Adelaide Strongwood appears in the leading role made its debut here last night, almost a year to the day after she shot and killed Michael Masterson, leading to a murder charge of which she was later acquitted.

---

8. American Mutoscope and Biograph was a film company, later known simply as Biograph, founded in 1895. Its studios were originally in Lower Manhattan, but in 1911 the company relocated to Los Angeles.
9. *Life of an American Fireman* was a short but influential narrative film made in 1902 for the Edison Manufacturing Co. and directed by Edwin S. Porter.

The motion picture, called "She Was Wronged," purports to be a dramatization of Miss Strongwood's case, but in fact bears very little resemblance to it, no doubt as a matter of artistic license.

Nonetheless, there were reportedly long lines at all of the nickelodeons where the film was shown, and even Miss Strongwood's harshest critics could not deny that she looked quite fetching and displayed considerable skill as an actress.

———

EXCERPTS FROM AN ARTICLE IN THE *NEW-YORK TRIBUNE*, JUNE 18, 1905

The marriage of Mr. Mark Grantham of New York and Miss Adelaide Strongwood, formerly of Minneapolis, was celebrated Saturday at Trinity Church in Manhattan, the Rt. Rev. James Peacock presiding.

Mr. Grantham, vice president of the American Mutoscope and Biograph Co., is credited with "discovering" Miss Strongwood, who has became one of the company's leading actresses in the new "story films" that are now the height of popularity.

More than 200 well-wishers attended the wedding, which was followed by an elegant reception at the Waldorf-Astoria Hotel.

———

EXCERPTS FROM AN ARTICLE IN THE *LOS ANGELES TIMES*, OCTOBER 29, 1912

The motion picture community is mourning the loss of Mark Grantham, a pioneer filmmaker and president of Biograph Studios, who died suddenly yesterday at his home in Hollywood.

Mr. Grantham, who was 50 years of age, was found dead in his sleep by his wife, the well-known actress May Grant.[10] The cause of death has not been determined, but Mr. Grantham was thought to have been in good health and gave no evidence of distress before retiring for the night.

———

10. May Grant was Addie Strongwood's stage name.

"I have lost my loving husband and my dearest friend," his wife said in a statement released through the studios. "I am saddened beyond all measure."

———

EXCERPTS FROM AN ARTICLE IN THE *LOS ANGELES EXAMINER*, AUGUST 24, 1913

May Grant, the popular star of Biograph Studios, has tied the knot with real estate tycoon Andrew Owens, whose extensive holdings make him one of the wealthiest men in California. The pair were united in a private ceremony yesterday at Mr. Owens's oceanfront estate.

———

The couple will honeymoon in Hawaii.

Larry Millett is the author of six previous Sherlock Holmes adventures (all but one also featuring Shadwell Rafferty) and is an architectural historian whose books include *Lost Twin Cities, Once There Were Castles: Lost Mansions and Estates of the Twin Cities* (Minnesota, 2011), and the *AIA Guide to the Twin Cities.* As a reporter for the *St. Paul Pioneer Press,* he covered many different beats and had the honor of writing clues for the newspaper's legendary Winter Carnival Medallion Hunt. He lives in St. Paul.